WITHOUT LIMITS
BOOK ONE

Skyla Raines

the lies we tell
OURSELVES

The Lies We Tell Ourselves

Cover Design: Design by Kage
Interior Design: Design by Kate
Formatting: Michaella Dieter
Proofreading: Michaella Dieter

BEFORE YOU READ

Please note this book has dark elements and contains themes which some may find difficult to read.

Your mental health is important, so if you need a more detailed content list, please check page 452.

"Tell me every terrible thing you ever did,
and let me love you anyway."
Edgar Allen Poe

CHAPTER ONE

Jamie

Dark fathomless eyes bored into mine, searching for any sign of hesitation, but they'd find none. I wanted this. I wanted him more than I could even say. This was the stuff dreams were made of—well, at least my dreams. He'd promised me I could have anything I wanted for my birthday, and my one wish was for my first kiss. A wish he was seconds away from granting.

Large calloused hands cupped my face, sending pulses of electricity across my skin as my heart pounded against my chest like it could burst its way right out of me. He licked his lips as his thumb brushed my bottom one before teasing it into my mouth. I took a shuddering breath as his taste burst across my tongue.

"You ready?"

"I've never been more ready in my life!" My words tumbled out of me as anticipation built inside me, lighting me up like a

Fourth of July display. "Don't keep me waiting," I whined, my lip pushing out into a pout that made him chuckle.

"Fuck! You don't know how many times I've thought about this." His words were soft like molasses as he closed the distance between us until I could feel his every exhale on my lips. Dillon cupped my jaw, adjusting the angle of my head, while his other hand sunk into my wild curls, anchoring me so I couldn't escape. Not that I ever would. I'd be a damn statue if that meant he'd hurry up and kiss me.

"Dillo—" His lips pushed against mine. I sucked in a gasp, my lips parting on instinct, and I felt the first tentative caress of his tongue against mine. A full-body shudder worked its way through me, causing him to chuckle into my mouth. "Shut up," I groaned as he took control of my mouth and mind as my body surrendered to him. I shuffled forward until I was straddling him, locking my legs around his waist and my arms around his neck.

"MOM! MOM!" I shouted as I pushed open the screen door and tumbled into the kitchen. "I kissed him. He kissed me. Mom!"

She stood at the counter chopping up carrots for dinner and looked over her shoulder. "That good, was it?"

"You have know idea!" I practically squealed as I pulled out a chair at the table and slumped down onto it, not sure my shaking legs could hold me up any longer.

"Sure, I don't." She winked at me before her eyes were back on what she was chopping.

"Do you think he'd be my boyfriend?" I asked, tracing the grain of the wooden table top with my fingertip.

"I'm sure—"

"I didn't raise no faggot." Dad's voice boomed behind me, making me jump in my seat and my spine straightened all at once.

"Larry—"

"Don't fucking 'Larry' me, you stupid bitch." His growled words slurred together as he stormed across the floor and back-handed me so hard I fell to the floor. My cheek burned like boiling water had been poured on it.

"He's just—" Mom's words were cut off by a howling cry as Dad wrenched her head backward by her hair. The golden strands fell to the floor, glimmering like fallen stars. I crawled out from under the table just as he kicked her legs out from underneath her, and she fell to the floor. The knife she had been holding clattered to the ground by his feet, the razor-sharp edge gleaming in the beam of sunlight.

"Run, baby. Run!" Mom screamed as the sound of breaking bones echoed around me, and the walls started to close in.

"JAMIE! You better be up! We've got to be on the road in a couple of hours," Aunt Clara yelled from the bottom of the stairs, freeing me from my perpetual nightmare. No matter how many times I was pulled into it, there was nothing I could do to change the outcome.

"I'm up," I muttered, even though she couldn't hear me and threw the blankets over my head. I wrapped my arms around my pillow, buried my face in it, and prayed I'd be dragged back into a dreamless sleep, because this exhaustion was kicking my ass.

Bang, bang, bang. "Jamie, don't tell Mama lies. I know you're not up yet," my cousin Jessie shouted as she thumped on my door. I love her, I do. I really do. But ugh, I'd hardly gotten a wink of sleep last night, and all I wanted to do was hide away from the world today. I spent all night tossing and turning as nerves churned in my gut so badly, I thought I was gonna be sick. "JJ, come onnnn," she whined as she pushed the door open a crack, letting in a bright beam of sunlight that I could see through the covers.

"Enough, Jessie, I'm coming," I groaned as I pulled my pillow over my head to block out the burning light.

"No, you're hidin'," she sang and jumped on top of me, pulling the covers off my head and batting the pillow away, making me huff. "I know it's scary, but college is meant to be fun, right?" Her innocence is something I envied, and I'd do everything in my power to protect her and make sure she isn't tainted by life.

"Yeah, sweet girl, it is, but it doesn't mean I can't be scared too, y'know." I sighed as she wrapped her little arms around my neck and curled herself into me as per our usual morning routine. I was a night owl for all intents and purposes, and she was, well, not. Jessie was a little ray of sunshine who rose at the ass crack of dawn and had apparently made it her life's mission to make sure I got up with her too. *Kill me now!*

Looking up at me through her thick dark lashes, her bright amber eyes seemed larger than normal, filled with an emotion I'd never seen in them before. "I'm going to miss you JJ," she sobbed into the crook of my neck, her words hitting my heart like a battering ram.

"I'll miss you too, my little sunbeam." I tugged on a strand of her curly brown hair and watched it bounce back into place as she peered up at me, her eyes filled with tears. "You'll be able to call me anytime. Aunt Clara says you can."

"But—"

I placed my finger over her pouty lips, shushing her. "Always, sunbeam." I kissed the tip of her cherry-red nose and kicked off the covers, blasting us with cold air. "But I need to have a shower and load up the car before breakfast." As if on cue, her stomach growled, and she let loose a giggle. One that filled me with pure joy—spread a deep-rooted warmth through me—something that had been missing in my life for so long. "Plus, it sounds like we need to feed the monster in your tummy before it tries to eat you." I wrapped my hands around her waist and hoisted her over me so her little legs kicked in the air, and she threw her arms out to the sides so she could fly. "Is it a bird? Is it a plane? No, it's my little sunbeam."

"JJ, stop!" She squealed, a bright smile lighting up her face that made my heart pinch. "Put me down. Put. Me. Down."

"No. I don't want the monster to eat me." I grinned as she huffed above me, putting her hands on her hips.

"Put me down! I'm hungry and Mama will get angry if I don't go down for breakfast." *Well played, kid. Well played.*

"Then beat it." I chuckled as I set her down on the floor, and she scampered off, slamming my door shut on her way out.

Heaving out a heavy breath, I kicked my feet out of my bed and sat up with a groan. I rolled my neck and stretched my arms up as I yawned. "Get it together, JJ," I grumbled to myself as I took in my small room. Well, what had become my room two months ago. Previously, it was Aunt Clara's writing room, but now the tiny space had become my domain, even though I'd hardly unpacked a single box and still lived out of my suitcase. Trying to resituate myself into a family I'd never known existed until five years ago was hard, and I'd only really gotten to know them over the last two years when... well, when everything irrevocably changed in my life for the second time.

"Enough." I ground my teeth, grabbed the clothes I laid out last night off the stool by my desk, and wandered down to the bathroom. The exposed wood floor was glacial on the soles of my feet, and the marble tiles in the bathroom were not much better, even though it was meant to be heated. I could only hope that once the shower was running, everything would start to warm up and I'd no longer resemble a vibrating popsicle as shivers racked through my body.

After that first gratifying pee of the morning, I put my clothes beside the towels on the heated towel rail and turned the shower on before finding myself staring at my reflection in the mirror. It was hard on a good day to look at myself, but today, it felt like someone was twisting a dagger in my heart. Everyone always said how much I looked like my mom. That would usually draw a little smile from me, but not today. Today, it made my chest feel tight, and my eyes burned. I had her eyes and her riot of bouncing blond curls, something which I'd come to learn ran in her family. My aunt and cousins had them too, although theirs were a dark black-brown, and mine were almost white blond.

"You can't change the past, baby. I want you to promise me you will look forward, embracing your future and all you can be. I'll be with you every step of the way." She placed her frail hand over my heart, the movement slow and jerky. I could feel the tremors through her touch like the ripples on a still lake. "I'll always be here with you, cheering you on."

A sob ripped its way out of my chest as the first tears burned down my cheeks. It should have been us—together—taking me to Briar U today. Instead, it's my Aunt Clara.

Swiping the tears off my face, I dumped my dirty clothes in the basket and jumped in the shower, allowing myself a few precious moments to wallow in my grief before I washed it all away and locked it up tight. I focused on taking deep calming breaths, Aunt Clara's voice echoing in my head as I did. "Out with the negative, in with the positive." It repeated as I watched the water and my pain spiral down the drain, leaving me feeling all kinds of numb.

Today was a new day, a new beginning, and hopefully the first step in the direction I wanted to take my life. Only time would tell, I guess. The world was my oyster—or so they said—but it's never as easy as all those self-help books would make you believe. It feels almost insurmountable to look forward when so much pulled me back to my past. It had sunk its claws into me and refused to let go. It weighed on me every second of every day. Fear. A fear that made me jump at shadows and a shiver work its way down my spine every time I heard a creepy noise. I shut my brain off and locked it down as I turned the shower off.

I grabbed my towel off the rail, dried myself off, and moisturized before slipping my clothes on. I'd gone for ripped skinny black jeans, worn through by wear and tear rather than design, and a tight-fitting pale-blue cropped top. I added a short-sleeved black button down over the top that had tiny blue applique flowers on it which I buttoned up to the bottom of the top underneath. It was one of my favorite outfits, one that teased the world at who I really was. But the truth was I didn't know who I was or wanted to be. My head was filled with big dreams and ideas, but I was too scared to embrace them.

I felt it was probably best to try and blend in today—every day—until I found my people or more importantly, myself. I wanted to feel safe and accepted. Apprehension sat in my gut and coiled through my body. I didn't know if I would ever reach that point, but I owed it to Mom to try. Nothing could deter me from brightening my face up with a bit of concealer under my eyes to hide the dark circles that aged me, or from adding a touch of highlighter and blush on my cheek bones. I would conform, but still be me. Just a little less today. Soon, I would be free to be myself and embrace every part of my soul. If only I could find a way to make that happen.

I dried my hair off with the smaller towel, then grabbed my mousse and flicked my head upside down so I could work the product through it, scrunching it in my hands before giving it a quick blow over with the dryer. I cast one last look at myself in the fogged up mirror and gave myself a wan smile and a nod. *"You've got this, baby."* Mom's voice echoed in my head, and warmth suffused through my veins as pride radiated from her words. *"Go get them and make me proud by showing the world just how wonderful you are."*

For the first time in years, I looked at myself without drowning in revulsion. My curls were tightly coiled and hanging just below my jaw, glistening like they were crafted in the light that streamed through the fogged-up window. My pale blue eyes were ringed in a gray so dark it looked black, and brought a pang of grief to my heart but also a feeling of home. I looked so much like her. Even though it cut so deeply to see the features that reminded me so much of her and everything I'd lost, today they buoyed me and gave me comfort. She may not be with me, but as long as I drew breath, she would live on through me.

Clearing my throat, I pulled a wavering smile to my lips. "I love you, Mom. Always have. Always will." I brought my fingers to my lips and blew a kiss at my reflection. I could see her beautiful face, white-blonde curls blowing in the wind as she smiled back, pools of bottomless love glittering in her eyes.

Back in my room, I pulled on my boho-style black high tops and shucked on my gray zip-up hoodie before grabbing the first of my boxes and loading them into the car. It took me about thirty minutes to get everything moved and packed up from my room. I swear Aunt Clara was tormenting me with the delicious scents that wafted out of the kitchen every time I passed. My stomach was a rumbling mess, but I couldn't tell if I wanted to eat something or if I was gonna throw up before I could take a bite.

The sound of happy voices filtered through the house as I shut the front door and took a seat at the breakfast bar in between my cousins Zack and Jessie, who were already stuffing their faces with pancakes, eggs, and bacon all drowned in maple syrup. It smelled like heaven but was a heart attack waiting to happen. They—we—were young and today was a celebration of sorts, so I supposed it was alright.

"Is there any left for me?" Aunt Clara chuckled as she pushed a plate across the counter to me. It looked and smelt amazing, but my stomach chose that moment to revolt as it tried to make its way up my throat as nerves simmered in my gut.

"Drink this, JJ." Aunt Clara's warm honey-brown eyes regarded me with understanding. "It's a big day, but you've got nothing to worry about, kid, you'll see." I huffed out a breath and downed the drink she'd given me. I felt every one of those little bubbles pop as I swallowed them down with a grimace. "It'll help settle your nerves and your stomach." I looked at her in disbelief as I grabbed the orange juice and a fresh glass, filling it to the top. I gulped it down as fast I possibly could to get rid of the aftertaste of whatever that mixture was.

"If you say so." I grunted, stuffing my face with a forkful of pancake and bacon to stop myself from telling her just how vile it was.

"My own special recipe," she said with a twinkle in her eye and squeezed my shoulder as she headed out the front door to check I'd done a proper job of loading up the car.

"So, mom said we'll be moving once you've left for college," Zack murmured around a mouthful of food. Nothin' like watching the kid's mouth be a garbage disposal to put me off my food.

"And how d'you feel about that?"

"I don't understand why we have to keep moving." He sighed and looked out the window, shoulders slumped. "We've moved more in the last two years than we ever have and I don't get it. I've only just started to make friends and feel good about school, y'know..." His words trailed off, and a lump of emotion clogged my throat, and my chest tightened. Guilt threatened to drown me, and I wished the ground would swallow me up.

I've brought so much change into their lives. It can't have been easy with all these adjustments they've had to make for me—because of *me*—and if that doesn't make me feel like the worst cousin in the world, I don't know what else could. I never asked them to uproot their lives when I met them two years ago, but Aunt Clara is something kinda special. She took

Mom and me in with open arms, never hesitating to do what needed to be done. Before then, I'd never really understood the importance of family, because it had been me and Mom against the world. But now, I know family is everything.

"I know it's not been easy, Zack, it wasn't for me either." His dark brown eyes pinged up to mine as if he hung on my every word. "Life isn't always easy, buddy." I cuffed him on the shoulder and made his lips twitch. "But sometimes, we've just gotta make the best of what we have. Love those who love us harder, hold them a li'l longer, y'know?" He bobbed his head before his eyes dropped to his plate.

"Yeah, sure," he replied, his voice thick as he twizzled his fork between his fingers like a drum stick. "I wish I'd have had more time to get to know Aunt Selene though." He sighed and sniffed before picking his plate up and dumping it in the sink.

"Yeah, me too," I mumbled into my glass of orange juice. Spearing the last piece of pancake on my fork, I used it to chase the few remaining drops of maple syrup around my plate when a little hand landed on my arm. My gaze tracked the pattern of Jessie's top up her arm until I met her questioning gaze, amber eyes burning with a depth of emotion most eight-year-olds couldn't possess.

"It's gonna be alright, isn't it?"

My hand ran through her hair and cupped the back of her head, making sure her full attention was fixed on me. "Yeah, sunbeam, it will be." I sighed, suddenly feeling a wave of tiredness wash through me. "You'll see. In the end, everything works out just how it's meant to."

"And what if everything isn't right? What if I'm not happy?" Her bottom lip quivered.

"Then it's not the end." I pulled her forward and placed a kiss on her forehead, breathing in her floral scent before exhaling. "But right now, you better get your shoes on and grab your bag or you'll be late for school."

"I wish you... I wish I knew you'd be here when I got home tonight," she grouched as she jumped off her chair and ran to get her stuff just as Aunt Clara's voice reached my ears.

"Zack, Jessie, get your school stuff and get out here. The bus will be here any minute." I snickered at the sound of feet thundering above my head as I grabbed their lunches off the counter and brought them to the porch. "Ah, thanks for gettin' those, Jamie." Aunt Clara smiled as she took their lunches off my hands.

"No problem." The bus pulled up a second later and my cousins appeared in front of me as if by magic.

"See ya, JJ. Have a good time, yeah?" Zack pulled me in for a side hug, then bounded down the steps to his mom, took his lunch, and joined his friends at the back of the bus.

"JJ?" came a quiet watery voice.

"I'm here, sunbeam." I crouched down in front of her and brushed the tears off her face.

"I'm gonna miss you."

"I know, sweet girl." She buried her face into the crook of my neck and wrapped her arms tightly around me. I could feel her sobs as they racked through her body. Knowing she wouldn't release me anytime soon, I wrapped my arms around her and carried her down the path to meet the bus.

"Come on, Jessie," Aunt Clara cooed as she rubbed a hand up and down her back. "You gotta get to school, kid."

"B-but I d-don't want 'im to go," she warbled.

"I know, but we'll see him soon, so don't you worry. Okay?"

"Okay." She nodded into my neck but still wouldn't let go, and it made my heart ache. I'd never had siblings, and this felt like I was losing a part of my heart all over again.

I crouched down till her feet hit the ground and gently pushed her back by her shoulders. Jessie's tear-streaked face looked up at me and a million words flowed through my head of what I could say, but none of them would come. I brushed back a wayward curl from her face, and kissed her forehead. "I'll see you for Thanksgiving." She blinked up at me as she slowly processed the words and nodded. "That's a promise, sunbeam." I smiled as much as I could. "So get on that bus and make lots of memories, then you can tell me all about it when I see you next."

"O-okay, JJ." She sniffled, kissed my cheek, and bounded onto the bus.

CHAPTER TWO

Jamie

We stood and watched the bus fade from view as it drove down the road. The world seemed unnaturally quiet now the kids had gone, like the silent lull before a storm. But the air felt electric and the blood in my veins hummed. Everything was about to change, again. I just hoped it was for the better.

"Don't cry, JJ." Aunt Clara brushed tears off my cheeks I didn't know were falling. "It's going to be okay." I sucked in a shuddering breath and looked into her eyes, expecting to see pity like I had done so many times in the past after Mom... but all I saw was love and understanding.

"I-I'm scared." The words tore themselves from my lips as she wrapped her arms around me. She hugged like a mom; tight, firm, and true.

"I won't lie to you." She pulled back, brushing my cheeks dry again. "It's not gonna be easy for you, Jamie." I sighed, chewing my bottom lip to hold back the cry that wanted to escape. "You've been through so much in the last eighteen years. Too much for someone so young." She cupped my face, the heat emanating from her palm warmed my cool skin. "But Selene..." She sniffed, and licked her lips. "Your mom would be so proud of who you've become and who you will be. She loved you more than life itself, sweetie. Never doubt that."

"I-I always thought it would be us..." My voice gave out, but I could tell she knew what I meant by the sad smile that lit her face. The plan had always been for mom to drive me to college and help me set up my dorm room, but as with many things, the best laid plans didn't mean shit. Life was cruel and had a way of crushing your hopes and dreams before they had a chance to come to fruition.

"Go live your life. Chase your dreams." Her thumb stroked across my cheekbone as longing filled her words. "Fall in love. Have that great romance you both used to sit and read about. Okay?"

I nodded mutely, struggling to breathe. My lungs felt like they were being crushed. And my heart? Well, that had been broken five years ago. That useless thing was nothing but a bruised effigy of what used to be a vital beating organ.

"Good." She squeezed my shoulder before releasing me. "Go get in the car. I just need to grab my bag and lock up."

I smiled, even though it felt like I was fighting quick drying cement on my skin. "Sure." I took one last look over the fields opposite me, watching as heads of corn chased the shadows of the clouds blowing overhead. The bright blue sky was darkening as a murky gray spiderwebbed across it above the clouds. I felt like my anxiety was polluting everything, staining it. The dry grass crunched under foot as I crossed the yard to my aunt's Honda, the black paintwork faded and pockmarked, but it was as reliable as they came, and given our current circumstances, that was something we needed.

Briar U was about a three-hour drive from Bentwaters

where we currently lived, and I was beyond grateful to be getting out of this narrow-minded backwater. Even though I couldn't admit it, I was hopeful Briar U being on the edge of a large city like Jamieson meant it would be more progressive. Maybe I'd finally find the strength to let go of childhood promises and do exactly what my aunt wanted me to do and open myself up to love.

I scoffed at the thought. I might not have advertised my interest in guys, but I must have put some kind of signal out into the world, because I'd been propositioned a handful of times in the last few years by closeted jocks. They were like my own personal brand of kryptonite. Big, built, and brooding made alarms blare in my head every time one of them cornered me in the hallways or the locker room. I didn't know if I wanted to scream and run, or get down on my knees and beg for mercy.

I'd kissed a grand total of one guy; the one who still owned every facet of my being. I'd promised myself that with this move being my fresh start, it was time to let go of childhood naivety. Of promises made and shared on my thirteenth birthday and get myself out there and see what a real relationship was like. I didn't like the hookup culture that everyone else seemed to rave about. I wanted a connection. I wanted something deep and meaningful, not just to scratch an itch—not that I'd had that other than with *him*.

The car door banging closed snapped me out of my meandering thoughts, and I linked back to reality. "You ready to go, Jamie?"

"Yup. Thanks for doing this for me."

"Don't be stupid, JJ. You're family. I'd do anything for you. Speaking of..." She reached into her bag and pulled out a massive manilla envelope and handed it over to me before shoving her bag into my footwell. "Daire gave me this for you. It's got a burner phone with his number pre-programmed into it." I glanced over at Aunt Clara as I fingered open the envelope. Apprehension marred her features. "I'm not saying you should need to use it, but—"

"I know," I interrupted her. I'd heard this speech so many times over the last few years, I could recite it in my sleep. "I'll use it if anything feels off." She smiled and squeezed my shoulder before starting the ignition. The Honda roared to life beneath us, and within minutes, we'd passed through the town limits and headed for the highway.

"Zack knows you'll be moving again."

Aunt Clara sighed like the weight of the world suddenly landed on her shoulders as I looked through the other documents Uncle Daire had given me. "I know." She cleared her throat and adjusted her sunglasses. "He heard me talking to Daire the other night about our new location." Amber eyes flicked over to me and glanced at the paperwork in my lap. My scholarship offer to Briar U was in the name of Jamie Bowen—my current name. I'd been Jamie something or other for the last five years, but I knew the score now; unlike when I'd first met Uncle Daire on *that* night. It was for my safety and protection. I understood it, and I was beyond grateful, but it sucked having to learn a new name every six months or so.

If I had to be honest with myself, I'm so damn tired. It's not a physical kind of exhaustion—it's in my soul. I'm tired of going through this shit, of nothing changing, of having to uproot my life over and over again. I'm sick of trying. It's not that I don't want to live, but more like it wouldn't be the worst thing if I fell asleep and didn't wake up. It's a silent battle I've waged against myself every day for the last two years. One I've hidden from the world, from those who love me. How would they react if they knew how broken I was, or how my dreams are haunted by memories I can't escape? I'm scared they wouldn't want me anymore, because I'm not sure if I can be fixed, or if I even want to be.

"How about some music?" Aunt Clara's voice cut

through the myriad of thoughts circling my anxious mind, pulling me back to what is meant to be a positive day.

"Sure. But only if I get to pick the station."

She snorted and ended up coughing her guts up. I smirked at her when I saw tears streaming down her face. "You always pick the damn station, kid," she croaked.

"I got a new one you're gonna love too." She scoffed as I flicked through the channels until I found the one I was looking for, and Sleep Token's *Alkaline* blared through the crackling speakers. It sounded like the subwoofer had blown, but somehow it enhanced the song in a way that made the rest of the world turn into a blur as we merged onto the interstate and ate the miles.

"What in the living hell is this?"

I couldn't help but laugh at the look of horror on her face. "This is Sleep Token. They're amazing!"

"They've got nothing on Linkin Park, kid."

"If you say so." I smirked, tipped my head back, and allowed my eyes to fall closed as she continued to mutter under her breath about my lack of musical taste. It wasn't long before my lack of sleep caught up with me, and everything faded away as the movement of the car lulled me into unconsciousness.

"Wow. This place is hella impressive, Jamie." Aunt Clara's eyes bulged as we drove down the main boulevard past the campus buildings in the direction of the dorms. As part of my scholarship, I got the full board program. That meant I had food and a room for the four years it'd take for me to graduate with my degree. I just needed to work out what my major would be. I couldn't decide between design, art, or architecture.

I was a creative at heart, much like mom and Aunt Clara, but I also loved numbers and nature. It was an odd combination of subjects that I enjoyed, but I loved the juxtaposition between the freedom nature and art offered versus the rigidity and order of numbers and architecture.

"The buildings are beautiful, the streets lined with trees, and gorgeous open spaces where you could sit and relax between lectures. I'm jealous. It kinda makes me wish I went to college."

"Ha! Good one. You've never stopped saying how much you hated school and the oppressive structure of it all."

She snorted. "I can't argue with that. I'm gonna need you to direct me to your dorms."

"I've got you. You want the second left. My building is in the same quadrant as the sports dorms."

"Guess they thought you scholarship kids would be a good influence on all those hotheaded jocks."

I shrugged even though she wasn't paying me any attention. "Yeah, maybe." It only took us a few minutes to find a space in the parking lot opposite my building, just enough time for me to put my mask on so Aunt Clara wouldn't worry about me. My throat was drier than the Sahara, and my stomach was filled with an angry swarm of wasps, but on the outside, I looked relaxed. I just hoped it was enough to put Aunt Clara at ease so she wouldn't linger and end up being late for Jessie and Zack when they finished school.

She turned the ignition off and turned in her seat to look at me. "What do you want to do first? Grab your boxes or check out your room?"

I sucked in a deep steadying breath as I pondered her question. "Let's grab some boxes then go check in with the RA. I'm guessing that's him standing outside the building." I tried not to laugh as I took in the stark contrast between the two buildings that faced each other across the lot. One was all sparkling white stone and windows that shone like mirrors, and the other a dull gray with windows covered in a film of dirt that looked like they hadn't been cleaned in well, ever.

"Sounds like a plan. Let's get to it." We slipped out of the car and loaded ourselves up with boxes. I only had six, so we'd only need one other trip, and all my worldly possessions would be in their new home.

We strode between discarded cars and around people who seemed to stop for no reason right in front of you and made our way to the guy in the royal-blue polo shirt. He was a jock, with broad shoulders and thick biceps that flexed as he turned the pages on his clipboard. His tanned arms were muscled and every little movement highlighted the veins that threaded his forearms. My mouth was dry, my tongue sticking to the roof, and the ability to speak evaded me as he held out his hand and chuckled. Pink tinged his cheeks as he took in the boxes braced in my arms. Pale green eyes looked at me through thick lashes, and his lush lips curled up into a devilish smirk. "Hi, I'm Taylor. I'm on the football team." Figured as much. They all look like gods, and this guy was no exception. Even so, he didn't hold a torch to the god that broke me. "I take it you're moving in today?"

Aunt Clara chuckled next to me. "What gave it away? The boxes?"

"Uh, yes ma'am." Taylor seemed a bit flustered before he regained control of himself. Weird. "All the team are helping out today at the dorms as we welcome this year's freshmen to Briar U."

"That's wonderful. So thoughtful..." Aunt Clara's voice faded away as my eyes caught on bright rainbow hair that bobbed along the sidewalk. It belonged to a small girl, with her arm wrapped around the waist of another taller girl with long black hair that went down to her waist. I smiled, and even though it was wrong of me to assume, I hoped this meant the school was LGBTQ+ positive. "Thank you so much, Taylor.

I'm sure we'll find it without any issue. It was the third floor, right?"

"Yup. Room three-oh-one. Any issues, you know where I am."

A throat cleared, and I snapped my gaze in the direction of the sound to see Aunt Clara smiling so wide it illuminated. "You ready, kid?" I nodded mutely, unable to connect my brain and mouth and followed her through the growing throngs of people. "I think you're really gonna like it, Jamie. It's got a nice feel to the place."

"Yeah," I croaked. I cleared my throat as we slipped into the cool building and made our way to the elevator and piled in along with two other kids and their parents. Everyone gave each other uncertain smiles as the numbers ticked on the display panel. The kids wore a similar expression as me, one of nervous anticipation, while the parents beamed like Aunt Clara. Only time would tell if these kids ever spoke to me, but I didn't hold out much hope. I struggled to make friends, let alone talk to someone new in such an intense setting. Thankfully, the elevator stopped on my floor—which was also theirs—before any inane small talk was required. Sweat beaded on the back of my neck as I trailed after Aunt Clara like a lost puppy as she counted down the numbers till she came to my room. My new home.

The door was ajar. I pushed it open with my toe to see one bare bed, the walls and desk surrounding it equally as stark on the right-hand side, whereas the bed on the left was covered in a riot of color. It felt like I'd need to sleep in my sunglasses. "I'll pop these on your bed, JJ, and go and get the last couple of boxes while you settle in and start to unpack, yeah?" Before I answered, Aunt Clara swept from the room, and I was left standing there like some kind of idiot, unable to move, clutching my box like it was a liferaft in a storm.

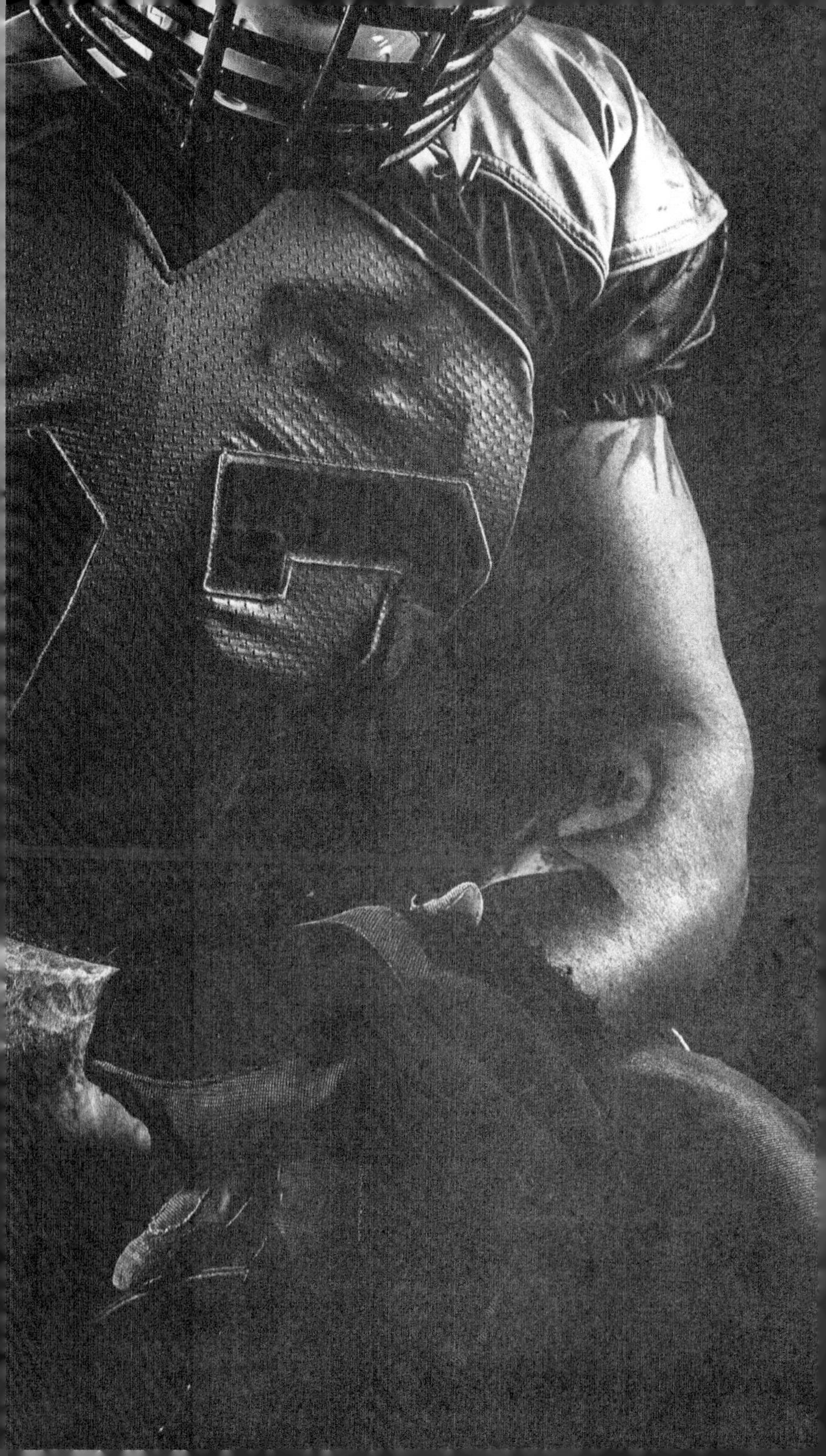

CHAPTER THREE

Dillon

Summer training camp finished two weeks ago and Coach shipped us all back to Briar U and immediately started our regular season training. Even though there was a hint of the seasons changing, with cooler mornings and nights drawing in, it didn't touch the scorching midday temperatures. Coach Grundy was a former NFL linebacker, and he worked us hard. He pummeled us into the ground, and if we set one foot out of line, he'd have us running suicides till we puked and then drag our asses back into the melee of practice without a second thought.

He was hard, but we respected the shit out of him, because we knew he could make NFL stars. He had connections, and for those of us with the drive and determination to push ourselves, he'd make sure we secured a foothold in the future we wanted. But right now, I wanted to smash my fist into his face. He was being an asshole. His words were spat with vitriol, hate, and ire, and cracked like a metal-tipped whip on our backs.

Sweat poured down my spine like a river and dripped into my eyes as I wiped my forehead with the back of my hand. I grabbed a cold drink out of the cooler and ran it over my face before taking a sip. The cool liquid flowed down my throat as I swallowed, but it felt as effective as a broken sprinkler in a raging inferno.

"Who pissed in his Cheerios this morning? I feel like I've been ripped a new asshole," Buchanan, our center, groused as he jogged up next to me to grab a drink while Coach was focusing on our defensive line. They'd been our weak link last season—the first one I spent on the varsity team as a breakthrough sophomore talent—and because of their repeated failures, we lost our chance to go to state. That failure had Coach riding the team harder than ever before, and I had to step up to the plate this year as the first junior captain of the Briar U Ravens.

"I heard he caught his wife with one of the history professors." Stevens chuckled as he grabbed a water from the cooler. "You know, doing the horizontal tango." He held the bottle before him and pretended to fuck it and slapped his ass.

"Such a prick." Buchanan snickered, watching Stevens being, well, Stevens. He's an immature idiot on his best days, but his spirit and ridiculous antics buoyed the team when energy and belief was low.

I snorted. "You're such a dick. Don't let him hear you talking about it, or you'll be cleaning the locker room for the first half of the season at least." Stevens shot me his favorite finger and continued to ride his bottle.

"That's if it's even true," Vieck, the best running back in the state, said and slapped Stevens around the head. "You can't always trust what the cheerleaders say. Stevens, you know this."

He snorted and we all turned and stared at him. "What?! I

can't help it that they get loose-lipped when I fuck 'em, can I? If there's anything you need to know, I can find out... my dick's magic!"

"Does he have a special wand too? To back him up when he falls short?" McCormack, our wide receiver, added. "Can't believe you nut sacks started without me."

"Just a quick water break, man. We've gotta get through the last hour of practice without fucking up. I just wanna hit the sack, my hamstrings are killing me."

Buchanan's head snapped to me, a fleeting look of concern crossing his face before he wiped it clear.

"Make sure you report to the physios after practice, Hargraves!" Jessop, our assistant coach's voice, rang out behind us as he strode out of the tunnel and onto the sidelines next to us. He gave us all a withering stare and sighed like we'd innately disappointed him. Fucking story of my life; never being enough for anyone to stick around or put the effort in with. "Finish up, then get back out there! You don't win titles by sitting on the sidelines, boys."

"Sir," I grunted as he stalked across the field and took his position at Coach's side. I dropped my bottle in the empties bucket and strapped on my helmet. "Right, guys, let's get back out there and show our defense what we're made of."

I rubbed my hands together, looking forward to making fucking Chad eat dirt. Prescott was our defense captain and hated my guts. He despised the fact I was a junior and team captain when all he got as a senior was the defensive cap and had to defer to me. But I fucking loved it.

"Whoop!"

"Let's kick their ass."

"Hell yeah, Cap!" The guys hollered as they fixed their helmets and ran out onto our side of the field. I knew Coach was planning a short face-off between the lines to end this morning's session. We'd discussed it while the rest of the team were in the locker room getting ready. He wants us to be unstoppable—our defensive line a brick wall, me to have sniper-level accuracy, and the rest of the offensive line to be a battering ram that obliterated the opposing defense. As captain, that responsibility rests on my shoulders. I might only be a junior, but I'm going to leave an indelible mark on this place.

"Hargraves, get your ass on the field," Coach bellowed, and I snapped to it, taking my position in the offensive hustle and laid out our play. The guys were hungry. They played hard and partied harder, but at the end of the day, winning was in our blood, and that's what we did best.

Coach blew the whistle, and like a perfectly choreographed dance, Vieck and McCormack sprinted through the defensive line, breaking through their weak spots like knives through butter. The defense broke apart and tried to rally by chasing them down, but it was like the guys knew it was over before it even began. I took a step back and worked out the force I'd need to make the distance to Stevens, who was completely open as pandemonium unleashed on the field.

Chad was closing in on me, but I didn't let the thought of the impending sack distract me. My arm snapped forward, the ball rotating in a fast spin as it flew in a perfect arc, dropping into Stevens' arms on the ten yard line. I lasted long enough to see him break into an unstoppable sprint before Chad's shoulder pads crashed into my gut, forcing the air from my lungs. He wrapped his arms around me and slammed me into the ground, the smell of wet dirt and grass searing into me. The impact was jarring, and I felt like I was floating for a second before he hauled ass off me and left me on the ground.

"Time to get up, Cap," Buchanan said as he held his hand out to haul me up. I wavered on my feet for a split second, the adrenaline pounding through me dulling the aches I knew I'd feel later. "You good?" He looked at me through the bars of my helmet with a grin. "We fucking did it."

"Fuck yeah, we did." I slapped him on the back and ripped

my helmet off before we jogged down the field to join the rest of the team. I snickered as the angry bellows from the coach reached my ears. "Wouldn't wanna be Chad right now."

"Yeah, he's getting whipped." The evil smirk on Buchanan's face said it all. We all hated Chad Prescott, but we had to deal with him day in and day out. The guy thought he was a god and the world's most talented player, when in fact, he was mediocre at best. But his daddy was minted and had invested heavily in the team—new uniform, training gear, and a private bus for us to use when we traveled, decorated in the team colors.

"Nothing less than that prick deserves," Vieck added as we stepped up next to him. I ran my fingers through my hair, pulling the wet strands from my eyes and blinked away the drops of sweat from my lashes.

"Head on the game, boys," I grunted. They nodded, shut up, and focused.

"How do you expect to take state playing like that?" Coach bellowed, his blue eyes like ice as he stared each of us down. It felt like we were looking down the barrel of a gun, and his finger was on the trigger. Our life and our futures were in his hands. "You're playing like a bunch of headless eejits, not my top-tier guys. You are all on probation. Everyone's starting place is in jeopardy if you continue like this! I will not have my name tarnished by association."

"But we're trying, Coach," Chad whined like a spoiled brat.

"Shut it, Prescott! You have no room to talk. That was the worst sack I've ever seen. You run slower than my grandma when she's using a walker. Hargraves shouldn't have been able to get that throw in if your game was en pointe."

"What the fuck ever," Chad muttered under his breath, loudly enough for me to hear. The prick. Judging by the red flush on the coach's cheeks, so did he.

"Prescott, you're on locker room duty for the foreseeable future."

"What the f—"

"Do not finish that, young man, unless you want to be stripped of your captaincy." Chad stayed silent, but if he were a cartoon character, there would have been steam pouring from his ears. He ripped his helmet off, threw it down the field in full diva mode, and stalked off toward the tunnel.

"Holy shitballs." Stevens whistled as we waited with bated breath for Coach to blow.

"I will not tolerate insubordination on my team. I don't give a fuck who your parents are or how much they donate to this college. When you're on my team, I demand your respect at all times, not just when it's game day. You are ambassadors of Briar U and you must—at all times—lead by example."

"Yes, Coach!" we shouted, as Chad's figure faded into the darkness of the tunnel under the stands.

Coach took a deep inhale and pinched his nose. "Now that's out of the way, I have arranged for you all to act as chaperones for the new students starting today." The collective groan that rang out made me chuckle. Nothing was worse than helping a bunch of away-from-home-for-the-first-time kids find their dorm rooms. I hated dealing with criers, and there always were on drop-off day. Fuck this shit! "On the whiteboard in the changing room, you will find your assigned buildings. The clipboards with room details are on the bench next to it."

"Just what I wanted to be doing after the session from hell," Vieck whispered in my ear.

"Tell me about it." It took everything within me to hold back the eye roll I was desperate to unleash.

"Well? What the hell are you doing standing there? Get your asses showered and get to it."

"Yes, Coach!" Chatter ensued as we headed to the locker room, mixed with pained groans and a hell of a lot of whining.

Christ, it was just my luck that I'd be stuck with a team that behaved like ungrateful kids. This was going to be a long year, and fuck me, it had only just begun.

"I CAN'T BELIEVE we got stuck with the scholarship kids," Buchanan moaned as we trudged across campus to our dorm. We had enough time to dump our shit in our rooms before heading over. I was lucky to get a single this year due to being team captain, but was still in the same building with the other guys so we could bond as a team. All the footballers were housed in a state-of-the-art building with a private gym, all the equipment donated by none other than Daddy Prescott. I'll admit it was nice as fuck—new, clean, and an en suite in each room. It made a nice change after the filthy communal showers in the locker room.

"Should only take a few hours, so stop your bitchin'!" I sneered as I pushed the button for the elevator. My guys were on the top floor of our building, and it was nice not to have to listen to idiots running up and down the halls at all hours of the night.

"I know, but I wanted to get laid."

I scoffed. "Your dick's not gonna fall off if it doesn't get wet for a few hours."

"True." Buchanan shrugged. "But he's a lover, and he's been lonely."

"That's what your hand is for," I snapped, looking over my shoulder and pulling my key card from my pocket to open my door. "Dump your shit, and I'll meet you downstairs in ten. I gotta hit the head first."

"Cool. See ya then." Buchanan disappeared through his door, and it felt like the first time I could breathe all day. My room was simply laid out with a bed, closet, and desk. I didn't personalize it like the other guys. I had no time for that shit. I was here for one purpose—to get scouted and drafted to the NFL. Nothing else was acceptable. Everything else was a distraction.

No sooner had my gym bag hit the floor, than my phone rang. The most obnoxious sound made my ears want to bleed, and my heart stopped. Shakes racked my body, and saliva pooled in my mouth, the acidic quality making my gut churn. I took a deep breath, braced my arm against the door, and clicked on the green phone icon on the screen. "Dad—"

"Don't you fucking 'dad' me. I heard practice today was shit. What's the meaning of this?" I stifled my sigh, knowing it would only lead to a verbal lashing. I closed my eyes as his rant continued and wished I was anywhere else but here. "Well? What the fuck you gotta say for yourself, kid?"

"Sorry, sir," I ground out, but it was as if he didn't hear my words or chose to ignore them, which is par for the course with him. I tuned out after five minutes as his tirade continued, barely aware of the grunts of acknowledgement I made.

My dad wasn't the worst parent in the world, but I wouldn't say he was the best either. There was no love in our relationship. I was a tool for him to reclaim his youth through. He was a second round pick drafted to the NFL his senior year, but while at practice, he damaged his ACL. Being the man's man he is, he played with the untreated injury during practice season until he was pulled up by the coach for poor performance. By then, he'd done too much damage to treat the injury. His contract was terminated and his dreams shattered.

When I was five, he threw me a ball in the backyard. I caught and returned it, and from that moment, he has pushed me to succeed where he had failed. The game comes naturally to me, and I loved playing at high school, but it's lost its appeal the past couple of years. Not that I'd ever breathe life into those words—it's his way or the highway.

"I expect to hear things have improved by the end of the week, or I'll be coming down to meet with Grundy myself. Clearly, his ability to discipline you idiots is failing."

"Yes, Dad." Silence greeted my words. The asshole hung up on me. Well, fuck him and the horse he rode in on. I've got too much to deal with as it is. I quickly changed into some black jeans, a band tee, and slipped on my black high tops. I take a second to glance in the mirror and run my hands through my wild hair with a bit of product.

"You said ten minutes, man. It's been fifteen," Buchanan says with a grin as he saunters toward me, leaving the girls he was talking to outside our dorm.

"Yeah, well, shit happens." My curt response wasn't a surprise. He gave me a knowing look, his bright blue eyes laced with sympathy and understanding.

"I know, Cap. But if you ever wanna—"

"No!"

"Well, alright then," he muttered, flicking through the pages on the clipboard that he held in his hand. "We're expecting twelve scholarship kids to turn up today."

"Great. Can't fucking wait."

"Try to put a smile on that ugly mug of yours, Cap." I tried, but it came out more like a grimace, judging by his reaction. "Oookay, maybe not, then."

I snorted, and my steps faltered as a wave of coldness rolled through my body, a bit like someone had walked over my grave. Goosebumps spread across my skin, and I clenched my fists and bit down on the inside of my cheek as the feeling intensified. I scanned the parking lot, eyeing the people and cars coming and going. Piles of boxes lined the entryway to the dorm block opposite ours. I scanned every face to see if I could pinpoint where this alien sensation came from, but I didn't recognize anyone.

I'd only ever felt this feeling once before, when I'd stumbled across a little blond boy being picked on by the two biggest pricks in school. His beseeching pale-blue eyes looked up at me from the dirt where he laid flat on his back as Mark Johnson straddled him, landing punch after punch. It was like time froze and the world stopped turning. Something coiled around my heart and made it stop beating, and I went full beast mode, almost like I'd blacked out as I hauled Mark off the boy with beautiful blue eyes and golden curls that looked like spun sunlight. It didn't come back into focus until I was sitting on the floor with this boy in my lap, his face buried in the crook of my neck, arms and legs wrapped around my body as he...

"Fuck this," I muttered to myself as I shook it off. That was a lifetime ago. I shut that train of thought down immediately and locked it up tight. "Right, what do we do now?" I turned to Buchanan to see he'd gone. "Fuck!" I ran my hands through my hair, tugging at the strands in a futile attempt to center myself.

"Thanks for joining me," Buchanan snarked. "I've ticked three off our list already," he said, slamming the clipboard against my chest. "You stand there and look grumpy." I rolled my eyes. Fuck my life. Were we done yet? "Just give me the room numbers when I give you the names, alright?"

"Sure."

"Sure, he says," he muttered, rolling his sleeves up his arms as he plastered a smile on his face as a young woman and girl walked up to him. They smiled sweetly, instantly hypnotized by his all-American smile. God, this afternoon couldn't pass quickly enough. I'd rather stick pins in my eyes than be surrounded by people.

CHAPTER FOUR

Jamie

I placed my boxes on the desk in front of the window, then collapsed on the bed and threw my arm over my face. I was equal parts exhausted and wired. I felt like I could sleep for a hundred years, but the thought of shutting my eyes filled me with a kind of existential dread. The door creaked, and the sound of footsteps drew my attention as I sucked in a deep breath. "Just put them next to the others on the desk," I mumbled.

"Aww, shit," a soft sweet voice said. "I'm sorry, I came empty handed." My eyes snapped open as his words registered, and I sprung off the bed like someone had lit a match under my ass.

"Ugh." My mouth went dry, and the entire English language evaporated out of my head, leaving nothing but tumbleweeds behind. I wiped my sweaty palms on my jeans and prayed the power of speech would return.

The boy in front of me cracked a smile, lighting up his face. His dark blond hair looked like he'd just gotten out of bed. Judging by the rumpled sheets on the other side of the room, it was entirely possible. But it was his sea glass-green eyes that caught my attention. They held a warmth in them I hadn't seen in the last few years, and I felt instantly at ease.

"Hey, I'm Malachi, your new roomie."

"Uh, hi." I licked my lips and held out my hand. Malachi looked down at it, then up at me, and back down again before tilting his head to the side. I rubbed my hand on my jeans again, worried I had dirt or something on it, when he lurched at me and wrapped me up in a warm hug. It's the kind a mom gives, and my eyes started to prickle with heat.

"None of that formal stuff here, okay?" He stepped back and cupped my face. Still mute, all I could do was nod.

"This is the last of it, kid." Aunt Clara's voice cut through whatever this was, and Malachi stepped back before turning his beaming smile on my aunt.

"Hey," he held out his hand to her, which she gladly took. "I'm Malachi, his new roommate. I promise I'll look after him and show him the ropes. I'm a junior here, so I know everything there is to know."

"Lovely to meet you. I'm Clara, and this is Jamie. What a sweetie you are." Heat spread across Malachi's cheeks at my aunt's words. "I didn't expect juniors to still be in dorms."

"It's part of our scholarship agreements. We have to stay in the accommodation provided, or we lose our funding."

"Oh," Aunt Clara said, dropping his hand like she'd forgotten she was still holding it. "I guess I missed that bit. Right, well, I won't cramp your style, boys." She gave a tight smile as if she could fool anyone that those weren't tears pooling in her eyes as she looked at me.

Without conscious thought, I threw my arms around her shoulders and hugged her tightly. "I'm gonna miss you. Thanks for everything you've done for me," I croaked, as the first tear slid down my cheek. I felt like I would lose the last connection to my mom when she walked out that door, so I clung on extra tight.

"Shhhh, kid. It's gonna be alright." She kissed the top of my head and ran her hands up and down my back. The continuous movement helped to soothe me. "I'm never further than a phone call away." She chuckled. "And you know Jessie will be phoning you once she's back from school."

"Yeah, I do."

Aunt Clara took a step back, braced her hands on my shoulders, gave me a final squeeze, and looked into my eyes. "She would be so proud of you, JJ. Don't doubt yourself, because she wouldn't want that. Live life, get involved, and enjoy this amazing experience."

"Sure." I sniffed, wiping my nose with the back of my hand.

"Right boys, I'll be off." With a wave over her shoulder, she slipped out the door, and when it clicked shut, I felt a shudder roll through me like a crashing wave. I felt untethered in a way I hadn't done before. So much had changed in the last five years, all of it beyond my control, but this felt too big, too impossible. Like I was in the Matrix, and Morpheous was giving me a choice—take the red pill and my life would stay the same, or take the blue pill and nothing would ever be the same again. I just didn't know if this change would be a good thing or not.

A throat clearing pulled me back from my mental spiral, and I looked at Malachi through my lashes. All pretenses of the confidence I'd tried to convince myself I had fled at that moment. "Umm." I licked my tear-stained lips and shrugged. "Sorry about that."

"Hey, Jamie, it's no biggie." He smiled that impossibly bright smile, and my lips curled in response. "How about I help you get unpacked, then take you for a coffee and introduce you to some more people like us?"

It sounded too good to be true. He wanted to help me unpack and introduce me to his friends? I'd never met anyone like that before. Now, that's a lie, isn't it? Well, no one other than him. But that was a lifetime ago, and it wasn't like I'd ever see him again.

I coughed to clear the lump in my throat. "Sure, sounds good."

"Sweet! What d'ya wanna do? Make your bed or unpack your clothes?"

I smiled. "I'll do clothes and all my junk. The bedding should be in the box—"

"Marked bedding?" Malachi snickered.

"Yup." I dragged my boxes of clothes over to the closet and started unpacking. I was pleasantly surprised to find hangers in there on one side for my tops and shelves on the other for jeans and pants. Luckily, there was enough space at the bottom for my collection of shoes. It was mind-numbing work, but it helped calm my lingering nerves, and in no time at all, my boxes were unpacked. My stuff littered the shelves, including little knick knacks mom and I had collected together, each one holding a special memory that helped me feel closer to her.

"Gotta say, that's an improvement. I was getting bored of staring at white walls and a mattress."

"Oh? What happened to your last roomie?" I said as I plopped down on my bed. The mattress was firm but had a soft top, not the kind of thing I was expecting in a dorm room.

Malachi mirrored me, sitting on his bed while changing his high tops for a pair of rainbow sneakers. My eyes caught on the bright colors, and I wondered if he just loved color or if he was making a statement. I looked up at him with the question on the tip of my tongue.

"I'm ace," he said, tying off his laces with a small smile on his face.

"I…I…"

"I could see the question on your face, sweet cheeks."

"Oh." I chuckled. "Sorry." My cheeks heated as mortification set in.

"Nah, don't be. Anyway, people like us have got to stick together." My mouth fell open and closed like a fish out of water. "It's okay, y'know? This is a safe space."

I sucked in a sharp breath and traced a pattern on my thigh, pulling the frayed threads on my jeans. "I've never told anyone. Well, no, that's not entirely true. I haven't told my family."

Malachi looked at me with understanding and compassion. "I'm sure your aunt would love you no matter what. She's got such a pure aura, y'know?" I nodded. I might not be able to see auras, but my aunt was as pure as they came. She loved fiercely, just like Mom, embraced everyone she met, and was always willing to help a stranger. Even though the last two years had been some of the darkest, most challenging of her life—thanks to yours truly—she still did everything she could for me. I owed her and Daire so much. I knew I'd never be able to repay them for all they'd done, but I could try and make them proud.

"I do." I hiccuped. "There's just been so much going on recently what with my mom and..." A vise wrapped around my throat, stealing my words. I chewed my lip, and my eyes fell closed. I didn't realize I'd started crying again until the bed dipped and an arm wrapped around my shoulder.

"Hey, I didn't mean to upset you," Malachi said softly.

"I know." I tried to swallow back my tears. "It's just it was always meant to be me and mom. We'd talked about it so much, how we'd road trip me to college and call in at a local mom-and-pop diner on the way up and eat burgers and dirty fries and end up with grease stains on our tops but we wouldn't care... b-because we were together." I looked up at him through my lashes. Sympathy etched his features as he wiped away my tears. It seemed that now they'd started, I couldn't find the off switch.

"That sounds awesome." He sighed. "I wish it was the same for me." I pulled away and turned to face him, pulling my right leg up to my chest. "My parents couldn't wait to be rid of me. They thought I was a freak—broken—when I turned sixteen and hadn't kissed anyone or even had a girlfriend. My pa tried to convince himself I was playing the field on the down-low."

"Oh."

"Yeah. It was alright until he went through my browser history and saw that I'd been researching the Kinsey Scale and what it means to be ace." He shook his head as if to get rid of the memory. "It all happened so quickly after that. I was told to pack my shit and get out. I've not seen or spoken to my parents or my twin sisters since that night."

"Oh Malachi, I'm so sorry." My heart broke for this sweet boy. I was horrified at how his family had treated him. I didn't understand how someone who was meant to love you unconditionally could be so cruel.

"I didn't raise no faggot," Dad's voice boomed behind me. I wrapped my arms tightly around my leg until it felt like I couldn't breathe, and my heartbeat whooshing in my ears.

"Eh, it is what it is. I just hope in a few years when the girls are old enough to think for themselves, they'll want me in their lives." He shrugged and hopped up off the bed, extending his hand to me. I slipped mine into his, and he pulled me up off the bed with a light giggle that seemed so at odds with the heavy conversation we'd just been having. "Anyway, enough of that heavy talk. We're new friends, and it's much too early in our friendship to be sharing the deepest darkest secrets." He cracked a smile.

"Not gonna argue with you there," I snarked. "And I do believe you promised me coffee, Malachi."

"Call me Mal, please. All my friends do." He wrapped his arms around me and kissed my cheek. "I can tell we're gonna be besties, Jamie."

"Cool. You can call me JJ, then," I muttered, as Mal dragged me out the door that closed with a resounding bang by the time we reached the elevator.

Mal smirked as he pushed the button. "What? You wanna take the stairs?"

"Hell no." The metal doors slid open and we stepped in before they could shut. I heard someone shout for us to hold the elevator and stuck my hand between the door, hoping the sensor was working and I wouldn't end up losing a hand less than an hour after I started college.

"Thanks, new kid," a girl with blond pigtails said. She had glitter in a band over her eyes, something I'd never seen before, but it looked stunning on her.

"I like your makeup," I whispered.

"Awww, thanks, short stack." She held out her hand. "I'm Lyssa. I've got every color of the rainbow if you ever want to try some." She gave me a bright grin and exited the moment the door opened and disappeared into the crowd.

I followed behind Mal as he led me through the throng of bodies that were still filling the parking lot and sidewalk. Boxes were stacked haphazardly, while others lay on their sides, the contents covering the cement beneath my feet.

"Move in day is always nuts," Mal said over his shoulder before linking our hands. I looked down to where his fingers were laced with mine, and a pang shot through my chest that I rubbed away with the knuckles of my free hand. "It's just so I don't lose you, JJ. I am not gonna maul you or nothing. Ace, remember. He winked. The pounding in my chest calmed slowly as the number of bodies around us started to thin. I wasn't used to large crowds, and with Mal holding my hand, I felt like everyone was looking at me. I glanced around and realized everyone was so wrapped up in their own lives, that we were nothing but inconsequential strangers passing them on the street, but Dad's words still echoed in my mind.

"Do you think you could give me a tour tomorrow so I don't get lost when lectures start?"

"For sure! We'll do it first thing in the morning. Actually —" He spun around so he was facing me and continued walking backward. "The person we're going to meet is the best tour guide ever, and she knows all the gossip too. You okay if I ask her to tag along?"

"Don't see why not?" I replied, my tone whisper soft.

Mal walked at a quick clip that made it impossible to take in the stunning grounds around me, but I was just glad to be outside stretching my legs. Anything was better than being stuck in that Honda. I wouldn't have lasted another hour in that car. Thank god I chose Briar U instead of Board Lake, which was a further two hour drive. In no time at all, the smell of coffee permeated the air and the low buzz of chatter greeted my ears.

"Bean There, hands down, makes the best coffee on campus. There are other places you can get some, but it's totally not worth it."

"It could taste like crap for all I care. I'm super desperate."

"Man after my own heart. I've only had two cups today!" Mal held the door open for me and as we stepped into Bean There, a wall of scents hit my face. I took a deep inhale, savoring the complex taste as it landed on my tongue. "What do you want, new roomie?"

"What?! No! I should get one for you since I'm invading your space and all."

"Nonsense. It's your first day. My treat."

"Umm." My eyes almost glazed over as I took in the drink options listed on the blackboards. "Wow."

"Right?! This place is a caffeine lover's heaven."

"It sure is." The weight of his stare on me made my heart thunder. I didn't like being under pressure or the center of attention, and at the moment I was both. It was just too much for me to wrangle my mind into making any kind of decision. "How about you surprise me, and I'll go grab a table?"

"Of course." Mal's smile was sweet and understanding. "If you head to the back and follow the rainbow, you'll find my sister from another mister, Ava. She's who we're meeting." I turned my head toward the back, followed the location Mal was pointing at, and saw the back of a rainbow head bobbing along to the music playing softly through hidden speakers.

"I see her. I'll meet you there." I swallowed down my fear, gritted my teeth, and headed over to the bobbing head. I cleared my throat and wrung my hands. "Hey, you must be Ava?"

"Oh. My. God. You must be *the* Jamie." The pixie with a rainbow bob squealed as she launched herself out of her seat and clung to me like a koala. I chuckled and patted her back while trying to unlatch her from me.

"Uh, Ava?"

"Yes?" She giggled, squeezing me even tighter.

"Umm, do you think you could release me?" I croaked, hardly able to breathe.

I felt more than heard her sigh. "Sure, I can," she sulked. "I just love hugs. Sowwy."

"It's, umm… all good. Let's have a seat and get to know each other while Mal gets our drinks?"

"Is he getting me one?"

"I, uh. I don't know." I shrugged.

"Mal!" Ava shouted so loud the café fell silent. "I want a double chocolate espresso." Mal's face lit up with a giant grin, even though he shook his head as he added another drink to the order being taken by the goth girl behind the counter. "Sooo, new bestie to be. How you doin'?"

"Did you just Joey me?"

Ava snickered. "Hell, yes!" She held her hand up for a high five, and I rolled my eyes while giving her exactly what she wanted. "Wasn't so hard, was it?" She nudged me under the table with her foot. "We'll look after you sweet summer child, don't you worry." Her words were infused with a confidence I didn't possess. I wanted to believe her, but I spent my entire life waiting for the other shoe to drop. It was only a matter of time—I couldn't outrun my past forever.

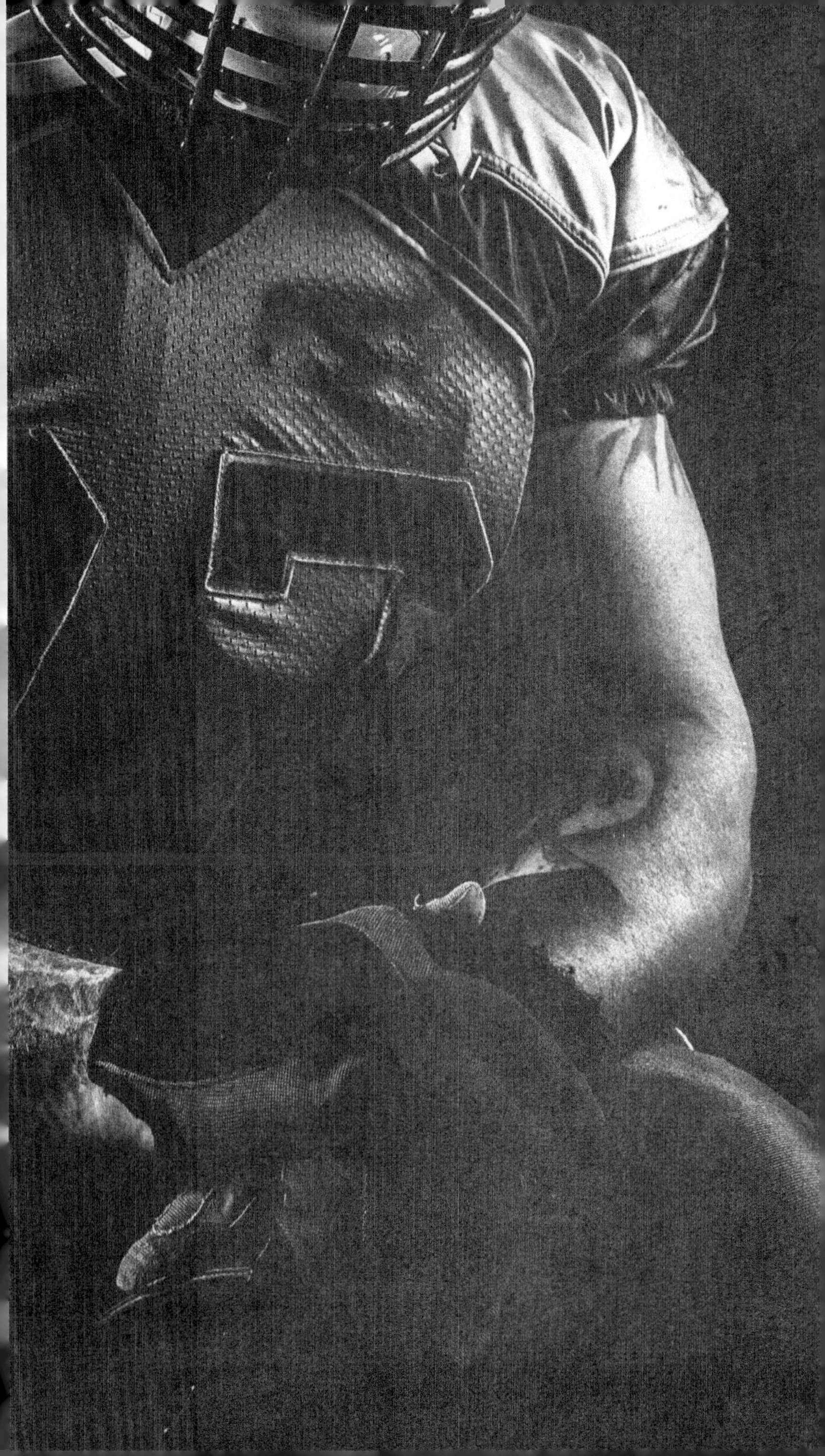

CHAPTER FIVE

Dillon

My five-thirty alarm wrenched me from a fitful sleep. My eyes were dry and crusted with grit as I blinked awake, and my room slowly came into focus. It was our last weekend off before the semester started, but I couldn't sleep the day away no matter how much I might have wanted to. I'd been off kilter since moving in day for the underclassmen. It was like the world was spinning in one direction, and I was falling in another. I hated feeling out of control. It had me feeling untethered and unsure, and I didn't have time for that shit. I was nothing if not single-mindedly focused.

I had to lead the team to the state championships, and I had to get scouted. Getting an agent and getting drafted was my goal. Nothing else mattered apart from that. My dad fought for me, pushed me harder than any parent should push their kid. But being drafted also offered me an escape route and a chance to live my life for myself and not be weighed down by the expectations of everyone else. Dad, Mom, Coach, my teammates, school. Of course, there would be expectations of whatever team I made it on to, but that would at least be my choice. I'd have control of my life for once, and that was something I'd never had.

The cold water of the shower power blasted my skin and rinsed away the sleepy cobwebs that still clung to my mind. It sharpened my focus and allowed me to get in the zone for my workout. Ten minutes later, I was dressed in black athletic shorts, a gray tank, and a backward baseball cap all with the Briar U Ravens crest on them. I was a walking billboard for Briar U, but I didn't really care. The gear was top quality and it helped us gain extra sponsorship that could be invested from our training team up.

It should have been eerie walking through the doors into the deserted state-of-the-art gym in the basement of our dorm building. The sensor lights flickered to life the moment I stepped into the pitch-black room, the machines humming quietly while the fans and A/C clicked on. No matter how hard they worked, the stench of musk and sweat was ingrained into every surface. It was gross, yet comforting. This place was more like home to me than anywhere else had been in the last five years. Ever since everything fell apart after we...

"Fuck that," I muttered to myself and locked the unwelcome thought down. I stepped on the treadmill, put in my AirPods, and started a gentle jog to warm my muscles up before stretching and hitting the weights.

I should have woken the rest of the team up and dragged their hungover asses out of bed—even if it was our only weekend off for the foreseeable future—but I valued the peace of working out on my own. I loved to run until sweat poured over my skin and my muscles burned like I'd been injected with liquid fire. For those few moments when my vision narrowed and it felt like my heart was going to give out, my mind was finally quiet. It was a reprieve I often chased but never found. Not since...not since *him*.

I was finishing up my final bench press reps two hours later when the rest of the team filtered into the gym, moaning and groaning as they shuffled around like a zombie hoard, downing iced water and staring at their phones. I racked the barbell, snagged my towel, and dabbed the sweat off my face before wiping down the bench. No one wanted to sit their ass on a wet bench; it was simple gym manners. Not many would say I had them, but I wasn't here to make friends. I was here for one thing only—to get scouted and to win.

I chugged down some water as my eyes darted to the guys finally getting on with their workouts. They were slower than molasses. "If you'd stayed in like I said last night, you wouldn't be feeling like you'd been hit by a mack truck this morning," I grumbled loud enough for them to hear me if the uptake of their shoulders was anything to go by.

"Where's the fun in that though, Cap?" Buchanan smirked at me in the mirror as he kicked up the pace on his treadmill.

"You should try living a little, Hargraves," Vleck grunted on one of the bikes. I gave him my favorite finger, making him laugh then gag. Serves him right.

"Have you all forgotten what tonight is?"

"Oh! Oh! I know that one," Stevens said behind me.

"Well?" I folded my arms over my chest and tapped my foot.

"It's, ahh?" McCormack looked up from his bicep curls in confusion.

"It's...IT'S OUR TURN TO HOST THE OPENING PARTY OF THE SEMESTER," Stevens all but yelled as the room fell silent a moment before a chorus of groans rang out.

"Exactly!" I chucked my empty bottle in the trash and

hung my towel around my neck. "I'm going to get the keys to the house and do an inventory log to make sure we get our deposit back tomorrow."

"Whoop." Stevens slapped my back and took an empty treadmill.

"Vieck, McCormack you need to make sure the kegs and liquor are delivered without issue." They both gave me a thumbs up before kicking up the pace on the bikes. "Buchanan, you got the DJ sorted?"

"Yes, Cap."

"Stevens—"

"I got the girls, Cap, no worries." He saluted, and I nodded.

The door slammed shut behind me as I left the guys to their workout, under no illusion they would probably stop five minutes after I left. My legs and arms felt like quick-drying cement due to not having done a warm down. I slumped against the wall, my chin hitting my chest, and I heaved in a deep inhale, allowing oxygen to filter through my lungs to my aching body.

I pushed myself too hard. I knew it, and by the looks my team gave me, they did too. But I couldn't be complacent; this year was my big chance. Coach told me the scouts would be coming to our opening game, and Dad was overjoyed when he'd heard the news. I just had to remain focused on the prize. I'd come too far to lose traction now, lost too much give up.

I carded my fingers through my sweat-slicked hair, pushing the long strands off my face and counted to ten and back again. It was one of my coping methods when I felt my anxiety levels spiking. I hated socializing, parties, and people. But tonight's party was all any of the upperclassmen were talking about since everyone came back to campus. It was another stress, another responsibility I didn't need but had somehow been lumbered with.

Chad "fucking" Prescott was pissed not only that he didn't make captain his senior year, but also that he wouldn't be the one responsible for hosting this year's opening party. He wanted his name to be synonymous with being the king of campus, but all his sour behavior was doing was turning everyone against him, making him hate me more. It wasn't my fault he was a shit player that only made the team because of Daddy's money, and the threat of the money train stopping was all that held his place.

Speak of the devil and he shall appear. The elevator door slid open to reveal Chad in the latest gym gear circulating on TikTok, instead of the required team gear the rest of us were wearing. My feet begrudgingly carried me forward, a grimace marring my face as pain lanced through my calves with every step. Chad smirked as he shoulder-checked me out of his way, malice gleaming in his eyes. "Look like shit, Graves." He never called me Cap or showed me an ounce of respect. "Sure you're up to this?"

"I got this," I grunted. "Nothing to worry your pretty little head over, Chad." I kept walking without looking back like he desperately wanted me to. I could feel his gaze burning into my back as I stepped into the elevator and turned to face him just before the doors closed.

Chad's hands were fisted at his sides as he stomped down the corridor to the gym. "Fucking stuck up prick." His cursed words reached me before the silver doors obscured him from my view.

There was so much I had to get done before tonight it was ridiculous. Not only did I have to sort everything out for the party, but I still needed to collect some books from the library for my nutrition course, and I had a meeting with Coach to go over the team for our first pre-season friendly next week. Thank god I knew my way around the building with my eyes closed, because I sure as shit wasn't paying attention to what I was doing. Before I knew it, I was standing under a scalding hot shower, washing the sweat off. I braced my hands against the tiled wall and allowed the hot water to work out the aches in my muscles.

My hand wandered down my chest, tracing the grooves in my abs before wrapping around my semi. It'd been weeks since I'd touched myself, or had any inclination to. I was a twenty-year-old red-blooded male, and even I knew my lack of drive wasn't normal. But I just didn't have it in me. I curled my fingers around my semi-hard shaft and gave it a tight squeeze before working my fist up and down my length with a couple of exploratory strokes. And nothing.

My inability to get hard niggled at me as I dried off and threw on some jeans, my Ravens hoodie, and shoved my feet into my boots. Maybe I could find a willing jersey chaser and get her to suck me off or fuck her ass until she screamed. Luckily, the guys didn't question the fact I didn't hook up much. I once told them I had a thing for older women, and that I used an app to meet local cougars desperate for the taste of a young jock. That'd earned me a round of whistles, back slaps, and "You da man, Caps." I wasn't naive enough to think my misdirection would last forever, so I occasionally took one of the campus sluts to bed to satisfy everyone enough to keep them off my case.

Fifteen minutes later I was in my truck, heading across town to pick up the keys for the 'party house' from Tristan. He was in his late twenties, graduated a few years ago, and had come into some money. Some say he got his trust fund, others say he got the money from dealing drugs. Honestly, I didn't care how he was able to afford one of the McMansions, just that this arrangement we had with him offered us the perfect solution.

It gave us somewhere to party so our dorm didn't get trashed, and we wouldn't get shut down by the dean. Richard Michaelson was an asshole. He ruled Briar U with an iron fist and hated to find out any of his students were having a life beyond sports or lectures. He'd almost shut down Greek Row several years ago, thanks to one very wild night that was still talked about today. So what if ten kids ended up in hospital with alcohol poisoning? It was college—the first time most of us had the opportunity to drink and live away from our parents. It's what we're meant to do.

The drive passed in the blink of an eye, and before I knew it, I pulled up outside Tristan's garage. He had a thing for classic American muscle cars and was all about restoring them. He didn't have time for "modern atrocities."

The bell rang as I entered the shop through the service entrance. I waved at the old lady at reception who didn't even look up from her magazine and made my way through the garage to his office at the back. I glanced at my watch before I rapped on the closed door. I had three hours before my meeting with Coach. I hoped to god Tristan wasn't on a call or doing whatever he did behind closed doors. It wouldn't be the first time I'd walked in on him getting his dick sucked, and I prayed today wasn't going to be another one of those.

"Enter," his muted grunt came through the door. I toed it open and slipped through the gap, breathing a sigh of relief when I found him smoking a joint. "Want some?" He took a drag and offered it to me.

"Nah. I'm good."

Tristan snorted, a thick cloud of smoke pouring from his mouth. "Fuck, I forgot you're one of those tight-ass jocks." I ground my teeth and bit back my retort. I didn't want to fuck up my life. "Take a chill pill, Dillon." He smirked. "Bet you don't do those either, do you?"

I shook my head. "No. I'm too focused on my future."

"Good for you, kid." He rolled his eyes and took another drag. Tristan stubbed out the roach and pulled his drawer open. "Money?" he asked as he rooted around in it and held out his free hand.

"It's all there," I said as I placed the envelope in his hand. Tristan made a lot from us college kids. Two grand to rent the house for twenty four hours and five hundred for a deposit when you booked it. He was making bank, that's for sure. Rumor had it this wasn't the only 'party house' he had. Apparently, he had them all across the state near colleges.

"Take a seat." It was on the tip of my tongue to tell him to fuck off, but instead, I sat my ass in that chair opposite him while he counted our money. The whole dorm put in for this. Vieck acted as party treasurer and handled the money. He just gave me the envelope and I delivered it. Personally, I thought I had the worst job, but no one agreed with me. They were all jealous. One day soon they'd realize I was the one getting the short end of the stick, but until that day came to pass, I'd keep my gob shut. "Is there anything else you guys need for tonight?"

"No."

"Still a kid of few words, aren't you, Dillon."

"I say what I need to." Tristan nodded and threw the keys at me. I caught them in one hand and rose to my feet, more than ready to get out of here.

"One of my guys will be stopping by—" I froze and turned to look at Tristan as he lounged back in his chair. "You know, in case you guys need any extras."

I closed my eyes and counted to ten and back down again. I knew what he meant by extras. Even though I hated it, there wasn't anything I could say. Tristan was a man you didn't cross unless you had a death wish. I opened my mouth, and he smirked at me. "We won't, but if you want to..." I shrugged.

An evil smile spread across Tristan's face. "You made the right choice, Dillon. See you tomorrow with my keys."

I nodded and hightailed it out of there before I gagged on the suffocating air. My chest pulled tight, and my eardrums pulsed with their own heartbeat, seconds away from exploding.

Only once I closed the door of my truck and stuck the key in the ignition did I allow myself to take a breath. My head crashed onto the steering wheel as I wrapped my fingers around it in a white-knuckled grip. "Fuucckk," I bellowed into the silence.

CHAPTER SIX

Jamie

The last few days were some of the best in my life. I felt safe and secure in a way I hadn't in as long as I could remember. Ava was the most amazing tour guide, just as Mal said. She took us around campus, and showed me the best routes to go from lecture to lecture to avoid the crowds. She'd quickly worked out my aversion to overcrowded, loud places and people in general.

You could get lost in a crowd but you could also be found, and there were just too many moving parts to keep watch on. It made my skin crawl and my anxiety spike through the roof.

I saw questions in her eyes and prayed she'd never voice them. I wasn't ready yet to talk to anyone about what haunted me. I didn't know if I ever would be.

After sharing a room for a few nights, Mal suggested I meet with the college therapist, due to my nightmares waking him up multiple times every night. I wasn't sure that was wise, and I rebuffed him every time he raised the suggestion. He accepted my unwillingness with a sad smile and didn't push the point too far.

I wasn't ready to share that part of myself and wasn't sure I ever would be. So instead, we danced around the issues we both had and avoided talking about. Me, my mom, and what haunted me, and Mal with the lack of contact with his sisters and his parents' disownment. We made a happy pair—or not—but we both put on a front and wore it like armor.

The late afternoon sun painted the sky with striking bands of orange, red, and gold, making the silhouetted buildings look like they were on fire as I crossed the main quad from the library and trudged toward my dorm. It had taken nearly a week for my final architecture books to come in.

Not that I minded; I loved the peace and solitude the library offered, and as far as I was concerned, not much beat the smell of books. Maybe bacon, or freshly cut grass, the smell of the earth after it rained, or one other that I resolutely refused to think about. Sea salt, musk, and sweat. One that was all man, even though when I'd last seen him, he was in that in-between stage—no longer a boy, but not yet a man. *Dammit.* Even my mind was against me, the damn traitor. I licked my lips as saliva pooled in my mouth at the thought of him.

I'd been an avid reader for years now, completely addicted to the escapism literary worlds offered. Nothing beat living vicariously through characters who overcame all the pain and suffering in their lives to find their happily ever after. It was a well-guarded secret that I was a romantic at heart, one who longed for a love worthy of Shakespeare's poetic words. I wanted the epic love, the fight to keep it, and everything that came with my favorite three act book plots. Although I hated the third-act breakup that seemed to be a common theme in so many romance books, I guess it added a touch of reality to each story, and reminded the reader that no matter how epic the tale, how strong the main character's love was, it was still balanced on a knife edge. One wrong move, one miscommunication, and the happiness they'd lost themselves in was ripped away.

"Hey, watch it, kid." The loud nasal voice froze me in my tracks. The next thing I knew, someone shoulder checked me, making me lose my footing and stumbled forward. My knees crashed into the sidewalk, my books falling from my arms as I reached out to brace myself before my face smacked into it. I felt like I'd been hit by a train. I struggled to breathe, my lungs refusing to expand as I tried to draw air in.

Dazed and confused, it took me a couple of minutes to pull myself together enough to grab my books off the ground and stand up. Groups of students that were previously chatting stared at me, watching and waiting to see what would happen next.

A girl in a short red dress stood before me, her long blonde hair swaying in the breeze. Her hands rested on her hips, head cocked to the side. "Look where you're going," she sneered, her red lips curled in a snarl. Her friends giggled and looked at me like I was beneath them. Maybe I had 'poor kid' branded on my forehead and that's why they looked at me like that. I didn't know but I was grateful for this opportunity more than anyone knew.

"S-sorry," I muttered and stared at the ground, waiting until they walked away. I heaved a sigh of relief when they moved on, but they weren't quiet. I heard every one of the insults they hurled in my direction and just like that, the glow dimmed on what had been a great day.

My fingers flexed on my books as nervous energy ricocheted through me, turning my knuckles white. I needed some space, some time to decompress and let down my walls. But I couldn't go back to my room because Mal and Ava were there, getting ready for a party they spent the day going on about.

My bottom lip quivered as I bit back the tears burning the back of my eyes.

I made a split-second decision and turned away from campus, focusing on putting one foot in front of the other. I walked until the voices of other students were nothing but a distant memory, until the cement path under my feet turned to grass, then leaf-littered dirt. Soon, I found myself in the woods that bordered the grounds and continued walking, even though my feet ached.

A study of maps of the local area one day in the library brought about a discovery of a lake located in the middle of dense woodland about twenty minutes from Briar U. Water and being surrounded by nature always calmed me in a way I could never articulate. It called to a part of me, resonated with my soul in some way that made me feel like I could breathe when it felt like the world was closing in around me.

Evening bird song filled the air, and cicadas chirped around me. The sounds of the forest enveloped me in a cocoon of safety as I followed an animal trail through the dense undergrowth. I could almost smell the water, feel its calm energy as I broke through the tree line and stepped onto a sloped grassy bank that led to the water's edge, where the freshwater lapped against a sandy shore line. The water was stained with the colors of the sunset; burning golds and reds faded to shades of amethyst and indigo as another day drew to a close.

I dropped my books and bag on a flat expanse of rock that edged the shore before collapsing, unable to hold myself together any longer. I sat with my knees pulled up to my chest with my arms wrapped around them, and allowed the tears I'd been holding back to finally fall.

The world blurred around me as I cried silently, the trees the only ones to witness my pain. I cried at the injustice of the world. I cried at the cruelty of humanity. I cried because despite how much I pretended, I was all alone in the world.

I missed mom more than I could ever put into words. I missed *him*. I felt like I'd been shot and five years later that wound still festered, refusing to heal. The pieces of shrapnel that had embedded into me that night were killing me slowly as they filtered through my bloodstream, heading toward what was left of that broken organ.

The shrill ringing of an unfamiliar phone pierced through the tranquil silence and had my heavy eyelids pulling open. "What the fuck?" I muttered, blinking in a daze, trying to see where the noise was coming from. It cut off before my brain was back online, then started again. The bottom of my bag vibrated against my foot, and I yanked the zip down and dug around through all the crap I'd accumulated. My fingers wrapped around the burner phone I'd all but forgotten about.

"I thought I told you to call after you unpacked and Clara had gone?"

"Hello to you too, Uncle Daire," I croaked, wiping away the drying tear tracks on my face.

"Jamie?" Concern laced his voice, and his tone softened. "You alright, kid?"

I snorted, the sound of snot popping in my nose echoed in my head. "Not a kid." I cleared my throat. "Y-yeah, I guess."

"You know I'm always here..."

"Yeah, in emergencies only." My tone had more bite than I'd intended it to, but I couldn't let go of my anger toward my uncle. He'd done so much for me and Mom, but in five years, I'd only met him once. He watched us from the shadows, and moved us around like pawns on a chess board. I knew it was necessary, but he never took the time to get to know me.

He sighed, the static on the line making it sound like he scrubbed his hand over his face. "You know why, JJ."

"I do... but it doesn't make it easier," I whispered, my throat clogged with emotion.

"Trust me, I wish things were different, but while—"

"I get it."

"But you're okay?"

"Yeah." I stretched my numb legs out in front of me and tried to wiggle my toes but couldn't feel a thing.

"Good. We're closing in, Jamie. It won't be long now, kid. Just stay vigilant, okay? Don't get careless."

"I won't."

"Promise?"

"I Promise."

"Good." The line went dead, and I dropped the phone back into my bag, just in time for the one in my pocket to start buzzing.

"Ugh." I groaned and leaned to the side to pull my phone from my back pocket. The screen came to life, the light so bright in the growing darkness that I had to blink away the stars that dotted my vision. I unlocked my phone and saw a message notification.

MAL

It's almost 7!!! Where the hell are you, Jamie?

Just at the lake, be there soon!

AVA

Sweet, sugarplum

AVA

...

It was never a good thing when the three dots stayed on the screen, especially when it was Ava typing. She was the kind of girl you could never have on loud speaker because you never knew what was going to come out of her mouth next.

AVA

I've got your costume ready.

Costume? Oh no! I said I'd go with you, but it's a no on the costume. Thanks.

Ava and Mal spent the whole time I'd known them persuading me to go to tonight's party. Ava knew I hated being surrounded by people, loud noises, and enclosed spaces. But she had begged, like literally got down on her knees and begged me to go. I'd eventually relented and agreed, but my stomach had been churning all day, and it felt like lead ran through my veins.

MAL

Oh, come ooon, JJ

AVA

It's all in the name of fun ;)

Sure!

MAL

Just hurry up or there will be no mimosas left. Ava is drinking from the jug.

AVA

STFU!!!

"ABOUT TIME, ANGEL BOY," Ava grouched as I walked through the door to find her splayed across my bed looking like a more colorful version of Cleopatra. Her costume was exquisite, and even though I'd expected nothing less, it still blew my mind and it made me feel like a fish out of water. I was so out of my depth.

I dropped my bag in the bottom of my closet, toed the door shut, and collapsed on my bed next to Ava. A smile that reached all the way to her eyes lit her face as she turned to look at me as she traced her index finger along my eyebrow, down my nose, and onto my lips. I tried to nip the pad of her index finger before she lifted it off my lips, but even in her intoxicated state, she had lightning-fast reflexes.

"Here you go, JJ." Mal leaned over Ava and passed me a cold glass filled with bubbling golden liquid. I arched my brow as I watched the glittering liquid swirling around inside the glass, having never seen anything like it before.

Ava smirked up at me and winked. "It's safe. I saw it on Amazon, and I just had to buy it. Looks freaking cool, right?"

"What is it?"

"It's a gold standard mimosa." She chuckled. "Oh, JJ." She wrapped her arm around my neck and pulled me in for a side hug. "You know how everything is better when it sparkles—"

"Or is a rainbow," Mal added.

"If you say so." I sipped my drink and ran my eyes over their outfit. Ava's was obvious, but Mal's left me confused. "So what are you, Mal?"

Ava snorted at Mal's affronted look and tried to hide behind her glass. "He's... he's..." She couldn't get her words out before she broke into a giggle.

"Seriously, you can't tell?" Mal slowly turned in a circle as I took in his low-slung blue jeans sitting just below the tight band of his boxers, and his open short-sleeved button down that exposed the slight definition of his muscled stomach.

"Have you used bronzer to give yourself abs?" I squinted, trying to get a better look. I couldn't deny the product added extra depth, making the fake six pack look real. Ava snorted, slipping off the edge of my bed and unceremoniously falling in a heap on the floor.

"Might have." Mal crossed his arms, puffed his chest out, and clenched his stomach. "Looks good though, right?"

"H-have y-you got it yet?" Ava wheezed.

I looked at her then at Mal again. My head tilted to the side as a flicker of recognition filtered through my brain. "I want to say it's on the tip of my tongue." I chewed the inside of my cheek as the answer buzzed around inside my head. "But... no?"

Mal cringed as Ava barked a laugh. "Oh, angel." She sighed and pulled herself back onto the bed, sitting criss crossed facing me. "I have one question for you... were you team Edward or te—"

"JACOB!!! Oh my god, you're Jacob Black!"

Mal rolled his left hand through the air and tucked his other hand against his stomach and took a bow. "Finally! Jamie, I was worried about you there."

"Oh shut up," I grumbled. "My eyes are sore." My head dropped to my chest, and I took a deep breath as my anxiety swelled inside me.

"Jamie," Ava said softly. "What's wrong, sweetie? You look like you've been crying."

I sniffled. "I'm good." I popped off the bed and grabbed the hanger off the back of the door and slipped into the bathroom to get changed. "Why are we getting dressed up?" I asked through the closed door.

"'Cause it's a costume party," she sang.

"Duh!" Mal chuckled.

I rolled my eyes at Ava's response, even though she couldn't see me. "Should have fucking guessed they'd keep something like that from me," I muttered to myself as I slipped on a white toga dress type thing, then battled with my lack of balance to buckle up some Roman sandals. "Ava, are these shoes yours?"

"You know it, angel. They fit?"

"Ah, yeah. I guess." To be honest, they were a bit snug, but at least they worked with the costume. I caught my reflection in the mirror as I slipped on my wings and took in my side profile. I rolled my shoulders and chuckled to myself when my wings moved, but then my gaze snagged on my face and I froze. "Shit." My face was flushed, my cheeks tear-stained, and my eyes were swollen. Thank god I hadn't put any makeup on before I went out earlier. But now, after seeing what I looked like, I had even less of an inclination to go out and be surrounded by drunk people.

"Hurry up, man. Ava wants to add some extra sparkle to you."

"And your halo! Don't forget that, Mal."

"Ow! What was that for?"

Ava's answering cackle scared me as I opened the door to find her poking Mal like a voodoo doll. He tried to bat her away with his hands, but he was as ticklish as anything and kept cracking up instead.

"You guys ready?" I turned and headed to the door. I had my hand on the handle, ready to make a quick escape.

"Not so fast, mister," Ava said as her hands latched onto my shoulders steered me toward my desk chair. Once I was situated to her liking, she grabbed her bottomless bag and pulled out foundation, concealer, mascara, and two pots of glitter. One, a holographic gold, the other, rainbow.

I swallowed. "All that for me? I knew I looked bad, but..." My throat felt thick, and it was hard to swallow. My anxiety pounded through me, ratcheting up higher with every passing second.

Ava dropped down in front of me, her blue eyes glassy, and rested her hands on my knees. "It's going to be okay, Jamie." She looked up at Mal. "Whatever happened today, you know you can talk to us, right?"

I nodded, unable to speak past the lump lodged in my throat, and placed my hand over hers and squeezed. She gave me a sweet smile, pointed to the items she'd put on my desk, and explained her vision while Mal put on some music. The soft haunting notes of Last Resort, the reimagined version, by Falling in Reverse filled the room as I sat back and let Ava work her magic on me.

Mal's phone buzzed, letting us know our rideshare was here as Ava did her finishing touches. Rainbow glitter flakes floated through the air, shimmering like the room was filled with magic. With nothing to do over the past twenty minutes, Ava's words had allowed me to lock down most of my anxiety. We slipped into the silver sedan waiting right outside our building, Ava in the front and Mal and I in the back. Campus passed by in the blur, the lights fading until we hit the outer limits of Whinthrope.

The streets were busy for eight-thirty on a Saturday evening, but then again, it's a college town and the semester was just about to start, so I guessed everyone was blowing off some steam before the real world hit us.

Trepidation crawled over my skin as the car slowed to a stop at the bottom of the drive of what looked like a modern McMansion-style home. As soon as we stepped out of the car, the thumping bass music hit us, and the windows lit up with an array of colors. Cars were parked haphazardly up the driveway and across the front lawn, making it difficult to get to the house.

Ava wore a wide smile, and Mal's sea-glass eyes sparkled with excitement. "It's gonna be fun angel. I promise," Ava said.

"We'll take good care of you and introduce you to some of our other friends," Mal added. He linked his fingers with mine as Ava stepped through the door and led us through the throng of writhing bodies into a modern kitchen. The pulsing beat of EDM music assaulted me, the vibrations rattling every surface and making bottles of liquor move across the white quartz countertop.

"What do you wanna drink?" Mal shouted in my ear. I could barely hear him over the volume of the music, even though his lips were brushing my ear.

"Nothing strong," I said as I turned to face him. From a distance, it probably looked like we were having an intimate moment, but there was nothing between us other than a budding friendship. I was already feeling the effects of Ava's gold standard mimosa as it sloshed around inside me, creating a light buzz.

"I've got you!" Mal kissed my cheek and sauntered around the island to where the red solo cups were and started mixing bottles of liquor with some fruit juices he pulled out of the large fridge.

I'd never been to a party like this. Not that I'd been to any in recent years, having never stayed in one place long enough to form any friendships. Ava bounced through the crowd with the goth girl from Bean There attached to her hip. The girl looked at Ava like she hung the moon. It was a look I recognized well, as it was one I'd worn once too.

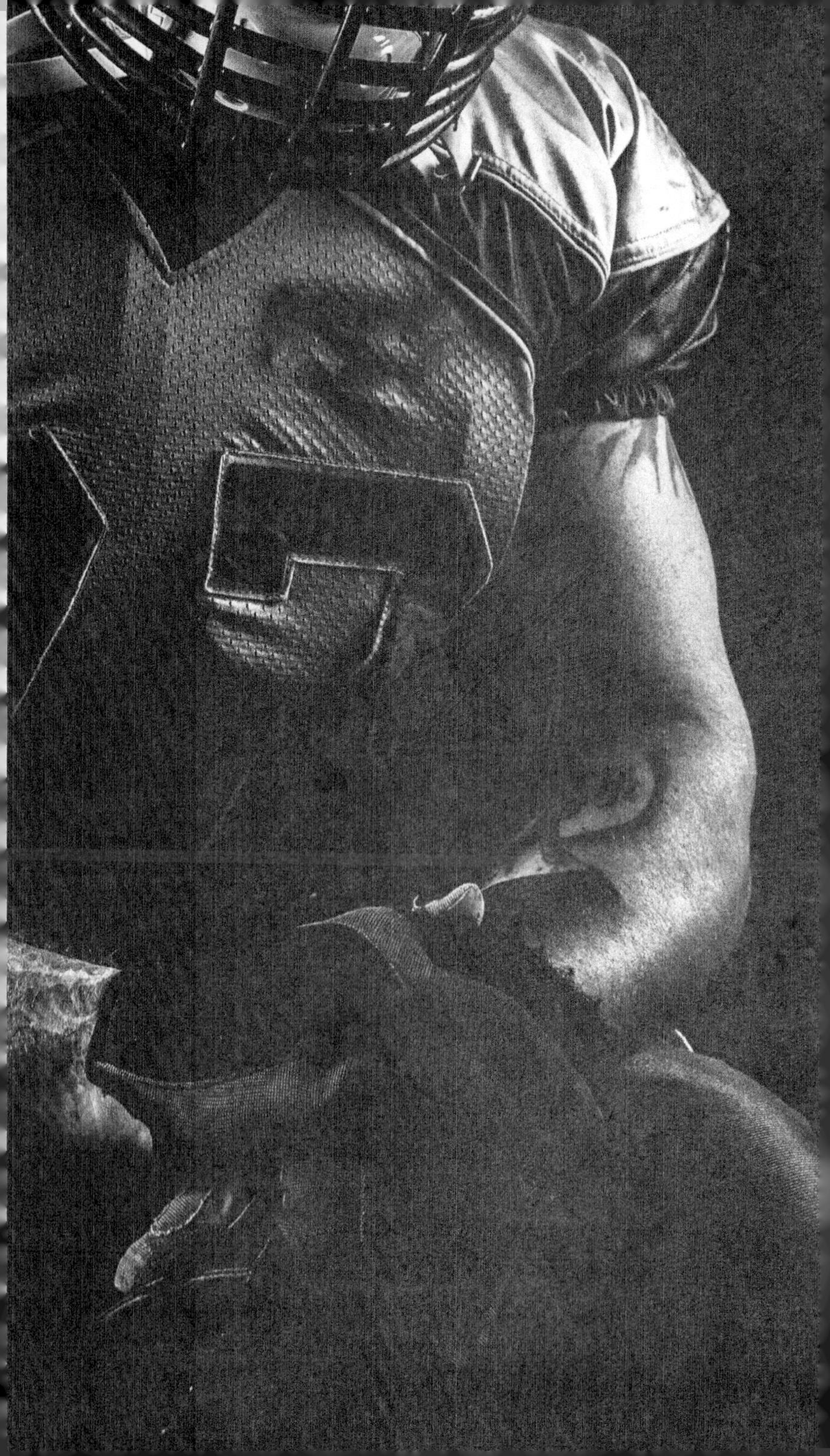

CHAPTER SEVEN

Dillon

EDM music pounded through the room, the base so heavy it vibrated through my legs as I sat at the edge of the dance floor with Elise writhing on my lap like I was a piece of furniture. Her long blond hair kept brushing over my face as she rolled her body to the beat. Her tight red dress—if the scrap of material could be called a dress—left little to the imagination, but she was all about appearances. She continued to rub herself on my crotch like I was some kind of pogo stick, but I was deader than a doornail. She irritated me more than a fucking mosquito.

Elise had spent the first hour sitting on my lap, holding court with her bitchy plastic friends, taking her role as queen bee to the nth degree. She was the 'IT' girl at Briar U. All the girls wanted to be her friend, and all the guys wanted to fuck her. She came from old money, and her daddy was a senator. She was addicted to power, but she was a vapid airhead who was still living in her high school years. The quarterback and the head cheerleader, her and me, that was her goal. I'd rather jump off a fucking cliff.

"Baby," she whined as her hand worked its way up my chest. "I'm gonna dance with Karri." She bit down on her over-inflated lip, trying to be seductive. "I'm going to put on a show you won't forget."

"Sure," I grunted, swallowing down a mouthful of my beer that was now warm because she'd prevented me from drinking it. I watched her saunter into the middle of the makeshift dance floor with her friend, Karri, a curvaceous brunette with an ass the size of a small country. They started grinding together, legs entwined, but I was more interested in how soon I could leave without raising questions.

"Fuck, that's hot," Vieck said as he sat on the arm of the chair I was sitting on, swigging his drink.

"Ahh, this is the life." Stevens groaned and adjusted himself before taking a seat on the sofa on my other side. I wanted to be anywhere but here. Fuck, this shit was boring. Talk, get drunk, fuck, then repeat at the next party. They were all the same, and as a junior, I was now done with this scene. I'd rather be at the gym.

"So, is tonight the night you're finally going to make her dreams 'cum' true?" Vieck snickered. "Get it? Cum, as in your cum."

"I get it, and no. Not interested."

"What the actual fuck, man?!" Stevens yelled. "She's the hottest piece of ass here and she's been begging you to fuck her since lat year."

"Don't care. Not interested." I tipped my bottle up only to find it empty. Fucking great.

"Leave him alone," McCormack said and handed me a cold bottle as he joined me and the rest of the guys. "Everyone knows Cap likes older women and doesn't play around with spoiled little girls."

"True, that. Can't beat an experienced woman who knows what she wants and isn't afraid to take control," Buchanan added with a smirk.

"Got somethin' ya wanna share, Buchanan?" Stevens asked, eyes alight with interest.

"Yeah, maybe you should try it. Then you wouldn't be dry humping every girl on the dance floor and making us feel sick all night."

"Don't knock my moves, man." Stevens waggled his eyebrows. "I've got plans tonight with Gemma." He pointed at a girl in a purple sequin dress. "And Ellen." He motioned to the girl next to Gemma in a black bikini. "They're twins." Stevens licked his lips and downed the rest of his drink. "See ya later, boys." He waved at us over his shoulder as he sauntered over to the girls, wrapped his arms around their shoulders, and steered them toward the stairs.

"He might be an idiot, but our boy's got game." Vieck chuckled.

"True," McCormack added. "Anyway, I'm off to find Stacie. That girl has a mouth like a vacuum, and I'm in need of a deep clean."

"Fucking ace, man," Buchanan said into his bottle. "I can totally confirm that."

"Don't look now, but here comes your snake," Vieck muttered. My eyes automatically landed on Elise as she strutted toward me like she was on a catwalk. *Fuck my life.*

Elise stopped in front of me and dropped to her knees, her hands sliding up and over my knees and down my thighs, heading for my groin. The guys were whistling and catcalling as she braced her hands on my legs and rolled her body so her fake tits rubbed against my crotch, and her face was in my line of view. It took everything to bite back my groan of frustration at the ridiculous display she was putting on.

"Hey, baby." She moaned like a cheap hooker, and her perfume smelled like rubbing alcohol, burning my nose.

"Wanna get out of here?" She looked over her shoulder toward the stairs and tipped her head. Her bedroom eyes had zero effect on me, but the guys whooped loudly and drew everyone's attention.

"Fuck!" I ground out and allowed her to pull me to my feet.

"I'll make you feel so good, baby," she purred and ran a red nail down my chest, making me shudder with revulsion.

"You want me to fuck you, little girl?" She giggled like it was Christmas morning and dragged me through the throng of dancers and up the stairs. My feet felt like lead, and my dick shriveled up inside my body.

"This one will do, don't you think, Dillon?" She smirked as her hand latched on to the handle of one of the seven bedrooms.

I fucking lost it. "No one calls me by my first name, you little slut," I snarled. My hand wrapped around her throat, and I squeezed. Her eyes were wide, pupils dilated as fear wrapped around her, but the crazy bitch just moaned.

"Oh yeah, baby. I wanna play rough. Fuck me so hard I can't walk."

"Shut the fuck up." I kicked the door open and dragged her after me. I used my strength to toss her on the bed as I shut the door. "On your knees, whore." Elise hauled herself up on her knees as I strode toward her, my hand on the button of my jeans, her eyes tracking my every move. I stopped in front of her and tipped her head back. "You do exactly what I tell you to." Bile churned in my gut and burned the back of my throat.

"Anything you want, baby," she whimpered. Elise wasted no time. She yanked my button open, pulled the zipper down and fished out my dick before I'd even taken a breath. "Fuck, you're—"

"Shut up, and suck it." I wrapped her long blond hair around my hand, positioned her head where I wanted it, and shoved my semi into her mouth until she gagged. "Suck it, or I'll fuck your face until you pass out." Tears streamed down her cheeks as she slurped on my still not hard cock. Even so, she could barely open her mouth wide enough as it was.

"Jesus," I growled with frustration, but she must have thought I was enjoying it as she moaned and started rubbing herself over her dress. "Fuck." I yanked her head back and threw her down on the bed.

Elise licked her lips and spread her legs. "You gonna fuck me with that monster, baby?" Fuck, her voice was like sand-paper against my skin. I rolled her onto her stomach, pushed the red material over her ass, and pulled a packet of lube from my wallet. I ripped it open with my teeth and poured it down her crack, working it into her ass with my thumb. "What the fuck?" she screeched.

"You wanted me to fuck you," I grit out. "Just doing what you wanted."

"Not like that, you fucking freak. Get the fuck off me," she cried and pulled her dress down. "Fucking perv."

I sneered at her, teeth bared. "Get the fuck out, you stupid bitch."

"Fuck you!" Elise righted her dress as she stumbled toward the door. Apparently, the alcohol she'd consumed hit her suddenly, as she started to stumble.

"Fuck," I muttered. Taking a deep inhale, I stared at the dark ceiling, wondering how this became my life. I tucked myself away, grabbed her arm, guided her to the door, and threw her out of the room and into the arms of some random guy dressed up as Indiana Jones. He smirked at me and started walking her down the hallway to the stairs.

I could feel eyes on me, everyone staring. "What?" I snapped. "She couldn't handle it." I played it off as best as I could, even though I was shaking and adrenaline was coursing through my body at an alarming rate. The guys jeered and most of the girls huffed and stomped past me, but a few sent heated gazes my way. I shook my head and clenched my fists to hide how much I was shaking.

I turned to walk toward the back staircase and some idiot walked straight into me. I shoved them away, not caring what happened to them because I needed to get out of this house. I needed to get away from everyone before I lost control.

The guy cried out as he hit the floor, and my body froze midstep. Something about that voice wrapped around me and held me prisoner in my own body. My heart pounded against my ribs, more erratic than it did mid-game, and my ears buzzed as everything and everyone else faded away. My eyes were drawn to the guy on the ground as flickering memories bombarded my brain. What the fuck was happening here? No. No, no, no, no! This couldn't be real.

"Little crow?" I rasped as the guy I'd just shoved to the ground picked himself up off the floor and turned around to face me. One moment. One look into those steel-ringed pale-blue eyes and my world imploded.

My hand came out automatically to touch his face, my body moved of its own volition as if the three feet that separated us were too much. My body ached to feel his, to feel his skin against mine. Electric. The magnetic force from our childhood had only grown stronger. It was like he was the air I needed to breathe. The world stopped turning. I stopped moving, and Jamie became the center of my universe.

The need to hold him in my arms burned through me. The desire to taste him saturated every cell of my being. I hungered to know everything about who he was now. A primal need consumed me. I needed to own him, possess him. Fucking consume him.

"D-Dil?" Jamie whispered, his wide eyes glistening as emotion pooled in his chalcedony orbs. He slowly got to his feet, drawn by the same force that was propelling me toward him. My heart thudded its way up my throat. I couldn't breathe. "I-I've missed you so much."

Jamie was standing right in front of me, his smaller lithe body within touching distance. Every wall I'd built around me shook. Every memory I'd kept locked down for the last five years bombarded my mind like artillery fire. Every hope and dream of us I'd kept locked down screamed at me to release them. This was everything I wanted. He was everything. Always had been. Always would be. He owned me, heart and soul, and had never known.

I took a step back, the anguish that bloomed on his gorgeous face was like a sucker punch to my solar plexus. Pain sluiced through me, altering me at a cellular level. I was lost to a dream, an unobtainable fantasy that would never become reality.

"Dill—"

"Who the fuck are you?" I growled and took a menacing step toward him. I hated seeing the flash of fear in his soulful eyes. They were like sunshine after a rainstorm. They were everything positive and warm in the world, and I was a hurricane full of wrath, hatred, and destruction. "No one gets to call me that."

Jamie flinched and took a step back, raising his hands in surrender. "I-I," his voice wavered. "I must have been mistaken." The first tear broke through the barrier of his lash line and trickled down his cheek. It felt like it was carving a canyon in my heart as I watched it fall.

"Get the fuck out of here," I bellowed. Jamie turned and ran down the stairs without looking back. The world flickered and faded before me. My lungs screamed for air. I couldn't breathe. I clutched my throat and stormed down the stairs. Buchanan and McCormack shouted after me, but I couldn't stay here a second longer. I couldn't risk exposing the truth.

I was terrified I would be dropped if Coach found out I was gay. I was heartbroken for hurting the one person I'd ever loved. And I was fucking angry he left me behind without a second thought.

“Pull it together. You have to stay focused. Protect yourself above everything else. Once you’re drafted then…” I shook my head. There would never be a then. I could never admit my truth.

I wasn’t worthy of his love when I was fifteen, so how could I be worthy of his love now, after what I was going to do to him?

I was going to hurt him, because what he knew about me was far too dangerous to be discovered.

I let that raging inferno of love inside me freeze over and molded it into hate. I turned my heart into an arctic winter and bottled up the pain that threatened to bring me to my knees. I’d hold it close to me, ready to be unleashed any time I felt my resolve weaken.

He abandoned me, broke me. Forgot me. I was simply going to remind him why and make him hate me, because I hated everything he stood for. I hated everything he was.

I fucking hated that he had the power to destroy me.

CHAPTER EIGHT

Jamie

"Little crow?" the voice so similar to the one that haunted my dreams said, but this was the voice of a man, not the boy I remembered. It was deeper, its timbre thicker. It ghosted over my skin like velvet, making goosebumps erupt across my body.

I picked myself up and turned toward him. The vision I saw stole the air from my lungs. It felt like I was having an out-of-body experience. He was the same, yet so very different. Dillon now stood close to six-five, towering over my five-foot-nine. I felt small but safe in his presence, like I'd finally found my home. My true north. He'd aged like a fine whiskey, and heat flushed through me, every nerve ending in my body becoming electrified. He was handsome at fifteen, but now, he was beautiful beyond words. His dark-brown, almost black eyes captivated me; it was like staring into the vastness of space, its enormity unknown. I could get lost amongst the galaxies and secrets they held. I'd once been the gatekeeper to his secrets, but I had a feeling I'd lost that right.

His broad shoulders were barely contained by the dark gray Henley he wore, the sleeves rolled up to reveal thick forearms dusted with dark hair. His hands flexed, highlighting the prominent veins and a tapestry of tattoos I wanted to trace with my tongue. I wanted to lick every inch of him. I needed to know his body better than I knew mine. I wanted to taste his pleasure. His love. Him.

Dillon ran a trembling hand through his thick black hair, the sides cropped close to his head, but the strands on the top were long enough to wind around my fingers when I kissed him. I wonder if he tasted the same? I licked my lips at the thought, while my heart thundered in my chest like a herd of wild horses.

We moved forward as if magnetically drawn to each other, both unable to fight the pull that only grew stronger with each passing second. "D-Dil?" I whispered, too scared to speak in case I was dreaming, and my voice would make his mirage vanish. "I-I've missed you so much."

Dillon took a step back, his face distorted in anguish. As if hearing my voice, even whispered, caused him physical pain. My eyes burned, and I blinked away the tears that wanted to fall. I felt like I was being stabbed repeatedly in the heart at his disgusted dismissal. I thought all my dreams were coming true, but what people often forget is that nightmares are dreams too.

"Dill—" I tried again, desperate to find the boy I loved in the man before me.

"Who the fuck are you?" He growled and took a menacing step toward me, a snarl slashing through his sinister lips. He was filled with hatred so vitriolic, it felt like a physical wound on my skin. Fear like I'd felt that fateful night flooded my body, and adrenaline poured into my veins and wrapped around my throat. "No one gets to call me that."

His words landed like a punch to the face, forcing me backward. I raised my hands in surrender as my heart shattered into a million pieces. "I-I," my voice wavered. "I must have been mistaken." A maelstrom of emotion blew up inside me. I lost the battle, and the first burning tear of agony seared into my skin.

"Get the fuck out of here," Dillon bellowed. My stomach revolted as the boy I loved turned into a monster that was the sum of all my fears. I did the only thing I could as the hope I'd clung to for years turned to dust at my fingertips. I turned and ran as fast as my feet would carry me. I pushed past couples making out on the stairs, lost my footing on the last few steps, and landed in a heap at the bottom. The girl in the red dress from the quad laughed and spat at me as I clambered to my feet.

The walls were closing in around me. I couldn't breathe. I clawed at my neck, trying to remove the invisible rope around it getting tighter and tighter every time I opened my mouth. I gasped for air as perspiration beaded on my brow and dripped into my eyes. I tried to push through the gathering crowd to the front door, but the bodies were too tightly packed, so I turned and ran toward the kitchen.

I saw Mal, Ava, and the goth girl chatting where I'd left them when I went upstairs to take a piss. Luckily for me, they were far too engrossed in each other to see me stumbling over my feet and rushing to the open back door. I slipped out of the kitchen and ran. I ran around the yard, down the drive, and along the street in the direction I thought we came from when we arrived.

At some point, I'd lost my wings. Right now, I wish I had them and they were real so I could fly away and never come back. Tears poured down my face, and the world around me blurred, but I didn't care. I had to put as much distance as possible between me and *him*.

All the times I'd dreamed of seeing Dillon again, it had

never gone like this. It might have been awkward and uncomfortable to begin with, but he never looked at me like he hated me. Like he cursed the day I was born.

My legs ached, and my muscles burned, but I kept pushing myself. I wasn't sure I'd ever put enough distance between us, but I had to try. Then, and only then, would I try and figure out what the hell to do now the one hope I'd clung to was gone. Ripped out of my fingers before it had even had a chance to grow roots.

There was a pain in my side so acute I felt like I could pull a knife out of it. Every movement made the pain spike. My feet were numb, and my body was slick with sweat, while my toga soaked through and clung to my skin. My ankle buckled, and I tripped and tumbled to the ground. My skin scraped along the sidewalk as I rolled to a stop against a wall.

I pulled my knees up to my chest, my left wet with blood as I wrapped my arms around my legs and buried my face in them. Tears poured down my face, and my teeth chattered as I was battered by the continual onslaught of emotions I didn't know how to process. The only thing I could think to do was purge myself of them, so I screamed. I screamed until my throat was raw. I screamed until my voice gave out. I screamed until I felt numb inside. The cool wind froze the sweat on my skin into a layer of ice, and I found myself begging for oblivion.

"JAMIE?"

"JJ? Where are you?"

"Jamie Bowen, can you hear me?"

"Please, JJ, answer me!"

I heard voices calling out my name, but it was like I was hearing them through water; every word distorted and far away. I tried to open my eyes, but it was like they weighed a thousand pounds. I couldn't lift my head, and grit and glass cut into the side of my face. I was too cold and weak to move. I thought the voices were getting closer, louder, but I wasn't sure. I couldn't think straight, and my mind was playing tricks on me. I was exhausted in the bone-deep, soul-draining kind of way.

The trouble was, I had no idea where I was. No clue how far I'd run or in what direction. I'd just followed my feet trying to outrun my past. A past I now wanted to forget, along with all the other bad things that had happened.

A bright light burned through my eyelids, making me groan. The sound made it feel like someone had poured acid down my throat as pain lanced through me.

"Shit. JJ?" The broken voice was clearer now. A warm hand touched my cheek and neck. "Hang on, okay? I'm going to get Ava." Footsteps sounded around me like boulders tumbling down a hill. I curled tighter in on myself and willed sleep to claim me.

I felt like I was floating, lights flickering in and out of the darkness. The bone-deep cold I'd been lost to started to fade as something soft and warm covered me. A whimper escaped as my body jolted. "Shh, angel, we've got you. We're nearly back to campus, then we'll get you a coffee and wrap you up in bed." Ava's soft voice soothed the swelling anxiety inside me, because I didn't know where I was.

"W-w-where a-am... I?"

A deep chuckle sounded by my feet, and it was then I realized firm hands were massaging my aching muscles. "We're in Tim's car, Jamie. He came with us when we discovered you'd disappeared. We tried to call your phone before we remembered you left it in our dorm."

"Mmhmm," was all I could manage.

"You scared the shit out of us, you know," Mal scolded.

"S-s-sorry."

"Hey, sweetie, it's okay. We were just worried about you and what had happened," Ava cooed as she ran her fingers through the tangled strands of my hair, her gentle touch comforting.

"We're here, guys," a voice said that I didn't recognize. It must have been Tom? Tammy? Tim? "Do you need me to help carry him upstairs?"

"What, you don't think I'm strong enough?" Mal snorted.

"You're hardly a chopstick. There ain't no muscles on your scrawny-ass bones." Tim snickered.

"Hey! I resent that."

"Boys!" Ava snapped. "Let's get Jamie inside and cleaned up, yeah? The RA would have left by now. So if you could carry him up, Tim, that would be great. Mal will get the doors."

"Of course, I will."

I don't know how they managed to get me out of the car when my muscles were locked up tight without bashing my head, but they did. The next thing I knew, I'd been laid on my bed, the soft glow of the lamp light giving our dorm a warm glow and offering an ounce of much-needed comfort.

"Well, if that's all, guys, I better head home."

"Thanks for your help, Tim," Mal said softly. I could just about make out him wrapping his arms around a blurry figure before the door snicked shut.

My bed dipped and Ava's rainbow hair filled my vision. "You alright there, Jamie?"

"Not really, no." My eyes started to well up again, but I was too tired to hide my tears as they started to fall.

"Oh, honey." Ava leaned forward, wrapping her arms around my neck. She held me in her arms, muttering soothing words into my ear. She pulled back and gave me a soft smile. "I'm sorry for pushing you to go tonight."

I licked my dry lips. "It's not your fault. You didn't cause this." I tried to wave my hand up and down my body, but I ended up smacking myself in the face, making her smile. It broke my heart when it didn't reach her eyes. I hate making people sad because I felt like I'd failed.

"Here." Mal holds a cup of coffee in front of me. "Ava, can you help him sit up so he can drink this while I take a look at his leg?"

"Sure."

"Thanks."

Ava hooked her arms under mine and helped me shuffle until my back was against the headboard, then passed me a steaming cup of coffee. The rich bean scent wrapped around softer tones of chocolate and caramel. "This smells super sweet." My nose wrinkled as I took another inhale of the dubious mixture.

"It's my famous I've-had-a-shit-night drink. Caffeine for an energy boost, chocolate and caramel for sweetness, and added sugar in case you're dropping from an adrenaline surge."

"Listen to Dr. Mal, Jamie," Ava said as she walked into the bathroom and returned with the first-aid box we kept under the sink.

I took a sip of my drink, noting the flavors as they burst across my tongue and groaned. "It's good, huh?" Mal said as he undid the Roman sandals that were cutting off my blood circulation. He pulled them off and flung them across the room. "Are you going to tell me what happened?"

I shook my head. "It's stupid... nothing. Don't worry about it, okay?"

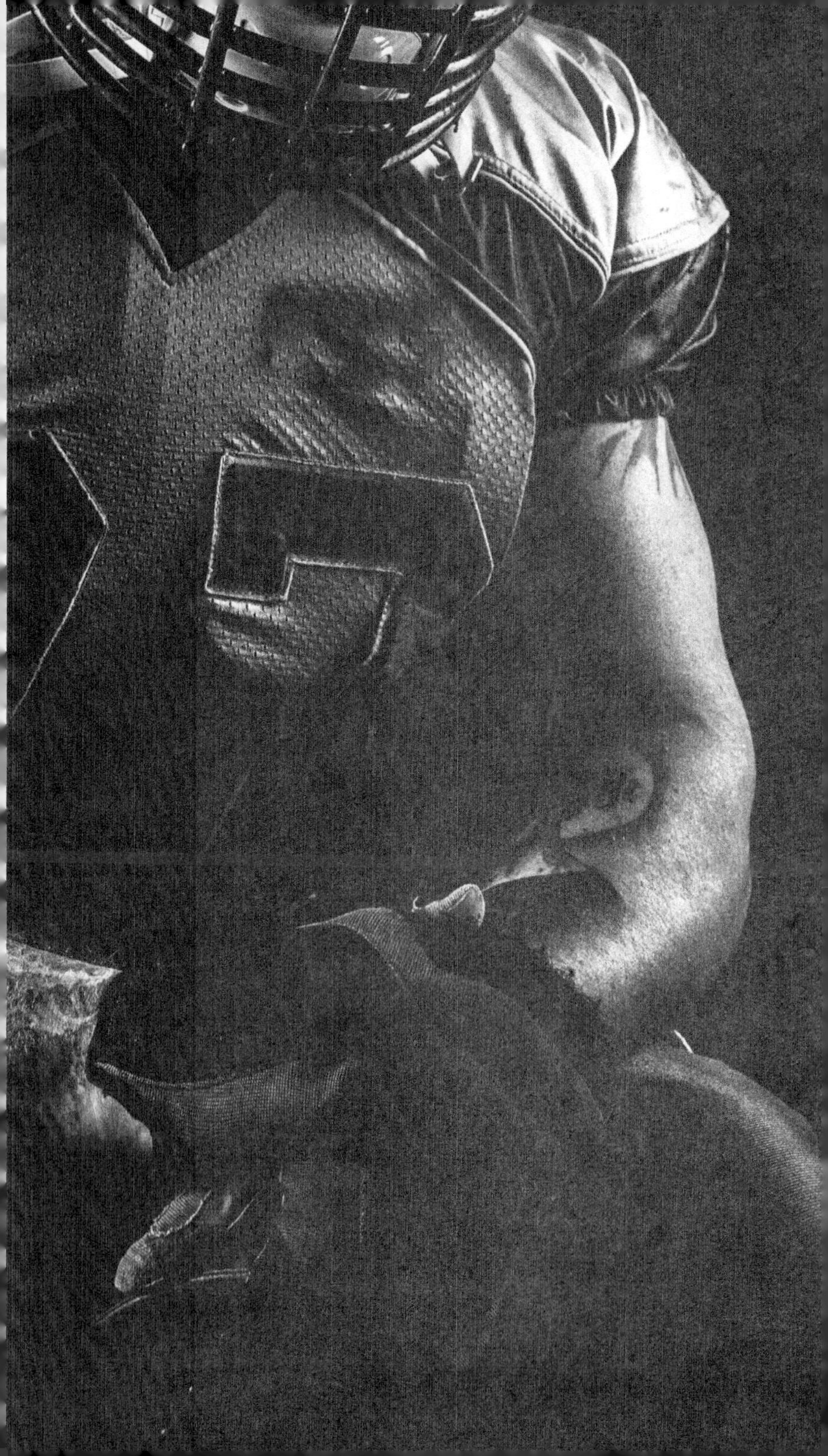

CHAPTER NINE

Dillon

I rolled the empty bottle between my fingers, the hollow weight of it echoing the feeling inside me. The smoldering flames of the fire pit licked into the night sky, illuminating a small part of the deck from the darkness beyond it. The party raged around me, people having the time of their lives, drinking, laughing. *Fucking.* I'd seen one too many poorly executed blow jobs tonight, and I needed to bleach my fucking eyes. The scent of pot hung in the air, and for the first time in my life, I considered taking a joint and numbing the pain infecting me.

A self-deprecating laugh clawed its way up my throat, making a group of girls that were smoking jump out of their skin. A malicious smirk lifted my lips as I enjoyed their fear. It was better than drowning in my self hatred. My head rolled on my shoulders, and I stared up at the ominous blackness above me, the empty bottle slipping from my fingers and clattering on the deck below.

I needed another fucking drink. "Hey, kid." I grabbed the sleeve of some guy walking past me, pulling him to a stop.

"What the fu..." He lost his voice when he caught sight of me. "H-Hargraves?" he squeaked in question, even though he knew who I was.

"Yup, that's me." I tried to smile but it felt awkward. I didn't make small talk to anyone, if I could help it. "Get me a bottle of tequila." The girl he was with huffed and stomped her foot. "What?!" I snapped.

"N-nothing." Wrapping her arms around herself, she looked at the guy she was with. "Let's just get it for him, k?" The guy nodded and dragged her into the house.

I threw another couple of logs into the fire pit. The flames were almost non-existent now, and it made me realize how cold it was. I shoved my hands into the pocket of my hoodie and continued to stare at the black expanse above my head, wishing the incessant noise around me would fade away, but I was never that lucky.

"H-Hargraves?" My head lolled to the side, and I peeled my eyes open. Fuck! When had they closed? The kid stood there shaking, arm outstretched, bottle of tequila in hand. "I got it."

I snatched the bottle off him, brought it to my lips and took a long swig. The burn was just what I needed. The kid was still standing there, fidgeting from one foot to the other. "What?" I snapped.

"I-I—"

"Yooou what? Just spit it the fuck out, will ya? I haven't got all day to wait on you!"

"I was wondering if." He licked his lips and pulled his shoulders back. I rolled my eyes, willing his bumbling to be over. "If you could, y'know, say hi to me if you see me around?"

I snorted. This kid was so ordinary he'd blend into a beige wall if he stood still for too long. I ground my teeth. "Fuck off!" I barked, and he scampered off like I'd thrown a grenade at him. "Stupid little prick."

The liquid in the bottle glinted in the moving light of the flames as if to remind me this bottle was in fact not empty and that it needed drinking. There was only so much I could process at the moment. All I wanted was to chase oblivion and forget tonight ever happened. I lifted the bottle to my lips and swallowed down one burning mouthful after the next until my lungs screamed at me to take a breath.

As the world around me blurred, my racing heart calmed and a soothing numbness spread through my veins. My eyes felt heavy as the exhaustion I spent every day ignoring grew stronger.

"What the fuck happened?" McCormack said as he dropped down in a seat opposite me. I rolled my eyes and brought the bottle back to my lips.

"Cap, seriously, who was that kid?" My head rolled in the direction of Vieck's voice as he took the chair next to me. I shrugged and carried on drinking.

"Daisy said he was a freshman," Stevens muttered, loading more logs onto the fire that had all but burned out. "Said you made him cry?"

Buchanan laughed, passing out beers to the guys before plopping down next to me. "Seriously, Cap, what the fuck?"

"Nothin'," I grunted.

"Michelle also told me that she saw Elise running down the stairs in tears." Stevens smirked and tilted his head, watching me too closely for my liking. "What did she do?"

"Or didn't, more to the point." I snorted.

"She get freaked out over that whopper you're packing?" Vieck raised his bottle at me before taking a drink.

"Somethin' like that." I tipped my head and closed my eyes, done with this conversation already.

“Seriously though, Dillon.” My eyes flew open as I glared at Buchanan. He raised his hands in mock surrender. “What happened with the kid?”

“Yeah! Everyone is talking about you going postal on him,” Stevens added.

I heaved a sigh. “Nothin’, I told ya.”

“Cut the shit, Cap.” McCormack leaned forward and rested his elbows on his knees. “This isn’t like you.” I grunted, making him chuckle. “I know you’re a prickly fucker, but this?” He waved his hand toward the house. “This was something else, right? Something personal?”

I couldn’t hide my wince even if I tried. I wedged the now half-empty bottle of tequila between my legs and carded my hands through my hair. “It doesn’t matter.” I sighed.

“It does, man,” Stevens said. “You know we’re here for you, right?”

“We got your back, Cap!” Vieck agreed.

“We’re a team!” McCormack nodded.

“Fuck off, all of you.” I took another swig of the burning liquid, and the world started to move all on its own.

“No,” Buchanan said, his tone brokering no argument. “You tell us what the hell that was all about, and let us help you for once.”

I pinched the bridge of my nose and tried to order the thoughts and feelings churning around in my mind. I couldn’t tell them the truth—that I loved and hated that boy in equal measure. That he knew a secret about me no one else knew—one that would most likely lose me my place on the team. Coach had never outrightly said anything against queer players, but there was enough undertone in his commentary to know he wasn’t an ally in any form, and the whole reason I was here would be ripped away from me in an instant. I couldn’t allow that to happen.

I might be an unsociable ass and generally hate everyone, but these guys were more like family to me. We’d all arrived as naive freshmen, and we'd partied hard and played harder to get where we are today. So I owed them something, some semblance of the truth. But not the whole truth.

“I know him from back home.”

“Called it,” Stevens whooped.

“Shut up.” Vieck laughed and whacked him around the head. “He'll never tell us if you keep butting in.”

I cleared my throat; it felt thick and dry. A bead of sweat ran down the back of my neck, even though I felt cold to the bone. “He... his dad.” *Fuck.* I raised the shaky bottle to my lips and swallowed down the liquid fire. Normally, cheap-ass drinks get better the more you drink, but this paint stripper only got worse. My fingers and toes started to feel numb as the alcohol spread through my body. “His dad beat me up when I was a junior, broke my arm and stuff. I ended up in the hospital for the weekend while they set the cast and monitored me for concussion.”

I looked around at the guys. Each and every one of their faces wore the same expression. Complete and utter shock, disbelief, and anger.

“He fucking WHAT?” Buchanan bellowed, his hands clenched into white-knuckled fists.

“Yup he told his old man I was bullying him.” *Lie.* “That he was afraid to go to school.” *Lie.* “That I'd threatened to break his legs.” *Lies!* All of it—fucking lies. I was the lowest of the low. Even if I begged on my knees, Jamie would never forgive me once he found out the truth.

“That fucking little shit needs to pay.” McCormack growled. He's always had a short temper—anything could set him off. You never knew if the guy was going to Hulk out on you at any moment. *If that's what you think he's like, I dread to think what you think of yourself.*

“What's the plan, Cap?” Vieck asked, wringing his hands together.

“Shit like that can't go unpunished,” Stevens added.

"We make him pay. Fuck him over so badly he leaves."

"Whoop! That's the spirit, Cap." Buchanan slaps me on the back. He takes the empty bottle of tequila and hands me an ice-cold bottle of water.

"What's his name?" Stevens inquiries. "I'll get my girl to look at his file and find out everything there is to know about him."

"Sounds good." My hands shook, and acid churned in my stomach, making me feel like I was going to puke. "Jamie Abernathy."

"Consider it done." Stevens nodded at me before sitting back in his chair and kicking his legs out.

I took a swig of water. The icy liquid soothed my sore throat but did nothing to stop the emotion burning the back of my eyes. I tipped my head backward and allowed my eyes to fall closed as the guys talked about their conquests for the night. I chose to ignore them in favor of the chaos in my mind.

There were four days etched into my mind that I could never forget, and they all centered around one blond-haired blue-eyed boy. They had each changed me in some way and molded me into who I was today, for better or worse.

SWEAT DRIPPED down my face as I arrived home from my morning run, my soaked top clinging to my skin. The early morning was already a slave to the mid-summer heat. There wasn't a cloud in the vast expanse of blue that made up the sky.

I sat down on the steps that lead to the front porch, my arms braced on my legs, my head hanging as I sucked in deep breaths. I prayed the gentle breeze would pick up and help cool me down, but it seemed I was out of luck. Mom and Dad were already gone for the day—Mom to the library where she'd work till noon, and Dad to the factory. It was a new job, and he hated it with a passion, but he'd been sacked from his last one. I wasn't sure why; I just knew he was pissed over it and had started to drink heavily. It made things super uncomfortable at home, so I did everything I could to stay out of his way. That included getting up at six every morning and going for a run before he got up.

The sound of an engine rumbled down the road, growing louder until it came to a sudden stop. The breaks squealed, making me wince at the high-pitched whine. I pulled my top off and used it to mop my face. My head snapped up when a car door slammed, and a large figure walked toward me. It was hard to see who it was through the hazy glare of the sun.

"Dillon," Mr. Abernathy growled.

I stood up quickly. "Mornin', Mr. Abernathy. Dad's not here right now. He's at work."

"I know that, kid," he spat. He towered over me even though I stood on the second step, and at seventeen, I wasn't small. I was over six feet and had finally started building some decent muscle with all the football practice I did.

"I'll let them know you stopped by," I said and turned to head toward the house. My dog, Buster, whined and scratched at the door.

"No." Before I knew what was happening, his hand wrapped around my arm and yanked me down the steps. My legs gave way underneath me, and I fell on the grass at Mr. Abernathy's feet. "Where the fuck is he?"

I pushed myself up and got to my feet. "I don't know who you're talking about." I crossed my arms and stared into his red-rimmed, bloodshot gray eyes. The volatile energy surrounding him made me take a step back.

"Of course, you know!" He growled, taking a step toward me, forcing me to back up again. "You two are practically joined at the hip. Don't lie to me, Dillon. Where the fuck is my son?" Spit hit me in the face as he sneered down at me.

"I told you, I don't know." I didn't, and it killed me. I'd gone from the biggest high of my life to rock bottom in less than twenty-four hours and now this. My first kiss with Jamie was

life altering. Earth shattering. For the first time in forever, something felt right, perfect even. But he had to leave to get home to his Mom as it was his birthday before we could talk about it. I wanted to be his boyfriend, even if we couldn't be out at school. He stole my heart the moment his lips touched mine.

I got up extra early the following day and walked to his house. It was only fifteen minutes from mine, less if you used the shortcut. But when I got there, everything changed. I knocked on his window like I did most mornings. Usually, he'd slide open the screen and let me in, but that day, nothing. I walked to the back door and knocked again, and nothing.

I'd tried the handle, expecting it to be locked, but the door opened. I slipped in, making my way down to his room, and gently pushed the door open so it wouldn't squeak. But his bed was empty. My stomach fell through my feet when I noticed his closet and drawers were open, mostly empty with a few clothes hanging out of them. His room looked like it had been ransacked.

I quickly made my way through the house, and every room was the same. It was like someone had ripped open every door and trashed every room. There was a dark stain on the kitchen floor.

I left twenty minutes later, tears streaming down my face, and my heart irrevocably broken. The car had gone. Jamie had gone. He'd left and not told me. Every one of my dreams had been ripped to pieces.

"I told you, sir." I sucked in a shuddering breath. "I don't know where he is. I haven't seen him in five days."

Mr. Abernathy scoffed in disbelief. "You're lying to me." He stepped forward, and I edged up another step, closer to the house. My heart thundered in my chest, thrashing against my rib cage.

"I-I'm not." I licked my lips, tasting salty sweat as it continued to drip down my face. My fight or flight instinct kicked in, and adrenaline surged through my veins. I needed to get out of here. The scent of alcohol surrounded Mr. Abernathy,

and his wife beater was soaked through with sweat as he vibrated with rage in front of me.

Before I could blink, his hand wrapped around my throat, and he pinned me to the front door. His face so close to mine, his nose brushed my cheek as he spat, "Tell me where that little faggot is." The blood in my veins turned to ice as I froze in his hand. He tilted his head as he regarded me. "You didn't know?" His voice was laced with suspicion.

I'd never told anyone I was gay, not even Jamie. But he knew, without me ever having to say a word. "N-n-no."

"Well," he said, spitting at my feet. "I wanna leave a message for that little faggot with you."

Confusion washed over me, but I nodded as much as his grip would allow. "O-okay," I rasped.

I hadn't even blinked before his fist crashed into my temple. The world went black. Pain ricocheted through me at multiple impact points like I'd been shot several times. The pain stole the air from my lungs as tears spilled down my cheeks. "Fucking nancy boy." Mr. Abernathy growled as I fell to the floor.

I curled up into the fetal position as he kicked my stomach. I wrapped my arms around my legs and tucked my head, trying to shield my organs. His steel-toe capped boots relentlessly kicked into me as he yelled profanities at me. The pain made blood and bile pool in my mouth. Every breath was excruciating as agony became the only thing I knew.

I thought it was bad when he kicked my stomach, but it was nothing compared to the moment he stomped down on my throwing arm. White-hot pain shot through my bone as it cracked. The sound echoed around me before I passed out. For a few blissful seconds, the world was silent.

My head was wrenched up off the floor by my hair. Mr. Abernathy grabbed my face, his fingers and thumb pushing my jaw open. His arm shook with his unrestrained anger as he bellowed at me, "I will fucking kill him. Make sure you tell him that. No son of mine will live to be a fucking faggot."

CHAPTER TEN

Jamie

Monday was here before I knew it. The alarm on my phone, although set to silent, vibrated like a jackhammer in my hand. I blinked awake, my eyes dry and crusty from lack of sleep. It was still dark outside, but the light from the streetlight near our window illuminated the room enough for me to see.

After not being able to fall asleep Saturday night—even though it was almost three a.m. before Ava went back to her room—I should have been exhausted. Instead, I was wired. I had tossed and turned, got up, fumbled with my e-reader, and at one point, threw it across the room. When it crashed into the door, Mal got up, picked my e-reader up, and placed it on my bed. Then, like the sweet-hearted guy he was, asked what movies I liked. I wasn't able to think of anything, because my mind was still laser-focused on what Dillon said at the party.

Instead of being put off by my introverted nature, Mal put

on Twilight and told me to get into bed with him. I must have looked like my eyes were about to bug out of my head, because he threw his head back and laughed at me. I'd never shared a bed with anyone else, so his suggestion caught me completely off guard. He'd assured me that he had no nefarious intentions; he just wanted to offer me some comfort and told me when his sisters struggled to sleep, he did the same and thought it might help.

Sunday morning, he plied me with a caramel latte and breakfast wrap from Bean There before spending the rest of the day snuggled in his bed. We were both able to get a few hours of sleep in between watching the whole Twilight Saga. Mal was a dork and a massive Jacob fan, so I guess I shouldn't have been surprised, considering he dressed up as him for the party and all.

I slowly extracted myself from Mal's arms, careful not to wake him. He needed his sleep, but because of me and my nightmares, he'd hardly had any. Remembering his words about his sisters, I made a mental note to call Jessie after classes. It had been nearly a week since I last saw her beaming grin.

After showering and dressing, I closed the door quietly behind me and headed toward Bean There where I was due to meet Ava. She wanted to walk me to my first course. Not many students signed up for the early-morning classes, preferring to sleep in longer. Unfortunately for us, the ones we needed for our degree started at eight, so we had no choice.

The cool morning air was a welcome reminder that the seasons were starting to change. Fall was one of my favorites. I loved the autumnal colors—golden yellows, burnt oranges, and vibrant reds, and the first frosts that crunched under your feet and the way your breath hung suspended in the air. Nature at its finest.

"Well, if it isn't my little angel."

"Hey, Ava." She handed me a to-go cup and smiled. The

early morning sun lit up the kaleidoscope of colors in her hair. "You ready for today?"

"Of course, I am! Who doesn't like getting up at the ass crack of dawn?" she snarked. "That's why this is my third latte this morning." I snorted. No wonder she was an Energizer Bunny every time I saw her. "I got you a caramel latte."

I took a sip and groaned. "This is delicious. Let me know how much I owe you."

She waved me off and sat down on one of the benches facing the main quad. "Sit with me, we've got time." She patted the space next to her. I dropped my bag by my feet and tried not to shriek when my ass hit the cold wooden bench. "So—"

Her tone said everything, and I rolled my eyes. "Not you as well?"

She looked up at me with an arched brow. "It's not wrong to care about your friend's wellbeing, Jamie." She put her hand over mine and squeezed. "And we care. Me and Mal."

"Did he put you up to this?"

She shook her head. "No. He said he was worried about you. We both are. We saw how you were on—"

I held up my hand to stop her from saying anything else. I turned in my seat and took her hands in mine. "I know, and I'm sorry that you did." I bit my lip as I took a deep calming breath. "That was, well, that was rough." I fumbled my words, not knowing what to say. "But I'm alright." She looked at me like she didn't believe me. "Honestly, I'm okay." I smiled. "I've been here a week and already made the best friends I've ever had." Saying that hurt more than I'd ever admit, but I plastered a smile on my face so she would believe me.

"Alright, if you're sure?" she said hesitantly. I squeezed her hand before letting go and taking another sip of my latte.

"I am. I'm excited about today." I beamed at her over my cup. Ava's mirroring smile settled something inside me, and a weight lifted off my shoulders.

"It's Architectural History for you, isn't it?"

I nodded. "I've heard good things about Mr. Tunaley."

"Yeah, you can say that again. The guy is a bit of a legend around here." She snorted. "Shame he doesn't teach the arts," she said, flashing me a bright smile. "I snuck into one of his lectures when I was a freshman just to see what all the fuss was about, and I mean, the guy is hot. Older, like late thirties, I think. He's got that refined air about him and always dresses in a three-piece suit." She leaned in closer. "Some of the jocks here could take a page out of his playbook, if you know what I mean."

I didn't really, but I just chuckled with her. Her light laugh was infectious like that. "Well, at least I'll know he's the one in a suit." I cracked a smile and finished my latte, already feeling lighter than when I got up. Ava was like a rainbow fairy godmother, and she didn't even know it.

"But in all seriousness," she said around a mouthful of burrito. "He's as straight as they come." I choked and swallowed that last mouthful down the wrong way. "Not like that." She whacked my arm. "Well, I mean he is, but that's not what I meant. He calls a spade a spade, but he's passionate about his subject. He even made me consider doing one of his courses, and I'm here for the creative arts program."

"I guess that explains your flare."

"Totes. Why live life in the gray?" She turned her dark eyes to me, and the weight of her gaze made me squirm.

"Uh oh," I muttered. "Don't look at me like that."

"Like what?"

"Like you know something I don't but should."

Her hands landed on my shoulders, pinning me in place. "Maybe I do? Maybe I see that you're hiding yourself away, burying your truth." Who the hell was this girl? I'd only known her for a few days, and it was like she could see right through me.

"I…I…" I lost my voice and tried to swallow around the

lump in my throat. Ava made me feel vulnerable and exposed, but ironically, also safe. There was this softness to her, an inherent goodness that had me wanting to rip open the vault doors and lay my secrets at her feet. But I didn't. I couldn't.

My phone vibrated in my pocket, three short bursts. It was my alarm reminding me I had twenty minutes to get to my first lecture. Pulling my phone from my pocket, I cleared the alarm and glanced at the notifications. I had messages from Mal and Aunt Clara. I opened Mal's first.

MAL

Good luck today! You'll be fine.

Thanks. Hope I didn't wake you?

MAL

smiley face emoji Nah, all good! Wanna meet for lunch?

Sure.

MAL

Sweet. Text me when you're out.

Will do.

I flicked to the thread with Aunt Clara.

AUNTIE C

Good luck today, JJ. She's proud of you.

Emotions I wasn't prepared for slammed into me, knocking me off center as a cool breeze lifted my curls. It felt like Mom was there with me, holding me, soothing me like she used to when I was younger. I wiped my eyes with the back of my hand, catching the tears that clung to my lashes before replying.

Thank you.

Just as I sent through my reply, a photo popped up in the thread of Jessie holding a cardboard sign with the words *WE LOVE YOU, JAMIE!!! MISS YOU!* surrounded by millions of little hearts.

Miss you too, sunbeam. Will call you when I'm done for the day.

AUNT CLARA

Sounds good, kid. Love you *heart emoji*

Love you guys too.

I tucked my phone back into my pocket and took a moment to lock my emotions down. The quad had filled since Ava and I sat down. Groups of friends walked together on their way toward different buildings on campus. Others headed in the direction of Bean There for that elusive first hit of caffeine and a quick hot breakfast. It was like watching a silent movie, the figures moving around the screen while your mind tried to work out what they were talking about. A loud laugh rang out, and the world snapped back into focus like an elastic band. I shook my head and looked over at Ava who was lost in her phone.

I cleared my throat and dumped my trash in the garbage. Ava peeled her eyes off the screen and tilted her head. "I've gotta go. I've only got fifteen minutes until my first class starts and it's roughly a ten minute walk from here."

"Alright, let's go. I've got to get to the dance hall anyway." Popping up off the bench, Ava slid the strap of her bag over her shoulder and dumped her trash. I smiled at her as she linked her arm with mine and dragged me along with her.

"I didn't expect there to be this many people around this early."

Ava's musical chuckle rang out. "I'm pretty sure every department has early starts." She inhaled a quick breath. "Plus, we're not far from the sports fields, gym, and dance center.

Those guys train from like six in the morning, so y'know, we're not the only early risers."

I groaned. "It wasn't like I was up at this time by choice. If I had my way, the day wouldn't start before noon. Anything before that is just plain rude."

"I hear you on that." She chuckled. "Anyway, we're here, angel."

I looked at her with wide eyes. Trepidation and excitement made a complex mix for my strained anxiety, but my smile held firm. "Thanks for walking me. You didn't have to."

"Nonsense." She chucked her thumb over her shoulder. "Besides, you practically walked me too. I'm just over there."

"If you say so. You wanna meet for lunch? I'm meeting Mal."

"Sure thing, angel boy." Ava wrapped her arms around me before giving me a quick once over. I wasn't in anything special, just jeans, a hoodie, and my high tops. "Hmm, we need to do something about that," she muttered as she turned away.

"What?" I called after her

"Tell you at lunch!" she shouted as the crowd of students swallowed her up, and I lost sight of her rainbow hair.

I didn't have time to ponder what she'd meant, because now I only have five minutes to get to my room and find a seat. So much for planning to have plenty of time on my first day. I shook off that thought and slipped through the still open door behind a group of girls and jogged up the stairs to the second floor of the building in search of room N305.

Luckily for me, I'd entered the right end of the building, and the first door I came to was the one I needed. A large metal desk sat at the front with a massive white screen behind it. Curving around it was the seating, arranged like an amphitheater, with each row having a long communal table. Half of the seats were filled with quietly chatting students. I'd read that this course was quite interactive, and I had high hopes for Mr. Tunaley's engaging lectures. I made my way up the stairs to one of the back rows and sat in the middle of five empty chairs, placing my laptop on the table. The clock above the white screen ticked over to eight o'clock and a pregnant hush fell over the collection of students as a door I hadn't noticed in the wall behind the desk opened.

"Good morning everyone, I am Mr. Tunaley." His voice boomed through the room, effectively silencing anyone who was still talking. "I'm excited to share with you my love of architecture, its history, different movements, and how it still impacts modern design. The course this semester will be split into architectural movements, modern engineering developments, and an end of unit design project."

Quiet conversation broke out as Mr. Tunaley sorted through the stacks of paper on his desk before handing them off to those in the front row. "Take one of each sheet and pass it on, please. You will shortly be receiving your syllabus, required reading material, and reference books. There is also a pop quiz on the online portal that I expect you to have completed before our next lesson." A collective groan rang out, but I couldn't wait. Academics was where I felt confident.

The next ninety minutes passed in a blur, and I found myself looking forward to my next lecture with Mr. Tunaley. As Ava said, he dressed sharply in a navy-blue three-piece suit with the whitest shirt I'd ever seen. But it was his easy-going demeanor that put me instantly at ease. He was a fun and engaging talker who seemed to value student participation.

I packed up my things and jogged down the steps, following the crowd and ready to dash across campus to Applied Mathematics. Numbers made more sense to me than words half the time, both written and spoken made me nervous. It still surprised me that I'd settled into an easy friendship with Ava and Mal. Usually, I was left on the sidelines. I was the kid always stuck on the friendship bench, and the last to be picked for a sports team when PE was a requirement.

The number of students had increased exponentially, and the halls were flooded with bodies. It made it difficult to navigate them, especially when I had to go against the flow. I managed to squeeze through a gap and hit the stairs without too much issue, but as soon as my feet touched the ground, I was shoulder-checked so hard I smacked into the wall, and the air was punched from my lungs.

"Shit," I muttered, slightly dazed as I braced myself and took a few deep, steadying breaths.

"Are you okay?"

"Huh?" I glanced up to see a red-haired guy standing in front of me. His plaid shirt hung open, revealing a tight white t-shirt that hinted at what lay underneath. A smile flickered at the corner of his lips, but it was his bright green eyes and the intensity of his stare that had me tongue-tied.

"You took a pretty hard hit there I just wanted to make sure you were alright?"

Flustered, I stepped back and ran my hands through my hair, my fingers catching on the knotted strands. Unnerved, I pulled at the drawstrings on my hoodie as a way to hide the tremor that ran down my arms. "Uh, yeah. I'm fine. Sure it was an accident."

"Mmhmm, if you say so." The look on his face said he didn't believe a word I was saying. Same dude, same. "I haven't seen you here before?"

I smiled, stepped away from the wall, and headed for the exit. The guy fell into step beside me, like we were friends. "It's, umm, my first day, if you couldn't tell." He chuckled and held the door open for me. His hand landed on the small of my back as he guided me through the throng of students bustling to get to their next class.

"I guessed as much, sweetheart." Heat warmed my cheeks,

and my eyes dropped to the pavement beneath my feet. "I'm Cory, by the way."

"I...oh...um, Jamie," I muttered, flustered and wishing the ground would swallow me up right this second. I wasn't good at this, small talk or making friends. I'd rather be left alone. I was more comfortable being on the outside looking in, than right here on the hot seat like now.

"Nice to meet you, Jamie. What do you have next?"

I licked my suddenly dry lips. "W-why?"

"Just wondered if you'd like to grab a drink with me?"

Oh holy god. Was he? Is he? No, surely not. I felt like my face was on fire. "Oh umm, errr, thanks, but I've gotta get to my next class."

"Oh, sure." Disappointment clouded Cory's features. "How about next time?" He sounded hopeful, and his confidence terrified me.

"Uh, yeah. Sure." I went to step away, but he grabbed my arm, halting my progress.

"Can I get your number?"

I looked up at him blankly, my mouth opening and closing rapidly. "Why?" I squeaked.

"So I can take you for that coffee." His green eyes sparkled in the sunlight. "Here, give me your phone." Why was on the tip of my tongue when Cory shook his head. "I want to give you my number. That way, when you're ready and want that coffee, you can let me know." Oh. Well, that made sense.

"Okay," I whispered and handed over my phone. Cory typed in his digits, his smirk growing into a blinding smile.

"Here you go." He started to turn away but stopped and looked at me over his shoulder. "Nice to meet you, Jamie." I smiled and waved. *God, why did I wave? What am I, twelve?* "Make sure to message me, cutie."

"What the fuck?" I breathed as Cory melted into the crowd. "That was so weird." I shook my head and hurried to calculus.

CHAPTER ELEVEN

Dillon

"Good practice, guys," Coach said as he walked into the locker room. Half the guys were chugging water like they'd been lost in a desert for years, while the other half stripped off to head for the showers. "Our defensive line is definitely tighter, but it's still too loose. Hargraves's guys are carving it up like butter. Prescott, you need to focus."

Chad turned to face me as he pulled his top off. If this were a cartoon, he would have been bright red with steam pouring out of his ears. "Yes, Coach," he snarled, eyes focused on me. The visceral hate in them was nothing new. He disliked me when I moved up to the varsity team, but now that I'd taken the captaincy from him, all bets were off. He was a ticking time bomb waiting to blow. I wouldn't be surprised if he threw a game just to make me look bad.

"Ignore him," Buchanan muttered as he sat next to me, unlacing his boots.

I looked down at him and raised a brow. "I'm trying, but the guy's a prick."

He snorted. "You're not wrong there. Anyway, let's hit the showers and get out of here. I need a damn coffee to help me stay awake for the rest of the day."

After showering and changing, we headed out across the quad toward Bean There, the best place on campus to get coffee that didn't taste like dish water. The first lesson had let out by the time we were done with practice, and there were people everywhere. Some ignored us, while others stopped and stared. The girls were the worst. They followed us around like street dogs begging for scraps. Most of the guys loved it—especially Stevens—but it irritated the fuck out of me.

"Don't look now," Vieck said as he shouldered his bag.

"Blonde devil incoming." McCormack chuckled. What the hell were they…

"Hello, baby." Elise sidled up beside me, wrapping herself around my left arm. I shoved my hand in my pocket and kept walking.

"Elise," I clipped.

"Missed me?" She pushed up on her tiptoes, trying to kiss my cheek. "No. Can't say I have. What do you want?" I growled.

"Just to spend some time with you." She bit her lip, trying to be coy, but she looked more like a rabbit chomping on a carrot.

I rolled my eyes as the guys snickered and sped up their pace so it was just me and Elise. Once there was a fair bit of distance between us, I stopped. She twisted herself until she was pressed up against my chest, and when she tried to loop her arms around my neck, my patience snapped. "Stop!" I barked and placed my hands on her shoulders, shoving her back a step and putting some much-needed space between us.

"Why, baby?" she mewled. "What's wrong?" She tried to step into me again, so I applied some pressure with my fingertips until she winced.

"What do you want?" I grunted. "Because as far as I'm concerned, there is nothing going on here. You had your shot on Saturday and you ran away like a little bitch." Why did girls do this? Get obsessed and clingy? It made my damn skin crawl.

"Ooh, burn," someone shouted as others broke into laughter. Great, we'd attracted a crowd like this was some kind of sick spectator sport.

Elise huffed and stroked my arms. "I wasn't feeling very well. That's why I left." Bullshit. I'd treated her like shit coz I wasn't interested, yet here the crazy bitch is. "I wondered if you wanted to go to the party on Greek Row this weekend?" She fluttered her lashes as her hands worked up my biceps.

"Fuck no. Take the hint, Elise. I'm not interested in washed-up whores." I pushed her away, not caring if she ended up on the ground or not.

"You're making a mistake, Dillon Hargraves!" she screamed, and stomped her feet attracting even more attention.

"The only mistake I made was giving you a second of my time." Laughter eddied around me, along with whoops and cheers. I swear I also heard someone say, "Ding dong the bitch is dead," but I didn't care. I wasn't here for her or them. I had one goal. Well, maybe two now as I had to get rid of the ghost from my past before anyone found out about me. The crowd parted like the Red Sea, and I breathed a sigh of relief when Elise's wailing faded behind the chatter of the other students.

"Well, that was more entertaining than anything I've seen in a long time," Buchanan said with a smirk. We grabbed one of the benches outside Bean There and waited for the rest of the guys to join us.

"Ugh. It is what it is," I said with a shrug, playing the arrogant jock role that was expected of me.

"You know she's going to get you back for embarrassing her," McCormack said, coming up alongside me and handing me my coffee.

I took a long drink, groaning as the rich liquid slid down my throat. After wiping my mouth on the back of my hand, I replied, "Don't care. She's not my problem. Elise can go cry to Daddy all she likes."

"You know she's connected, right?"

"I'm not afraid of her, Vieck. I'm too valuable to Briar U for them to do anything." Arrogant maybe, but it was the truth nonetheless. They didn't have a backup quarterback that could replace me. Davies was a sophomore, but he was still green. Far too green to be a threat to me. Coach knew how hyper-focused I was and used that to his advantage. He wouldn't kick me off the team any time soon.

"If you say so," he muttered into his latte.

"Anyone know where Stevens vanished off to?" I ran my gaze over Vieck, Buchanan, McCormack, and the rest of the team that decided to tag along, and all of them shook their heads. I hadn't seen him since we showered, but he'd been bouncing around like a damn puppy before that. The guys broke into conversation about practice and the weights season we had later this afternoon. We had two weeks until our first preseason friendly, and we needed to come out hard, so conditioning was at the forefront of everyone's minds.

"Cap! Cap!"

"Speak of the devil, and he shall appear." I looked up and followed McCormack's gaze. Stevens sauntered toward us with a big grin on his face.

"Where the hell did you go?"

"I went to see a man about a dog." He chuckled.

"What the—"

"Shh, Cap, I've got good news." Stevens smirked. "I went to see my person who does back office admin for the administration department. They have access to the student directory and all their records. And I hopefully have what you want in these files."

I nodded. "That was fast."

"Well, after what you said on Saturday, I paid them a little visit and voila." He spread four folders out in front of me. I scanned the names, but none of them matched Jamie Abernathy. My stomach dropped like a lump of lead. I'd seen him! He was here. But if there was no matching record, what did that mean?

"I know the names don't match, but this one—" He thrust a folder at me, flicking it open to a photocopy of their student ID. My heart stopped mid beat, and my blood whooshed through my ears. "This one fits your description of him."

I reached out with a shaky hand and snatched the file off Stevens. I could feel the weight of everyone's eyes on me, but I ignored it and the pickle of goosebumps that spread across my skin. If we did this, there would be no going back. I knew that. I knew this would irreparably hurt him—my little crow. But without a shadow of a doubt, the secret he knew had the power to destroy me. Without football, what was I? I didn't know, and I sure as fuck didn't want to find out.

"That's him," I muttered as confusion grew within me. Why was my Jamie registered here as Jamie Bowen? Had his parents gotten divorced? Is that why he and his mom vanished one night, never to be heard from again?

"Sweet." Vieck grinned. "What's the plan then?"

"Well..." I shared a conspiratorial look with Vieck, McCormack, Buchanan, and Stevens before launching into my plan for how to get rid of my little problem. This would be the hardest thing I've ever done—not that they knew it. I felt so much guilt over lying to them about why I hated Jamie, but at the end of the day, there is no 'I' in team, and here at Briar U, it's every man for himself. I was going to make sure I was the last man standing—no matter how much it hurt the boy I loved.

Morning lectures passed in the blink of an eye. Apparently, my showdown with Elise was the talk of campus if the conversations I overheard were anything to go by. I found it amusing the amount of disgusted looks I got from her sycophant followers, but to me it was like water off a duck's back. I had much more important things to do than worry about people's opinion of me.

The late afternoon sun was out in full force, the heat beating down like I was walking in a sauna. I wiped the sweat off my brow as I headed toward the gym for my afternoon weights session. My mind ran over everything I had planned for my little crow when a group of students caught my eye. Jamie's blond curls shone like spun strands of gold in the sunlight. He threw his head back and laughed, light and carefree. The smile curving his lips made my heart squeeze. At one time, that smile belonged to me, but now it was out there for everyone to consume. My gut twisted as envy slithered through me.

On Saturday, Jamie looked beautiful. Fragile, yet ethereal. The gold glitter flakes that covered his face over his eyes accentuated the color of his hair, and his smokey eyeshadow brought out the depth in the steel band that ringed his pale-blue eyes.

One look at him had stolen my breath and released every tarnished memory I'd had of him from the deepest recesses of my mind. But today, the image before me brought forth the urge to claim him as mine. He was mine. Mine to love. Mine to destroy.

No one got to touch him but me. No one got to hurt him but me.

I'd never admit it, but my jealousy grew as I took in the group he sat with. Or, more importantly, who was wrapped around him. Jamie may have a heart bigger than anyone I'd ever known, but he was also terrified of meeting new people, let alone talking openly to those he knew. But the boy sitting before me seemed confident, adjusted, and content.

I fucking hated it.

I exhaled a ragged breath and clenched my fists, nails digging into the palm of my left hand while the bottle in my right groaned under the pressure. My jaw clenched so hard, I was amazed my teeth didn't turn to dust as jealousy turned to visceral anger. The guy wrapped around Jamie nuzzled into his jaw before tilting his head in an intimate gesture. The two were nose to nose, and I knew as sure as the sun would rise tomorrow, that the guy with dark blond hair was going to kiss what was mine. Fuck no.

Without conscious thought, I pulled my arm back and launched the bottle in my hand, aiming for the guy who was about to learn I didn't share my toys. The bottle landed with precision, smashing into the side of the douchebag's head. The accompanying scream made me smirk as I made my way through the little copse of trees to the back of the group.

"Hargraves?" Someone called after me, their footsteps trailing in my wake, but my eyes were laser focused on the guy wrapped around Jamie. He was older, that was clear. I'd seen him around before, but like everyone else, he just blended into the background of unimportant faceless people that existed around me.

"Dillon!"

I turned on a dime, a snarl curling my lips. "What?" I demanded as a guy with red hair stumbled to a stop beside me.

He braced his hands on his knees, panting. "Taylor said you needed my help with something?"

I canted my head to the side and looked at the guy as confusion washed over me. "Did he say why?" My brain was still focused on the guy Jamie was tending to.

"No, just that I was the guy you needed." He shrugged and kicked the dirt, looking all kinds of uncomfortable.

"Right." I shook my head and tried to focus but... Jamie. *No, not now.* "Buchanan said you're taking journalism and working for Briar U press?" He nodded his assent, and his gaze wandered over me, the unmistakable heat in his eyes making my hackles rise. "I need you to follow someone. I want to know everything about him. Who his friends are. Where he goes, what he eats, routines, everything. Also, I want background on all the people he hangs around with. I want you to be his shadow. Know him better than he knows himself."

With a raised brow the guy looks at me. "I...umm... that's a bit extreme, isn't it?"

"What's it matter to you?" I crossed my arms over my chest. "I'll pay for your time if that's what you're worried about."

"No, no." He put his hands up. "I mean yeah, obviously, I want to be paid. But you basically want me to be his stalker?"

"Just not with nefarious intentions," I said, making him chuckle. "What's your name?"

"Cory." He held his hand out, and I shook it. "So what did this guy do to you?"

"That's not your concern." I squeezed his hand tighter.

"Hey, I'm within my rights to ask if you want me to invade some guy's life and dig up everything I can on him."

I stepped up to him until our toes were touching and used my height against him. "It's no concern of yours. Just do it. You're being paid to do a job, that's it."

Cory stepped back, hands up. "Alright, alright. Give me two weeks."

I rolled my eyes. "Send me what you can dig up online

ASAP then come find me in two weeks when you have everything else."

"Okay. Cool, cool. Sooo, who is this unfortunate soul?"

I heaved a sigh, grabbed Cory's shoulders, and turned him towards the group. Jamie stood with his hand outstretched to bottle guy and pulled him to his feet. It looked like whatever the group were doing was now breaking up. I itched to move to follow him, to know and possess everything about him.

"See the guy with blond curls?" Cory nodded. "Him. Jamie Bowen." Not Abernathy as I knew him, but Bowen. Doubt crept into my mind that I could have been mistaken, but he recognized me on Saturday. It was him, but why was his name different?

"Oh, Jamie? He's a cutie, right?"

A growl escaped me. "Excuse me?" Fear coiled around my gut, tightening with each passing second. Did he know I was gay? Was he after Jamie? *FUCK.*

"I met him earlier. He'd been shoved into a wall by... some jock." His eyes widened as he looked at me. "Y-you did that."

"Maybe." I shrugged. "Not personally, though. I was at practice."

"Sure, sure. So, get to know him and give you everything. Done."

"Good." I went to step away. Jamie was on the move, and I couldn't let him get away from me. Cory grabbed my arm.

"Just don't hurt him." My gaze drilled into Cory. I knew he had more to say. "He seemed like such a sweet guy." He shoved his hands into his pockets. "Like he wouldn't hurt a fly. So be nice."

"Fuck off," I growled and left him standing there, trepidation coming off him in waves. There was only one place I needed to be, and it wasn't here, with Cory.

My little crow didn't know it yet, but I was coming for him.

CHAPTER TWELVE

Jamie

"There she is," I cooed as Jessie's face appeared on my phone. "How are you, my little sunbeam?" Her luscious brown curls danced across the screen as her image flipped, and it felt like the world was spinning.

"Oops. Sorry, JJ." She giggled. God, I'd missed that beaming smile of hers. It had been far too long since I'd seen her face. I spoke to her briefly on Monday when I'd gotten back to my dorm, and Aunt Clara sent me a couple of photos of her and Zack, but that had been it as far as communication from my family went. It was like I'd been forgotten. The old saying, "out of sight, out of mind" felt like it applied to me.

"What are you doing, you little cray cray? Hope you're not being a superhero without me?"

Her laughter filled the air around me, making me feel like I was home. "I thought it would be fun to talk to you upside down."

"Huh, that's different," I remarked. "So, what's new with you?"

"Nothin'."

The edge to her voice made me think otherwise. Jessie was always full of life, going at a million miles an hour, but she didn't talk about things that upset her. "You sure, sunbeam? Your smile must be hidden behind a cloud."

She huffed a breath and the cutest little pout appeared on her face. "Mama packed up my room again and said we're goin' on a road trip somewhere new..."

"And?"

"I don't wanna, JJ. I like it here. I've gots friends. Suzie-Mae, Joelle, and Patty. We played in the pool yesterday at Patty's and had cake 'cause it was her birthday and... and then all my toys were gone when I got home."

Guilt ate away at me, even though I wasn't there anymore. I knew I was the reason for the move; Aunt Clara confirmed that was the plan once I was settled at Briar U. Hopefully, this constant moving wouldn't last much longer. It wasn't fair how much my life affected theirs. They deserved a home, not a stop gap. They needed the chance to set down roots, the chance to grow, be kids, and make friends.

"Well, I think it's exciting. I've moved to a new place for college, and you're moving to a new place too." I smiled at her as the world flipped again, and she sat upright on the couch. "You can tell me all about your amazin' new home, and I can tell you about all the cool stuff here? Deal?"

"I'm not so sure."

"I think it'd be really cool, Jessie."

Sounding more like an adult than the child she was, she responded, "I'll think about it, but the same goes for you."

"Of course, sunbeam." I smiled at her, and my heart clenched with how much I missed her.

Her face grew larger on the screen until all I could see was her eyeball. A chuckle escaped me at the sight. "Where are you?" she asked curiously.

"Can't you tell? Your head is almost popping out of my phone." Her laughter was brighter than the sun.

"No, silly." Jessie stuck her tongue out at me, and I did the same right back, making her giggle-snort.

"I'm sitting under a tree, waiting for my friends Mal and Ava to get out of their classes, so we can go grab dinner. Then I'm off to the library to research a paper I've got for History of Architecture."

A yawn split her face so wide I could see her tonsils. "Food sounds good." As if on cue, her stomach rumbled like thunder. "But books and stuff sounds boring."

"Ha! Yeah, it can be, but I'll tell you a secret," I whispered conspiratorially to her.

"What?" she mimicked.

"I kinda like it." Her amber eyes popped wide open as she stared at me. "I like books and libraries."

"You're so weird, JJ." Her stomach rumbled again, and I could hear Zack's voice in the background yelling for her to wash her hands. She rolled her eyes at me. It took every ounce of control not to laugh at her.

"Jamie, who are you talking to, grinning like that?" Ava asked as she plonked herself down next to me and grabbed my phone. "Oh, hello cutie. Who are you?"

"You look like a rainbow fairy!" Jessie squealed, clapping her hands, her grumbling stomach all but forgotten. "Do you really have rainbow hair?"

"I sure do. So you like it?"

"I love it!! You look real pretty."

Ava's cheeks tinged with a soft pink blush. "Well, thank you. You look like a princess with your long hair."

I grabbed the phone off Ava. "Jessie this is my new friend Ava—"

"Fairy Ava." I rolled my eyes at Jessie's sass.

"Ava, this is my little sunbeam, Jessie."

"Hey Jessie, it was lovely to meet you, but I need to drag Jamie to get some food. I'm starving."

"Me too." Jessie giggled. "I gotta go. Mama is shoutin' for me."

"Bye—" before I could finish, the screen went black, and Ava burst out laughing. She flopped backwards onto the grass and tucked an arm behind her head.

"Get down here." She tugged my shirt until I was lying next to her, and we stared at the clouds. "Mal's running late. He had to stay behind and ask Mr. Powell some questions." I flicked my gaze over to her and checked our group chat, but there weren't any messages. "I saw him when I cut through his building. There was a whole group of nerds asking questions."

"No problem."

"So, is Jessie..."

"Don't look at me like that." I snickered. "I'm too young for kids." I rolled my eyes at her smirk. "She's my cousin. I live with my aunt. Or, you know, I did before I came here."

I didn't know what kind of reaction I was expecting. Maybe I thought I'd see pity in Ava's eyes or she'd ask questions but no, she surprised me.

"Oh, sweet. Is it just your aunt and that lil' cutie, or are there more of you?"

"There's also my cousin Zack but that's it." Linking her fingers through mine Ava gave them a quick squeeze.

"I live with my Nanna. Mom and Dad died in a car crash when I was five. I was in the accident too, but I don't remember it. They said my car seat saved me." My heart went out to little Ava losing so much so young. "It's all good though." She hitched her shoulder up as she turned to look back up at the clouds. "I mean, I don't really remember them, but Nanna has lots of photos and tells me stories all the time. So, I guess I know them through her more than my memories."

My eyes fluttered shut as I processed everything she said. "Well, now you have me and Mal. I mean, what more could you want?" My words had the effect I was hoping for when Ava cracked up, melting away all the tension from the moment.

"Hey guys," Mal said, dropping down to sit at our feet. I squinted against the afternoon sun and shielded my eyes with my hand. The bruise on his cheek had faded to a greenish yellow and was still a point of contention between us. I wanted him to report the incident, but he refused. "God, what a day. I was thinking we could go off campus to eat instead of staying here?"

"Heck, yes!" Ava jumped up and grabbed her bag before turning to look at me. "You coming, JJ?"

I opened my mouth ready to answer, but Mal cut me off. "Thought we could go to The Smoke House and get barbecue?" Mal said, brushing the grass off his jeans as he got up.

"Uh." I sighed. "I would, but I kinda need to go to the library as I've got a paper to write."

"You sure? We can always go tomorrow?"

"I'm sure. Thanks, Mal. I'm just gonna grab something from the cafeteria, then head down. I'd rather get a head start on this than rush it."

"Such a good boy." Ava snickered. "Are you sure?"

"Yes, Ava." I hugged them both and grabbed my bag. "If I can get most of it planned tonight, then maybe we could do something tomorrow?"

"There's a party on Greek Row?"

"Ava," Mal cautioned, his tone all but telling her to zip it.

"What? It could be fun."

My stomach flipped at the thought. "I think I'm all partied out for the time being. I don't want to run the risk..."

Mal grimaced. "We'll talk tomorrow and sort something out?"

"Sure," I ground out.

They walked me to the library before hugging me goodbye. I felt buoyed after speaking to Jessie, even though I didn't make it out with Ava and Mal for dinner. Nothing was going to put a dampener on my mood. Truth was, I couldn't really afford it. Instead, I planned on grabbing a sandwich on my way back to my dorm.

The sound of the door closing behind me echoed through the cavernous space of the library. It took my eyes a few seconds to adjust to the muted light, but something about the atmosphere in here soothed me. The domed ceiling was an amazing piece of architecture that drew my eye as soon as I walked in. It never got old. Suspended from their peaks were cut glass chandeliers that cast rainbow fractals over the overstuffed shelves that filled the building. Interspersed between row upon row of books were tables peppered with students. There was a surprising number of people in here, considering it was the first Friday of the semester.

Was it weird to feel a sort of camaraderie with people I didn't know just because they were here working on their assignments when the rest of the student body was out living it up?

I was a homebody at heart, even though it had been years since I'd had one. It was one of the only things I truly craved. I didn't think home was a place defined by its position on a map, marked by longitude and latitude. No, to me, home was a moment in time. A memory. A person. An unattainable dream that had been ripped from my grasp when it was almost tangible. I'm sure I'm cursed to hope for things that can never be.

"Nothing worth having is ever easy." It was one of mom's favorite sayings. I missed her so much, and it hurt to think I'd never get to see her smile again or be enveloped in her arms.

My thoughts seemed to want to pile problems on top of problems. I had so many, it was easy to get lost in them. I over-thought. I over cared. I over loved, and I over trusted people, which ultimately meant I got over hurt.

Shaking off that train of thought, I made my way to the section of the library I needed, then sought out an empty table. I dumped my bag on the table, parked myself in a chair, and pulled out my laptop. I logged onto the intranet, and it took me a few minutes to find Mr. Tunaley's portal and the details of the assignment he'd set. Now, all I had to do was decide which topic I wanted to write about. *"Explore how architectural design is influenced by the philosophies, methods, and technology of the fine arts"* or *"Explore how the current culture and intellectual theories have influenced modern-day architecture."*

"Easy," I muttered to myself. "Not!" I shoved my laptop across the table as frustration burned through me. I tipped my head back and stared at the ceiling while the minutes ticked past. Maybe I should just flip a damn coin. Releasing a weighted breath, I hauled my laptop back to me and pulled up the list of suggested reading material. Maybe I'd find the answers in there. If not, I'd see what book I found first and hope it had the solution to my current problem. It's not like procrastinating would help me get my degree.There, choice made.

The looming bookshelves seemed to watch me the farther I walked into the stacks. My finger trailed along the spines as if the physical connection could help me decide what question I was going to pick. Ha! Who was I kidding? A heavy sigh punched out of me when I saw the book I was after, but even stretching up onto my tiptoes, I couldn't reach it. Sometimes it really sucked being short.

I was about to turn back and grab my chair when the air seemed to shift around me, and the temperature dropped. The delicate hairs on my arms and the back of my neck stood on end as my skin prickled with goosebumps. I sucked in a shuddering breath and glanced up and down the row but saw no one. Nothing seemed out of place. Trepidation crawled down my spine and spread across my skin, making me shiver.

"H-hello?" I croaked and waited. I couldn't hear anything, and the ensuing silence only served to ratchet up my frayed nerves. I licked my dry lips as the feeling of being watched intensified, and the erratic pounding of my heart tried to tattoo itself onto my sternum.

"Is someone there?" Great, now I sound like every cliché murder victim in a cheesy horror movie. I scoffed at myself. Stuff like that didn't happen in real life; it was just my overactive imagination.

"Stop being an idiot," I scolded myself and stepped up onto the bottom shelf, praying it didn't break under my weight. I rolled up onto my toes and braced the knee of my right leg on the shelf above, my fingertips skimming the spine of the book I needed. "Just a little bit farther." I bit my lip as I focused, managing to grasp it and yanked it backward off the shelf. I lost my footing and slipped, falling backward. It felt like everything was happening in slow motion but also rushing so fast I couldn't focus or brace for the inevitable impact.

A yelp ripped out of me as I smacked into something hard. No, not something, someone...if the low oof was anything to go by. "Watch it," they growled as thick arms wrapped around me from behind before lowering me onto my feet. Large hands braced my hips as I got my balance.

"Fuck." I gasped and rubbed my hand over my chest. I clutched on to the damn book in my arms like it was a lifeline as I tried to draw air into my lungs.

"Next time," the husky voice chuckled, "use the ladders. That's why they have them."

I looked over my shoulder, my eyes locking with the dark fathomless depths of Dillon's. All traces of humor vanished off his face as it contorted in anger. "T-thank you," I stuttered, feeling the blood drain out of my face.

Dillon's chest heaved as his stare bored into me. He

clenched his fists so hard, his knuckles bleached white. I swallowed around the lump in my throat as tension thickened the air.

"What do you think you're playing at?" he growled, the rasp in his voice like a visceral touch as he stepped into me, backing me up against the bookshelf. "What are you doing here, little crow?" The demand was unmistakable as the wood bit into my skin.

My eyes shuttered closed, and I shook my head, unwilling to look at the man who wore the face of the boy I once loved. *You still do,* a little voice whispered in my mind. "S-s-sorry."

"That's not good enough," he bit out. I shivered at the intensity of his closeness, and every nerve ending came alive. His body heat seeped into me as he braced one arm beside my head, and I inhaled his musky sea salt scent. Heat unspooled in my stomach, something that had been dormant for years. I gasped when his other hand wrapped around my throat, his fingers biting into my skin. Dillon yanked my head up so I faced him. "You don't belong here, little crow."

"I...I..." Every word that sprang to mind dried up on my tongue before I could say it.

"You need to leave." I blinked up at him, at a loss of who this person was before me. Gone were the kind eyes that used to greet me every morning. Gone was that smile that used to make my heart skip a beat. "Now!" He clenched his fingers tighter, making it impossible for me to breathe.

My heart thundered in my chest and echoed in my ears. My lungs screamed for oxygen as the edges of my vision started to fade to black. But I couldn't look away from his desolate eyes. They hypnotized me, called to the brokenness that I hid behind my smile.

"D...D..." I rasped. My book slipped from my hands, landing with a resounding thud. I managed to wrap my fingers around his, relieving the intensity of the pressure against my throat. "D-Dillon... please."

A snarl curved his lips, and he leaned into me, chest to chest. His taut nipples brushed against mine, and his hot breath danced over my lips. His knee slipped between my legs as he caged me in, with only the thin layer of our clothes separating us I burned up inside. "No," he breathed, lips almost brushing mine. "You need to leave."

"No." I shook my head as much as I was able but it barely moved. My strength faded as the darkness around me closed in.

"Get out of Briar U before I hurt you so badly, there will be no coming back." His words sliced right through me and carved agony into my bones. But his eyes. Oh, they told another story, one from a lifetime ago. I saw an echo of the love I had for him reflected back at me.

"I… c-ca…"

Dillon growled and bared his teeth while his fingers pulsed around the column of my throat. My heart stuttered, and everything faded to black.

Scorching heat seared my face, abrasive and demanding. I sucked in a breath when the pressure relented, and my eyes flew open. It took a few seconds for my brain to catch up with what my eyes were seeing. With what my body was feeling.

Dillon's fingers sunk into my hair, controlling the angle of my head. The hand that had squeezed my throat until I blacked out was now teasing the skin along my thundering pulse. A groan reverberated through the air, surrounding us as unyielding lips slammed down on mine. His tongue demanded entry to my mouth, pushing past the seam of my lips.

I gasped at the intrusion as he invaded my mouth, and his tongue wrapped around mine. A shudder worked through me as liquid heat filled my veins. I couldn't reconcile how something that should be so intimate, so tender, made me feel owned and dirty. I loved him, but he didn't love me.

Dillon lapped at my tongue, tasting and teasing me while

simultaneously breaking me to pieces. Tears burned in my eyes and collected along my lash line, but I refused to let them fall. His hips rolled against me, and the rigid hardness of his length pressed against my stomach. Our height difference had never been more apparent to me than it was at that moment.

I was helpless to do anything but let him defile me. To allow him to take what he wanted and sate the thirst he needed to quench. Every brush of his lips was a rusty nail driven into my heart by his bare hands.

"Jamie," he whispered as his lips slipped from mine. The reverence in his tone stole what little air from my lungs there was left. For a split second, I saw the boy I once knew before the cold mask of hate settled over him again. I wanted to reach out to him and beg him to stay, but the iciness of his glare silenced me.

The static buzzing in my ears nearly drowned out the sound of our ragged breaths. "Dil—"

"Shut the fuck up! Get away from me, you fucking little faggot. I don't want to ever see you again." Dillon shoved me, and my knees hit the floor, the carpet burning through my jeans. My shoulders hunched up to my ears, and I wrapped my arms around myself as I crumpled inwards, my heart shattering into a million pieces. A blanket of coldness wrapped around me, chilling me to my core.

The first tears fell as I watched the boy I'd loved since I was eight, walk away from me like I was nothing to him.

CHAPTER THIRTEEN

Dillon

I was a piece of shit. I knew it, but I had never been more disgusted with myself than I was right now. My heart was hammering its way out of my body whilst simultaneously breaking. I was a fucking mess. His soft cries sunk into me like claws, ripping me open and bleeding me dry.

"Fuck!" I ground out, making a table of students jump in their seats, their books and laptops flying. Normally, I'd find that kind of shit funny, but tonight, it made me feel hollow and worthless.

I punched open the doors so hard they crashed into the brickwork, and the glass panels shook as I exited the library. A group of kids dived out of the way as I stormed towards them. I couldn't breathe as the suffocating vise around my lungs grew tighter and tighter.

My legs felt shaky and uncoordinated as I tried to block out the sounds of the world around me and focus on the rise and fall of my chest with each inhalation. I needed to trust in my body, that it was doing what it was meant to. Otherwise, I would spiral too far, and I wouldn't be able to bring myself back. There were far too many people around for a Friday evening. Didn't these people have lives they could be off living, instead of being here pushing me closer and closer to the point of no return?

The smell of damp soil saturated my senses as I fell to my knees under the cover of the trees, far from prying eyes. My fingers dug into the earth, gouging tracks into it as I braced myself on my elbows. The first garbled cry tore its way out of my chest, dragging my shattered heart with it. Maybe it would be a good thing if I killed that useless muscle now as it would save me from suffering this kind of torment again. I wasn't a masochist. I didn't enjoy pain, but I understood it. I understood suffering and faking it every day.

Hargraves didn't do therapy. The one time I told my dad I thought I was suffering from panic attacks and anxiety from Mr. Abernathy's attack, he laughed in my face and called me weak.

"WHAT THE HELL is wrong with you, boy?" he ground out and grabbed me by the front of my Henley. "Real men don't cry like little pussies, do they?" His stale breath made me want to vomit, but I swallowed it down.

"N-no, sir." I sniffled.

"Then what's all this on your face?" He wiped away my tears, looked at his glistening fingers with disdain and smeared them across my face. "Are you a little girl? Or are you going to be a real man?"

"I'm a man," I choked out, my throat feeling like cut glass as the anxiety inside me swelled like a savage storm. "B-but, Dad, it keeps happening." A fresh wave of tears spilled down my face as shame set in.

"You're a man, are you?" He shoved me back and laughed, mocking me as I stumbled over. My skin was crawling, like a million needles were sinking into my skin. "You're weak," he spat. "Pathetic. No son of mine."

"No... Dad." I crawled after him, latching onto his pant leg. "Please, mom said maybe I should talk to someone."

"What the fuck?" His fingers sunk into my hair as he yanked my head back so he could stare into my eyes. "Listen to me, and listen good. Hargraves don't do therapy. It's a load of poppycock."

"Y-yes, sir," I murmured, even though every breath was a losing battle.

"Now suck it up. Lock it down, and get up. Today is the day you become a man."

THE BARK BIT into the back of my head as I sucked in deep inhales and rejoiced as I felt my lungs finally inflate. The rush of oxygen to my brain made me feel like I was floating, and I grabbed on to the emotional reprieve with both hands for however long this fleeting moment would be.

My phone vibrated in my pocket, and the world snapped back into focus around me. Fuck. I hated myself, but this was for the best. I had to get him to leave. I mean, what did Jamie expect by strolling back into my life after five years like nothing had happened? That I'd fall to my knees and worship the ground at his feet? Hell, no. Too much time had passed. There was too much stagnant water under that bridge, one I wasn't prepared to cross to find out his truth. Nah. The safest thing to do was blow it up and save myself.

The screen lit up to show eight missed calls and a message.

CORY

He lives in the dorm block next to yours. Room 301. Here on a full scholarship, but there are no transcripts from previous schools. No address history. Nothing. Your boy is a ghost.

Thanks. Keep digging.

"What in the actual fuck. Nothing makes any sense." I sighed and scrubbed my hand down my face, dirt and grit biting into my skin. I probably looked worse right now than when I walked off the field at the end of a game. Brushing that thought aside, I hauled my ass up and brushed myself off. My stomach rumbled and exhaustion draped itself over me like a second skin. It was a feeling I was used to, but my blood still felt electrified after that kiss, and I knew I wouldn't be able to sleep. The best thing I could do now was head to the gym and lose myself in the burn of my muscles until I couldn't stand. Working myself to the point of passing out might not be healthy, but it was the best damn coping mechanism I had and no one could tell me otherwise.

The walkways around this part of campus were all but deserted this time of night. I mean, who the hell wanted to be around here at ten on a Friday night? Not anyone with sense. It was a peaceful evening with a slight chill in the air that signaled fall was nipping at summer's heels. I pulled my hood up and toyed with the drawstrings when a shuffling figure caught my eye.

Concealed by the shadows of the arts building, I held my breath as I watched the lone figure stumble along. They weren't walking like they were drunk; maybe they were under the influence of something else? I wouldn't be surprised—it was easy enough to get your hands on any type of drugs you wanted in a place like this. All you needed were the right connections.

A cold gust of wind smacked me square in the face and carried with it the wet sniffling sound of someone crying. Something in my heart lurched at the sound as an echo of Jamie's soul-shattering cries from the library filtered through me. My breath caught when the figure moved through a pool of light cast by the street light that illuminated the walkways. Golden curls glinted like sunbeams before being lost to the darkness once again.

My feet moved without conscious thought as I trailed my little crow across campus. Concealed by the shadows, he'd never know I was watching over him. If he felt my presence, he never acknowledged it. I loved him and hated him in equal measure. I wanted to make him mine and never let him go as much as I wanted to bury him and never see him again. But this innate part of me wouldn't relinquish his safety to anyone else. If he got hurt, it would be because I hurt him. If anyone else tried, they'd pay with their fucking life.

The parking lot by our dorms came into view, the bright hive of activity a stark contrast to the rest of campus. People went to and from their dorms, some on nights out with friends or going on dates, and others coming back inebriated or having just finished a shift. I'd had a job my first two years here, but now I'd made the varsity team, I wasn't allowed. I was singularly focused on the team and my performance. At least, I was meant to be. But I knew how fickle an athlete's career could be, so instead of taking easy electives or general studies, I was taking nutrition and sports management. It offered me a number of avenues if I wasn't drafted or ended up with a career-ending injury.

Jamie's head snapped up, and he looked in my direction. My heart worked its way up my throat at the thought of him seeing me here. He discreetly wiped at his face with the sleeves of his oversized hoodie, ran his fingers through his hair, and pasted a plastic smile on his face. A growl rumbled in my chest as envy swamped my senses. Who could pull that smile from him?

I gritted my teeth and locked my jaw to prevent myself from calling out to him and making myself known. My blunt nails dug into my palms as I clenched my fists. Adrenaline flooded my veins. I was ready to take out anyone who dared touch him. "He's fucking mine." A random girl walking past gave me a double take when she heard my harsh words. Luckily, my face was hidden so she had no idea who I was.

It was like watching a car crash in slow motion. You knew the inevitable sucker punch was coming but sheer morbid curiosity made it impossible to look away. Copper burst across my tongue and seared my taste buds as I watched Jamie be enveloped in arms that weren't mine.

Fuck, it hurt more than I'd ever admit.

The blond guy from earlier buried his face in Jamie's hair. I was too far away to tell if they were talking, or if he was still crying or not. They swayed on the spot like they were dancing to music only they could hear. It was painful. Torture. The guy stepped back and cupped my little crow's face, cradling it like it was something precious. His thumbs swiped across his cheeks, removing the tears I put there.

I could still smell his sweet caramel scent. Feel the tentative brush of his lips against mine. Feel his slender toned body against mine, underneath mine. He was at my mercy, and I took everything I could in one stolen moment. One mistake. Minutes I'll never get back, ones I should forget, but I'll hold on to for the rest of my life. Nothing has ever felt as right as that kiss did. But this is real life, not a place for dreams... no matter how much I might wish things were different.

"You're a worthless piece of shit, Dillon," I reminded myself. I was the devil to Jamie's angel. He was my balance, my missing piece. Without him, I would sink and drown in the darkness I fought so hard against until one day it consumed me.

Blondie said something that made Jamie laugh, the lilting chuckle all I could hear. He sprung up onto his tiptoes and wrapped his arms around the guy who—unbeknownst to him—was now number one on my shit list. I prayed Cory found some dirt on him, and I could unleash my temper on a worthy target. It took everything in me to keep my feet glued to the spot as they walked toward the dorm building next to mine, arms wrapped around each other, like a couple. Objectively, they looked good together. If I had anything to do with it, they never would be.

"Fuck this," I gritted out and stormed into my building, deciding to take the stairs to my room. I didn't want to see anyone on a good day, let alone having to describe why I looked ready to commit murder. This wasn't the field; that look would raise all kinds of red flags. Unfortunately for me, the world decided to shit on me as I reached the landing at the top of the stairwell.

"Well, if it isn't Mr. Perfect."

"Get lost, Chad. I'm grabbing my stuff before heading to the gym. Maybe you should think about getting a workout in," I snapped and eyed his bulging gut.

He snorted. "Don't think so. I've got a free ride on the team."

"Nobody's place is guaranteed. You know that. You think your money keeps you safe?" Chad smirked before taking a swig from his beer. He thought he was untouchable. I stepped closer to him, and the stench of booze coming off him turned my stomach. "Well, let me tell you a little secret, Chad. Your time is running out with Coach. One more fuck up, and you're history."

"Fuck you, Hargraves."

I should have seen it coming, but my brain was sluggish and hazy from my panic attack, delaying my reactions. When the pain exploded in my cheek, I felt the impact in my teeth. Blood coated my tongue. I dragged it across my teeth, staining my gums red, and bared them at Chad. "Is that all you've got?" I raised my hands and made a come hither motion, begging him to take another shot before I annihilated him and put the prick in his place. "What are you waiting for?" I taunted and licked my lips. "Are you afraid?"

"Why would I be afraid of someone like you?" he sneered and looked down his nose at me.

"You should be very afraid, my man." Buchanan's voice cut through the air with a level of confidence I could only envy in my manic state. "You know Cap's undefeated. If you've got a score to settle, or just fancy gettin' your ass handed to you like the little bitch you are, Chad, I suggest you speak with Vieck about the next fight night."

"Yeah, sure." Chad scoffed and stepped right up to me, his nose a hair's breadth from mine. "We're not finished here." His finger jabbed into my sternum.

"I think you'll find we are," I spit, watching with satisfaction as some splattered on his face. "The next time you want to take a swing at me, you'll be looking up at me from the flat of your back, Chad."

"Whatever."

"Nah, man. That's a promise."

"Fuck you," he snarled as he headed down the stairs.

"You're not my type. You're pathetic." I flinched as the words left my mouth, my Dad's voice on a continuous loop in my head. "Fuck!" My hand snapped out, and the drywall buckled under the unrelenting pressure of my fist. I didn't feel my skin shred until Buchanan pulled my hand out of the wall.

"Seriously? You let that dick get to you?"

I shook my head. "Wasn't him." I grunted as he slowly pulled bits of board from my skin.

"Then what was it?"

"Don't wanna talk about it. Heading to the gym." I tried to pull away, but Buchanan's grip tightened. Rage and self loathing surged through my veins. I was at the brink of no return, and I needed to burn off the adrenaline I was drowning in or I'd make a stupid mistake like finding Chad and beating the living shit out of him. "Get off. I need to run this off, B."

Buchanan released a weary sigh and let me go with a shake of his head. The look in his eyes told me he understood what I couldn't put into words. I had my hand wrapped around the door handle when I heard him say, "This isn't over, Dillon."

CHAPTER FOURTEEN

Jamie

"I swear someone was following me, Mal." I sniffed as he guided me into our building. The warmth from his hand at the small of my back radiated into my chilled skin, even through the layers of my clothes. The bright light stung my sore eyes, every blink like sandpaper. I wished the tears would stop falling, but they had a mind of their own. I wasn't weak. I hated that people could see me like this. That Mal saw me like this.

Everyone relied on me to be their stronghold in a storm. I was the one who brought the sunshine on their darkest days, who could be relied upon to help take care of people and fix their problems. Putting everyone before myself made me feel like I was neglecting the broken parts of me that desperately needed someone to take care of. But inevitably, no one really cared. I never wanted anyone to feel the way I did.

"It's alright, Jamie." The soft tone of Mal's voice was

comforting, and the fact he believed me without question helped ground me. "Let's get you back to our room and into bed. Unless you want a shower first?"

I didn't know what I wanted. I couldn't focus on anything, as my mind was racing a mile a minute. "I...umm." My teeth clacked together as another full-body shudder worked its way through me.

"You don't need to decide now. Let's just get you inside and warmed up." I caught the concern in his eyes and the slight downturn of his lips.

"Okay." I didn't realize we were back in our room until he gently pushed me down onto my bed and pulled off my shoes.

"Arms." I lifted my arms as he slipped my bag off and placed it on my desk. Tilting his head, Mal looked me over and nodded before disappearing into the adjoining bathroom. "I'll get the shower started. You think about what movie you want to watch when you get out, okay?"

Tears trickled down my cheeks, showing no sign of stopping any time soon. I was almost numb to them now. I sucked in a shuddering breath and blinked myself out of the daze I was lost in. Moving on autopilot, I folded my hoodie and put it on my chair, kicked off my jeans, deposited them in the hamper, and grabbed my fluffy rainbow kitty pjs. A ghost of a smile flickered on my lips as my fingers toyed with the fluffy material.

"You good?" Mal asked, concern threading his tone as I slipped past him. I nodded mutely, clutching my pjs tightly to me. "I'm gonna go grab us some drinks and something for you to eat. I'm assuming you didn't eat?"

Guilt churned in my gut. "I'm not hungry, but I'd take a hot cocoa with—"

"Marshmallows and cream? I got you, boo."

"Thank you..." my words trailed off into the silence as the door clicked shut, and I was left alone with my thoughts and broken heart.

The hot spray of water pounded against my cold skin, goosebumps chasing the droplets as they fell over me. I allowed myself this moment, this quiet reprieve to open the locked box in my mind and replayed every memory of my time growing up with Dillon. His open smile. Every kind word he whispered in my ear. Every time he showed me what I meant to him without words. What it felt like when he finally kissed me. Then, I added my second kiss with him and slammed the lid shut, vowing as my eyes fluttered closed I would never open it again.

I was finally starting to find my feet at Briar U, considering the first two weeks fried my brain and put me through an emotional wringer. High school had been a breeze by comparison, but I was never one to back down from a challenge. I'd promised Mom I would live my life to the fullest and not shut myself away after she was gone. It was the easiest promise to make, but the hardest one to keep. But I owed her everything, and I refused to renege on the last promise I made the woman who gave up everything for me.

"You're going to come tonight, aren't you, JJ?" Mal asked, falling into step beside me as I left calculus and merged with the flow of bodies heading outside. The temperature had dropped over the last few days, and the first leaves had started to turn golden brown.

"Tonight?" The wind whipped around us, nipping at my skin. I wrapped my jacket around me, my arms hugging my chest as I tried to remember what was happening tonight but kept coming up blank.

"Yes." His chuckle made my lips quirk. I peeked up at him through my lashes and caught his indulgent eye roll. "You've forgotten, haven't you, little bookworm."

I shrugged and shook my head because, yeah. "Maybe."

"There's no *maybe* about it." He poked my side. "I can tell by the color of your cheeks that you did." I snorted and bit back a smile. "Every time you lie, you go as red as a tomato."

"I do not."

"Oh yes, you do." He held open the door to Bean There for me, and the blast of heat that hit as we stepped inside was more than welcome. "She's over there." Ava sat at a table in the back corner, waving like a maniac at us with three steaming cups in front of her.

"If it isn't my favorite two people."

"Hello, rainbow fairy," I said as I wrapped my arms around her petite frame before slipping into my seat and shucking off my coat.

"He forgot, Aves," Mal said as he slipped in next to me. The look of outrage on Ava's face was enough to have me breaking into a laugh.

"How?! Why? Do you not love me?" she chastised. "My little angel, tonight is going to be so much fun. I promise."

I must have looked as confused as I felt, because Mal said, "You remember when I said Ava was president of the LGBTQ+ club?"

"Mhmmm." I hid behind my latte, taking a long, drawn-out sip before I could face the incredulous looks on their faces. "I'm sorry, I've had a lot going on... it's been a bit of an adjustment."

"Sure. Sure." The weight of Ava's probing eyes on me made me shrink back into my seat. "Anyway, it's the first mixer tonight where all the members get together. It's nothing formal, just a group of us with drinks, nibbles, and some music."

"Gives us a safe space to be ourselves and talk to like-minded individuals without fear of judgment or reproach," Mal added.

"And you think I need to go?" I toyed with the zip on my bag, refusing to meet their eyes, knowing what I'd see.

"Yes."

"I think you do," they said simultaneously.

"Oh."

"JJ, my angel." Ava's hand landed on mine, giving it a motherly squeeze. My shoulders sank as I finally met her dark eyes. "We all know about your unending crush on *he who shall not be named,*" she said, using her fingers for air quotations.

"I... I'm not..." I licked my lips, trying to find the right words. "I'm not denying that, and it's not that I'm not out, per say. I've never said either way, other than to my Mom." Those words hurt more than I wished to admit. "But I've never..."

"Never what, Jamie?" Mal's soft voice made my cheeks heat.

"I've never felt that way or even a remote flicker of feeling toward anyone but *him*."

"And there's nothing wrong with that," Ava said in the no-nonsense voice she got when she was about to go to battle on something she felt passionate about, but Mal cut her off.

"Aves is right, there isn't. It could mean a few things, to be honest," He waved his hand in front of me before closing his thumb. "One: it could be that you're still in love with him and refuse to look elsewhere." He put down his index finger. "Two: you simply might not have found someone who gives you butterflies. So, tonight might be a great opportunity for you." His middle finger lowers. "Three: you might not feel that spark of connection with someone—"

"You saying I might be demi?"

"It's a possibility." He spread his hands wide. "I can't tell you, but what I—ouch! Why did you kick me, Ava?"

"We!"

Mal cocked his head to the side and looked at her before understanding bloomed on his face. "What we can do is be here to support you and answer any questions you might have."

"Exactly! That's what BFFs do, Jamie."

Emotion burned the back of my eyes. I tried to blink it away, but the world turned hazy, and my throat was thick. "T-thank you."

"So you'll go?" Ava bounced in her seat, unable to contain her excitement.

"Yes, I'll go."

They fell into conversation about what the plan was for tonight. I nodded and hummed at what I hoped were the appropriate times, but I didn't hear a word. A feeling I couldn't name took root inside me, consuming all of my attention. We ordered lunch and set in place a study plan for the rest of the week, but it was like I wasn't really there. Before I knew it, we were heading out for the last classes of the day.

The wind picked up while we were at lunch, and the sky was blanketed with tumultuous dark clouds. A trickle of foreboding skittered down my spine, making the hairs at the back of my neck stand on end.

"Excuse me, are you Jamie Bowen?"

I spun around to see a guy dressed all in brown holding a package. "I... um... yeah?"

"Could you sign here, please." An electronic device materialized in his hand as he gave me the parcel. I signed, although it didn't look anything like my signature and handed it back to him. "Thank you."

"What's that?" Ava peered at the box in my hand before poking it with her finger. "Kinda fancy having something hand delivered to you and not left in your mailbox." I didn't miss the hint of accusation in her tone.

"I haven't got a clue. Maybe it's because I needed to sign for it?"

"I doubt it. The guys on the desk normally sign for everything then keep a copy or photo on record as proof of receipt."

"Let him open it, Ava, before you launch an acquisition," Mal joked, wrapping his arm around her shoulders and steering her toward one of the benches lining the sidewalk.

I sighed and followed after them. The sensation of being watched had me looking over my shoulder, but I couldn't see anyone looking directly at me. Groups of students stood around chatting, not paying me any attention. I shook it off and went and sat with my friends, turning the box over in my hands. "Anyone got anything that will open this?" The inconspicuous brown box was tapped up so well, I'd never be able to get into it without a hell of a lot of help.

"Here, use this." Mal produced a small penknife. "Don't ask," he said when I raised my brows at him in question. I shook my head and sliced the tape at the edges and then along the top where the top pieces had been pulled together.

The unmistakable weight of someone's gaze on me flared, and my stomach felt like it was filled with wasps. I darted my eyes around, and they snagged on a group of jocks standing over by the main quad. It seemed like they were looking everywhere but me on purpose, their posture too stiff. Everything about that group felt off. Was I on to something, or was it my overactive imagination?

"Are you going to open that, or what?" Ava goaded me, eliciting a laugh from me.

"I was waiting to see if you got impatient enough to do it yourself."

She scoffed and crossed her arms as Mal leaned over the back of the bench, curiosity etched in his features. "Hurry up. Don't keep us waiting."

Exhaling, I brushed away the feeling of apprehension and pulled the box open. A loud bang boomed and echoed through me like I'd been shot. A scream pierced my ear drums and everything went dark for a split second as the whole world disappeared.

"Holy shit."

"Jamie, are you alright?" Trying to hear past the ringing in my ears was almost impossible, like I was on the other side of bulletproof glass. My body vibrated as adrenaline surged through me. My hands were shaking so much, the slick box slipped from my fingers. I tried to open my eyes, but thick viscous liquid covered my features and glued my hair to my face. The heat of it had my gut churning and bile sitting on my tongue.

"I-I-I... c-can't open m-my eyes," I managed to get out between the chattering of my teeth. I licked my coated lips and copper burst across my tongue.

"Shh, it's okay. I've got you, Jamie." Mal's soft voice became clearer the longer he spoke to me in his calm, comforting tone. "Just stay still, and don't move, alright?" There was a rustling noise, like someone was removing clothing. Something soft brushed over my face, making me flinch. "Keep still, JJ, I'm just cleaning you up a bit."

Cleaning me up? Why? What was going on? Seconds stretched into minutes, and even though I couldn't open my eyes, they itched and burned. My breathing grew faster and faster, my chest tight like a weight sat on my lungs.

"There you go. Try to open your eyes now?"

Tentatively, I peeled my eyelids back. Black dots burst across my vision as the bright glare from the sun made me squint. "W-what happened?" I lifted my hand to my face, the tremor running through it made it hard to control. "What's that?" I hissed as I stared at the deep red staining my fingers. "Is... is that b-blood?" I skewed my eyes shut and sucked in a few deep breaths before opening them again, praying I'd been having a nightmare. My hand was still red, and whatever it was, was quickly drying on my face. "Mal? Ava?"

An arm wrapped around my shoulders as a shudder racked my body. "I don't know, JJ," Ava said gently, turning me to face her. Concern clouded her eyes as she wiped her thumb over my brows.

"Is it paint?" I shook my head. It was too dark, too thick. "B-blood?"

"No. Well, not real blood," Mal said, staring at his stained T-shirt clutched in his hands. "I called the SRO to come speak to you about this." I shook my head. I didn't want anyone to know about this. It was embarrassing. Humiliating.

"Jamie, there's a note," Ava said, a hysterical lilt to her voice.

I grabbed it from the box sitting at my feet just as Mal said, "Don't touch it!"

"Too late." My voice was hoarse and strained. I picked up the red splattered paper and flushed hot and cold as the sprawled words on the note registered.

THIS IS ONLY THE BEGINNING.
LEAVE BEFORE IT GETS WORSE FOR YOU.

"What the hell does that mean?" The words carved their way up my dry throat. I looked at my friends, their expressions mirroring each other. Confusion. Anger. A touch of fear. "We need to go. I need a shower and get changed or I'll be late for my class."

"Jamie, do you think you're in the right headspace to go?"

I flinched like I'd been hit at Mal's words. Logically, I knew he didn't mean it that way, but I was fine. Shaken, sure, but I had to keep going. That's one thing Mom taught me; keep going in the face of adversity. Fake it till you make it.

"I'm fine."

"Sweetie, you're shaking like a leaf and crying." I looked up at Ava and she nodded. "You are, JJ. I think you're in shock."

"I..." I didn't know what to say to her. I couldn't tell that I was, because I didn't know how I felt. What did that mean? I huffed a breath and shook my head, dropping it so it hung between my shoulders and stared at the ground.

“We need to stay for the SROs before you can go.” I ignored Mal as he and Ava discussed what was best for me. My gaze wandered to the groups of people staring at me, taking photos and pointing. Some were laughing at my misery. Some looked shocked, but it was the group of cheering jocks that snagged my attention. They seemed far too happy with what happened, high fiving and slapping each other on the back.

Only one member of that group wasn’t joining in. His face was as white as a sheet, dark eyes clouded by shadows. He held my gaze for a few seconds before breaking our connection. Shoulders hunched, he turned and walked away, leaving me once again to stare at his retreating form. With his silent dismissal, I finally understood all the ways I could die while still breathing. *Did he know this was going to happen?*

It took nearly an hour for the SROs to document and interview me, Mal, and Ava before I was allowed to go back to my dorm and shower. Mal offered to come with me, but I insisted he should go to his class. It took far more convincing than I had the energy for, but finally, he relented and dragged Ava with him.

I desperately needed some time by myself to process what had happened. The SROs initially tried to say this was a prank gone a bit too far, but their attitude changed after reading the note and becoming increasingly concerned about what the red liquid was.

It felt like years had passed by the time I was opening the door to my dorm. All I wanted to do was fall face first into my bed and forget this day ever happened. But I couldn’t do that until I washed all this stuff off. It had partially dried and was so tacky it stuck to everything like glue. I managed to peel my top and jeans off, taking half my skin with them before a black envelope in front of the door caught my attention.

“Is this some kind of joke?” I bent down, snagged it off the floor, and flipped it over. It wasn’t addressed to anyone. Weird. I half considered dumping it in the trash and forgetting about it, but morbid curiosity drew me to it. The need to open it became more of a compulsion. Before I gave myself a chance to back out, I ripped it open and upended the contents on my bed.

Sensible? Definitely not, but I couldn't help myself. "What the...?" I inhaled a sharp breath as four polaroid photos of me landed on my rumpled blankets. All taken here on campus, on different days. Some from far away, others from up close. A sick feeling revolted inside me as fear crawled over my skin and settled into my bones.

My hand shook as I dug my phone out of my bag. My brain screamed at me to call Uncle Daire, because what if this was him? What if he'd finally found me?

But what if it wasn't? What if it's another prank? Do you want to waste his time?

My legs gave out from under me, and I crashed into the floor. My phone skidded across the room and under my desk as I pulled my knees up to my chest and cried.

CHAPTER FIFTEEN

Dillon

The last two weeks had been a hell of my own making and things only seemed to be escalating. They were spiraling beyond my control, and all I could do was sit back and watch the destruction. Jamie was a ray of sunshine that was trapped in eternal darkness, one I had caused. It was my fault for giving the guys carte blanche over what they did to him, and the student body were a bunch of twisted sycophants when it came to the football team, willing to follow any directive they issued.

Stevens took the proverbial bull by the horns after I lied to them about why I hated Jamie so much, and I was racked with guilt over it, drowning more and more every day. I thought Stevens was easy-going, but apparently, that was just a mask he wore. Once that was ripped off, he was the most cruel, vindictive individual I'd ever met. He scared the shit out of me—and that was saying something. His first major offense was the exploding box he had couriered to Jamie during the middle of the day. It was orchestrated so the whole team would be there to witness the events as they unfolded. I ended up walking away in shame as Jamie sat there frozen in shock as blood dripped down his face. The headline the following day in the Briar Chronicles was still a trending topic on campus and followed me around like a bad smell. *Box blood bomb: Freshman Prank Gone Wrong or A Cry For Attention?*

Every time I closed my eyes, the events of that day and every one since haunted me. I don't know where Jamie found the strength to keep going, but every day there was a smile on his face, and he treated everyone he came into contact with a level of kindness they didn't deserve. I was too afraid to talk to him directly, so I became his shadow. He never saw me, but I know he felt my eyes on him. He constantly looked over his shoulder when he was walking around campus and didn't even feel safe bracketed between his friends.

The guys had been planning something the last few days, but I'd ignored them and focused on our grueling training and conditioning schedule. It was either that, or I'd beat the shit out of every one of them. My already frayed temper was balanced on a knife's edge, and if anyone so much as breathed near me the wrong way, I would explode. Coach capitalized on it on the field, and it led us to a nail-biting 24 – 21 win in our preseason opener against Amhurst Hall. We celebrated the win, but it felt hollow, considering our defensive line fell apart, adding more fuel to the fire of my building feud with Chad.

"You've got calculus next, haven't you?" I looked up from the sports science assignment I was working on when Stevens slid into the chair next to me.

Keeping my voice hushed, I cast a surreptitious glance around the library. "Yes, why?"

"Oh, nothing really. It just means you'll have a front row seat to what we have in store next for your boy toy." The twisted smirk that spread across Stevens's lips sent a chill down my spine.

"Are you going to clue me in on this?" I asked as I packed up my books.

"Nope." My glare made Stevens chuckle. "There's such a thing as plausible deniability here, Cap. The team needs you, especially after that game." He wasn't wrong there. We might have pulled a win, but it was a mess, and Coach was riding our asses after the defensive line crumbled.

I grunted in response and kicked back my chair. "Are you coming?"

"Nah, but I'll see you in an hour though." Stevens winked at me before turning his attention to his phone, effectively dismissing me.

It wasn't far to the mathematics building from the library. The late afternoon sun hung low in the sky, elongating the shadows and making them take on a sinister edge. Everything had changed on campus, yet somehow, it was still the same. If I was the introspective type, I believe I'd realize it was me that had profoundly changed since the semester started, but I wasn't that kind of person. I didn't believe in that kind of shit anyway.

The room was empty when I slipped through the door about ten minutes before our lecture was due to start. I made my way up the steps and took my usual seat at the back where I could be left alone. We didn't have assigned seating, but as time passed, I realized no one had moved from where we sat on our first day, whether it was a conscious decision or not.

My heart beat erratically and trepidation coiled through me as I drummed my fingers on the table. Jamie hadn't noticed we had this subject together, and with the way things currently were, I hoped he didn't. Nothing good could come from it, and I had a feeling that after today, everything would change again. Whether it would be for better or worse was still to be decided. Sitting at the back gave me the perfect opportunity to watch unencumbered as he interacted with the others. Always the introvert, he would barely acknowledge the guy sitting next to him unless we were made to discuss the problem presented on the whiteboard.

The room filled with noise as students filtered in and took their seats. I pulled my laptop out of my bag and checked the group chat to see if anyone had let anything slip about what they were planning today, but it was quiet. Eerily quiet. And that unnerved me more than anything. Before I could focus on the tension growing inside me, Mr. Velecote walked in and silence fell over the room.

"Morning, everyone. I hope you all took the time to read and review everything we've been working on the last two weeks, because today we have a pop quiz." A collective groan rang out along with a few muttered curses. I shoved my laptop back into my bag and waited for the paper to be passed along the rows.

The door creaked open and somebody stumbled through, capturing the attention of the room. My heart lurched up my throat when I realized the disheveled person was Jamie. Cheeks flushed, clothes askew, he looked like he'd been dragged through a bush backwards. He caught himself on the front row and righted himself before straightening his clothes.

"Nice of you to join us, Mr. Bowen."

"I-I'm—" Jamie stuttered, gasping for breath.

Velecote's voice took on a biting edge, which was completely out of character for him. "I'd have thought you'd know your time table by now and manage to be in the right place at the right time. Perhaps you could drum up an ounce of respect for me and your fellow students and arrive on time in the future." Jamie folded in on himself and tucked his chin into his chest.

"What are you waiting for?" Velecote bellowed. "Take your seat this instant, or you'll get an automatic fail." Jamie flinched like he'd been physically struck, his knees shaking as he shuffled to his seat. I white knuckled the wooden table so hard I'm amazed it didn't crack under the pressure. It took everything within me not to haul my ass down to the front and introduce Mr. Velecote to my fist.

"S-sorry, sir," Jamie responded meekly as he slumped in his seat.

"Now that you've had your afternoon delight..." That earned a round of chuckles. Mr. Velecote looked down at his wrist, his thumb and index finger poised around the watch face. "You have forty-five minutes to complete the quiz, but when your time is up, you're done whether you have completed it or not. Your time starts now."

I chanced one last glance at Jamie before working through the inane multiple choice questions on the first page. Time merged into one big blur, the questions blending into each other. It was difficult to focus when I knew something was coming, and my gaze kept landing on Jamie. He sat slumped in his seat, curled over the table, but nothing could hide the way his body vibrated—whether through fear or anger, I could only guess. I was ready to throw the test when an alarm sounded. My heart stalled mid-beat, my only thought was to get to Jamie and wrap him in my arms. To keep him safe, no matter what it might cost me.

There had never been a fire drill when lectures were in session before, so this had to be a real incident. Noise exploded in the room, footsteps thundering on the floors as everyone rushed toward the exit. Except for Jamie, who cowered in his chair while Mr. Velecote loomed over him. I was singularly focused on the object of my obsession when four men dressed in all black and wearing ski masks stormed into the room. Frozen to the spot, all I could do was watch as everything unfolded. Three of the guys surrounded Jamie and pinned his head and arms to the table. Try as he might, he couldn't fight them off. I could tell he was screaming but couldn't hear anything above the wailing alarm.

Pain bloomed in my chest, spreading outward like poison with every raging beat of my heart. I stormed down the stairs, ready to confront the men, when my eyes snagged on the fourth guy shaking hands with Velecote before he slipped out the faculty door.

"No fucking way." I clenched my jaw and balled my fists, ready to take a swing. This was what Stevens had planned? As if he could feel my eyes on him, he turned and waved in my direction, motioning for me to join them. "What the fuck are you doing?"

His low chuckle sent shivers across my skin. "I told you to stay tuned." Malice coated his usually playful voice, and it made me realize that I didn't really know anyone past the facade they presented on the surface. "If he doesn't leave after this, I have one more idea that will end him."

Refusing to give credence to his words, I turned my back on him and watched as the others hauled Jamie to his feet and pulled a sack over his head. Jamie fought with everything he had, and I just stood there like a piece of shit as they dragged him out of the room, his feet trailing on the ground.

"Come on, man, we don't have a lot of time."

I followed behind Stevens as my stomach revolted, and bile burned the back of my throat. My chest felt like it was being crushed under a ton of weight. Guilt slithered over my skin, coating me in an icy tar. I was disgusted. I was retched. I fucking hated myself as I stood by watching and doing nothing to help the boy I loved.

The edges of my vision started to darken as shadows swallowed the light from my world. I trailed behind them down the corridor, every step becoming harder as my feet tried to fuse with the ground to prevent me from being part of this atrocious act. I was the one who should be condemned, because I started this. I told them to make him leave. I was the one who set the devil free. The continuous blaring of the alarm acted like a countdown timer, covering Jamie's screams.

One of the guys held the janitor's closet open, swinging the keys around his finger like this was a normal everyday occurrence. "Come on, come on. We've only got about three minutes before they turn it off."

Stevens chuckled behind me. "Has Spencer got the containers ready?"

"You know it," the guy on the door said with a chuckle.

"Good. Throw him in."

It felt like an out-of-body experience as they threw Jamie into the small dirty room that smelled like stale smoke and chemicals. I was frozen to the spot, my body locked up tight, every muscle begging me to move, to make it stop, but I couldn't. I was trapped in a cage of my own making, screaming at them to stop inside my mind but unable to do anything.

The thud of Jamie's body as it crashed into the shelves lanced through me, fracturing every part of me. Fear wrapped around my throat like a boa constrictor, stealing the air from my lungs as I was pulled into a memory, one I had long since forgotten.

THE ROUGH PLANKS of the front steps bit into my legs as I waited for Jamie. It had been two days since we'd seen each other, because his parents had dragged him out of town for some unknown reason. I knew he'd gotten back last night, because I'd seen their truck out front, but he hadn't been allowed out. When I'd turned up, his Dad was yelling, so I crept around the back and knocked on his window to see if he could sneak out. His red-rimmed eyes had said everything he couldn't, but he promised he'd come and see me today.

Light footsteps made my head snap up as he approached, and a wide grin lit up his face as he sat down next to me. "Hey," he said softly as he bumped my shoulder.

"Hey." I chuckled. "What do you wanna do today?" I looked

down at him expectantly, waiting for his answer as he toyed with a piece of rye grass between his fingers.

"I dunno. How about we play at the abandoned house? See if we can find anything worth keeping?"

"You just want to see if there are any treasures you can add to your hoard," I joked as his cheeks stained a pretty pink. I shook off that thought, jumped to my feet, and held out my hand. His soft palm slipped into mine, so much smaller—delicate really—and I hauled him to his feet.

Jamie scuffed his shoe in the dirt and shoved his hands in his pockets. "Can we take your bike? Mine is, well..."

His voice sounded small and sad so I did what I always did. I tried to make him smile. "O'course we can." I smirked. "The question is whether you can balance on the seat and not topple us this time."

Jamie laughed so hard, he clutched his stomach and bent over. "That was one time—"

"And we ended up in the creek!"

"I know, I know." He wiped a tear from his eyes. Even though tears swam in them, they sparkled brighter than I'd seen in weeks.

"Race you to the back." Before I'd finished speaking, I ran to the garage and pulled my bike out. Jamie hopped on behind me. The ride to the abandoned house took us about twenty minutes through the winding back roads that no one really used anymore. We spent most of our time dodging the growing pot holes and laughing every time I had to swerve when the road broke beneath my tires.

"This place will never not be cool," Jamie said with wonder in his voice. He loved this old building even though I thought it would make a better bonfire. "One day when I'm older, I'm gonna build us a house like this."

I turned to look at him with a funny feeling in my chest. Us? He'd said us. I wondered what that meant to him. Did it mean the same to him as it did me? Jamie was my everything, the center of my world. But was I his?

"That sounds cool," I said as the porch boards crumbled beneath our feet. "Just promise me it won't fall apart like this one."

"Like I would design us a bad house?!" The affront in Jamie's voice had me cackling as he shoved me through the open front door and into the wide open entryway covered in dry leaves and trash. Graffiti covered the walls, and an old mattress was dumped in one of the front rooms.

"Well, I won't know till I see it, will I?" I said.

"That's true." He snickered. "It'll be a surprise. I'll just say one day, 'Oh Dil! I've got something to show you,' and bam! There's our home."

My heart skipped on the word home. That's what he was to me. Home. "Sure, can't wait. Hey, wanna play hide and seek?"

"Okay. I'm hiding first though," Jamie called to me as he ran past the stairs. I shook my head and started counting. By the time I'd gotten to thirty, the house was silent save for the wind whipping through the broken boards. Even though the windows had been white washed, I could still make out the dark clouds swelling across the sky as the temperature started to drop. I could taste rain in the air as a storm rolled in.

"Ready or not, here I come," I shouted as I strode through the house and out to the back deck. Jamie had an affinity for nature —he'd be outside surrounded by trees or water as often as he could. I didn't know if he was trying to escape something or just loved being outside more than anything. He might be my best friend and tell me almost everything, but I knew he kept secrets from me. Just like I kept some from him.

"Jamie, where are you?" I called after half an hour of searching for him. His small frame made him a master at this game. It frustrated me no end, but all I wanted was to see him smile. "Jaammmiee?"

A faint giggle carried on the wind as I headed back toward the house and searched every room. Where is he? The only place I hadn't looked was the old storm shelter under the house. We'd both been a bit freaked out when we checked it out the first time we came here and had never gone back.

I grabbed the rotten door and pulled it back, staring into the darkness beyond. "Jamie?"

"Ahhhh, crap." His voice floated up from the dark depths. "Dil, I'm stuck."

"I'm coming!" I shouted and jumped right in, the old wooden beams groaning when I landed. I blinked a few times, waiting for my eyes to adjust to the near darkness before moving. "Where are you?"

"Over here." Jamie's voice sounded pained as I followed it farther into the extensive shelter. Old shelving units were toppled over, and piles of old clothes gave the damp air a musty tinge that tickled my nose.

"Little crow?" I whispered as I saw Jamie sitting in the corner. "I've found you."

"Well, I kinda gave it away when I called you," he whined. "My leg's stuck Dil. The floor gave out." Just as the words left his mouth, a cracking groan rendered the air and the board beneath my feet crumbled.

"Shit, Jamie," I screamed as the corner he sat on shattered, and he disappeared. I threw myself onto my stomach, trying to find him. "Jamie? Jamie? Please answer me."

"I'm down here," he cried. "I'm... I'm okay." Sure enough, about ten feet down, Jamie was wedged under broken planks. "I can't get out Dil. You need to get my mom."

"I'll be as quick as I can. You gonna be alright while I go and get her?"

"Y-yeah?"

IT TOOK seven hours to get Jamie out. He'd been alone and terrified all that time. I didn't have a phone, and Jamie's mom wasn't home. None of the neighbors knew where she was. By the time I finally found her, hours had passed. Once we got back to the house, Jamie was hysterical and couldn't stop crying. The doctor had to sedate him, because he was shaking so badly.

Jamie's hysterical scream snapped me back to the depravity of the present. His head cracked on the concrete floor, his body jolting from the force as he skidded into the unit storing toxic chemicals. The guys laughed as Jamie's screams turned to pained whimpers, each one like a bullet to my soul. They pulled everything off the shelves. Cleaning supplies, buckets, and tools scattered across the room as they fell to the floor. Jamie curled into the fetal position, his arms braced over his head to protect himself as things landed on him, making him grunt.

A loud whistle pierced the air, silencing everyone. They all left the small room and turned off the light. "This is my favorite part," Stevens whispered into my ear as someone else appeared with two large buckets filled with water.

"What the fuck are you going—" My words froze as they threw the contents of the buckets into the room, drenching Jamie and flooding the floor.

"Get the lights," someone shouted, and my heart turned to lead. I didn't deserve to breathe the same air as Jamie after this. I knew what it would do to him. It would fuck him over more than I intended. All I wanted to do was scare him enough so he'd leave, and my secrets would stay hidden. So I could live my life and get out from under my dad's control.

The door slammed shut, the click of the lock an ominous sound as the alarm fell silent. In the blink of an eye, everyone scrambled out, darting in different directions. Jamie's haunting wails stalked me as I ran from the building.

My heart was pounding so hard it was about to shatter my ribs. I ran until my knees buckled, and I crashed to the ground, gasping for breath, my body tight and aching. I dragged myself under the trees for cover. My stomach revolted as bile surged up my throat, and I emptied the contents of my gut until I was retching on nothing but air.

I rolled onto my back. Sweat dripped down my temples and soaked through the shirt on my back. Tears seared my eyes as guilt ate away at me. "What have I done? What have I done?" I was the worst of the worst. I might not have thrown him into the janitor's closet or doused him with water, but I am the reason he is suffering. I am weak. Pathetic. A disgusting excuse for a human being. I will be condemned for the rest of my life for what I allowed to happen today, all because I wanted to keep my truth a secret. But I've done it at the expense of the most amazing and loving person I've ever known. I might hate him, but does he really deserve this?

CHAPTER SIXTEEN

Jamie

The silence was so thick and heavy it suffocated me, clawing its way into my lungs and stealing every particle of air. My throat was raw, burned from the inside out from every scream that was wrenched from me against my will. Blood dripped from my nose and coated my mouth, staining my lips as I dragged my tongue over them. The slightest movement ached and echoed though me as I slowly cataloged every pulsing point of pain that blazed with white-hot intensity.

I tried to move, to call out for help now the blaring alarm and abusive words had stopped, but it was too much. The fragile grip I had on my consciousness started to fade and slip through my fingers. At least if I let go, the pain would stop, and I'd feel some semblance of peace. I wondered if this was how Mom felt every time Dad beat her. I would listen to her screams from the safety of my closet until the house fell under an unearthly silence that flushed my skin with goosebumps, and I would selfishly pray she'd still be alive the following day. I knew I was too small to survive my father's brand of love. It was a weak and selfish thought, but I needed her. I still do. I miss her so much.

"You're stronger than this, Jamie. Don't give in. Get up, baby. Get up."

"Mom," I wheezed, my arm outstretched on the cold cement floor, reaching for a ghost that wasn't there.

I didn't know how much time had passed since they locked me in here. It had lost all meaning. It could have been minutes, hours, days, even. They left me to endure. To suffer. They wanted to break me. To make me run. What they didn't know was I had nowhere to run to. When you've spent years running from the devil, a lesser monster holds no power. And that's all they were—a bunch of assholes on a power trip. I didn't understand why they had it out for me, only that they did.

"Jamie? Oh fuck. Jamie?" Dillon's voice was etched with anguish. I'd been so lost in my marauding thoughts and pain, I hadn't heard his approach.

"W-what." I licked at my dry lips. "What a-are you d-doing here?"

"I..." A breath shuddered out of him. I felt the air move as he fell to the floor next to me, his knees landing close to my head, the scuff of denim on the concrete floor like sandpaper on my brain. "Fuck, little crow..." His words felt like a physical touch, something tangible I could cling to in the darkness. A spark of hope.

"D-Dil... p-please..." I wanted him to wrap his arms around me. To feel safe. To go back five years when the future looked bright and full of possibilities. I wanted too much, even though I knew I could never have it. I'd prayed for another chance with him, for us. But we were on opposite sides of the board. We were enemies. There wasn't a line drawn between us; there was a canyon that grew wider every day. I just didn't understand why, and maybe I never would.

"Shhh, little crow, I've got you. I'll get you out of here and make sure you're safe." His words were whisper soft, a gentle caress. A promise that sounded so sweet I couldn't resist. I breathed them in, committed them to memory, and then buried them.

"O-okay," I managed to grit out. My teeth chattered as my body recoiled from violent convulsions. My wet clothes clung to me like a layer of burning ice, numbing my skin but intensifying the pain that shot through me. His hands slipped under my legs and wrapped around my chest, causing my breathing to hitch as he jostled me.

"Try to relax, baby. This will hurt, but I'll be as gentle as I can be." His feet shifted around me, heat radiating off his body as he painstakingly maneuvered me off the floor. A scream tore free from my lungs as he lifted me bridal-style into the air. He jostled me in his arms as his grip wavered until gravity pulled me into his body, and his arms locked around me.

I felt like I was flying, soaring above the clouds, even though I was trapped in darkness. Safe, yet my head was facing an unending abyss. "D-Dil? Can y-you..."

"Oh shit, hang on." His firm muscles strained and rippled as his hands shifted on my abused skin. A jolt shot through me as he pulled the bag off my head, and I tasted sweet, sweet air. I sucked greedy mouthfuls down into my lungs as stars danced across my vision, unable to focus on anything. "Are you okay?" His tentative question was threaded with fear. He knew. He could see me, but he asked anyway.

I couldn't speak. Every word turned to ash on my tongue as a wave of nausea rolled through me, and the taste of copper in my mouth turned to acid. I nodded, a barely perceptible movement, but the look of understanding in his sorrow-edged eyes let me know he understood.

I curled into the sanctuary his body offered as he moved on silent feet to the open doorway. The bright light of the corridor was blindingly bright and made my eyes water. I blinked to clear the welling tears as too many emotions battled inside me, threatening to overwhelm me. I rested my head against his chest, focusing on the erratic pounding of his heart as he stalled for a second, his body swaying as if he was paralyzed. I felt more than heard him suck in a deep inhale, and then he was running. His footsteps were like a metronome, swaying us from side to side as he raced through the building toward the exit on nimble legs.

The world blurred around me as he moved faster than my brain could process. The world flickered in and out of focus around me like the old-fashioned black and white movies. Dillon's panted breaths were hot against my chilled skin. They were the only thing that let me know this was real, and I wasn't dreaming. "Shit," he ground out as the sound of voices rang out around us, and the air buzzed with anticipation. The chatter of students grew louder and louder until Dillon cursed again and abruptly changed direction. "We're going to have to go by the sports fields, because everyone has been corralled in the quad. You're goin' to have to hang on a little longer, little crow."

I don't know if I closed my eyes or passed out, but they snapped open as a wave of warmth washed over me. A door banged, and I became hyper aware of my surroundings. The stale smell of the dorms filtered through my nose, and his thudding footfalls were now muted by carpet. Lights flashed above me as we moved swiftly along the corridor toward the elevator, the soft ding perfectly timed as the doors slid open. I caught a glimpse of my fuzzy reflection. I looked like shit, but after what I'd been through in the last few… hours? Minutes? I wasn't surprised in the least.

"Here you go," Dillon muttered as he pushed the door open to my room. His head swung from side to side before he looked down at me. "Which one?"

Which one is what? Oh, bed. He meant bed. "The right," I rasped. He softly placed me down as if I was something fragile and precious, then removed my shoes and socks before starting on my pants. The button was undone, the zipper halfway down before my brain kicked in. "S-stop." My hand shot out and grabbed his arm. If he could feel the ferocity of the shakes running through me, he didn't react to them.

"Jamie?" The pained tone of his voice tugged at something inside me I didn't want to look too closely at. "*Please,*" he begged. "We need to get you out of these wet clothes. I… I can't —" He turned away in frustration, hands fisted in his hair as I gingerly pulled myself up onto my elbows, my eyes enraptured by him. He paced back and forth, burning a path in the carpet. No matter how many times he retraced his steps, I couldn't tear my eyes away. He was beautifully broken, fierce and deadly. But right now, he looked small and lost. He looked like mine.

"I can do it myself." My breathless words were softer than a summer breeze, but Dillon heard them and froze. His shattered eyes trained on me as his chest heaved, shoulders rising and falling. A myriad of emotions played across his face, eyebrows scrunched as if he wanted to say so many things but couldn't find wherewithal to articulate them. He stepped toward me with an arm outstretched. I held up my hand, and he turned to stone. "I-I can manage. Y-you should go."

"Jamie." His pained exhale was almost enough to make me change my mind, but I locked that feeble thought down. He'd done enough; too much, really. I was vulnerable, raw and exposed in a way I never wanted him to see. He acted like he hated me one minute, then became my dark knight the next. I was getting whiplash. It was a total mind fuck. What I needed was silence, rest, and sleep. With him hovering, I wasn't going to get anything.

"No, Dillon. You need to go." It hurt to say those words, and if the look of devastation that flickered across his face was anything to go by, he felt it too. But I couldn't do this. Not with him, not now. "Just go. Please."

His hand wrapped around the handle, and he slowly pulled it back, his eyes a vortex of agony. I bit down on my cracked lip, the pain helping to keep my emotions in check. All I wanted to do was reach out to him and beg him to stay, but I knew it was the wrong thing to do.

"Can I…" He shook his head and slipped out the door like a thief in the night, like he was never here. The Dillon I knew still existed—I knew it in the marrow of my bones—but he was buried beneath the pain and the anger he carried. Was he crying out for me as much as I was for him?

I'D SPENT the last week hiding out in our dorm. Mal had been an absolute saint, and if it wasn't for him, I'm pretty certain I would have packed up and left. When he heard what happened, and I didn't answer my phone, he burst through our door like his ass was on fire, threw himself on the bed, and wrapped me up in his arms until I stopped crying. When I finally did, he looked me over and arranged for one of the medical students to check me over. That's how I ended up with a prescription for some seriously strong painkillers that knocked me out for nearly three days straight.

Today was the first day I felt remotely human. I ached like I'd been hit by a bull, but I couldn't keep hiding. Mom never did. She dusted herself off and got back up again. She told me I was her reason for fighting, her reason to keep on going. It made me feel special but also like a curse. All I'm left with are painful memories and unanswered questions. Did she stay all those years because of me? Am I the reason she got hurt to begin with? I'll never know, but I can't help but wonder.

The pills went down easily as I sipped on my water and focused on what I needed to take to the art studio. I grabbed my sketch book, charcoal sticks, and pencils before slipping my bag over my shoulder. The halls were quiet as I headed out of the building. It was strange not having to duck and dodge large groups of people. It was nice to be able to just be in the moment without the distraction of everything around me being so loud I couldn't think.

My mind had been working overtime the last few days, trying to understand why Dillon was the person who found and rescued me. It doesn't make sense. How did he know I was there after the building was evacuated? The last thing I remember clearly was Velecote looming over me as the room emptied around us, the only sound louder than the stampede of feet was the wailing alarm. I can still hear it ringing distantly in my ears, like some kind of haunting tinnitus.

It's like I've got all the pieces of the puzzle, but they're not fitting together. Maybe I'm looking at it all the wrong way. Just like in art, perspective is everything. I want to know the answers, but also I fear they might be the final nail in the coffin. I've got myself caught in a catch twenty-two situation. Damned if I do, damned if I don't.

My phone vibrated in my pocket. Thank god for my ten minute warning alarm—I don't know where I'd be without it. Time management has never been my strong point. I turned it off before checking for any messages, but the screen is blank for once. A small smile lifted my lips at the background photo of my little sunbeam. I sucked in a deep breath and brushed off the melancholy clinging to me like a second skin. It's a new day and all that.

The art rooms were always a hive of activity, and today was

no different. The smell of old paint and oils saturated the air, permeating every surface. To many, it might be overpowering, but to me, it was a comfort I refused to let go. I settled at my table and waited for Mrs. Wright to tell us what our next project would be. Gina, the girl that shared my table, slipped into her seat.

"Hey, Jamie." She smiled sweetly at me, her fiery-red hair illuminated by the sun streaming through the windows. "I heard you had a bit of trouble recently. You doin' okay?"

If only she knew the truth. Mal told me no one knew what went down after the alarm was set off, and I took some comfort in that. "Yeah." I sighed. "Just had the stomach flu. Knocked me out for a few days." I hoped that was enough for her. I didn't really know her beyond the few interactions we'd had in class, and they'd been painful enough. I liked people, but I found it unbelievably hard to talk to them. I sucked at inane, surface-level chatter about the weather and classes, and the more someone pushed for an answer, the more I shut down. Mal and Ava were the only two people I had ever immediately felt comfortable with. Lie.

"Alright, everyone." Mrs. Wright clapped her hands together to gain our attention. "Today is going to be fun," she said as she cast her eyes over the room. They landed on me for a beat before moving on, and air wooshed out of me when she turned her back. "I'd like you all to go outside this afternoon and look at natural structures..." I tuned her out as she continued, my mind focused on being outside. I knew exactly where I was going to go. I needed somewhere peaceful where I could work without getting disrupted. "I want you to look at form, how its natural composition supports the structure, and really try and convey that depth in your work. You can use any medium you like."

Five minutes later, I strolled across the green expanse of lawns that separated the main part of campus from the sports fields. The shrill sound of a whistle belted through the air moments before the bellowing roar of a team in the middle of practice took over. I didn't know who was out there, and I didn't especially care, as Mal had hinted the issues I'd had on campus were because of the football team. One member to be precise, but there was no way of verifying that fact because apparently what happened at football practice, stayed at football practice.

I scoffed and kicked a stone that bounced along the grass until I lost sight of it. The light today was perfect. The skies were overcast, and gray clouds were marled across the vast expanse of blue. I could get lost in the ever changing patterns they created, but sadly, they weren't my focus today. There was an old gnarled oak down by the lake that would be perfect...

A pained cry rendered the air, followed by a sharp gasping breath. "Hello?" I called out, treading carefully across the grass. The world fell silent, and even the bird song seemed to have ceased as I strained to hear the sound again. When nothing happened for a while, I shrugged it off and kept walking in the direction of the lake.

"Fuck!" My head snapped to the right, my interest piqued, and I turned to head in the direction of the rasping voice. "No. No. No," they chanted, each word growing more and more pained, their agony palpable. Twigs cracked under my feet as I broke through the tree line, slowly heading toward whoever was hiding in the woods. From what I could hear, it sounded like someone having a panic attack. Their stuttering, gasping breaths ratched up my own anxiety with every step.

I couldn't explain what drew me toward them, other than their suffering pulled on something inside me, and I had this overwhelming urge to make sure they were alright. I'd suffered a fair few panic attacks in my time, and it was one of the worst things to endure alone without someone or something there to anchor you and help you fight back. Someone to hold you, to guide you as you worked on pulling yourself back from that ledge.

"I-I...I'm sorry... I'm sorry... I-I-I..." A low groan helped me cross the last of the distance between us, and what I found made me feel like I was free falling from a thousand feet with nothing to catch me when I crash landed.

Dillon sat on the ground, knees pulled up, arms wrapped around them, head buried in the space between them. His breath hitched with every labored inhale, and my heart squeezed in sympathy and ached with confusion. What happened to bring someone I thought of as so strong to this point? Frenetic energy radiated off him as he rocked side to side.

Unsure what to do or how to help without making things worse, I crouched a few feet in front of him. As if sensing me, he lifted his head and stared at me through unseeing eyes. Tears tracked down his flushed cheeks, but it was the swirling darkness that had hold of his eyes that made it impossible to breathe. I reached out to him, the need to wrap him in my arms tangible. My fingers tingled as I brushed the damp strands of hair off his face. "Dil?" I said softly, so as not to exasperate his emotional turmoil.

Dillon blinked, unleashing a fresh wave of tears as his lips trembled. I want to wipe them off where they clung to his plump bottom lip but apprehension held me hostage.

"Dillon? Can you hear me?"

He blinked again, and some of the shadows cleared from his eyes like a breaking storm. For a fleeting moment, recognition sparked in his ebony eyes, but it was gone before I could react. He gasped, fingers clawing at his throat like he was struggling to draw in a breath.

My legs crumbled, refusing to support me as he broke right in front of me. I refused to be a silent observer any longer and crawled across the ground, twigs and stones cutting into my skin. Kneeling at Dillon's feet, I tentatively put my left hand on his knee. Electricity danced across my fingers and shot down my arm like a lightning bolt. “Shhh, Dil. I’m here,” I cooed softly and teased my fingers through his hair. Leaning into my touch, Dillon’s rocking slowed as my fingers gently grazed across his scalp. His eyes fluttered closed as soft comforting words passed my lips. The tension locking up his shoulders eased, and so did the steel band around my chest.

CHAPTER SEVENTEEN

Dillon

Gentle fingers teased through my hair, sending waves of electricity across my skin as the world splintered around me. Everything narrowed down to the sensation as it worked from the front to the back of my head, just like Jamie used to do when we were younger. After a long day of school and a hard practice, we used to disappear to the creek out the back of his house and just sit there for hours. It was heaven and hell in equal measure, and they say the road to hell is paved with good intentions. Maybe this is my penance, one last torturous glimpse at heaven before I fall.

"How did it go today?" Jamie asked softly as he sat down in the long grass at the bough of a tree and patted the ground next to him.

I looked into his pale blue eyes, the edges burning with

molten steel, and released a heavy exhale. I plopped down next to him and shuffled in the dirt until my head lay across his thighs. "Coach was pissed." I sighed as his fingers worked through my still damp hair. Stoke by stroke, his gentle touch soothed me, and made my muscles ache a little less as I stared up at the leaves dancing in the breeze.

"What did you do?" The accusation in Jamie's sweet voice was unmistakable.

"What makes you think it was something I did?" I parried.

"Because if Coach was pissed at someone else, you would be laughing about it. Not stiff enough to shit diamonds."

I choked on the spit that got lodged in my throat, making Jamie hum a chuckle. "Did you seriously just say that?" I grinned up at him as he trailed his finger down over my nose before working on the pressure points by my eyebrows.

"Sounds like it, doesn't it?" He shrugged. "Besides, it made you laugh."

"True. I can't argue with that." My eyes fluttered shut as my mind started to let go of all the pressure and responsibility that sat on my shoulders. "Jamie?"

"Yeah, Dil?"

"Thanks."

He shifted underneath me, so I lifted my head, ready to sit up and take my weight off his thighs, but Jamie clucked his tongue at me and pushed down on my forehead before he continued running his fingers through my hair. The little hairs on my arm stood up on end as goosebumps spread across my body, and my skin came alive.

"SHHH, Dillon, I've got you. Come back to me. Lean on me, let me help you." His voice never ceased to amaze me even if it was only in my head. Fuck. I wished he was really here, but I haven't seen him since he threw me out of his room.

The last week has been excruciating. The walls have been

closing in, suffocating me. The pressure on me has reached boiling point, every single one of my responsibilities weighing me down with chains made of lead. I wanted to reach out to him so many times. I needed to see his face. His smile. See for myself that he was fine as the guilt over what happened ate at me like a cancer, but I couldn't. I've had eyes on me constantly.

Coach had been demanding, pushing the team harder and harder, but like a house of cards built on quicksand, the harder he pushed, the faster we fell. There's a discord among the team that's tearing us apart, with Chad being the instigator of the divide. I knew he hated me, but he loved to win and be the center of attention, so I don't know why he's driving us into a wall we won't be able to come back from. After every failed practice, my dad called to berate me, belittle and demean me. He threatened to come to Briar U and show me how it was done. What he really meant was that he'll beat some good ol' fashioned sense into me. It wouldn't be the first time. But he preferred to use words; his tongue was sharper than a blade, cutting me down like a machete. He'd sooner stab me in the back than watch his dream of me going pro fail. I was nothing to him but a stepping stone and dollar signs.

I couldn't cope. I just wanted it all to stop. I'd tried to focus and trained so hard my muscles were as burned out as my mind. I couldn't sleep, because my anxiety never let up. It was there pushing and pulsing like a living entity growing inside me. Even when I closed my eyes, all I could hear was Coach and my Dad shouting, taunting and maiming me with their disappointment.

My eyes were screwed shut so tightly that fireworks burst behind my closed lids like strobe lights. My breaths sawed in and out of my lungs, dragging a ball of shattered glass with each exhale.

"Dillon, I want you to focus on my voice." Jamie's soft, lilting voice was like a beam of sunlight in the darkness that was my mind. "I know you can hear me. I need you to breathe with me." Something solid pushed against my sternum, and I wrapped my hand around it on instinct, clinging to it like a lifeline. "That's it Dil, you're doing so good."

If only he was real. If only he was real. If only he was real. The chant ran through my mind, blocking the toxic thoughts as I focused on his voice. Even though I was delusional, he was here, helping me whether he was real or not. I'd take any moment in time he granted me, because I knew once he discovered the truth, he'd never look at me again. Like Icarus, I would willingly fly closer and closer to the sun just for one more chance to bask in its light.

"I'm going to help you get your breathing under control, okay? Just listen and do as I say." My breath caught in my throat as it squeezed tighter. "Breathe in. One...two...three." The vise around my throat got tighter as every second passed. "That's great. Now breathe out. One... two... three... four. That's great, Dil you've got this. Again."

I don't know how long I was lost in the darkness, listening to my hallucination of Jamie talking me through one of the most terrifying panic attacks I'd ever had. I wanted to claw at my throat as I fought to get air into my lungs, but his firm grip on my hand helped calm that destructive instinct. Sweat beaded on my brow and dripped down my temples. My shirt clung to my sweat-slicked back by the time I felt the rough bark bite into my skin. My legs were numb, my arms and hands locked up tight, my muscles stiff, cold, and aching. I couldn't move, but Jamie's presence remained constant, and he was the center of my focus. The eye of the storm. The one thing that pulled me back.

"That's it, Dil. You're doing so great for me." His warm hand cupped my face, his thumb feathering over my damp cheek. I choked on a sob as my breath caught in my throat, the salty taste of my tears on my tongue. I wanted so badly for him to be real.

The ringing silence in my ears dissipated, and a cool breeze brushed over my skin. I slumped to the side, my body drained and exhausted. My head landed on something soft but firm. It smelled of musky caramel and made my mouth water. Even in this semi-lucid state, I still clung to my fantasy. I wished he was real.

A lilting chuckle tinkled through the air. "I'm here, Dillon. I'm as real as you are." I felt the teasing scratch of nails against my scalp, and I shuddered, nuzzling into the softness that pillowed my head. A sharp intake of breath had my eyes snapping open. Blinded by the brightness, I blinked away the fog that obscured my vision, and slowly but surely, the world came back into focus.

"Little crow?" The delusional fever dream still clung to my mind like fractured cobwebs.

"I'm here, Dil." A warm hand cupped my cheek and maneuvered my head until I was staring into the eyes that haunted my dreams and owned my heart. Ones I pretended to hate but worshiped from afar.

"H-how?"

"I was on my way to the lake to do..." He shook his head, and his curls bounced around his jaw line. "That's not important." I opened my mouth, but he placed his finger on my lips, silencing me. "I heard you cry out. I mean, I didn't know it was you, but yeah. You get what I mean." A smile curved my lips at his bleeding heart.

"I do," I croaked, my throat itchy and dry. I rubbed at my neck with my hand, trying to alleviate the pressure.

"Oh." He leaned over, unzipped his bag, and produced a bottle of water and handed it to me. I sat up slowly. The world wavered around me before I braced myself against the tree at my back and drank down the cool water as Jamie continued to explain how he found me. How he pulled me out of the grip of a panic attack and coaxed me into being able to breathe again. Fuck, he was too much. Too good for me.

He was damn well perfect, and I was a toxic fuck up of epic proportions.

I brushed the back of my hand over my mouth, wiping away the water I'd spilled down my chin while Jamie laughed at me. "T-Thank you, Jamie. Really." I reached out and laced my fingers through his, my thumb gently stroking over his. Fuck, I wanted to kiss him. I wanted to show him how I felt without words, because I'd never be able to articulate this burning need inside me.

"Come." Jamie popped up and pulled on my hand until he dragged me to my feet. I wobbled for a second, my knees threatening to buckle as wave after wave of exhaustion battered me. "I know you're tired but I want to show you somewhere. It's where I go when it all gets too much. I think you'll like it. It...it reminds me of home." He looked up at me expectantly, his eyes twinkling in the dappled light filtering through the trees.

"Home?" Our home hasn't been the same for five years—not since he left and abandoned me. Wrath stirred in my gut, churning the contents of my stomach. I sucked in a deep breath and locked away the hate, allowing myself this moment with him, because only an idiot would believe we would get a happily ever after. I'd have to settle for a fleeting happiness for now. Live in the moment. I'd grab it with both fucking hands.

"Yes." He bounced on the balls of his feet and slung his bag over his shoulder before leading me on a meandering path through the trees. His soft hand wrapped around mine, growing slicker the longer we walked, and his breathing grew shallower as a tantalizing pink blush stained his cheeks.

"Nervous?" I joked as he nibbled his plump bottom lip. Memories of how full and soft it felt against mine played through my mind as I blindly followed him farther into the woods. I'd never ventured this far before. I didn't even know if we were still on campus grounds but right now I didn't give a fuck. I was with the only person I could ever be myself with, and that had to count for something, right?

A coy smile lit up Jamie's face as he looked at me over his shoulder. "Kinda," he mumbled. "Not far now. I hope it helps you like it does me. There's something kinda magical about it."

A chuckle slipped past my lips, and he stuck his tongue out at me. "If it means something to you, I'm sure I'll love it." *Like I love you.*

"Ha! Alright, well, we'll see. Close your eyes."

"You're joking, right?"

Jamie shook his head, a somber expression on his face. "I never joke about things that are important to me. You know that, Dil." That I did. Whether or not it was a conscious choice, Jamie had built a wall around himself that was a mile high and an ocean deep. In all the years I'd known him, I'd been his only friend. *You could have been more too.* He was all things sunshine and light, perfectly polite and friendly to everyone he met, charming them with his smile and bewitching them with his beautiful eyes, but he never let anyone in. I'd never questioned it when I was younger, but now all I had were questions.

"Promise you won't lead me into a hole?"

He shoved my shoulder. "Obviously not."

I inhaled and my eyes fluttered closed. "I'm at your mercy now, so be kind." The double entendre wasn't lost on me, but Jamie just hummed and guided me along. The ground changed and sloped under my feet, but he never let me fall or stumble. He guided me around objects in my way and coaxed me to climb down a bank before helping me step up onto something solid. The air felt cooler and smelled fresher. Purer, somehow.

"That's it. Now, sit down." My head whipped in his direction, and I arched a questioning brow.

"Trust me, remember?" I nodded my assent and folded

myself down on the solid surface. It was cold and rough under my hand as I used it to steady myself. Jamie huffed a breath at me. I could almost feel the warmth of the smile on his face and my lips quirked.

"Can I open them now?"

"Yes," he whispered, his soft lips brushing against the shell of my ear. I let out a shuddering breath, not expecting him to have been that close to me. I could feel his body heat radiating off him even through the layers I wore.

I peeled my eyes open and allowed them to adjust to the glaring brightness. It took a couple of seconds for my brain to fully process what I was witnessing. My mouth opened and closed like a fish as I failed to find words for, well, everything.

My heart thundered in my chest. I felt closer to Jamie than I had in five years. Not just physically or geographically, but emotionally. One of our favorite places growing up was the creek behind his house, closely followed by the beach where we'd whiled away hours of our childhood during the long hot summers when we were left to our own devices.

Emotion clogged my throat, and tears pricked my eyes. I'd thought I was all cried out after my panic attack, but now a fresh wave was upon me. Jamie stared at me with those wild beguiling eyes of his, and something inside of me snapped. My hand cupped his smooth cheek before my fingers sunk into his hair and angled his head. "Thank you, little crow," I breathed against his lips.

The tip of my tongue teased against the seam of his full lips, pleading for entry. He gasped and shuddered at the sensation, and his hands curled around the nape of my neck, pulling me closer. His lips parted, opening up for me, offering himself up for me to devour. I licked into his mouth and groaned as his tongue tangled with mine. Blood whooshed in my ears as I lost myself to the feel of his mouth against mine.

I swallowed down the soft whimpers that worked their way up Jamie's throat as he laved his tongue against mine. His sweet caramel scent saturated my senses until we broke apart, gasping for breath. He had never looked more beautiful than he did right now, with his cheeks flushed a deep red and his lips swollen and slick from my saliva.

"Dil," he breathed before pulling me back down to him. I lost myself in the molten intensity of his pale-blue eyes as wonder and lust flooded them. "Kiss me." He didn't have to ask me twice. I tightened my grip, tangling my fingers in his hair as my mouth smashed down against his. My tongue speared past his lips as I owned every inch of his tempting mouth.

"Fuck, baby." I groaned as his tongue wrapped around mine. I kissed him until my lungs screamed and burned. I drank down every soft mewl and needy moan until black dots danced across my vision. "Jamie." I sucked on his full bottom lip and rolled it between my teeth, pulling it back and releasing it with a pop.

"More," he whined as I kissed a path across his jaw and up to his ear, sinking my teeth into his lobe. Jamie turned his head and arched his neck, baring his throat to me. His pulse thundered against his delicate skin as I ran my tongue from the base of his neck to the sensitive skin just below his ear and blew on his overheated skin until he shuddered.

I traced my nose along his neck, inhaling his sweet scent mixed with salty sweat. The combination was intoxicating and had me desperate for things I'd never done before. Things I'd only ever dreamed of doing with him but had never dared to hope for. I wanted to taste him, to kiss and own every inch of his skin. I needed to trace every freckle with the tip of my tongue. I guided Jamie down onto his back on the rock he'd guided me too mere minutes before and slipped his bag under his head.

Confusion flickered across his face, and fear coiled in his eyes. He braced his hands on my face, his thumbs stroking across my cheeks and down through the stubble that covered my jaw. "I love feeling your scruff against my face." His cheeks flushed a deeper shade of red, and I licked my lips, tasting him on me and groaned.

"Jamie?" His pupil-blown eyes locked onto mine, his soft breaths panting against my lips. "Please, let me taste you. Just let me have this? You. Me. Let me hold on to it before you hate me?" I buried my face in the crook of his neck, peppering the delicate skin with biting kisses as I waited for him to answer.

Jamie tipped his head back, and my teeth scraped over his Adam's apple, making a full-body shudder roll through him as I positioned myself between his spread legs. He gasped as my weight settled over him. The sensation of his hard length brushing against mine tore a moan from deep within my chest as I rolled my hips against him.

"I..." he croaked and licked his slick lips. "Y-yes." His eyes practically glowed, illuminated by the setting sun as the sky turned from a marbled gray-blue to golden pinks.

"Really?" Hope lit me up from the inside as lust turned my blood to quicksilver.

"Yes." One word that had the power to change the world and destroy cities. My cock throbbed in my shorts, the tip slick as precum pooled from my slit.

"Thank fuck," I groaned as I pushed his hoodie up, exposing his little body. Corded muscles that looked like they were carved from marble glistened under sheen of sweat. I kissed down his chest and sucked a nipple into my mouth. The nub hardened under my touch, and I suckled on it until his head thrashed and moans spilled from his kiss-bruised lips. I chuckled and licked across his chest before sinking my teeth into the other one.

"Oh, god. Ahh." Jamie groaned and threw his head back as his hips lifted, searching for some much needed friction. "More. Please," he whimpered, and who was I to deny him? I kissed, licked, and sucked my way down his ribs, tracing each one with my tongue and making him shiver and writhe underneath me. I marked his skin as I sucked it into my mouth, making him arch his back and push himself closer to me. His fingers clutched at my hair, the damp strands sliding through them as he lost purchase.

"You smell so good, little crow," I hummed, tracing his hard length with the tip of my nose. My mouth watered at the tempting scent of his arousal, the sweet and musky scent everything I'd ever wanted but never had. "Fuck. I can't believe I get to do this with you."

"Please," he ground out, lifting his hips and thrusting his jeans-covered cock against my face. "Fuck."

I chuckled against him and held him down with one hand braced on his hip as I licked across the sensitive skin above the elastic band of his boxers, pulling at it with my teeth. A devilish, guttural moan sawed out of Jamie's parted lips as I flicked open the button on his jeans and pulled his zipper down, one tooth at a time, my fingertips ghosting over his length as I lowered it. I mouthed his cloth-covered shaft and lapped at the wet spot by his leaking tip.

"Shit. Fuck. Yes. Please," he babbled, consumed by lust. Jamie lifted his hips, and I pulled his pants and boxers down in one go. He didn't even flinch when his bare cheeks landed on the cold rock face.

"You're fucking beautiful, baby," I whispered with reverence. His cock was long and slender but absolutely perfect. I licked my lips as I took in his flushed glistening glans and his bare balls. They were drawn up tight, already hugging the base of his dick and I hadn't even touched it. "Fuck. That's the sexiest thing I've ever seen."

"Please."

"Anything for you." I kissed up one thigh and then the other as my fingers trailed across the hint of abs on his flat stomach, leaving a trail of goosebumps in their wake. Electricity crackled across my skin every time I touched him.

I buried my face in his groin, inhaling his scent. It was

stronger here; musky and all man. All Jamie, and perfect. A sweet whine came from Jamie as he started to chant, "Please." His glowing eyes watched me with an intensity that sucked the air out of my lungs. "I want you to keep your eyes on me, baby. Okay?"

"Yesss," he hissed as I licked him from root to tip, teasing the underside with my tongue. I moaned against his shaft, the vibrations causing his dick to twitch against my swipes. A wicked smile split my face as I circled his crown before dipping my tongue into his slit.

"Fuck, yes." I groaned as salty precum burst across my tongue. I wrapped my hand around his length, angling his pulsing cock just where I wanted before working up and down his length, giving it a slight twist on every alternate upstroke as I sucked one of his balls into my mouth.

"Holy fuck!!" His legs shook as I switched to the other tight ball and rolled it around in my mouth, covering it in saliva before releasing it and watching it drip down his crack. "I-I need..."

"I've got you, baby boy," I assured him as I wrapped my lips around his head and suckled on his tip like he was my favorite flavor. Newsflash—he was.

"Ahh," he moaned as I toyed with that sensitive spot just below the tip. "More. I need more. DILLON."

"So demanding." I chuckled and took his hard length into my mouth, sucking him all the way down until I triggered my gag reflex. My throat convulsed around him, and my eyes watered.

"YES." Jamie moaned so loud, birds took flight from neighboring trees. Not that he noticed anything other than the way my lips stretched around his perfect length or the attention the tip of my tongue paid to his slit.

"I want you to come in my mouth, little crow." He threw his head back and groaned. "You like it when I talk dirty to you, baby?" He nodded sweetly, biting his puffy lip as he consumed me with his eyes.

"I… I…"

He thickened in my mouth as I rolled his balls in my hand, and his salty taste grew stronger on my tongue, making me moan. His body tensed underneath me as he fought his oncoming orgasm. "Don't fight it, little crow. I want you to come for me." As if he'd been waiting for those very words, Jamie thrust his hips up, choking me on his cock as it hit the back of my throat. Tears spilled from my eyes at the intrusion, but I fucking loved the way he owned his pleasure.

"Yes. Yes. Yes. Yesss," Jamie screamed, his hips stuttering as lashes of cum launched down my throat. "Oh god, oh god." His thick length continued to pulse in my mouth, and I sucked until I'd swallowed down every last drop.

"I like knowing you're inside me now." I looked up at him as I licked his length clean. His glistening flushed face, blown-out pupils, and fucked out expression stole my breath. "One day, I'm going to eat my cum from your tight little hole." Jamie's answering whimper told me everything I needed to know. "Fuck, you're perfect."

CHAPTER EIGHTEEN

Jamie

I was on cloud nine one minute, then free falling off a cliff the next. I was so goddamn confused I didn't know which way was up. Who was the real Dillon? I'd had glimpses of the boy I'd known but that wasn't him anymore. Well, not completely. He was more complex. There were layers to him now, pieces I didn't know existed, and it worried me. Something was looming over every interaction we'd had, something that could change everything.

I'd been kissed with a passion that burned me inside out. I'd felt his mouth on parts of me no one else had ever touched. He'd made me feel wanted and precious, and then he changed on a hair trigger. I'd foolishly thought after that day by the lake we'd become more, but the next time our eyes locked across the quad, my heart was ripped out all over again. I'd waved at him, and he looked right through me with a sneer curling his lips before turning his back to me.

Those lips had become the star attraction of my dreams. I could remember the taste, texture, and feel of them. The lips that had kissed every inch of my body. Lips that had wrapped around my cock and sucked my soul out of it. I still wore his marks. A litany of bruises decorated my skin but they were fading every day, and selfishly, I wanted more. I liked that they were proof we had been together like that. It felt like he was slipping through my fingers like water.

He destroyed me.

He healed me.

He fucking confused me.

Mal had taken it upon himself to lecture me about valuing myself and respecting my boundaries. He thought someone had forced themself on me, pushed me to do things I didn't want. He knew I was a virgin, that I'd only been kissed once. I felt so guilty hiding so much from him, but until I understood what was going on how could I talk to someone about it?

"Hey baby boo." I looked up from my book as Ava plopped herself down on one of the armchairs opposite me. I'd discovered this little unused corner in the library hidden away behind the stacks, and it'd become somewhat of a refuge for me on the days that were too cold to go and sit out by the lake.

"Hey, Aves." Her smile brightened as I looked at her. Something about her expression made me squirm in my chair. "Sooo," she said, clapping her hands. "Tonight?"

"Yes?"

"You're coming out with me and Mal."

I chuckled. "Oh I am, am I?"

"Hell yes! It's this month's LGBTQ+ mixer that I've spent all week organizing. And since you missed the last one..."

I knew what she wasn't saying. I was still so raw over the whole incident. The blood bomb had derailed the plans we'd made to attend the first mixer.

"What she means," Mal added as he took a seat next to me

and dumped his satchel on the coffee table, "is that it's time you got out there and met some new people. Made some friends."

Anxiety swirled inside me. "I've made new friends." I gestured towards them. Mal smirked and Ava huffed, crossing her arms over her chest.

"Listen up, angel." Her voice took on a sharper edge. "You are the best and I love you." I rolled my eyes as she took on her "mom" tone. "But college is about expanding your horizons, learning about yourself and finding your people."

"And I've done that, haven't I?"

"No." Mal scrubbed his hand down his face. "You have, but who else do you talk to other than us?" His stare bored into me, and I rolled my bottom lip between my teeth. It's not like I could tell them about Dillon. I shook my head. They wouldn't understand.

"Exactly," Ava said. I sucked in a breath, about to refute what she said, but she held a hand up. "And we don't mean talking to people in class when you have to." My shoulders slumped as Mal chuckled.

"That's exactly what we mean, JJ."

I took a deep calming breath, pinched my nose, and exhaled. "Alright. Okay." It cost me more than I cared to admit to relent to their wishes. I wasn't a social butterfly. I didn't need a massive circle of friends. I was happy knowing a few people really well, then hundreds a little bit.

"Sweet. So now you're in, angel, it's time to go and get ready."

I looked down at my rainbow high tops, skinny jeans and hoodie. "What's wrong with me?"

"Nothing." Mal shook his head. "But—"

"But we've seen you look at what some of the guys on campus wear." I arched my brow, waiting for Ava to continue. She blew a raspberry and flicked her rainbow hair out of her face. "You look like you want to try more than skinny jeans, Tees, and hoodies."

I shrugged. "Maybe."

A cunning smile lit up her face. "Well then, my bestie boo." She got up and held her hand out to me. "We're going to pay a friend of mine a visit." I looked at her extended hand, apprehension niggling in my chest. I rubbed over the tightness in my chest but didn't move.

"Come on, JJ. Levi has some crazy mad skills. He's doing fashion design and we're certain he'll have something that's perfect for you."

AFTER GRABBING a quick bite to eat, we arrived at Ava's friend's industrial-style apartment. Levi turned out to be an interesting person. He fluttered around like a sparkly pixie, with flawlessly applied makeup and glow-in-the-dark fluorescent pink hair. I was so envious, I couldn't find words.

"You know, Jamie," he mused, walking around me and giving me a thorough once over. "You could totally be a model. Your bone structure is exquisite, and your body is bangin'." I felt light-headed with how quickly blood flooded my face. I felt as neon bright as his hair.

"Um." I licked my suddenly dry lips. "I'm not sure..." I shrugged and slipped my hands in my pockets to stop from wringing them.

"Hey, there's no pressure here, babe. Just saying. If you change your mind, I'd love you to model my new line for my next show."

"Sounds fun!" Ava elbowed me. "I'm doing it too. We could walk together, right?"

"Sure, babe," Levi agreed and Mal chuckled at the horrified look on my face.

"Only if you're comfortable, JJ." He wrapped his arms around my waist and pulled me into him. His quiet support helped me relax as he rested his head on my shoulder. "So, are you happy to let pixie-boy dress you?"

"Heard that!"

"Yeah," I breathed. "His work is amazing."

"Knew it!" Ava squealed and ran off into the clothes rails. "Levi, I'm going hunting." His chuckle rang out as Mal shook his head.

Levi was something else, but he was such a kind and considerate individual. He'd ordered Mal to go and find something for himself and led me over to his work station, which consisted of a white dressing table with the biggest Hollywood mirror I'd ever seen. The table top was covered with an expansive array of makeup that made my heart flutter and my fingers tingle with excitement. He took the time to ask me about what I liked and what I wanted to try. He talked me through the different materials he used to make his designs and showed me what he thought would look best on me. He felt like my very own fairy godmother. I'd never felt so seen and valued as I did the hour Levi devoted to me.

"There. Perfect." He kissed my cheek and stepped back. "You were made for the runway, babe."

I gasped at his blunt honesty and looked at myself in the mirror. "Thanks, Levi." I got up and hugged him, luxuriating in the feel of the silky material as it glided over my skin.

"Are you ready to show your adoring fans?" He winked.

"Never." I chuckled as he grabbed my hand and led me out to where Mal and Ava waited on his mismatched couches with a glass of sparkly bubbles in their hands. Mal's wolf whistle nearly deafened me, and Ava gasped and looked like she was about to cry.

"Holy shit, angel. You look hot as hell." She fanned herself and twirled her finger for me to spin around. "Show me the goods, bestie boo."

I laughed at her infectious excitement and spun around. "What do you think?" I turned to look at Mal who sat, mouth agape, not saying anything. He rubbed his eyes, and a blinding smile lit up his face.

"I... just... wow, JJ. You've always been gorgeous in that kind of sweet boy next door, wallflower kind of way, but like this." He huffed out a breath. "I'm going to need to beat guys off you with a baseball bat."

"You're funny." I flushed and bit my lip.

"Seriously, babe. You're a freaking knockout," Levi said and handed me a glass of bubbles. The sweet and sour tang burst over my tongue as I took a sip, hoping it would calm the butterflies rioting in my stomach. "So, is there anyone special in your life? Maybe he'd like a photo of you?" My mind immediately went to Dillon, but we weren't anything, were we? He blew hot and cold, and it was confusing as fuck.

I shook my head before downing the rest of my drink. "No," I said in a small voice.

"Well, after tonight, you won't be short of admirers, babe." Levi hugged me before leaving to get himself ready, and I walked over to the full-length mirror placed against the far wall. Mal and Ava were debating something about the LGBTQ club, and didn't notice the tears pooling in my eyes as my heart ached.

I stared at my reflection. I looked like me but different. Classier, more confident, a bit like Jamie 2.0. I was in a pair of tight leather pants that looked like they had been spray painted onto me—leaving nothing to the imagination—along with a sparkly thong underneath. But it was my top and makeup that made me feel out of this world. I'd spent so much of my time looking at confident gay guys and always wondered what it would be like to feel silk or lace against my skin, but I'd never had the confidence or opportunity to try. It was like Levi had plucked my dreams right out of my head.

I had a tightly fitted black fishnet crop top underneath the most amazing holographic mesh long-sleeved shirt that clung to me like a second skin. It shimmered between electric blue and the most vivid violet I'd ever seen. To complete my look, he gave me dark sultry eyes that shimmered in the same tones as my top. It made the dark gray ring around my iris stand out so much against the pale-blue, it looked like I was wearing contacts. He'd highlighted and contoured my cheeks so well, it was almost like I'd had plastic surgery. My bone structure looked amazing.

Mal's head appeared over my shoulder with an indulgent smile on his face. "You ready?"

"I am now." I grinned, feeling excited for the first time today.

"So, WHERE IS THIS EVENT HELD?" I asked as we walked arm-in-arm across the quad. The evening temperature had dropped as night fell, but the low cloud cover seemed to be keeping the cooler temperatures at bay for a little while longer.

"In one of the main faculty function rooms," Ava said. Our steps slowed as movement at the periphery of the quad caught our attention. A large group headed in our direction, consisting of the football team and the girls who seemed drawn to them like moths to a flame.

A leggy blond in a tight-fitting black pantsuit sauntered over to us and sneered. "Ugh, if it isn't the pathetic rainbow parade. What are you freaks doing out at night?"

"Ignore her," Mal ground out through gritted teeth.

"Come on, Elise, don't waste your breath," said a girl with long silky brunette hair. Two more crossed in front of us as the group disappeared into the shadows. But it was the group of guys wearing Briar U hoodies that made my heart beat faster than a hummingbird's wings. The air felt electrified around me, and the hairs on my arms stood on end. My eyes instinctually searched for Dillon's. I could feel the weight of them on me as we continued in the direction of the main building.

He cocked his head, and his eyes heated as they ran over every inch of me. It felt like a physical caress, and my body reacted to him on instinct. He licked his lips before jolting, as if he'd been struck by lightning. He froze mid-step when one of the guys he was with wrapped a hand around his arm and whispered in his ear. Time slowed down as I waited with bated breath to see what he was going to do. I wanted him to walk up to me and claim me with a kiss for everyone to see, but that was a dream. And dreams rarely came true. His gaze shuttered and all traces of burgeoning lust were wiped away. In the blink of an eye, Dillon changed. He hunched his shoulders, fisted his hands, and turned on his heel, storming back toward the dorms.

"Well, that was interesting." Ava's words cut through the growing tension as the rest of the footballers followed in Dillon's wake. "But it's time for drinks, my lovelies."

"Wow, Aves, this is amazing," I said as we stepped into the eloquently decorated room, noting the intimate seating areas and the food and drink stations. "I didn't realize there would be so many..."

"That's because you live under a rock, angel." She smiled and squeezed my hand. "I'm going to go and grab us a drink," she said over her shoulder. "Mingle." She wiggled her eyebrows before melting into the crowd.

I didn't know what to do with myself. I felt like I was floundering standing in the middle of a room full of people and completely isolated. Anxiety crawled across my skin, as if I was swarmed with ants. I sucked in a deep calming breath and moved into a quiet corner away from all the vibrant energy.

"I haven't seen you here before," a low voice rumbled behind me. My breath caught in my throat, and I spun around, coming face to face with a man with bright blue eyes and a charming smile.

"That's because I've never been." I ran my gaze over him as recognition hit me. "I know you!" I blurted.

He chuckled. "Not in the biblical sense I hope, because I'm sure I'd never forget someone like you." Heat crept up my neck all the way to my ears. No one's ever been so forward or obvious with me.

"No, no. Nothing like that." I bit my lip and looked anywhere but at him. "You... you were there at move in day and told me what my dorm was."

"Oh." Shock rippled over his features before they settled into that charming smile. "I'm Taylor."

"Jamie." I shook his outstretched hand. The calluses on his palm made me think of Dillon, and my gut sank.

"Hey." Taylor tucked his finger under my chin and lifted my head until he could see into my eyes. "I just want to..." He shook his head before looking at me again with a furrowed brow. "I know you've had a tough time recently, and I just wanted you to know I haven't had any part in it. Whatever issues he has with you, he should resolve them himself."

"Who's he?"

"I think you know." A smirk teased the corner of his mouth, his eyes imploring me to piece together a puzzle I had no frame of reference for. "I've seen how he looks at you when he thinks no one is looking. Whether it's fear or something else, it's eating away at him." He shook his head. "I hope it gets sorted out before someone gets hurt."

"I..." Taylor placed his finger over my lips to silence me and placed a kiss on my flushed cheek.

"He's an idiot for not seeing what's right in front of him. And hey, if it doesn't work out, come find me." And with that, he was gone, swallowed up by the ever expanding crowd filling the room. The pulsing beat of EDM music flowed through me as I tried to piece together everything Taylor said to me, but I kept coming up blank.

"What in the everloving..."

"Here you go, angel," Ava said, handing me a red solo cup. I looked at it and arched my brow. "Campus rules. Anyway, what did Taylor want?"

"I don't really know. He was rather cryptic about everything."

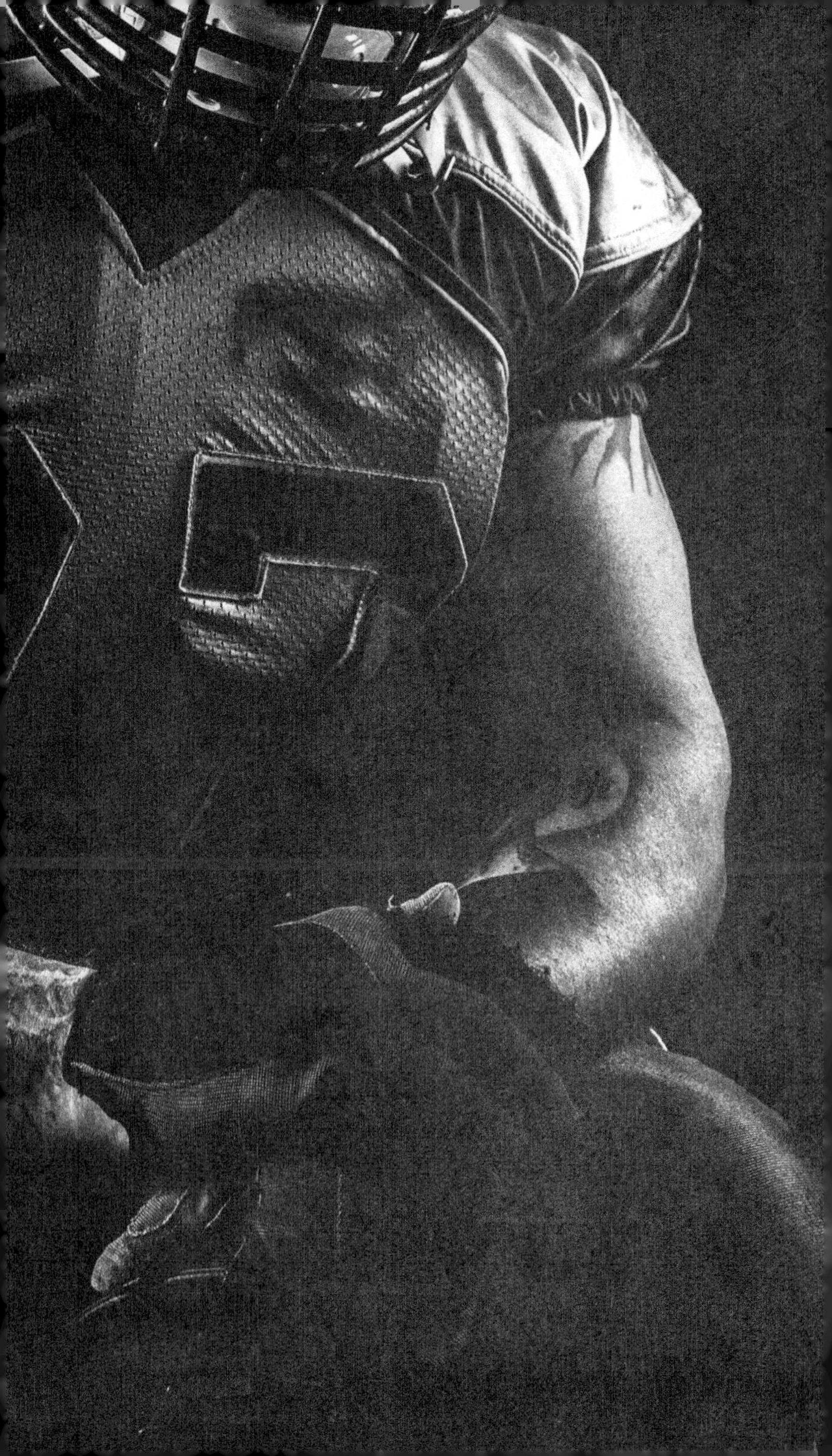

CHAPTER NINETEEN

Dillon

"Cap, look out!" Buchanan yelled, and for a split second, everyone slowed down like they were running in molasses. Each passing second was tracked by the *buh-bump* of my heart against my ribs as anticipation and adrenaline surged through me. Beads of sweat trickled down my temples and slicked my back until my undershirt stuck to my skin. I gritted my teeth, muscles tensed, and watched the play unfold before me.

Buchanan was twenty yards down the field from me to the right while McCormack sprinted in the opposite direction in an attempt to split open the defensive line. I rocked back onto my right foot, pivoted on my toes, and lined up my throw to Vieck—who had somehow managed to find open space. The ball left my hand on the perfect arc for it to be delivered directly into his waiting arms as he ran a breakaway toward the end zone.

"Fuck, yes," I growled, pounding my fist on my chest and ripping my helmet off, ready for the line change. The second string weren't as strong, but Coach had us playing mixed matches against them, not only to push us but also to see if anyone showed enough talent to usurp us from our starting spots. He'd put the whole team on notice after we lost our game last weekend.

"Cap! Fucking move!" Stevens bellowed. The urgency in his voice registered, and the world snapped back like a rubber band and resumed at full speed. I managed to blink before I was lifted off my feet as tree trunk-like arms wrapped around me and I crashed into the grass under a shit ton of weight.

"You stupid fucker," Chad spat at me and kneed me in the gut as he stood up. "You're going down, and you're gonna fucking stay down, Hargraves." He dusted off his cleats and sauntered down field while I lay paralyzed.

"Fuck!" I smashed my helmet into the earth. Today was going to shit, and I had a feeling it was only going to get worse.

AFTER A DRESSING down from Coach of epic proportions, I stormed out of the locker room while the rest of the guys were still in the shower. Coach glared at me the whole time he was reaming the guys like I was personally responsible for them playing like they were a fucking peewee team. If I'd have stayed in there a minute longer, my fist would have found its way into a few faces, and I'd probably have been kicked off the team. Which sounded really fucking appealing right about now.

My stomach growled, reminding me that I hadn't eaten anything other than a protein shake after my early session in the gym. Rather than heading to the dorms to dump my shit, I changed direction to the cafeteria. I should be early enough to get a decent amount of food. The guys could chew me a new one when they came in. I just didn't give a fuck.

The one thing you could rely on at Briar U was the outstanding array of food they made available to the athletes here. May was probably the only person on campus I wasn't a raging asshole to, and she smiled at me as I dragged my tray along.

"Long time no see, Dillon. You doin' alright?"

"Could be better, May." She gave me a sad smile, understanding shining in her eyes. Her son had been on the hockey team when he matriculated here, so she knew how tough it could get for us, not just physically, but psychologically.

"What sounds good today?" I pointed out everything I wanted, loaded up two plates, and grabbed a water and Gatorade. After paying, I swept my gaze over the room and headed for the empty table in the back corner. All I wanted was some damn peace, away from prying eyes. I wanted to eat without every fucker coming to tell me how much they loved me or how shit they thought I played. I wanted to scream at them, *"Trust me, I know I sucked. Every dick with a mouth told me the same. How about you join the team, and then you can tell me how shit I am."* But no, I was the one who had to lead by example as the captain. If the Ravens won, people loved us, but if we lost, everyone became a fucking critic.

"Fuck." I growled and slumped onto my chair. I kicked my aching legs out under the table, and picked up a slice of pizza. I polished off the three slices and was about to start on my pasta when the one person I couldn't get out of my head walked in. Jamie stole my breath whether he was in skinny jeans and an oversized hoodie, or skin-tight leather pants and a see-through mesh top like the other night.

When he was walking across the quad, arms linked with his friends, it was like the world faded away, and the only thing I could see was him. No one else existed. My feet had moved of their own volition, and before I knew it, I was striding towards him until Buchanan grabbed my arm and stopped me. I wanted to knock him the fuck out. I wanted to claim Jamie as mine right there and then. But I didn't. I couldn't. He was going to hate me when all this came out, but I'd hate myself more.

He was a drug, and this was one addiction I never wanted to be cured of.

Jamie was a walking wet dream and he had no goddamn clue. Girls, guys, and every asshole in between watched him, wanted him. My little crow broke hearts without even trying, but he was untouchable. I'd made sure of that. People could mess with him, but no one could touch him without finding themselves ostracized on campus, much like he was. It seemed everyone had got the memo. Everyone but Ava Barnes and Malachi Edmunds.

My eyes tracked his progress through the different stations. May lit up when he reached her, and it warmed my heart. Even after everything I'd put Jamie through, he still brought sunshine wherever he went. And I just kept digging my own grave deeper every day.

"Oh shit," I muttered as I lifted the Gatorade to my lips and downed half the bottle, eyeing the fucking queen bee bitch strutting in like she was on a damn catwalk. Her gaze met mine and a malicious grin slashed across her face, turning my blood to ice. I clenched my jaw so hard I was amazed I didn't crack a tooth. Unease slithered through me as Elise practically bounced through the line with a fully loaded tray, her gaggle of sycophants strolling behind her. They were like a pack of rabid wolves baying for blood and stirring up unrest wherever they went. Their numbers seemed to swell as they followed in Elise's wake. Students parted like the Red Sea to let her through, and she held the rapt attention of everyone in the cafeteria, student and faculty alike.

It was like I was stuck in the Matrix, suffering from déjà vu. I could see exactly what she intended to do, but no matter how fast I tried to move, the distance between me and Jamie didn't get smaller. It was like every student got in my way. I watched in horror as she dumped what could only be described as a vat's worth of marinara sauce over Jamie's head. A crowd massed around them, cheering her on as the final drops of sauce fell over his head and dripped down his face. Phones, cameras, and laptops were trained on him. My phone blew up with notifications, most likely from what just transpired.

His gut-wrenching cries hit me like artillery fire, stealing the breath from my lungs and nearly knocking me off my feet. I tried to push my way through the hoard of spectators, but I couldn't get through. Every way I tried to move, someone blocked my path. Fury heated the blood in my veins as adrenaline surged through me. I needed to make her pay as much as I needed to save him.

Jamie slipped and fell to the floor, coating himself in even more sauce. Elise howled with laughter until tears melted the makeup off her face, revealing her for the monster she was. The feral grin she turned on me made me sick to my stomach. I fucking hated her and everything she stood for. She'd spent years trying to force me into being hers, but her presence made my skin crawl. I'd rather swim in lava than spend a minute in her presence.

"You fucked up this time, bitch," I growled and wrapped my hand around her throat. A collective gasp rang out and made my spine stiffen. How could I have forgotten we were surrounded by a mob of students?

She smirked at me like this was the funniest thing ever. "I think *not,* Dillon." She dragged a long blood-red nail down my chest, and I shuddered with revulsion. "You're the one with your hand wrapped around my throat. I'm the poor helpless girl, half your size." She whispered, "All I'd need to do is start begging, and then you're off the team. I can even make sure you're kicked out of Briar U. So tell me, what do you want to do?"

I sucked in a sharp breath as her threat landed and the knowledge of everything I stood to lose. I was in shark-infested waters with her—she was as dirty as her old man. I was trapped with no way out. No one was ever safe around her, and right now, she could end my life before it even began. "This is over," I snarled and dropped her like the sack of shit she was. I walked away as she started wailing, doing anything to control the narrative, to make herself the victim.

The corridor was quiet when I made it out of the cafeteria, the eerie silence a shock to the system. I looked left and right for any sign of Jamie, but I couldn't see him anywhere. My heart was working its way up my throat. I wanted to smash something. I clenched my fists as I tried to think where the closest restroom was. Maybe I should be logical and start there.

"Dillon!" Buchanan shouted as he ran towards me gasping for breath. "I think he's heading back to the dorms. You need to help him."

"Shit," I cursed and broke into a run. I didn't get far before I heard Jamie's hollow cries. I skidded to a stop and rounded the corner on silent feet. There he was, curled in on himself and tucked away in a shadowed alcove. I dropped to my knees, hands outstretched, and slowly shuffled toward him. Jamie didn't move, didn't react to my presence at all. My heart shattered at his hapless cries. "Little crow? Can you look at me?"

Jamie sucked in a wet breath and raised his head. A river of tears had washed some of the drying sauce off him, but it did nothing to hide his anguish. His distraught features were pinched, his eyes red-rimmed. He looked fucking broken, and I broke alongside him. This all happened because of me, but I couldn't deny that Elise took some kind of sick pleasure in humiliating him in front of half the student body. Just thinking about it made my stomach revolt, and a fresh wave of anger swelled inside me.

"Come here, baby. Let's go and get you cleaned up." Jamie shook his head but didn't fight me when I hauled him into my arms. He felt so perfect against me, like he was made for me.

"T-thank you, Dil." A wan smile ticked up his lips as he wrapped his arms around me and buried his face in the crook of my neck. He inhaled a deep breath, and it stirred a primal part of me, making me smile because he found my scent comforting.

We luckily made it to the locker room without anyone seeing us. He didn't deserve this, no matter how shitty our past. He deserved better. I was childish, emotionally stunted, and fucking terrified I'd lose my shot at the only life I could see as an escape. I was a fucking selfish prick. Initially, I didn't care how much this hurt him, but now? Now that it's real, I can't do it. I can't make him suffer any more than he already has. I want to come clean, be a grown up, and find out why he abandoned me. Hurt me. Betrayed me. But I'm terrified of losing him all over again. Even when I want to make things better for him, I always make it about myself.

I shouldered our way through the door, careful not to hit Jamie's head on the frame and made our way past the lockers to the showers. My body vibrated, knowing I'd have to strip him out of his clothes to help him wash. My desperate cock thickened as images of his sweet body filtered through my mind. My fingers itched to touch his soft skin, and my lips begged for another taste. Just once more, then I'll tell him the truth. But first, I need my fix. *Selfish. Selfish. Selfish.* But nothing was going to persuade me otherwise—he was my drug of choice, and I'd do anything for another hit.

"You still with me, little crow?" I whispered against his head. The tremors running through his body had started to calm, and his cries had softened to quiet sniffles and hiccuping gasps. Using the shower wall for support, I leaned in and flicked it on, giving it a chance to warm up before I took us under the spray. "Jamie?"

"I-I'm okay," he murmured and nuzzled into my neck. The gentle puffs of his breath eased some of the rage inside me, and a smile curved my lips as he melted into me.

"We're going to need to wash this off, baby." I chuckled, trying for some levity, and he snorted. "As much as I love marinara sauce, I don't fancy it being the only thing I can smell for the rest of my life." Another quiet grunt came from him as his fingers started to tease the hair at my nape. I loved it when he touched me like this; I'd suffered from withdrawals after he disappeared. He used to touch me all the time; it was like he couldn't be apart from me. I'd refused for years to admit how much I'd craved it. Missed it. Needed him. Always needed him.

The sauce had started to dry, and it was tacky enough to irritate my skin. Our clothes would be stained beyond repair. I kicked my shoes off, and with Jamie still curled in my arms, I opened my locker and blindly reached in for my wash caddy. My fingers wrapped around the plastic handle, and I breathed a sigh of relief. I didn't want to search Coach's lost and found box, because that shit might have been there for years.

Steam billowed from the shower stall as I stepped in and closed the door behind us. My bare feet slapped against the tiles as I walked us straight under the pounding water. Jamie let out a screech worthy of a horror film victim, that made a laugh burst out of me.

"S-shut up," he gritted out. He pulled back far enough for me to see his red-rimmed eyes. The pain that resonated in their pale depths was like a sucker punch to the chest, but the teasing smile fluttering on his lips pulled me into the here and now. "A shower in our clothes? That's... novel."

"Fuck you." I pinched his ass, making him yelp. His fingers teased through my hair, making me groan as they scraped across my scalp. Jamie's breaths became labored and the air thickened around us. "I'm going to put you down now and get these clothes off of you." My mouth was dry at the thought of slowly peeling layer after layer off his delectable body.

The intensity in his eyes grew heated the longer he stared at me. He licked his lips and slowly slipped down my body. It took everything in me to bite back the groan that wanted to escape as he pressed against my aching cock. Our height difference had never been more apparent as I bent down and captured his lips with mine. They were as pillowy soft as I remembered, and when his tongue teased across my bottom lip, pulses of electricity flowed through me. I felt his touch flow through every inch of my clothed body.

"Dillon." He moaned as his tongue wrapped around mine. My hands cupped his face, thumbs wiping away a combination of water and sauce as I backed him up against the wall. My heart hammered in my chest, trying to reach out to him. I lost myself to the sensations his lips and tongue forced upon me, the feel of his small lithe body against mine. I slipped my leg between his and pulled him closer as he rolled his hips against me. The tantalizing brush of his hard length against mine turned me feral.

I traced my fingers over his face, mapping his features as my lips continued to devour him. I took and took, but I needed more—it'd never be enough. I kissed my way across his jaw, used my hand to angle his head backward, and sunk my teeth into his sensitive lobe. His answering groan was all the encouragement I needed to know he was as lost to the moment as I was.

With my thundering heart beating loud enough to be heard above the sound of the pounding water, I licked, sucked, and nibbled my way down the delicate skin of his neck. I sucked on his fluttering pulse as my blood turned to liquid fire. "More," he breathed as his cold fingers slipped underneath my drenched top.

Frustration and need had a growl tearing its way up my throat at not being close enough to him. I needed his skin on mine. It was the only balm to the ever-present guilt threatening to drown me. I shook it off and leaned back, wrenching my lips from his soft skin. Jamie's head tipped back, his hungry gaze mirroring my own and echoed in my soul. I reached behind me, pulled my hoodie off, and threw it across the cubicle, shivering when the water hit my overheated skin. I groaned at the intensity of the moment and licked my lips when my eyes caught on the purple bruise blooming on his neck. I'd marked him, claimed him as mine, and the evidence of it stoked the lust-fueled inferno raging inside me.

"Your turn," I rumbled as I worked his ruined top up his torso. I wanted to lick and suck on every inch of his alabaster skin that was revealed to me. It had been too long since I'd worshiped him. His top landed with a thud somewhere behind me, and we were drawn back together with a magnetic force that refused our separation. I would go to war for this feeling.

"Dillon," he ground out when we snapped back together. The contact elicited a full-body shudder to roll through him as my lips traced his collar bones. "Yesss." The hissed sound spurred me on as I sucked his hard nipple into my mouth, laving it until he writhed beneath me. His fingers dug into my back and shoulders, struggling to find purchase thanks to our slick skin. "More," he demanded.

More I would give him. He was intoxicating. One touch, one taste, set off a chain reaction in me that wouldn't be satisfied until I'd had every part of him. I sucked a path of bruises across his chest, then pulled his other nipple into my mouth as my hands trailed a feather-light touch down his side as he mewled, whined and whimpered. I undid the button of his pants and worked the zipper down. The teeth fought against me as I pulled the hard nub through my teeth, making him shout my name. He was so loud, if anyone was in the corridor, they'd have heard him.

I chuckled against his skin, goosebumps spreading in my wake as I licked my way down his abdomen. His muscles flexed under my ministrations as I dropped to my knees. I looked up at him from my prone position, and a feeling of rightness flooded through me. My little crow deserved the best of everything, and I was going to show him with my actions since words failed me.

Jamie nodded his assent to my unasked question as my fingers curled around his pants and I yanked them down. "Fuck!" I growled at the vision of his hard cock pushing against the cup of a lacey black jock. I kissed a path up the inside of his thigh, and when my nose brushed his thick length, his breath hitched into a garbled moan that had my cock throbbing with need. I ignored it. This was about him, not me. I never wanted to be a selfish lover where he was concerned.

"You smell so good, baby." I buried my face in his groin and inhaled his musky caramel scent. It was dark and decadent, and my mouth watered with the need to taste him. "Up," I said, slipping his soaked shoes off his feet so I could rip his pants off his legs. My hands shook as I worked them up the back of his legs and sunk my fingers into the perfect globes of his ass. It was full and firm and would look fucking amazing with my cock disappearing between its lush cheeks.

"Turn around. I need to taste you." Jamie's cheeks flushed, and he licked his lips. I ran my nose along his solid length and mouthed his leaking tip through the fine material. His deep moan echoed around us, only heightening our arousal. His dick jerked against the side of my face as he slowly turned and planted his hands against the wall, his golden curls clinging to his flushed face as he glanced over his shoulder. He bit down on his full bottom lip and pushed his ass out towards me like the fucking offering it was.

Jamie might look like an angel, but he was ruled by his desire. His dark pupils blotted out his usual pale-blue eyes and replaced them with lust-filled pools of darkness that I wanted to drown in. I ran my hands up the back of his trembling legs and trailed my thumbs along the cleft of his cheeks. I pulled him closer and bit down into his supple flesh. Jamie threw his head back and thrust his ass in my face.

I pushed his legs apart and settled between them. I nipped and sucked at his sensitive skin until he begged me to eat him out. "D-Dillon... Dil... please." He groaned as I teased my finger over his taint and between his cheeks. His hole fluttered under my touch, making me smile into his skin. "Ahh, please. Dil..."

A flush worked its way up his shivering skin as I pulled his cheeks apart, licking my lips at the sight. His tight pink hole made my mouth water. He was fucking perfect. I teased my fingertip around the rim. He was smooth, with not a hair in sight. I leaned into him, breathing in his musky scent before spitting on his entrance and working it around with my finger.

My cock pulsed against the zipper of my jeans, the bite of pain pushing me higher. I could come from looking at his perfect pink hole and soon, I'd paint it with my cum. I pulled myself out and groaned as the tepid air hit my engorged length. I gave myself a few light strokes as I tried to decide if I wanted to keep teasing him or eat him out like it was my last meal.

Impatient and needy, Jamie thrust his hips backward and begged. And fuck, it was a high I'd never known. I might have been the one on my knees, but he was in control. I was his slave; the sinner who would make the golden angel fall.

"Fuck! Please, Dillon. T-touch me. I... I can't take it...n-need to come." Taking pity on him, I released my steel length and buried my head between his cheeks, kissing his puckered hole. I nipped and sucked at his skin and flicked the tip of my tongue around his rim, pushing him further and further into lustful delirium. "D-Dil…p-please."

"With pleasure," I growled and reached forward to tug on his heavy balls.

"Fuck, yes." It seemed my angelic boy liked a bit of pain with his pleasure. "Ahhhh. Please. Yes!"

The first lash of my tongue against his tiny hole made me feel things, things I had no right feeling. It stirred a primal need inside me to mark him. Claim him. Own him. To fuck him and coat his insides with my seed and then plug him up so I was in him always.

Jamie cried out and cursed with every tantalizing lick I gave his entrance, his body strung tight as it thundered toward oblivion. His musky taste spread across my tongue, and my heart swelled ten times too big for my chest. I knew this was where I wanted to be. He was it for me, and as that realization sunk in, my eyes stung with the overwhelming emotions.

I wanted to possess him and keep him, but I knew I was on borrowed time. I might be his—had always been his even if he'd never known it. But if I was being brutally honest with myself, I knew I couldn't keep him. When he found out I'd deceived him, he wouldn't be able to look at me, let alone touch me or even want me. He'd hate me as much as I'd hated him. But little by little, he'd chipped away at the pain I'd buried beneath my hate until nothing existed but him. I feared he'd look at me and all he'd see was a monster, not the person he thought he loved. The person who would always be his. The other half of his soul.

The tight ring of muscle softened as I teased it with long hard strokes and light teasing flicks. I worked my finger around it in tandem with my tongue, the dual sensations more drugging then the next.

"Dillon!"

I chuckled as he sunk his hand into my hair and rode my

face. I stiffened my tongue and pushed inside him as he thrust back into me.

"Fuck! Yes!" Jamie bellowed as I entered him for the first time. His walls clenched around me, muscles pulsing with need. His intense flavor saturated every part of me, and I felt like I was flying high, untethered by his pleasure. *Fuck!* Jamie rode my tongue like he was created to, his rhythm hard and fast as I sucked and slurped against him before working my finger in.

Jamie threw his head and shouted as he squeezed the living daylights out of me. He arched his back, the view nothing short of pornographic as water sluiced down the gully of his spine and collected in the dimples at the base of his back.

"Fuck. You taste like heaven, little crow," I cooed as I fucked two fingers into his greedy hole. "I can't wait to feel your walls squeeze my cock to death." His answering moan was everything I'd dreamed of. "But right now, I want you to come on my tongue."

"Yesss."

"Fuck yourself on my tongue, baby. Imagine it's my cock and come on my face before I paint my release on your back."

"I-I'm close, D—" I stole his voice as I sunk my tongue back into his tight wet heat. I slipped my hand between his legs, and his walls tightened to the point of breaking my fingers. He screamed my name as his release consumed him. My hand cupped his pulsing length, and his hot cum seeped through the lacy material. I groaned into him as his body locked up tight, his taste intensified as he convulsed, pleasure stealing him away. I continued to wring his orgasm out of him until he went slack and collapsed back into me.

He slipped down the wall, flushed red, panting, and looking utterly fucked out. His eyes were glazed, and his mouth was a perfect little O. He collapsed against me, his eyes fluttering as he slowly came back into his body.

"Welcome back, beautiful." I leaned in and kissed him.

The gentle brush of lips turned feral as he devoured my mouth and moaned when he tasted himself on me like it was manna from heaven.

I pulled back, breaking our life-affirming kiss when dark spots danced across my vision, and my lungs screamed. Hauling myself up on my knees, my release barreled down my spine, electrifying every nerve in my body. One stroke, two, then the world went dark as my orgasm consumed my body and soul. It was like I was watching from outside my body as the first rope of my cum landed on his glistening face. Jamie opened his mouth as I continued to work my length in tight hard stokes, imagining I was coming deep inside him as I painted his face and mouth with my seed.

He licked his face, chasing the cum that dripped down his features before the water washed it off like it was his last meal. My spent dick gave an appreciative twitch, but I was out for the count. "Wow," I breathed against his lips before I licked into his mouth. Our combined taste sent me back to heaven as I wrapped my arms around him.

"Fuck, that was..."

"Yeah," I agreed and got to my feet, pulling him up with me. I locked my knees so we didn't land in a boneless heap on the shower floor. "Now that I've made you into a filthy little whore, I need to clean you up. Then, I'm going to wrap you in my clothes and put you to bed." Jamie whimpered against my lips, and I kissed him into submission. What I wouldn't give for it to be my bed he slept in.

Soon, I promised myself. *Soon.* My little crow would be mine in every way. Even if it killed me, I'd make him mine.

CHAPTER TWENTY

Jamie

"Hey, JJ, could you grab my mail for me? I want to jump in the shower before we head out." Mal's muffled voice came through the closed en suite door, and a sigh slipped past my lips as I slumped against the wall.

"Sure thing." I pulled myself together and rapped my knuckles on the door before swiping his mailbox key off his desk and headed downstairs. I'd never believed in curses but given everything that has happened over the last five years, I'm starting to think they're real. I thought I was strong enough to withstand even the most violent storm, but I'm not sure I'm strong enough to survive the rest of the year.

If it was just the students I had to deal with, maybe I would be okay, but it was the invasive photos that were unraveling my fraying nerves. It started off with four photos on my first week that were slipped under my door in an unmarked black envelope, but now they appeared almost every day. It was only a matter of time until Mal stumbled across one. I was amazed he hadn't yet. I had a box buried at the bottom of my closet filled with them. In the last few days, they'd taken on a more sinister edge. Whoever sent them scratched out my eyes and mouth with a sharp tool that tore through the paper. The creep factor pushed my anxiety to the brink, and I constantly felt like I was looking over my shoulder.

How someone could hate me enough to slowly torture me into a mental breakdown was beyond me. I'd been tempted to go to the faculty about the photos, but after the blood bomb debacle, I worried I'd be laughed out of there and called an attention seeker. I'm not. All I wanted was the chance to live my life on my own terms, but that seemed like a pipe dream. However, the thought of going to Uncle Daire made me feel like a failure, like a scared little boy who was haunted by the atrocities of his abusive missing dad. I didn't want to even entertain that rabbit hole. So instead, I stayed silent, bottled it up, and locked it away to face another day. I was the one people turned to when things got tough. I was the one who made people smile. They didn't have the bandwidth to deal with my problems.

I was fine. *Fine!* I'd keep saying it until it was true. Fake it till you make it and all that.

The soft ding of the elevator pulled me from my musings and the bright morning light greeted me as I stepped out into the main lobby of the building. It was surprisingly busy for not quite ten a.m. on a Saturday. Unless you were into sports, most students stayed in bed till the afternoon. I found it amusing to watch people and try to work out what they were up to or where they were going. It was clear to see who was doing the shuffle of shame. They staggered around in last night's rumpled clothes, and someone was even missing a shoe. A shoe?! A few of the girls still had the remnants of their makeup on and resembled someone from *The Rocky Horror Picture Show*. The men, however, seemed to have taken on a ridiculous swagger.

I tried not to laugh—but failed miserably—as one guy stumbled right into the closed elevator doors. I buried my face in my phone and hurried over to the wall filled with boxes where our mail was stored. It always reminded me of a mausoleum with its many rows of locked metal doors. I searched for Mal's name and opened his first, pulling out a number of envelopes wedged between a stack of junk mail. I tossed the leaflets into the nearby trash can before slipping the envelopes into my bag.

The key got jammed in mine and took a while to get it to open, but it eventually gave way. I hadn't looked in mine since I'd started because I knew Aunt Clara hadn't sent anything. But curiosity got the better of me today, and it was the perfect way to waste time while Mal used up the hot water for the whole floor. As expected, it was full of crap too, which I dumped in the trash. But when I went to close it, something hidden in the back corner caught my eye. I reached in and pulled out a small black box.

Bile burned the back of my throat, and a buzzing filled my ears. My hands shook so hard the box slipped through my fingers and landed on the floor with an ominous thud. My legs felt like jelly, and my knees buckled as I stumbled backward, crashing into the stair rail. I gripped on to it and used it to lower myself onto the bottom step. "What. The. *Hell.*" I braced my elbows on my knees and sunk my fingers into my hair as I flushed hot and cold. Perspiration beaded on my brow and trickled down my spine. My breaths sawed in and out of my lungs, fueled by my erratic heartbeat as I tried to ground myself, but I knew there was nothing I could do to stop the oncoming panic attack.

"Here, take this," a quiet voice said as a brown paper bag

appeared in front of me. I grabbed it with shaky hands and held it over my mouth. I flinched when a cool hand landed on my back. "That's it, just breathe in and out. In and out."

I tried as hard as I could, but my breaths stuttered and caught in my throat, making breathing impossible. It felt like razor-tipped vines were coiling around my legs, and the walls were closing in.

"Hey. Hey, look at me." The soft voice got sharper, more commanding, but I was trapped and couldn't move. Cold fingers pushed my chin up until I was blindly staring at a shadow. "That's it, Jamie, look at me. Focus on me. I've got you. Now, I want you to listen carefully. Don't think about anything else, just do as I say."

I latched onto the authoritative voice and made it the sole focus of my narrow world. It took time, but I was able to take control of my body, and my breathing slowed down enough for me to fill my lungs. The pressure surrounding my throat ceased, and even though it was still raw and every breath burned, I came back to myself.

"There you go. How are you feeling?" I shook my head to clear the spots from my hazy vision and gasped when I saw who was crouched down in front of me.

"C-Cory?"

His smile lit up his face brighter than his fiery hair. "Surprised it's me?" He chuckled and shifted to sit on the stairs, his back to the wall facing me. Cory pulled his left knee up to his chest and braced his arm across it. I was worried I'd see judgment in his eyes, but I saw nothing but compassion.

"Yes...no...maybe?" I licked my dry lips and brushed back the hair stuck to my face with a trembling hand. "I guess... I'm just surprised, really." I shrugged, feeling uncomfortable, but the soft smile on his face quieted any lingering anxiety. "Why are you here? This isn't your dorm."

"No, it's not." He sighed and rubbed a nervous hand

down his thigh, refusing to look at me as a soft flush worked up his neck. "Full disclosure?"

"Always."

"I came here to see you." My shock must have shown on my face, because he laughed and shook his head. "Honestly. I hadn't received a text from you, so I came to see if you wanted to go for that coffee." Hopefulness laced his words, and my knee-jerk reaction was to say yes, because I hated to let people down. But as the word formed on my lips, Dillon's face flashed in my mind.

I still didn't understand what was going on between us. I knew he liked me, maybe not as much as I liked him, but there was definitely something 'more' between us. But no matter how close we got physically, it felt like he was holding a part of himself back.

"Um—"

"Oh god." Cory ducked his head. "You're seeing someone, aren't you?"

"Well, it's complicated."

"Always is, isn't it?" He said quietly and tipped his head back against the wall. "Fuck it. I'm gonna shoot my shot." I smiled at his words. "I'm not complicated, Jamie. I really like you—"

"You met me for like two minutes." I chuckled.

"True. But I'm good at reading people and you're a nice guy and hot as fuck, with the most gorgeous eyes I've ever seen. So, what do you say? Wanna get a drink with me sometime?"

My face was literally melting from my blush. I was flattered and all, but I'd only ever had eyes for one person. To me, no one would ever compare to Dillon. Even if I didn't know where I stood with him, I could never entertain being with anyone else, let alone leading that person on. I sighed. "I'm honored." Cory cringed. "But I don't think that is for the best. We could be fr—"

"Oh my god, you're going to friend zone me." He clutched at his heart as if he'd been shot. "That's cruel, Jamie," he joked and rubbed his eyes. The glassy sheen in them made my breath hitch. I felt like shit upsetting people, but this was for the best.

"Sorry." I reached out and grabbed his arm. Cory looked at me from under his lashes. "But thank you for being here and helping me through that."

"No problem. Are you good now?"

"Yup."

Cory looked at his watch and pushed up off the stairs. "Well, I'd better be going. See you, Jamie." He winked and walked away with his shoulders hunched up by his ears.

I sighed as I pulled myself up, a wave of exhaustion washing through me as I wobbled on my feet. I glanced around the lobby and found it empty and prayed no one saw my epic meltdown. "Fat chance of that." I scoffed and brushed that thought aside and picked up the offending item. The box was small and unassuming, but I knew it was from whomever had been leaving the envelopes under my door. Taking a deep breath, I opened the box slowly in case it decided to explode all over me too. Thankfully, it didn't.

Nestled inside the black silk lining was a small clear USB stick. Nothing else, not even a note. Everything about it made me sick. My phone vibrated in my pocket, so I shoved the box to the bottom of my bag and ignored it. That was a problem for future me. I pulled my phone out and gasped when I realized it was nearly eleven. Mal was probably wondering where I was. The message icon blinked at me so I clicked on it and pulled up our thread.

MAL

I'm done, where are you?

MAL

JJ seriously, where are you?

MAL

Goddammit, Jamie. I'm coming to find you! Don't move!!!!!!

I'm in the lobby.

Just as I sent the message, the elevator dinged, and Mal strode out with a frantic look on his face. His eyes darted in every direction until they landed on me. I swallowed as his features flushed with what looked like anger.

"What the hell?" He walked up to me and wrapped his arms around me. I melted into his embrace, needing his strength. Mal must have felt something, because when he drew back, he rested his hands on my shoulders and looked into my eyes. "Are you okay, JJ?"

"Yeah." I nodded. "Well, I am now you're here." That got a smirk out of him, and he stepped back and bowed.

"At your service, m'lord." He snickered before casting a cautious eye over me. "Are you sure you're okay? You look a bit flushed."

"Yeah, I'm good. A bit..." I struggled to find the right words, so I went with a few. "Shocked and confused, really."

Mal cocked his head and wrapped an arm around my shoulders, steering us in the direction of the doors to the parking lot. "What's that supposed to mean?"

I told Mal all about Corey as we made our way to his car and headed to the mall. Mal wanted to get some new clothes because he was tired of his current wardrobe, and the changing seasons were the perfect excuse to update it. Last night, we'd both gone through everything we had and bagged up any clothing that was suitable for donation.

It was nice to get off campus for a few hours, and I was looking forward to spending some quality time with Mal. Things had been so hectic recently, that we'd only seen each other in passing, and it kinda sucked. He was my best friend—

along with Ava—but sometimes she was just too much for me, and I needed Mal's calming energy to balance me.

Once we'd dropped off the bags at the thrift store, Mal dragged me to his favorite stores, and we spent hours trying on anything and everything that caught our eye. I got a few shirts that Mal told me I had to get, or he'd buy them for me. The sales assistant chuckled at our antics while she rang up our purchases before Mal dragged me off to a lingerie store that blew my mind. I was like a kid in a candy shop. There were so many items I fell in love with, but I somehow managed to wrangle myself under control and only got a couple pairs of lace and silk briefs, and a matching crop top and jock set that made me feel exquisite. I secretly hoped I'd be able to wear them for Dillon, but only time would tell.

"Ugh. I'm all shopped out," Mal whined, bags dragging on the floor.

A laugh burst out of me, and Mal narrowed his eyes before sticking his tongue out at me. "How about we get some lunch?" That was how we found ourselves sitting at a booth in a vintage 80s mom-and-pop diner a short while later. Wendy, our server, came and took our orders and brought out our milkshakes. They were absolutely divine; thick, creamy, and full of flavor. I drank mine so fast I ended up with brain freeze, much to Mal's amusement. But I was skilled at ignoring his ribbing.

While we drank, I flicked through my messages with Aunt Clara but focused on her update on Jessie and Zack. I snapped a couple of photos of where we'd gone for lunch and promised to call my little sunbeam when we got back to campus.

Eventually, Mal asked the question that had been on his mind all day. He might have thought I hadn't noticed, but I'd caught him staring at me with a puzzled look on his face all day. He'd go to say something, then shake his head and walk away.

"Jamie?"

I smirked. "Finally worked out what you want to ask?"

He snickered. "You got that, did you?"

"Bit hard not to when you kept looking out like a fish out of water."

Mal burst out laughing, spraying his mouthful of milk-shake all over the table and me. "Oh my god. I'm sorry, JJ."

"I'll let you off if lunch is on you," I joked.

"Of course, don't be silly. That was..."

I rolled my eyes and looked at him. "That was a joke."

"Maybe." He shrugged. "But, regardless lunch is on me because—"

"There's something you want to know." It wasn't a question; it was a statement. Mal tipped his drink toward me and nodded. I sighed and sat back against the bench seat. "Alright, shoot."

"What's the deal with you and Dillon Hargraves?"

I choked on the mouthful of mint chocolate chip shake, my eyes watering as I tried to swallow. Mal had to get up and smack me on the back as I hacked up my drink all over the table. "Straight to the point there," I croaked and dabbed a napkin at my watering eyes.

"No point not to be."

"I guess." I glanced at my watch, refusing to look at my best friend. The weight of his unrelenting gaze pressed down on me. He had me cornered. I had no choice but to be subjected to his interrogation. "How long do we have?"

"As long as you need, JJ." I tipped my head back, closed my eyes, and drummed my fingers as tension coiled inside me. "Look, I'm not pressuring you to tell me," he said softly. "If you want to keep it to yourself, that's your right. But I'm your friend, aren't I?"

"Obviously! You know this." My words came out more forcefully than I'd intended them to. I was frustrated, confused, and so goddamn lost when it came to Dillon. I loved him. Always had. But that wasn't the issue. He blew hot and cold. When we were alone, he was more like the boy I used to know. But when we saw each other around campus, he was the arrogant, hateful, quarterback king who looked at me like I was nothing. It hurt, more than I cared to admit.

I was fucking everything up. Me and Dillon. Me and my friends. I was unintentionally keeping everyone at arm's length while drowning in fear and anxiety. I know I should tell Mal everything, but if the worst was to happen and my dad materialized, I didn't want him to get caught in the crossfire.

I was lost. It was like I was trying to climb up a glass wall and every time I made it a couple of feet closer to the top, I'd slide back down with all the broken pieces of my soul.

Mal gave a terse smile while twirling his straw around in his shake. "I do, but I also know there's a lot of stuff you don't tell me." I eyed him with suspicion. "And if it's 'cause you don't think you can trust me, that hurts. I'm not gonna lie." I winced at his pained tone. "I'm a vault, JJ. You're always there for me and Ava, so let us be there for you. Let me be here for you. Right here and now."

He was offering me an olive branch, but was I brave enough to take it? "I do trust you, Mal." I placed my hand over his where it rested on the table top and gave it a gentle squeeze. "It's... it's just complicated..."

"I'm good with complicated, you'll see." He shot me a winning smile. "Go on, talk." He squeezed my hand back. I took a deep fortifying breath and steeled myself, choosing to be brave and open myself up. I told Mal our history from the day I met Dillon until today and everything else in between—minus a detailed description of the times when it had all turned to sex.

"I got a text from him asking me to meet him at the party house for his birthday next week," I said as Mal stared at me with wide eyes. The look of utter shock on his face had me belting out another laugh. They say laughter was good for the soul, right? Well, being with Mal was better.

"Wow!" Mal called Wendy over and asked for something stronger to drink. He'd spent the last twenty minutes white-knuckling his shake glass. "Well, shit."

"Yeah," I breathed. It was nice having some of the weight lifted off my shoulders, but the confusion I felt only intensified.

"Here you go, hon," Wendy said, placing Mal's beer on the table. "And I got you this." I looked up at her as she placed another shake in front of me. "You looked like you needed it."

"Thanks." My shoulders slumped as I pulled the glass closer to me. A hand landing on my shoulder made me jump.

"It'll all work out in the end, sweetie. The best things in life are those you fight for." I titled my head, and she smiled. "The question is, are they worth it?"

"At the moment, I don't know. It's complicated."

"Then uncomplicate it."

"It's not—"

She cut me off. "At the end of the day, it is. Either you like them enough to try, or it's too much trouble, and you walk away. Simple, really." Giving my shoulder one last squeeze, she left and said she'd be back shortly with our food.

"I mean, she's not wrong," Mal added.

I let out a long breath. "I know. I do. But I don't know what I want. In an ideal world—"

"Jamie, there is no such thing as an ideal world. The world, your life, is what you make it. Do you want to be with Dillon? Ignore all the issues you think you have. It's a simple question. Do you want to be with him?"

"Yes!" I unequivocally wanted to be with him. He was the sun, the moon, and all the stars in the sky. My world began and ended with him. Always had. Always would. That wasn't the issue I had—it was whether or not he wanted me.

"I can see the cogs turning in your brain, JJ."

"Ha, you could say."

"You said he invited you to his party?"

"Yup."

"Go." My eyes bugged out of my head as I stared at him. "Go and ask him. Get the answer to all the questions going around in your head."

"Alright, but only if you come with me."

"Deal!"

CHAPTER TWENTY-ONE

Dillon

"I hear you're celebrating your twenty-first tonight?"

Fuck, how did he find out about that?! I scrubbed my hand down my face and cursed the day I was born. I didn't even want to celebrate my birthday; I just wanted to have a night alone with Jamie. But oh no, the team posted flyers all around campus advertising the captain's twenty-first, how it was going to be "the" party of the year, and if you missed it, you might as well pack up and go home. Fuck. My. Life. "Yeah, that's right."

Tristan leaned back in his chair, his gaze assessing me while he stroked his new goatee. "There going to be a big turn out?"

"So I'm led to believe."

"Hmmm." He leaned over and opened his drawer, pulling out the keys and a little baggie of white powder. "How about some birthday bumps?"

Fuck! I knew I should have made Stevens come and get the damn keys. "Ah, sorry. Can't. Athlete."

"I don't remember giving you a choice, Dillon." Tristan placed his hands on his desk and loomed over it, trying to intimidate me. Physically, I could take him in a fair fight, but this guy was fifty shades of fucked up, and I knew he was packing, along with the two guards on the other side of the door. "Don't be rude, or your party house goes up in flames with everyone in it." He poured the powder out on a silver tray and cut it into four little white lines.

"It's not like that." I tried to placate him. "It's just they run random drug tests, and one positive means I'm off the team. I can't—"

"We couldn't have that now, could we?" he mocked before inhaling a line. He sniffed and wiped his nose before licking the residue off his finger. "You're the best quarterback Briar U has ever had. We couldn't lose our golden boy that way." He cocked his head to the side, his pupils blown so wide there's not a hint of his dirty-brown left. "However, if you turn me down again..."

He didn't need to give credence to his threat; violence rolled off him in waves. I swallowed down the nausea rolling through me and took the proffered metal straw as he slid the tray over to me. "I made you two small ones."

I opened my mouth, a refusal on the tip of my tongue, when he flashed me a photo of Jamie sitting on the grass of the quad. A malicious chuckle oozed past his lips. "I can hurt you in more ways than one."

"I don't know why you're showing me that," I growled and bent over the tray, doing the one thing I'd promised myself I'd never do. I plugged my left nostril and inhaled. Fuck, it burned. The buzz was quick and a smirk flickered at the corners of my lips before I fell back into my seat. The sensation of the residue dripping down my throat and onto my tongue made me shudder, the chalky taste turning my stomach. Now I was back to square one—about to empty the contents of my gut all over his floor.

"Maybe you have got some balls after all, kid," Tristan goaded. "Take these and don't fuck it up too badly." I went to hand him the cash, and he shook his head "Consider it a present."

This was not good. Now I owed him, and one thing Tristan was known for was collecting his debts. "Thanks," I growled between clenched teeth as the sickening feeling of dread settled beneath my skin.

All Tristan did was smirk and wave me off as he settled back in his chair, phone to his ear. The door opened before I could reach it, and fresh air from the open bay blew across my face. "Oh, Dillon?" I rolled my eyes at Tweedle Dee and Tweedle Dum as they stood sentry outside the door and glanced over my shoulder, keeping my face blank. "I'll see you tonight." I nodded and walked out without looking back.

STEVENS HAD APPOINTED himself the party planner. All I had to do was get the keys and pay the deposit for the house. Said money burned a hole in my pocket all the way back to campus. I was in two minds as to what to do with it. It felt dirty, like I'd taken a back hander, and I didn't want to keep it because I knew the repercussions would be dire. Instead of making a decision myself, I put it to the guys to decide what to do; either keep it for our next deposit, or to use it for tonight. Stevens decided to book a DJ, and it was agreed by unanimous vote.

"This guy's sick, right?" Stevens shouted in my ear as he looped his arm around my neck and dragged me into the kitchen for a drink. "What's your poison tonight, Cap?"

It was my twenty-first, so legally, I could have anything.

But I had plans for tonight, as long as a certain blue-eyed golden-haired boy came. "Just a beer."

Arching his brow, Stevens looked at me like I'd grown two heads. "Are you sure? I went all out and got top shelf spirits." He grabbed a bottle of gold label tequila and waved it in my face. "This stuff is the shit, Cap. You really—"

"No." I shut him down instantly. "I'm not planning on getting wasted. We have a game next week, and you know Coach doesn't need any help finding reasons to bench us."

"Oh, I know *I* don't." Stevens sneered at me and grabbed a cold bottle from the fridge. "Here. So are you planning on hooking up with Elise tonight?" Just her name made my skin crawl and my balls retreated into my body. Instead of answering, I took the bottle from him and downed it.

"Cap, can I have a word?"

"Sure." I breathed a sigh of relief as I followed Buchanan out the bifold doors and onto the back deck. "What's up?"

"Not much. You just looked like you needed a rescue." I scoffed and walked over to the fire pit. The night was warmer than I'd expected, but the temperatures would drop as the evening wore on. Watching the flames helped calm the calamity exploding in my head. I knew shit was about to go down, and I just prayed I wasn't dragged down with it.

"Thanks." I clapped him on the back and took a seat on one of the loungers.

"This brings back memories." B smirked at a group of girls walking past before turning to look at me. Thankfully, it was still quiet in the yard. The party was just starting to kick off inside, so we had some time for him to say whatever was on his mind.

"I suppose."

Sighing, Buchanan passed me another beer. "What's going on, Dillon?" I blanched and looked up at him, grinding my teeth. "Nothin'."

"Try again, man. You forget I know you. More than those

asshats in there." A loud cheer erupted as Vieck was hauled up by his feet to do a keg stand.

I snorted. "You're not wrong there."

"Is it just what happened with Tristan? Or does it have something to do with Jami—" I slapped my hand over his mouth.

"Shut the fuck up," I growled, leaning into his space. "There's nothing to talk about."

"I bug ta difa," he garbled against my palm before licking it.

"What the hell!"

"Stop being a child, Dillon. There's too much at stake for you to be a dick. You like him. You—"

"I don't."

B threw his hands up in exasperation. "Seriously?!" He looked at me with narrowed eyes. "You think I'm blind? I have eyes!" He carded his hands through his hair and rolled his neck. "I've seen how you look at him, Dil. If the others pulled their heads out of their asses, they'd see it too. But they're too blinded by the seed of hate you planted in them."

"Fuck off, B. This doesn't concern you."

He pushed up from his seat and got right in my face, teeth bared. "It does when it's fucking you over." He snatched the front of my hoodie and pulled me in closer. "I don't know what happened between you, but I'm here if you need to talk. You never know, I might be able to help."

"Is that a fucking joke?" I pushed him back and started pacing, everything playing over and over in my mind. I had hated Jamie when I first saw him. Five years worth of pain and devastation crashed into me like a tsunami, pulling me down into the dark abyss. It set my volatile anger free, and it consumed me. I wanted to ruin him—make him suffer like I had—so he'd leave, but my stupid heart took flight when I saw his steel-ringed pale-blue eyes. They've haunted me every moment since.

He was intoxicating, but obsession was toxic. I couldn't allow us to crash and burn.

I needed him more than my next breath, but I stood to lose everything I'd been focused on for the last five years if I followed my heart. But could I live with myself if I didn't? If I gave up the chance to have a life with the only person I'd ever loved? Would I live my dreams or die slowly day by day as I became bitter and rotten to the core?

The question wasn't was he worth the sacrifice, but was he worth the truth?

My heart knew the answer. I just had to convince my head.

"No, joke. I get it, you're confused—"

"I'm not," I snapped. I was fucking terrified. I was drowning, and I couldn't find the surface. There was a wall of water in every direction, penning me in.

"Well, well, well," Buchanan mused and slapped me on the shoulder. "Looks like fate has decided for you."

"What the?" I turned the way he was facing, and my heart beat its way up my throat as butterflies swarmed in my stomach. "Wow," I breathed as my eyes roamed over Jamie. Buchanan's guttural laugh made me want to punch him.

"He's something else." B pinned me with a knowing look. "If you don't want him, they will be lining up around the block for him."

I grunted and flipped him off before I stalked across the grass to where Jamie stood with his sidekicks. They were like shadows, never leaving his side. And believe me, I knew that, because I stalked his fine ass all over the campus grounds. He might not have seen me, but if I wasn't in class, on the field, or in the gym, I was watching him. Cory had come through with everything he could find on Jamie "Bowen," but it only went back five years. It wasn't the whole truth, not by a long shot. My boy had skeletons in his dark closet, and I was determined to find them.

"Uh oh," the annoying rainbow pixie muttered under her breath as I drew closer.

"Ava." The look of surprise that flashed across her face made me smug. "Malachi." I nodded at the guy standing on Jamie's other side. "So nice of you guys to come and celebrate my birthday." Being polite to them was like pulling teeth. Why couldn't they just fuck off? I wanted Jamie. All of him. Alone.

"Next time, say it like you mean it," Ava clapped back like a snappy puppy with small dog syndrome.

"How about we go and get a drink, Aves? And let these two..." Malachi's words fizzled out as he rolled his hand in our direction before dragging a prickly Ava toward the house. I felt her heated gaze on me until I focused on my little crow, and the entire world melted away.

I stepped into the cover of the shadows behind Jamie, hooked my fingers through his belt loops, and pulled him into me. He was wrapped in a cocoon of his delicious caramel scent, and just a hint of it had my blood rushing south and my mouth watering. My heart was hammering, and nervous energy poured off me in waves as I feared someone might see us. But when Jamie's back was flush with my chest, he released a little sigh and melted into me.

I dragged my nose along the column of his neck, inhaling his sweet scent. He arched his neck, giving me full access to his soft skin, and I peppered kisses up to his ear. I breathed a sigh of relief that he was back in my arms. "I've missed you." My lips brushed the shell of his ear, and he shuddered.

Jamie looked up at me from under his dark lashes and chewed on his bottom lip. It felt like I was balanced on a tightrope while I waited for him to speak. He finally put me out of my misery. "I've missed you too, Dil." He turned in my arms until we were chest to chest, and his closeness short-wired my brain. My world began and ended with him.

Jamie's hand snaked up my chest, sending bolts of electricity across my skin and cupped the nape of my neck. He pushed in closer to me as if he was trying to fuse us together. I had to bite back the groan rumbling in my chest when his hard length brushed against mine. His nimble fingers carded through my hair and he pulled me down so our lips were a hair's breadth apart.

"Happy birthday, babe," he breathed before slamming his mouth against mine. I gasped into his dominating kiss as his tongue licked across my bottom lip, eliciting a needy moan from me. I hungered for his taste. My lips parted as a fever stole over me, and I spun us around and crushed Jamie into the fence.

"It is now," I growled against his slick lips and pushed my thigh between his legs, encouraging him to roll his hips. I luxuriated in the feel of his hardness moving against mine as his body heat burned me through the layers separating us. I gripped his jaw and maneuvered his head until I could take control of our frantic kiss and devour him.

Jamie mewled as he rocked against me, the tempo of his thrusts increasing as I tasted every corner of his mouth and wrapped my tongue around his. We dueled and fought back and forth, and no matter how aggressive and demanding I was, he never faltered. Jamie was a lit match, and I was a vat of kerosene. It was only a matter of time until we detonated.

My tattooed hand pawed at his clothes until my fingers touched burning skin. I needed to feel all of it against me. I needed to sink inside him and never leave. I'd never craved anyone with the ferocity I did for him. He was my savior and my undoing. I didn't care how far we fell as long as we did it together.

I feasted on his full lips and sucked them into my mouth, gladly swallowing down every whimpered cry and wanton moan. I'd forgotten how to breathe as I surrendered to Jamie. Who needed to breathe anyway? I kissed him until my lungs screamed, and my legs were on the verge of buckling. I pulled back from him and sucked in drugging lungfuls of air. I had to brace my hand on the fence beside his head as my chest heaved, and stars danced across my vision.

"T-that...was..." Jamie panted and rested his forehead against my chest. My whole body pulsed with need, and I could barely think. His hands slipped down and anchored on my hips. He held on to me like he was afraid I was going to vanish.

A rambunctious laugh pierced the lust-filled bubble we'd lost ourselves in, and we jumped apart as the rest of the party filtered back into focus around us. What we had done was not only dangerous but stupid. There was still a target on Jamie's back, and I was on the precipice of losing everything. Being out in the open like this was just asking for trouble to find us.

In the muted light, I could just make out Jamie's swollen glistening lips and glazed eyes. He looked seconds away from blowing his load as he smirked up at me and stroked his hand over the obvious bulge in his skin-tight pants. My eyes tracked his tongue as it ran across his puffy lip, but it was his moan that snapped my control. I grabbed his arm and yanked him until he fell into step beside me. We used the shadows for cover to cross the yard, avoiding the other partygoers and slipped inside the house without anyone seeing us together.

We took the back stairs that were out of bounds to everyone bar me and the guys. I opened the first door on the left and dragged Jamie into the primary suite. My hands shook as they slid down his body and cupped the full globes of his ass. As if he could read my mind, Jamie jumped up and wrapped his legs around my waist. He was as close as he could physically get, but it still felt like there were oceans between us. I wouldn't be satisfied until I was buried deep inside him.

His lips parted as he gasped, and in the blink of an eye, I had his back pinned against the door, and my mouth slammed against his. There was nothing gentle about the savage way I kissed him. I was like a starved man, and he was my only sustenance. My tongue fucked into his mouth, owning him, forcing his body to surrender to me. My skin burned with need as every roll of his tongue against mine threatened to incinerate me.

"I need you naked." I nipped and sucked a path down his neck, painting his skin with a watercolor of bruises.

"Yesss," Jamie breathed and rolled his head back, baring his throat to me. My teeth scraped over his Adam's apple, and his throat convulsed against my lips. Images of my cock buried deep in the tight wet heat of his mouth played through my mind.

"Off," I grunted, reduced to single syllable words as my desire, my all consuming need, obliterated my brain cells. Pinning Jamie to the door with my hips, my hands grappled the bottom of his sleek button down and ripped it up his body. Buttons pinged against the door as I wrenched it over his arms and let it fall to the floor. "You're utter perfection, baby." I tongued his hard nub, drawing it between my teeth, then sucking into my mouth to ease the burning ache.

Jamie mewled, the back of his head thumping against the door as I switched to the other nipple and flicked it with the tip of my tongue. "Fuck, Dill. Please." He panted, his hot breath teasing my skin and sending shivers of desire through me that had my heart in a chokehold.

"Bed," I ground out and sunk my teeth into the flesh of his peck. I tightened my hold on his firm ass as Jamie's arms wrapped around my neck and blindly walked over to the bed, tossing Jamie down onto the covers. He bounced once before I was on him, kissing, licking, and sucking every inch of him, driven wild by his supple body and consumed by the salty taste of his skin. I reached back and ripped my hoodie off, letting it fall from my fingers as my hands went to the button of his pants. His chest rose and fell with shuddering breaths, his pale-blue eyes flickering between mine as he traced his index finger over my chest. I followed the movement of his finger as it reverently mapped out the tattoo covering my heart. I saw the unasked question in their depths and the moment he realized the bird he'd been mesmerized by was a crow. My body was a tapestry of my memories of him, and one day I would tell him, so he would know it's always been him.

"No." Jamie's hand landed on my chest, stopping me in my tracks. Ice sheeted my skin, and my heart turned to dust.

"Fuck! Little crow, I'm sorry." Emotion clogged my throat as I struggled to breathe. My heart hammered as fear and shame pulsed through me. Tears pricked my eyes, and I buried my face in the crook of his neck, his sweet caramel scent taunting me.

"Hey, babe? Dil? Look at me." Soft hands cupped my face and pulled me back to him. Jamie brought my forehead down onto his as his breath stuttered out of him.

I licked my lips as the first tear dripped from my eye. "I'm so, so, sorry, little crow." I sucked in a gasping breath.

"I'm not." Wide eyes stared up at me. The strength and determination in them was impossible to ignore. "I don't want to stop, stop." I cocked my head in confusion as I pulled back so I could see all of him. Jamie smiled and my heart thawed at those beautiful eyes. "I want to taste you. I want... no, *need* to give you a taste of the pleasure you've given me." A scarlet flush worked its way up his chest to the tips of his ears.

"Whatever you want, baby," I whispered, terrified I was about to shatter from the intensity of his words and the lust churning in his eyes.

"On your back, Dil."

I'd never moved so fast as I dropped on my back and worked my way up the bed until my back rested against the headboard. I didn't want to miss a second of this. Jamie smirked at me as he pulled himself up onto his knees, flicked his button open and pulled the zipper down, revealing a tiny black fishnet jock. His hard length was clearly visible between the open diamonds, but it was the glistening bead of precum that had my mouth watering.

Somehow, he managed to shuck his jeans and shoes off without getting off the bed before slowly crawling toward me. Jamie arched his back and my eyes devoured the sway of his ass until he settled on his knees between my spread legs. "Fuck." The growl tore from my chest with an intensity that left me breathless.

Jamie spread his legs wide so his knees were under my thighs and planted a hand behind himself for support. "Do you like what you see, babe?" His soft tone taunted me as much as his actions had my rock hard cock pulsing against my zipper. "Watch me?" he questioned, but the way he looked at me said I didn't have a choice—it was do or die. A smirk kicked up the side of his flushed lips as Jamie licked the underside of his index finger before sucking it into his mouth. Watching his lips wrap around it almost had me coming on the spot.

"Fuck, little crow. You're gonna make me come."

"That's the plan, Dil," he crooned. In the most seductive move I'd ever seen, Jamie pulled his spit-slicked finger from his mouth and trailed it down his chest, teasing the peaked nub of his right nipple before trailing it down his stomach to where his flushed dick was trying to break free. He teased the glistening tip, covering the digit in his arousal.

"That's so damn hot." I panted, desperate for a taste of him.

Jamie winked and pushed up so he was looming over me. Sweat glistened on his skin as he trailed his finger over my lips. His hot breath fanned my skin as he said, "I want you to taste me as I taste you for the first time."

"Oh fuck!" I banged my head against the headboard and a devilish chuckle seeped from him. I squeezed my eyes shut and started to count down from a thousand to stop my impending orgasm as it barreled towards me.

I didn't need to have my eyes open to feel his every movement. My skin was electrified; his every touch zapped right to my cock. The pop of the button of my jeans sounded loud in the quiet room. The teeth on the zipper being pulled apart as Jamie slowly undressed me was like a countdown timer that set my soul on fire. My body pulsed with need. It was heady being at his sweet torturous mercy.

"Up," he breathed over my aching length as he pulled my jeans and boxers down just enough for my cock to spring free. It smacked down on my abs with a wet slap as precum poured from my slit and slicked up my skin. "Fuck, yes." Jamie licked my shaft from the root to the tip, making my dick jerk from the wet heat of his tongue. I wasn't going to survive being in his mouth and down his throat if this is how I reacted to one swipe of his tongue.

"Fuck, me. I'm not gonna last, baby."

He chuckled and nuzzled against my length before lapping up the liquid on my stomach. "Mmmm." He groaned, licked his lips, and stared into my eyes. "You taste so good." Before I could suck in a breath, Jamie lifted my heavy cock and flicked his tongue over the tip dipping it in the slit.

"Ahh. YES," I shouted, on a hair trigger and ready to come. I was acting like a horny teen, having his first blowjob.

With his tongue circling my crown, Jamie peeked at me from under his lashes. "I've never done this before, so tell me if it's not good." My brain stuttered and misfired when his words eventually registered.

"J-Jamie?" I couldn't compute his words.

He shook his head. "The only person I've ever kissed is you."

I sucked in a breath, ready to question him further, but he wrapped his lips around me and swallowed me straight down to the root. "FUUCCKK," I bellowed and wrapped my fingers around his curls, wrenching his head back. "Never?" He shook his head, an indecent smirk on his face before he sucked me right back down. "Oh god. Oh god. Oh god." I sunk my teeth into my lip, trying to fight my body as I flushed hot. Waves of euphoria crashed over me, and my balls drew up tight, hugging the base of my dick.

Jamie pulled back and sucked in a rasping breath, tears shimmering in his eyes. “Come. I need your cum now.” He took me back in his mouth, using the perfect amount of suction that made electricity shoot down my spine when a wet finger trailed up my taint and rolled my balls. I was fucking done for. I was dead.

My orgasm slammed into me so hard, my vision went black as my soul flowed through my dick. Ropes of cum shot into the tight heat of Jamie’s throat. His guttural groan was loud enough to rival mine. The vibrations rolled through my pulsing cock, prolonging my orgasm as euphoria drugged me.

“What the fuck is this?” My eyes flew open to see Chad standing in the doorway, shoulders rising and falling with the ferocity of the ragged breaths tearing out of him. He stormed toward me, fists clenched, knuckles white as he swung at my face. If I wasn’t still lost in the euphoric waves of the most intense orgasm of my life, I might have been able to react in time. "You’re a fucking faggot?” he spat in my face as his knuckles crashed into my cheek with the force of a Mack truck.

“Fuck off, Chad,” I bellowed at him as Jamie whimpered and clutched my leg like it was a shield. “Shhhh, baby, I’ll get rid of him.” I was just about to push off the bed when footsteps thundered down the hallway in our direction. I breathed a sigh of relief, but it was premature as Chad started to rain down blows on my face.

CHAPTER TWENTY-TWO

Jamie

Chad's hate-filled voice pummeled through my blissful orgasmic haze like a brick to the head. I coiled in on myself and clutched Dillon's leg like it was the last defense between me and the end of the world. The sound of flesh hitting flesh had me squeezing my eyes shut and a whimper ripping out of my mouth.

The sound of thundering footsteps and raised voices grew louder and louder with every second that passed. My heart pounded in my skull and adrenaline flooded my system, making me shake so hard my teeth chattered. Dillon let loose a pained grunt and shoved me off him, the movement forcing me off the bed. I crashed to the floor with a shout. The impact forced my breath from my lungs, and copper burst across my tongue.

Fear consumed me, turning the blood in my veins to ice as images of my dad beating my mom half to death choosing this moment to assault my mind. One after another, they flashed behind my eyes in vivid technicolor. Bile churned in my gut and coated the back of my throat.

"What the fuck are you doing?" someone shouted. "Vieck, get Chad the fuck out of here." I cowered, pushing myself flat against the carpet as each barked word felt like a physical blow.

"Ahh, shit. Stevens, get in here and help," another voice ground out, strain evident in their tone.

"Chad. Chad? Chad! Come on, you dick, cool it. Or you'll be on the bench."

"Fuck you! I will not be benched for a fucking fa—" A loud thud echoed in the silence as something heavy hit the floor. I flinched at the sound it made when it landed. Tears leaked from my skewed-shut eyes as I whimpered.

"How much does he weigh? Ugh."

"Three hundred or so, I reckon. He's a big boy."

"Haha. You can say that again."

"Stop wasting time and throw his ass outside. The rest of you clear out while I check Cap over." Heavy footsteps were accompanied by a low groan as bodies moved and followed instructions. A foreboding silence filled the room, and tension coiled through my body like a compressed spring. The pressure in my lungs didn't abate as a shuddering breath stole through me.

"Dil, sit down. I need to clean you up."

"Fuck off, B. I need to find him. *Shit*. Fuck!" I could just imagine Dillon carding his hands through his hair and yanking on the strands as frustration ate away at him. "Little crow, are you okay?" The soft words were closer than I'd expected, and the tentative hopefulness in his tone almost killed me.

The air around me felt charged, and apprehension slithered over my skin as I felt Dillon's presence next to me. I refused to open my eyes, even when he stroked his fingers up and down my arm in a soothing motion. I wanted to lean into his touch and find solace in his arms, but I couldn't. Not yet.

It was too raw. I was undone and vulnerable in a way I wasn't prepared for him to see. A garbled whimper left my lips, and I shook my head, unable to find the words to express myself.

"Jamie, please open your eyes. Come on, baby. It's okay. He's gone." I wanted to believe him, but my mind rebelled, triggered by the fight that had broken out. All I could see was my dad's face as he promised mom it was all over. *Lies.* That it had been a mistake and would never happen again. *Lies.* The pitch of his voice had burrowed under my skin and echoed through my mind. I hated it. I hated him for making me fear Dillon's closeness, for making me want to recoil from his touch.

"Maybe he needs some space, Dil?"

"Fuck off, B. This doesn't concern you."

"Well, I'm here, so it kinda does." I could hear the shrug in his voice but it didn't make me want to venture outside of the space I'd created for myself in my mind. Here, I was safe. Here, I was untouchable.

"Baby," Dillon breathed, his hot breath like a caress on my skin. His lips brushed over my cheek, and I shuddered. "I'm here, okay? Chad's gone and won't be back." He kissed my temple in the sweetest way. It was a simple brush of his lips, one you'd miss if you blinked, but I felt it all the way to my heart. "Can I hold you?" I considered his request, the pained tone of his gravelly voice, and chose to be brave, to trust that he would never hurt me. I nodded the barest of movements.

Dillon's strong arms wrapped around me, bracketing me in the safety of his embrace. The heat of his body dulled the sharp edges and thawed me from the inside out. I was safe. I was finally home. The place I'd been searching for for the last five years found me. Chose me.

"T-thank you."

"Anything for you." He kissed my cheek, and the ghost of a smile played over my lips.

My eyes fluttered closed as the exhaustion I'd been

pushing down became too much to ignore. I needed to give my mind a chance to reset and rest. The trouble with suffering from nightmares and flashbacks from some of the worst moments of your life, is that it infected you like a cancer. It took root in every facet of your mind, body, and soul. People might see how it affects you physically, but they couldn't feel the relentless mental anguish that holds you hostage, or the way it made your mind play tricks on you, forcing you to question everything.

I was tired, and not the type a weekend's worth of sleep could fix. I was emotionally drained and running on empty. My soul ached, and it felt like my bones were turning to dust. I just needed someone to hold me together, to love me even on the days when it was impossible to open my eyes.

"Put him on the bed, Dil. Let me check you over." Dillon's grunt made me want to laugh, but I couldn't move. I was weighed down by the world.

"I've got him," he snapped as he lifted off the floor and tucked under the covers on the bed. Warmth suffused my heart at Dillon's tenderness. Fingertips brushed the hair off my face, and he placed a kiss to my forehead. I wanted to melt in my semi lucid state.

"B..." Dillons aching sigh made my heart clench.

"Don't, Dil. Tell me when you're ready, okay?" The sound of a zip being undone made me flinch, and the pregnant pause that followed as everyone in the room held their breath was suffocating. "Tip your head back, or it's going to run into your eye."

"He's gonna pay for this. No one gets to touch him or hurt him like that."

"Alright, big guy, calm down. You can go all caveman on Chad later. Right now, you need to get dressed and get out of here. Take him home, Dil. He needs you."

"I know, B. But someone insisted on cleaning up my face."

I smiled at Dillon's amused tone. "What I don't understand is why he came up here in the first place."

"Um, well, Tristan turned up and brought some of his crew to join the party."

"Fuck!"

"Yeah, you could say that. He brought some heavy shit too, so you know it's going to get messy."

"I need to get him—"

"No! You're going back to the dorms and taking care of what matters. If people here fuck themselves up, that's on them, not you. Not us. Got it?"

"Sure. Catch ya later, and thanks, B."

"Anytime, Dil. You know that."

I listened to Dillon's soft foot falls as he moved around the room before the bed dipped, and he kissed my nose. "Hey, little crow. Open those beautiful eyes for me. We need to go."

I peeled one eye open and stared into his ebon depths. Ones that had previously been filled with glacial hate now brimmed with concern and maybe, possibly, something much more powerful.

CHAPTER TWENTY-THREE

Jamie

Dillon yanked the covers off me. "Hey! That was mean." I wrinkled my nose at him.

"I know, I'm sorry." The smirk on his face said otherwise as he pulled me up and slipped a hoodie over my head. I buried my nose in the material and inhaled his sea-salt scent. I couldn't help the groan that slipped from my lips.

Dillon chuckled. "Now is not the time for that." I snickered and stuck my tongue out at him as he worked some butter-soft sweatpants up my legs. They were massive and hung off my feet by several inches.

"I look like an idiot," I grumbled. Dillon sunk his teeth into his bottom lip and shook his head instead of answering me.

After putting my shoes on, he pulled me from the bed and laced our fingers together. His rough calloused palm swallowed mine, but I loved how we looked together and how damn hot that rose tattoo on his hand looked. We were opposites in every way, but it was like we were made for each other.

"No. You look like mine." The possessive growl in his voice made every nerve in my body spark to life ,and my heart did a backflip. "You ready to get out of here?" A small smile played around my lips but instead of answering, I pushed up onto my tiptoes, grabbed the toggles of Dillon's hoodie, and pulled him down to me so I could fuse his lips with mine. His sharp inhale made me preen as I licked into his mouth. His taste burst across my tongue, making me groan. I needed this. Needed him to make me forget.

I pulled back and couldn't help the chuckle that left me as I took in his dazed expression. "Yes."

"Well, alright then." He cleared his throat and adjusted himself before giving my hand a gentle squeeze.

The party was in full force when we made it down the stairs, and even though no one paid us a blind bit of notice, we stuck to the shadows. We slipped out of the party house like thieves in the night and stole away in Dillon's truck. As we drove across town, I wondered if it would always be like this—him and me—hiding in the dark. A secret that could never be shared with the world. I shook my head and stared out the window, watching the streetlights pass us by and let that thought go.

Campus was quiet when we arrived, which wasn't surprising since it was nearly one in the morning. Like a gentleman, Dillon got out of the truck and opened my door for me, taking my hand as I hopped out. Before I could head to my building, he pushed me up against his truck and devoured my mouth until I was a panting molten mess of need. "I couldn't help myself. You're irresistible." His mouth curled into a grin.

I blushed as his words lit me up from the inside, "Um, thanks." His answering chuckle gave the night some much needed levity, and I could finally breathe.

We crossed the lot, arms brushing with each step, but it was like a wall had been erected between us—a space neither of us could cross. Before my mind could start to spiral, Dillon stopped and turned to me. "Will you come up?" He nodded his head toward his building, and my heart took flight. "Don't look so shocked, little crow." He cupped my face and brushed his thumb over my bottom lip, pulling it down. Dillon groaned and squeezed his hard length under his pants. "I can't get the image of your lips wrapped around my cock out of my mind, and it's driving me insane."

I smirked. "It was fun."

He shook his head and grabbed my hand, practically dragging me along behind him as I struggled to keep up with the urgency of his long stride. I don't remember entering the building or the ride to his floor in the elevator. The world around us ceased to exist until he threw me on his bed, and his large body blanketed me.

"I didn't bring you here for this," he breathed against my lips. The heat in his eyes and the gravelly tone of his lust-filled voice turned my clothes to ash. "I just didn't want to let you go." He bit his lip, a groan stuck in his throat. Dillon rested his forehead against mine as I breathed in his exhale. Each inhale had me embedding him in my lungs, closer to my heart than he could ever physically be. I wanted to drink him down and fuse him with my blood, make him part of my DNA so no matter how much distance was between us, he'd always be with me.

His face was silhouetted against the darkness, and as I stared into his dark eyes, I forgot how to breathe. "I want it all with you, Dil." He sucked in a sharp inhale, and he trailed trembling fingers down my cheek. "I want you to have all of me. Everything I am is yours." I licked my lips. "I couldn't imagine ever being with anyone else."

"Jamie." My name on his lips was a prayer. A promise. An oath that was tattooed on my heart. "I want everything with you too." His lips brushed mine, and it felt like he was caressing my soul.

"Make love to me, Dillon. Make me forget," I pleaded as I peppered biting kisses down his neck, teasing his stubble with the tip of my tongue. "Make me yours in every way."

"Fuck. Me." He groaned and settled between my legs. The weight of his erection burned through the layers that separate us, but it wasn't enough. I needed more. Always more.

"Off. Off. Off." My hands scrabbled at his back, yanking and tugging his hoodie but falling to remove it. I growled in frustration. I was consumed by the need to feel his skin on mine.

"Patience, baby." He sucked the pulse point of my neck to the point of pain before laving it away with long torturous strokes of his tongue. My fingers sunk into his hair, and I pulled his head back to mine. I nibbled his bottom lip with teasing bites and flicks of my tongue, pulling back every time he tried to claim my mouth and take control. I wanted him to burn like I was. I wanted him consumed with the need that seared through my veins.

We lost ourselves in each other. Each brush of his lips against mine, every owning touch of his tongue stoked the fire raging inside me to an inferno. We moved with a synchronicity of lovers who'd been together for years. The push and pull of our carnal desire rendered me incapable of thinking beyond our next touch.

My world narrowed down to him and me. Us. The air between us. Two souls trapped in mortal skin, begging to be reunited. To be freed. "How can you be so perfect?" He whispered kisses across my chest and down my stomach, leaving a blistering trail of goosebumps in his wake. He stripped me of my clothes in the most sensual of ways. Dillon's fingers grazed my heated skin and hooked on the top of the sweats I was wearing before pulling them down my legs. An appreciative growl tore from his bruised lips when his eyes locked on my jock. "Fuck."

"Dillon." I begged and pleaded with my words, hands, and eyes. "Please touch me."

His dark eyes burned with the power of a thousand suns as he kissed and nipped his way up my legs. My muscles twitched as his lips teased my skin, and my cock grew painfully hard when his hot breath ghosted over the material of my jock. "So perfect." He ran the tip of his nose along my length, inhaling deeply. The rumbling groan that passed his lips vibrated along my shaft, making my dick twitch. His rough hands kneaded the sensitive skin at the juncture of my thighs, and he chuckled as I shivered.

"Sensitive," I said with a stuttering breath.

Dillon's wicked smile was like a bullet to the heart as he leaned down and captured the top of my lacy jock and suckled my leaking tip through the material. "Mmmm," he moaned. My hands fisted the sheets on his bed. His every touch lit me on fire, and I was fast approaching the point of spontaneously combusting.

"Dillon. Please."

"You beg so sweetly, little crow." With a final kiss to my straining dick, he grabbed the top of my jock and peeled it down until it hugged me under my balls. "Perfection." Adoration and wonder bled from his whispered words. "Hold your legs for me baby, while I get you ready for me."

He pushed my legs up, hand under my knees until they touched my chest. His hot wet tongue worked its way up my dick from root to tip. I threw my head back and let out an indecent moan. My entire body vibrated as he sat back on his knees and peeled his top off. My eyes roved over every inch of skin he exposed. Thick well defined abs, a smattering of dark hair that trailed down into his pants. He flicked open the button of his pants, looked up at me through his lashes, rolled his bottom lip between his teeth, and winked.

"You're beautiful, Dillon."

A look of confusion flickered across his dark features as he shucked off his pants and boxers. His thick length slapped against his abs, leaving a glistening wet trail. I licked my lips, remembering the weight of his dick on my tongue and his musky taste in my mouth.

I trailed my eyes over his perfect body as the weight of his heated gaze on my most intimate part felt like a physical caress. He looked at me with fascination and a carnal hunger that made me wetter than I'd ever been. I didn't know how I was going to take him, but for him, I'd try anything.

"You're wrong, Jamie. You're the beautiful one here."

Dillon braced his arms either side of me and stole my soul when his lips locked onto mine in a searing kiss that rendered me speechless. His tongue wrapped around mine, and I was lost to the sensation of his touch, and the safety I felt as he caged me in and took control of me. When he broke the kiss, both of us were left gasping. Not giving me the chance to reboot my brain, he nipped his way down my neck, scraping his teeth over my Adam's apple and sucking on my collarbone. Lips and teeth bit, sucked, and grazed their way down my chest and stomach.

I gasped when he wrapped his lips around the flushed crown of my cock, suckling on it and pushing me to the edge of no return before pulling off with a resounding pop. I dug my fingers into my thighs as full body shudders rolled through me in ever increasing waves.

Dillon laid down on the bed between my legs. One hand grabbed my ass cheek, opening me up to him while a finger teased across my skin from my spine, along my cleft, and circled my entrance. I rocked my hips, needing to feel him inside me. Hot breath brushed my skin as he chuckled at my eagerness.

A wanton moan tore out of me as his hot wet tongue circled my puckered hole. He started with a long tantalizing swipe over my entrance before switching it up with little flicks and drugging sucks. The orgasm that had abated roared to life. Lightning skittered over my skin, down my spine, and straight to my full aching balls, which drew up and hugged the base of my dick with a pulse of their own.

"Oh my fucking god," I shouted when Dillon suctioned his mouth over my hole and sucked it like he would my cock. My hand slipped off my leg and wrapped around my throbbing dick. I managed two strokes before he growled. "Hands off what belongs to me. No one gets to touch my cock but me."

"Fuck me. I need to c-come."

"All in good time, baby. All in good time."

My ass was throbbing in time with my cock when Dillon's tongue pushed past the tight ring of muscle. My body locked up tight at the intrusion before bliss flowed through me in drugging waves. He fucked my ass with his tongue until sweat slicked my sin, and I was begging like a whore. His finger teased my rim before it slipped in alongside his tongue and stroked my walls.

"Fuck. Fuck. Now, Dillon. Now," I demanded and thrust my hips into his face as I tried to ride him from the bottom.

Another finger entered me, and the burn was everything I needed to stop me from splintering into a million pieces. "Such a greedy little hole." Dillon's voice was pure sex. My eyes fluttered open to see him kneeling between my legs, eyes fixed on where his fingers entered me. He was enraptured, like a man possessed with a singular focus. Nothing else existed to him but his finger in my ass. It was hot in the extreme. I'd dreamed of moments like this, but they had nothing on reality.

"Jamie?" My eyes snapped up to him at the hesitancy in his voice. "I need to feel all of you." He licked his lips, groaning at the taste of me on his lips. "I had a full panel before the semester started. I haven't been with anyone..."

It took my misfiring brain far too long to work out what he was saying, but I eventually put the pieces together. "I want that too." I shuddered as his finger stole over a part of me that made electricity pulse through me. "I-I've never done this, so I'm safe... I don't want anything between us. Ever."

His eyes were wide, his fingers in my ass slowly scissoring and stretching me. "E-Ever?" he rasped.

I shook my head. "No. We promised to be each other's firsts, remember?" Guilt had his open eyes shutting down, and he started to withdraw his fingers from my ass. I clamped my walls around him, keeping him where he belonged. Inside me.

"I-I..." Dillon shook his head.

"Hey, look at me," I said softly. "That was a promise made as a child who didn't know what the world would throw at us. I'm not angry you lived your life, babe. In fact, I'm glad you did. I wouldn't have wanted you to suffer."

Dillon's eyes glistened in the muted light, but the anguish that crashed into him was a palpable force. "I... I never enjoyed it. Any of it. I did what I had to, to forget about you." He winced as the words left his lips. They landed like a sucker punch, but I pushed them aside and focused on him. This moment and us. We would never be the same after this, after I gave him everything I was. My heart was on the line once again, but I trusted him not to break it.

"That's in the past, Dillon." I held my hand out to him and cupped his cheek. "Tonight is about us. It's the beginning of our story." He turned his head, nuzzled my hand, and placed a kiss on my palm before pulling his fingers from me. The click of a bottle cap made me tense. Cool liquid trickled down my crease and pooled around my entrance.

"I can't wait to feel your body suck me inside you." Slick fingers pushed inside me, coating my already stretched walls. Anticipation swelled inside me like a storm. He covered his length in lube and pinched his tip until he flinched. I looked at him with questions in my eyes. "I don't want to come before I'm buried balls deep inside you, baby."

"Oh."

"Are you ready? I'll go slow. I don't want to hurt you."

A blush heated my cheeks at the thought of his dick being inside me, but it had nothing on the way I hungered for the connection. The way I craved to feel him pushing inside me and owning me. "I'm ready, babe. Please."

He swiped the blunt head of his cock up and down my crease, every pass had my fingers sinking deeper into my skin until his head notched at my hole. His dark eyes were obliterated with lust, filled with a need so fierce it rivaled my own. I nodded my head and bore down as he pushed into me. The burning stretch made me gasp and tense. Dillon wrapped his hand around my softening length and stroked it as he rolled his hips in time with his strokes until he was buried to the hilt inside me.

"Ahh. Fuck. Jamie," he shouted. His cock throbbed inside me as he heaved lungfuls of air, trying to calm himself. I let go of my legs and wrapped them around his waist, crossing my ankles behind his back and pulling him in closer, forcing him deeper. Fuck, I loved being so full of him.

"Dillon. Please. Fuck me. I need you." His eyes widened, and I nodded, silently begging him. "Please."

"Fuck. Hold on, baby, because I can't be gentle with you. I need you too much." With his words still ringing in my ears, he pulled back until just the tip was inside me before thrusting back in one smooth forceful thrust that pushed me up the bed. A look of reverence stole across his face as perspiration beaded on his brow. I lost myself to the feel of his thick length dragging along my walls as his pace grew more forceful, more demanding, until the sound of skin slapping on skin drowned out our moans.

Grabbing my right leg, Dillon pulled it over his shoulder and changed the angle, deepening his strokes as his fat cockhead hit my prostate on every stroke. "Oh god. Oh god. Oh god," I chanted in between gasping breaths as he fucked the air right out of me.

"There is no god here. Just me, Jamie." His large hand wrapped around my throat as he loomed over me. The possessive hold pushed me higher as his hips slapped my ass with every fierce thrust.

"D-D-Dillon," I groaned and threw my head back. Liquid head pulled at the base of my spine and my cock thickened further. "I-I'm gonna..." His next thrust fractured my mind as my orgasm detonated inside me. I clamped down on his cock, making him groan, but I couldn't focus on him as my vision whited out and thick ropes of cum spurted from my pulsing dick.

"That's it baby, come on my cock." Dillon fucked me through my orgasm, pushing me higher and higher until it felt like I was floating among the stars. He cursed, his thrusts stuttering before his body locked up tight, and he shouted his release. Hot cum filled me as my walls spasmed around him, clamping down on his dick and refusing to let it go. He lived inside me now. "Fuuckk, Jamie."

MY EYES FLUTTERED as a warm cloth ran over my stomach, along my soft cock, and between my cheeks to my aching hole. "I'm so sorry, baby. I was so rough with you, but I couldn't help myself. You consumed every atom of my being. All I saw was you, all I could feel was you, and I lost myself. I'm sorry."

I kissed him to shut him up. He tasted like mint as his tongue licked along my bottom lip. Dillon pulled back when I opened for him and chuckled when I huffed. "Happy birthday, Dillon."

"You need to sleep, little crow. So do I. It's nearly sunrise."

His voice faded into a dream, one where we were happy and living together. I don't remember falling asleep because reality felt like the very best dream.

When I opened my eyes again, bright sunlight blinded me until I was seeing stars. I screwed my eyes shut and pulled the covers over my head. The movement of the sheets assaulted me with the scent of sex and Dillon. A wide smile bloomed on my lips as memories of the previous night filtered through my mind. It was so perfect, it felt like I'd gone to heaven, but the twinge in my ass made it real.

"Holy shit." I giggled as joy radiated through every cell in my body. I felt like I was floating. I didn't want this blissful moment to end, so I shut my eyes, breathed in our combined scent, and let my memory give me a blow-by-blow replay. My dick thickened against my stomach. I wrapped my hand around it and gave myself a few strokes before swiping my thumb over my leaking tip. It didn't take long before I spilled all over myself. I sighed as euphoria made me go lax, easing the nervous energy starting to creep up on me.

I had stuff I needed to do, like find my phone, check on Ava and Mal, and finish a calculus assignment. And where was Dillon? I called out his name, but there was no answer. I pushed the sheet down my legs and gingerly slid out of bed. "Dil?" Doubt crept in when I was met by silence. He wouldn't take my virginity and leave me, would he? I shook my head. He was a top athlete, so was probably doing athletic stuff. I shuddered at the thought.

A nice hot shower would be the best thing to do while I waited for him to come back. I waddled to his bathroom, the ache in my ass only growing more and more apparent, but I couldn't help the smile on my face as I stepped into the cubicle and turned the water on.

The shower worked its magic. My skin might have been as red as a strawberry, but my muscles were liquefied. I felt lighter as I searched through Dillon's closet and helped myself to a clean pair of sweats. I had to roll up the waistband so I didn't trip over them or have a wardrobe malfunction, and they still ended up pooled around my feet. I grabbed a shirt off the floor by his side of the bed, because I wanted to be wrapped in his scent. It made me feel closer to him.

I found my bag discarded on his desk. I don't remember bringing it with me from the party house, but my world began and ended with Dillon so I'm not surprised. A bomb could have gone off, and I wouldn't have noticed. As I pulled my phone out, it buzzed in my hand, and the screen lit up."Oh shit." Twelve missed calls and twenty texts from Mal and Ava made my good mood plummet.

I clicked into our group chat and died.

MAL

Jamie, where are you?

MAL

Seriously, Jamie, call me!

MAL

Where the hell are you???

MAL

Please. Please call me, Jamie. I'm worried about you.

AVA

FFS angel, let us know you're alive!

MAL

He's not at the hospitals or police stations.

AVA

JAMIE!!!!

Hey guys, sorry, my phone died. I will see you soon.

MAL

You better come home soon.

AVA

Thank fuck you're ok.

It wouldn't be long until I was back; they could wait a few minutes. I turned my phone off and dropped it in my bag. My gaze snagged on the little black box I'd all but forgotten about. I don't know what made me do it, but I pulled it out and looked at the USB stick.

"It's now or never," I muttered to myself.

I pulled it out and slipped it into Dillon's laptop on his desk and turned it on. The silver laptop looked brand new, like he'd barely touched it. The screen flashed to life without any password security. I clicked through the menu until I found the right program to assess the USB and clicked on the folder.

It took a couple of minutes until it loaded, and I wondered if we'd go for breakfast or lunch when he got back. That thought died a thousand deaths as my eyes locked on the grainy image on the screen. It was me lying in bed in my dorm. I sucked in a shuddering breath and pressed play. My stomach churned as the minutes ticked by. Ice sheeted my skin, and I was cold to the marrow of my bones as I watched myself and Mal come and go from our room.

My stomach churned when the camera angle changed to one in a different corner of my room, showing me dressing, doing my homework, and playing on my phone. "Oh god. Oh god. Oh—" Vomit surged up my throat. I broke into a run and managed to get the toilet seat up before it rocketed from my mouth. The words "I FOUND YOU!" flashed in red behind my closed eyes, and the world spun off its axis as I flushed hot and cold before another wave of nausea hit.

"Jamie? Where are you, baby?" Dillon's voice pulled me from unconsciousness. I groaned and pulled myself up from the chilly tile floor where I must have passed out. Why does my mouth taste like ass? Memories hit me, and I stumbled toward the sink. I couldn't stay here. The USB stick was still in

Dillon's laptop, and I had to go search my room for cameras. With my heart pounding against my ribs like a herd of elephants, I quickly brushed my teeth and slipped out into his room, purposefully keeping my back to him.

"Hey," I muttered, shuffling to his desk and slipping the USB into my pocket. Thick arms wrapped around me and pulled me into his body. Instead of melting like I wanted to, I stiffened.

"Jamie? What's wrong?" Tension bled from him, making it almost impossible to breathe.

I pushed out of his embrace and searched for my shoes. "Nothing," I said sharply and winced. "I've just, erm. I've gotta go. Got stuff to do." I found them under the bed, slipped them on, and grabbed my bag.

"Baby, wait. Please." His agonized tone almost killed me, but I couldn't stay. I had to know who had been in my room. Was it real? Another prank? I didn't know what the hell to think. "Jamie? Please look at me."

Big fucking mistake. The absolute worst. Dillon looked wrecked at my dismissive attitude. "Look, I'm sorry, Dillon." He recoiled as if my words had physically struck him. "Last night was great and all. B-but I've got to be somewhere. Sorry." The words came out all wrong, and my heart splintered as his hitched breath resonated around the room.

"Great. He said g-great—" The last words I heard broke into a soul-shattering cry as I pushed through the door and let it slam shut behind me.

"What have I done?" I whimpered as tears seared down my cheeks. The acidic tang of bile lingered in my mouth, getting stronger with each panicked breath I sucked in as I ran. Ran from the one person who would protect me above all else. I was safe with him. He was my home. But I loved him too much to drag him into this. I loved him enough to protect him from my world.

Even if that meant hurting him.

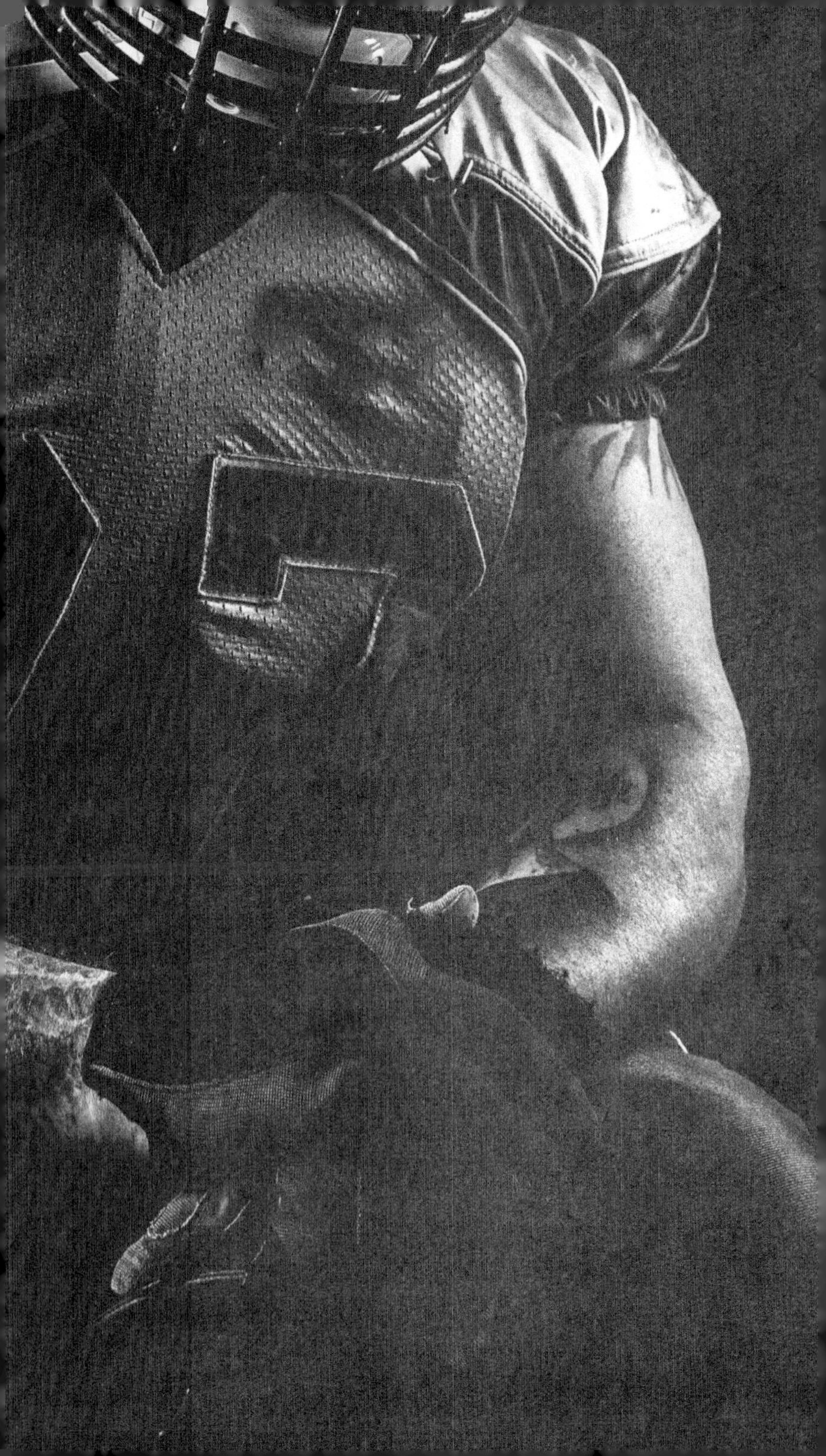

CHAPTER TWENTY-FOUR

Dillon

DILLON

Let me know you're ok, little crow.

DILLON

Haven't heard from you since this morning. Just wanted to know if you're free to have a chat.

DILLON

Jamie, it's been over a day. I know you've read my messages. Just reply.

DILLON

Please?

DILLON

I have no regrets. I wouldn't change a thing that happened between us. Please, Jamie. Just let me know you're ok and you don't hate me.

DILLON

You can't hide from me forever! I know where you live!

DILLON

FFS Jamie. I can't believe you're behaving like this.

DILLON

I thought I meant something to you.

DILLON

I thought you cared.

DILLON

So very mature… NOT!!

DILLON

FUCKING HELL, JAMIE! ANSWER YOUR DAMN PHONE!!!!

"Jesus." I scrubbed my hand down my face as I stared at my messages to Jamie. It had been four days since he ran from my room with tears streaming down his face. I don't think he even realized he was crying. It was like he wasn't there—he answered me on autopilot, but his mind seemed a million miles away.

I'd never considered myself capable of being a stalker before, but my actions over the last weeks have proved to the contrary. After Cory dug up everything he could on Jamie, I learned his schedule by heart. I knew where he was meant to be every hour of every day. So I've been where he should be every day, but no dice. It was like he'd become a damn ghost, and his fucking friends shut me down every time I asked about him. Their lips were sealed tighter than any vault in existence. And as much as I hated them for that, I was happy he had people that would go to bat for him without thinking.

I checked my watch as students swarmed the corridor, heading to their next class, but as my eyes ping-ponged from face to face, the one I needed to see wasn't there. Jamie had five minutes before Velecote would start the lesson and considering the way he had it out for Jamie has only gotten worse, I prayed he'd make it on time. I heaved a sigh and pushed my damp hair out of my eyes. Tension rippled through my muscles, making the ache from practice intensify.

I leaned against the wall opposite our room, ankles crossed and arms folded over my chest. The volume of people had rapidly decreased in the last couple of minutes. I was just about to head in when the doors at the end crashed into the wall, the sound reverberating through the nearly silent corridor. My head snapped up, and my eyes latched on to Jamie. Even in his flustered state, he was still the most beautiful thing I'd ever seen. His bag was slung over his shoulder, and his cheeks were flushed like he'd been running, but it was his rigid posture that set off alarm bells in my head.

"Jamie." His shoulders slumped when he turned toward me. He kept his head down, refusing to meet my eyes as he scuffed his shoes on the floor. I wasn't having this. When I was with him, he'd look me in the damn eyes. I stepped up to him, tucked my finger under his chin, and nudged it up until he was forced to look at me. His eyes were bloodshot, red rimmed, and seemed to vibrate with anxious energy.

That look alone had some of the anger in me abating, but like the surging tides, a new wave of emotion threatened to pull me under. Someone had made him cry. Someone had hurt him that wasn't me, and there was no lifetime where that was acceptable. He was mine. *Mine.* Anger and fury coiled through me. I would make whoever had made him feel this way pay. I touched my tongue to my teeth, shut my eyes, and counted down from ten in a futile attempt to control myself.

"Where have you been, little crow?" I growled and breathed in his sweet caramel scent. With each deep inhale, color filtered back into the world and something that had been missing slotted back into place. He was here, with me. My little crow. Mine.

Jamie wrenched his head from my grasp and cast a surreptitious glance up and down the corridor before his eyes flicked to the door to our class. Mr. Velecote was just entering the far end of the building, talking to some blonde woman. I couldn't make out who she was, and quite frankly, I didn't give a shit. My attention was wholly focused on Jamie.

Clearing his throat, he pulled his phone from his pocket and turned off an alarm. "Going in there." He nodded to the door and turned away from me.

I grabbed hold of his bag to stop him walking away from me. No one turned their back on me or dismissed me like that. "Not like that, you're not," I growled and stepped up behind him. My hand touched his side, and Jamie jumped a mile in the air.

"What the hell did you do that for?" He spun around, breaking my hold on him. His chest heaved and he narrowed his eyes at me.

"I want answers." Jamie scoffed, stalked away from me, and had his hands wrapped around the handle when I said, "I want you to sit with me today."

He froze but didn't look back at me as I closed the distance between us. "Thanks, but I'll pass."

I leaned into his back and had to bite back a groan at the feel of his body heat seeping into me. "I mean it. He gave you shit last time. The least you can do is sit with me."

"How do you know? You're not even in this—"

"I said I was, so I am," I countered. "If you paid more attention to the rest of the room, you might have seen me." Watching Jamie from afar was mesmerizing, but it had nothing on how it felt to be the center of his all-consuming attention. That was fucking addictive.

"Yeah, sure," he mocked. He was acting like a petulant little child. Was he going to stomp his foot next? It took everything in me to smother the grin that was tugging at my lips when I felt the fight drain out of him.

"Don't believe me?" I breathed against his ear, and he shuddered. I reached around him and opened the door. Mr. Velecote's footsteps were growing louder by the second. "I'll prove it to you. But Jamie?" He stepped into the room but glanced at me over his shoulder, chewing on his bottom lip and disbelief shimmering in his eyes. "Next time you dismiss me like that, I'll punish you."

An indigent squeak slipped from him and this time, I chuckled. I placed my hand at the small of his back and steered him into the lecture hall. Tension radiated off Jamie as every set of eyes followed our progress and hushed whispers broke out. I ignored them, and when he went to sit in his usual seat, I wrapped my hand around his wrist and hauled him up the steps to where I sat. Confusion flickered across his face, and his mouth opened to question me, but I shook my head at him, and it snapped shut.

"Move," I grumbled at the guy in a beanie who'd taken the seat next to mine.

"Aww, man, really?" I glared at him so he'd get the fucking message. He jumped up like I'd lit his ass on fire, and my lips twitched.

Jamie scoffed. "You're such a dick. You know that?"

"I do. Sit." I nodded to the seat next to mine and waited. "Jamie." The command in my voice had him slumping down next to me just as Velecote walked into the room. Jamie busied himself getting set up, resolutely ignoring me. That was fine. He was where I could see him, and it calmed the rage simmering too close to the surface. I'd get the answers I wanted, whether he liked it or not. I could be patient and bide my time. I've had five years worth of practice, after all.

The lesson was boring as fuck as Velecote droned on in his monotone voice. It made my ears bleed. Jamie huffed and puffed, but every time I looked at him, his eyes were glued to the images on the whiteboard. Not at me. Never at me. It made my jaw tic. I wanted his eyes on me like there were on my birthday.

"Make sure your notes are up to date as I'll be clearing the board in two minutes." Velecote said. "Then, I want you to watch a short presentation on our next topic." The lights started to dim as he cleared the board off. *Shit.* I'd have to get the work from someone else as I'd ignored everything else in the room but the perfect boy next to me.

"Are you going to talk to me?" I leaned into his personal space, inhaled his delicious scent, and ran my knuckle down his cheek. Fire-filled eyes bore into mine before darting to the font of the room.

"Eventually," Jamie said, making that admission sound like it'd cost him more than I knew. "There's a lot we need to talk about." His words made me shiver, because he wasn't wrong. There was a fuck ton of skeletons and secrets between us, but that didn't stop my single-minded focus. Jamie was mine—any other outcome was unacceptable.

"Is there something you'd like to share with your fellow students, Mr. Bowen?" Velecote's voice boomed in the now silent room. You could have heard a pin drop. But all I could focus on was the hitch in Jamie's breathing and the tremor running through his body.

"No sir. I just—"

"That's enough. Eyes front, or I'll make you stay behind after class."

I clenched my fist tight enough to snap the pen I was holding, and a growl rumbled my chest. "That fucker—"

Jamie's hand landed on my arm, stealing my focus. It was only then that I realized I was halfway out of my seat. "It's alright, big guy." His tentative voice shook me to the core. "He's just got it out for me. Not everyone is gonna like me, you know that." But they did, and that was the problem. He was the walking definition of sunshine—kind, sweet, and caring. He'd give the shirt off his back to a stranger if they needed it. He was the best of humanity wrapped up in one perfect package, and he'd chosen me. Fate was a cruel fucking master. My chest ached as guilt wrapped around my heart.

I scrubbed my hand down my face and whispered to myself, "What the fuck have I done?"

This is all my fault, and I felt like shit because of it. I had to speak to the guys and call this off. Things had gone too far already; involving the faculty had never been part of the plan. Stevens had a lot to answer for. That bastard was avoiding me even more than that fuckface Chad was. Guilt decimated me. It was like being stabbed repeatedly in the heart by a rusty blade and unable to escape. I created this shitstorm and I had to fix it—without him finding out before I could tell him.

"Oh my god, that's him."

"He sure can take it."

"What a whore."

The room felt electrically charged, and Jamie froze next to me. My gut plummeted through my feet as mocking laughter echoed around us. I pulled out of my meandering thoughts and nearly threw up in my mouth when my eyes locked on the image on the board. "Fucking hell. I'm going to puke." The words were out before I could stop them. Jamie flinched before packing up his stuff.

I couldn't tear my eyes away from the image on the screen. Someone had very skillfully manipulated a still from either a porn site or an Only Fans account. It was as hot as it was fucking disturbing. Jamie being double penetrated by two massive guys—bulging glistening muscles and all—with his head thrown back in ecstasy while they held his lithe body between them as they kissed over his shoulder. The words "FUCKING LITTLE FAGGOT" were written above the image. I knew this was fake, but fuck, who ever did this had done an amazing job.

My heart pounded like a war drum. I was out for fucking

blood. I didn't care how many bones I'd have to break. I'd find out who did this. The noise volume rose exponentially as Jamie retched beside me. My hand shot out to hold his, but my eyes remained resolutely focused. I knew he was a virgin. It was the singularly most spectacular moment of my life when I sank into his tight heat. When he gave all of himself to me—it was a gift from fucking heaven. I finally understood why sex had made my skin crawl before, but I'd done it to make sure I fitted in. That my secret was safe. But with Jamie, it was life-altering. Life affirming. It was like coming home after being lost for years.

"D-Dil." His broken voice shattered my heart. Tears spilled down his face as the rest of the room howled with laughter and snapped pictures of him. "I..."

"I've got you, baby." I cupped his face and rested my forehead on his. I felt like I was the king of the word when he sighed and melted into me. "Let's get out of here." Jamie stumbled on legs that wouldn't hold him as I snatched up our bags and led him down the stairs to the door.

"Where do you think you're going, Mr. Bowen?" The accusatory tone in Velecote's voice had me seeing red. I wanted to rearrange his face with my fist until he was unrecognizable. Jamie's shattered whimper held me back.

"We're leaving. I'll ensure the dean hears about this." Without waiting to hear his response, I guided Jamie from the room before he had to endure anymore of that shit. His legs collapsed as the door slammed shut, and the silence in the corridor was a welcome reprieve.

"I... I d-didn't... D-Dil—"

"I know, baby. That image was photoshopped. I'll find out who did it and make sure all traces of it are deleted." His watery smile gutted me. I hated that he was hurting. Hurting because of me. Because people had gone wild and turned this into so much more than it was ever intended to be. I couldn't wait for the day I left this place, and if I had my way, I'd be taking Jamie with me.

"Dil." He cupped my cheek with a shaky hand and licked his lips. "Make me forget. *Please.*" I kissed his forehead as tears poured down his cheeks. His agony and humiliation saturated the air.

"I will, little crow." I adjusted him in my arms so he could wrap his legs around my hips. Luckily, classes ran for another twenty minutes, which would give me enough time to get him squared away in my dorm. "First, I need to get you out of here and somewhere safe."

"Okay. I trust you." *Fuck, baby, I wish you didn't.* The countdown timer was dangerously close to zero, and I prayed I wouldn't be one of the casualties when it detonated.

CHAPTER TWENTY-FIVE

Jamie

"Jamie, you're being unreasonable!"

"The hell I am, Uncle Daire. I'm *fine*. Everything is *fine*." I'm the biggest goddamn liar who's ever lied. Everything was so not fine. I wanted to buy a cabin in the woods and never see another person again. I fucking hated the world. I couldn't leave my dorm without people pointing, whispering, and laughing about me. After that damn calculus class, that image had been everywhere. It went around Briar U like wildfire between students and faculty alike. Dillon somehow found someone to remove the digital footprint as I'd heard it was doing the rounds on social media platforms. Thank fuck I didn't have any social media accounts, but once it's out in the world, it's never really gone. No matter how many times Dillon said it was taken care of, I still see it every time I close my eyes.

My life felt like a David and Goliath battle, but unlike

David, I didn't have a sling full of stones. I only had myself, and I wasn't exactly made for war. I wanted to vanish. I wanted to disappear so completely, not even I would remember myself. No feelings. No memories. Just the freedom of oblivion.

With a heavy sigh that made me imagine him pinching his nose, Uncle Daire tried to reason with me again. "I'm not saying you need to lock yourself in your room or anything. I just need you to take precautions—"

"I know, I know." I cut him off and plopped down on my bed with a bounce. My eyes burned with the depth of emotion I kept pushing down. I'd face it one day, but today wasn't that day.

"I'm not sure you do, Jamie." His voice grew deeper and sterner with every word. "Your father was seen at Clara's old house. The. One. You. Lived. In!"

"I know. I heard you, but I'm not there anymore. I left nothing behind. Your team swept the place and did a deep clean. Nothing would have been left behind for him to trace us with."

"That's true, but—"

"You also said you had the school records wiped. So again, there's nothing there." He sighed again. A loud thud echoed down the phone line, making me jump. "Did you just hit something?"

"You're driving me crazy, you little shit." I could hear his smirk in his voice as he chastised me.

"I know I do." I carded my hands through my damp hair, pulling it hard enough to hurt. I wanted to scream and cry. To punch something. I wanted to fight for once and not have to run. I wanted to be brave, but I felt like a coward.

Guilt weighed heavily on me for taking my frustration out on him. It wasn't Uncle Daire's fault I'd spent the last five years in witness protection, running from my dad. It wasn't his fault that I'd never been able to stay in one place long enough to make real friends and have a life that didn't involve looking over my shoulder. But I did now. I had so much more. And what he just told me made it feel like my chance at a life was about to be ripped away again.

"I know it's hard, Jamie. I really do. But this i my job—"

"And it's my FUCKING LIFE!" I shouted loud enough for anyone in the corridor to have heard me. The tears I'd been trying to hold back burst free, carving agony into my flushed skin. "I just... I... want it to be over." A wave of exhaustion washed over me, and my eyes fluttered closed.

"I know, kid. This has been a long time coming, but it's good news."

"How the hell is this good news, Uncle Daire?"

"He's slipped up, Jamie. We've seen him. That means we can track him and finally put the fucker behind bars for what he put you and your mom through. God rest her soul."

"Yeah. But..." I licked my lips, tasting the salt of my tears on them as words failed me. It all felt so pointless. It turned out my dad was good at hiding, so good he deserved a medal. In the last five years, there'd been six sightings of him. The last one was after Mom's funeral, and that was two years ago.

"It'll be over soon kid, I promise."

"I hope so, 'cause I'm not sure how much longer I can live like this without going insane."

"I know, kid. Trust me, I do."

"I do trust you. It's just—"

"I know." His mournful tone made me want my mom. I wanted to cry in her arms and have her run her fingers through my hair and tell me it was all going to be alright. My mom had a super power—she could fix anything—and oh, how I needed her strength right now.

"She'd be so damn proud of who you've become, Jamie." How did he know I was thinking of her? "Just keep the burner with you at all times, alright? I'm sending some boys your way to watch over you." My breath hitched at the thought Dad might finally be ready to carry out what he threatened all those years ago. "I won't let it come to that. I promise."

"Don't make promises you can't keep, Uncle Daire."

"I don't intend to break this one, JJ. Look I've gotta go, kid. Keep safe and keep your wits about you. Take care."

"HOLY SHIT, angel! I'm so fucking sorry you're going through this." Ava sat with her legs crossed at the end of my bed. Tears pooled in her eyes as her hand cupped her mouth, shock written across her features.

"Now I get why you always changed the subject when I asked about your family." Mal hiccuped a sob and wrapped his arm tighter around my shoulders. Thank god we were leaning against my headboard. If I'd have been standing, my legs would have buckled, and I'd have collapsed.

This had been the most painful conversation I'd ever had to have with someone who wasn't family, who hadn't heard about it first-hand from my mom. Having to witness their reactions gutted me. I was terrified they'd look at me differently. Judge me. Fear me. Recognize what being around me now represented.

I sucked in a shuddering breath and dried my eyes with the back of my trembling hand. "S-so, now you can see why I don't really feel up to going to the Halloween party."

"Oh, angel."

"JJ, we completely understand. Do you want us to stay in with you?" Ava nodded as Mal spoke.

"N-no," I rasped. Mal reached over and grabbed my water off my desk. The cool liquid felt amazing as it soothed my sore throat. "I don't want my life to impact yours. I don't want to be a burden or put you in danger any more than I already have."

"JJ, you're not a burden."

I felt like one. What college kid wanted a friend like me? I reached up and squeezed Mal's hand where it rested on my shoulder. "Go! Go have fun and then fill me in later."

"Are you sure?" He looked into my eyes, searching for the truth in my words.

"Yeah, I will be. Just gonna grab some food and come straight back here."

"We can—"

"Ava, no. Thanks, but no. You guys need to go to the party. You've put far too much effort into your costumes. You both look amazing, and I don't want you to have wasted all the effort you put in."

A small smile played across her black lips, and she nodded. "Okay. If you need us, text me."

"I will." I hugged each of them, holding them a little longer and tighter than I would normally. I felt raw and exposed. "Now go and have fun." I pasted a wavering smile on my face and willed the tears flooding my eyes not to fall. With a final hug from Mal, they were off down the corridor, leaving me all alone.

I breathed a sigh of relief when the door snicked shut and flopped face down on my bed. I hadn't come to the decision lightly to tell them what was going on, but if anyone was going to notice the change in me, they would. Not only because they spent so much time with me, but also because they paid attention where others didn't. They'd have noticed if I started acting weirdly. So I went with the lesser of two evils and just prayed that being my friend wouldn't hurt them.

After a quick nap, I felt strong enough to piece myself back together and put on the armor I wore every day. I wasn't about to let my dad's ghost ruin my time here at Briar U, even if it was only fleeting. I might have more to lose than I ever have before but that also meant I had so much more to fight for. I just had to work out how to fight someone I couldn't see.

I hurried out of my dorm building and across the quad, wrapping my arms around my middle as the full moon peaked out from behind the dark clouds dusting. Campus was eerily quiet due to Halloween, as the majority of students were at The Cave for their legendary All Hallows Eve Rave. I only had ten minutes to get to Bean There before they shut. I'd discovered by accident one night that they discounted all the pastries that weren't sold during the day just before closing, and one of the best things to eat after baring my emotional damage was sugar-covered confectionery. I wasn't fussy as long as it was sweet, sticky, and yummy.

"Stop being such a wimp, JJ," I scolded myself for jumping when the streetlight above me flickered. "It's just your mind playing tricks on you." I wrapped my coat tightly around myself, my breath fogging around me like a cloud. The temperature had started to drop the last few days, and today it was even more noticeable. The wind bit at my cheeks, making them burn as it blew through the trees and the sound of dry leaves skittering along the sidewalk made the hairs on the back of my neck stand on end.

I was being paranoid, twitching at every little sound like someone was about to jump out at me and drag me into a bush. Uncle Daire's call had messed with my head, and I kinda hated him for it. The snap of a branch behind me had my steps faltering and my heart racing. I slowly turned around to face the direction the sound came from, but I couldn't see anything but a solid wall of darkness.

"Seriously, pull yourself together." The words froze on the tip of my tongue as a glowing face appeared in the darkness. Large orange eyes that looked like they were illuminated by the fires of hell, and a wide open mouth with sharp teeth stared back at me. The head tilted to the side in a psycho serial killer move, and my blood turned to ice. My breath caught in my throat, and I wrapped a hand around my bare throat and felt my Adam's apple grated against my palm.

Consumed by fear my feet were welded to the ground. I was screaming at myself to move but no amount of self flagellation seemed to make my body cooperate. Time seemed to slow down as the glowing head floated toward me. Seconds ticked by as it got closer and closer, and all I could do was stare at it as I stood completely immobile.

My heart hammered, its thundering echoed in my ears, my eyes locked on the face moving closer to me. When it was on the verge of breaking through the shadows, it stopped. A hysterical cackle burst from me as it cocked its head to the side again like an evil movie villain.

The weight of their gaze was tangible. My body vibrated with fear, while adrenaline flooded my system. I waited for my fight or flight instinct to kick in but it didn't. A piercing whistle sounded in the distance, making me jump like I'd been electrocuted. The sudden movement made my aching muscles burn.

"Run!"

A scream tore its way out of my throat at the distorted voice emanating from the masked figure. They stepped into the pool of light stretching across the ground from the nearest streetlight. Instead of moving, I shook my head as tears pricked my itchy eyes.

"This is your last chance. Run, or I will hurt you." I shook my head again, trying valiantly to convince myself this was a joke. That it wasn't real. That I was tucked up in my bed.

"You were told to run." I whipped around to see an eerily similar mask, this one in blue, coming from the other side of the sidewalk.

"I...I..." I clenched my fists hard enough for my blunt nails to sink into the flesh of my palms. That bite of pain was enough to clear my foggy mind and unlock my body, and feeling slowly came back to me.

"Time to run, boy toy," Orange Mask goaded, inching closer.

"This is going to be so much fun." Blue Mask tipped their head back and howled like a wolf. "I'm going to enjoy hearing you scream."

"F-fuck... y-you," I gritted out, my heart beating so fast I thought it was going to explode.

"Oh, no. It's you that's fucked." Orange Mask cackled, the static quality to their distorted voice fueling the fear blooming inside me. Like a scene from a horror movie, more and more illuminated masks of different colors appeared in the darkness surrounding me. They moved as one, closing the distance between us, leaving one clear escape route open to me.

"Fuck!" I whimpered, squeezed my eyes shut, took a deep inhale, and counted to three. I cast a final glance around, counting ten masks surrounding me, then turned on my heel and ran. I was running blind. I didn't know where to go as I whipped past the campus buildings. The quad seemed darker than it should. It took my brain too long to realize the majority of the streetlights were out. No one could see me being chased. And it hit me then. No one would be coming to save me. I was alone.

Catcalls, whistles, and screams bayed for my blood. They were hot on my heels, their thundering feet making the ground shake beneath me as I tried to escape them. I might not have been able to see that well, but I knew I was getting closer to the sports fields. Chancing a glance over my shoulder, my heart shot up my throat as the number of masks chasing me had doubled. They fanned out into a semicircle, herding me like cattle.

I pumped my legs, my muscles bunching as I pushed them as hard and fast as I could. Breaths sawed in and out of my throat, slicing into my lungs as every inhale felt like swallowing shards of ice. I clenched my fists as my arms swung at my side, determined to get away from the masked hoard chasing me.

"Run, little faggot."

"I found you!"

"You're going to regret ever coming here."

"Run, little rabbit, run."

"Shut up! Shut up! Shut up!" I screamed. Tears flowed freely from my eyes as a wave of boiling hot nausea flushed through me. I bent over double and braced my hand on a tree as the contents of my stomach surged up my throat. Their thundering feet on the ground sounded like a cavalry charge.

They were hunting and I was the prey.

I wiped my face with the back of my hand, swirled spit around my mouth, and spat out the acidic taste burning my taste buds. I almost swallowed my tongue when I caught sight of more figures all dressed in black racing through the shadows. When they hit the path, I did the only thing I could do.

I ran like my life depended on it.

CHAPTER TWENTY-SIX

Jamie

I might not be the fastest runner—god knows I wasn't built for sports—but I was fast when I needed to be. I was small and agile, so I used my build to my advantage. As I neared the sports courts, I slipped between the chain link fences that separated two of the tennis courts and dropped to my knees, hiding behind the low solid wall separating the courts. I leaned back against it, sucking in a heaving breath to center myself.

I counted to ten before rolling onto my stomach and commando crawled along the patch of dirt, praying I could get to the little shack before anyone found me. Grit bit into my hands and scraped along my stomach through my clothes, and my knees felt like they were bleeding. Every time I moved, pain eddied through my body, pulling a whimper from deep inside me. In the silence of the night I could hear them as they swarmed around me over the thudding of my heart in my ears.

By the time I reached the end of the courts, I was covered in sweat. The distant sounds of my hunters' shouts as they moved farther down the fields let me breathe a momentary sigh of relief. "You've got this," I whispered to myself as I pushed up onto my feet.

Not knowing how much time I had before they came back here looking for me, I ran blindly in the direction of the rundown groundskeeper's storage building and prayed to every god in existence that I'd get there before I was caught.

"He can't be far away." A distorted voice sounded way too close to comfort, and my heart shot up my throat. The cloud covering the moon cleared enough for me to see four figures dressed head to toe in black heading towards me.

"It's now or never.'" I gritted my teeth, dug deep into my mental reserves, and ran with everything I had. My vision blurred as sweat dripped down my face. The building was within touching distance when cold hard dread slithered down my spine.

"He went that way."

"Quick, I can see him!"

My leg buckled underneath me and I crashed into the corner of the building. White spots burst in front of my eyes as I fell to the ground just outside the open door. "Shit." I bit down on my lip and dragged myself though the small opening and quickly sat with my back to it. My hands were shaking so violently, it was almost impossible to get the bolt across the door. My slick fingers couldn't grip it, but by the grace of a god I didn't believe in, it snicked shut before vomit filled my mouth and coated the floor.

My phone vibrated in my pocket, and the screen lit up through my pants. For the first time in what seemed like hours, I thought I might be able to get out of this without getting seriously hurt. I needed help. I desperately needed someone to come and save me from this nightmare. "Fuck!" I whispered as it slipped out of my hand and cracked on the cement floor. *Please, please, please, don't be broken.*

"He was just over here."

My heart beat so hard, even my eyeballs pulsed. The grass crunched under their feet as they drew closer. I held my breath and covered my mouth with my hand so I didn't make a sound. The door behind me groaned, and I jerked when they threw themselves against it."Fuck. It's locked."

"Is there another door?"

"No, there's just that one. And if it's locked he can't be in there. Only Jerry has the key."

"Alright, let's move on. He can't have gotten far."

Sweat poured down my temples and dripped into my eyes. My tee clung to me under my hoodie and coat, my body drenched in perspiration. My fear permeated the room as I shook uncontrollably. My lungs burned from lack of oxygen, but I held my breath until the only thing I could hear was silence before letting out a ragged exhale.

I blindly patted the ground, trying to find my phone. My fingers brushed the metal case, and I wept tears of joy. I grabbed it and called the only person I could think about. The only one that mattered. I knew in my heart he'd do anything for me.

"Hello?"

"D-Dillon?" I croaked, my dry mouth and thick tongue making it almost impossible to get my words out.

"Little crow? What's wrong? Where are you?"

"I-I n-need you... h-help."

"Where are you?"

My breath caught in my throat, and it felt like it was closing up. I shook my head, unable to answer him as fresh tears scolded my face. "I...I..." Anxiety ripped through me, my lungs protesting as I tried to suck in air. I was hyperventilating and shaking. Dillon's crackled curses were the only thing I could focus on as the world closed in around me.

"Shit! Baby? Can you hear me? I'm coming. I'm coming. Just stay on the line." Silent tears poured down my face. "Even if you can't talk, I need to hear you breathing." He sounded frantic. Doors crashed. Footsteps echoed. His panted breaths rasped through the static of the line. "Just keep breathing, baby. I'm coming."

I clutched my phone to my heart and kept pressing the screen so it stayed lit up. I'd never been a fan of the dark, but tonight had just turned my fear into something real. I pulled my legs up to my chest and wrapped my arms around them. It felt like the world was swaying around me, the floor moving in the opposite direction to the walls. I buried my face into my knees and tried to focus on my breathing.

"JAMIE, CAN YOU HEAR ME?"

Not like this. Not like this. Not like this. Not like this. Not like this. Not like this.

"Jamie, baby. I need you to open your eyes and look at me. Please. *Please,* show me your beautiful eyes."

Not like this. Not like this. Not like this. Not like this. Not like this. Not like this.

Soft lips brushed across my face, the gentle rasp of stubble against my skin sending shock waves through me, making my breath hitch in my throat. But something had sunk its claws into me and refused to let me. I was screaming inside my head but couldn't move.

Not like this. Not like this. Not like this. Please not like this. Not like this. Not like this.

"Little crow...p-please... come back to me. I need you. I'm so, so sorry."

Please, please, not like this. Not like this. Not like this. Please not like this. Not like this.

"I never meant for this to happen." Agony laced his thick words and pulled at something deep inside me. My pain recognised his; we were like twin embers fighting against the darkness that wanted to extinguish our light.

"I was scared, baby. So fucking scared that you being here would ruin everything. I never meant to hurt you. I'm sorry." The sound of flesh hitting flesh made me flinch. "Shit. Sorry. I didn't mean to scare you."

Not like this. Please, please, please not like this. Not like this. Not like this. Please not like this.

"Oh, god. I need you to stop shaking. You're freezing cold. Wet with sweat. If you can hear me, little crow, I'm going to strip you off and put you in the shower. I'm going to hold you in my arms until you come back to me."

It was like an out-of-body experience. Dillon's gravelly voice was muted and distant. I was vaguely aware of what he was doing to me, but I couldn't react. I was trapped inside my body, but it didn't feel like mine anymore. I was just a passenger pushed into the background.

His words percolated through my mind. *I was so scared you'd ruin everything.* Darkness claimed me even though I fought against it. *I never meant for this to happen.* A barely perceptible echo of his pain felt like a razor blade slicing across my skin.

"I'm sorry."

Nothing.

"I never meant to hurt you."

Nothing.

My body ached, every muscle burning even though I was caught in that barely conscious state when your brain didn't know if you were awake or still dreaming. My mind felt heavy, like something important weighed it down, but that knowledge was just out of reach. But the existential dread clawing at my lungs was all I needed to know.

"Hey there, my beautiful boy. Are you back with me?" Heat flushed through me, concealing the way I ached, and I peeled my eyelids back. I winced as the air hit them. Each blink felt like I was scraping sandpaper over them, making them water.

"D-Dil?"

"I've got you. I'm never fucking letting go." He was wrapped around me, legs entangled with mine, and arms enveloping my middle, holding my back to his chest. His fingers bit into my skin and even though it hurt, I melted into him. I felt safe.

"You came for me?"

A pained sound cut through the quiet of his room. "I will always come for you, Jamie." He sounded like he'd swallowed glass, like every word hurt to say. "Always." He kissed a path across my bare shoulder and buried his face into the crook of my neck. His shuddering inhale rolled through me. I felt it everywhere.

"I was s-so scared." My eyes stung, and my tongue stuck to the roof of my mouth, but it was imperative I got the words out before they burned me to the ground. "What did I do to them to make them hate me so much?"

Dillon's hold slackened like he was withdrawing into himself. His heart beat through his chest into mine, each one shattering me from the inside out."I-I don't—"

"Don't lie to me, Dillon. I've always been able to tell when you lie." He slipped out of the bed, and I immediately felt his loss. I was cold, bereft. I closed my eyes and fought the mountain of emotion rising inside me and focused on the sound of his feet shuffling on the floor, the rasp of material on his skin as he pulled on clothes. His erratic, labored breathing. His weighted sigh hung heavily over us.

It was suffocating.

I was like a soldier on the front line, not knowing if these were my final moments.

Memories of last night flicked through my mind, a broken movie montage that didn't make sense. It didn't happen to me, did it? Dillon's broken voice was the only thing I could focus on as the images in my head faded into the fog.

"I never meant for this to happen."

"I never meant to hurt you."

"I'm sorry."

"What did you do?" I rolled over, sat up, and shuffled in his bed until my back rested against the headboard. Naked apart from boxers—his—I felt too exposed, so I pulled the sheet up and tucked it under my arms. "Dillon?" My fractured voice was whisper soft, but his head whipped up like I'd struck him. Tears shimmered and clung to his lashes as oceans of pain raged in the dark depths of his eyes. "What's wrong? Talk to me."

Dillon blinked up at me through unseeing eyes and for once, I was grateful for the distance between us. He sat on his desk chair with his elbows braced on his knees. His chin rested on steepled fingers, and his lips trembled as the first tear fell from his wide eyes. "Just know that I love you, little crow. Always have. Always will." *I love you too.* But I didn't have the strength to give credence to my thoughts.

I'd dreamed about the first time Dillon told me he loved me. I expected to feel the kind of euphoria addicts talk about. I never expected to feel like this—like he was shredding my soul with his bare hands. I tilted my head to the side and waited for him to finish. I could tell there was more he left unsaid. Like an iceberg with hidden depths, he'd only given me a crumb of what lied beneath.

Dillon sat up in his chair with his head tipped back and stared at the ceiling. His chest rose and fell with shallow pants. Fingers carded through his hair until he yanked it hard enough for the strands to break before fisting them in his lap. "That night when I first..." He shook his head and tried again. "I hated you! Hated you so much! Fucking hated you and everything you stood for! And then you turned up here and looked at me with those pale-blue eyes." He clenched his jaw, and a muscle ticked in his cheek.

I sucked in a sharp inhale that burned my lungs and opened my mouth.

"Don't. I have to get this out." I shook as his pain lanced right through me. "You fucking left me. You kissed me, then fucking disappeared." An inhuman noise tore from his lips and tears flowed down his cheeks like a river. His red-rimmed eyes chipped away at my heart. "Did I mean so fucking little to you that you could just walk away and treat me like I was nothing?"

"No," I gasped, my hand reaching for him. He flinched even though he was on the other side of the room. "It wasn't like that." I licked my lips, tasting the pain of my salty tears. "That's not what happened—"

"How would I fucking know?!" He threw himself out of his chair, stalking across his room like a caged beast ready to explode. "YOU. LEFT. ME," he bellowed. "You left me, and I had no one. I was all alone with my pain." He punched the wall, his fist going straight through the drywall. "Five fucking years, Jamie." He moved toward me with blood dripping down his fist and a snarl curling his lips. Eyes that only moments ago looked at me with nothing but seething hate.

"That's not what happened," I cried. "You need to listen to me," I begged. Fear coiled around me as he ripped the sheet off my body and yanked me off the bed. I hit the floor so hard, it forced the air from my lungs.

"Five fucking years, and not a word." He wrapped my hair around his fist and yanked my head back. His whole body shook, and his rage was suffocating. "How fucking hard was it to pick up a phone and called me? To write me a letter and explain why you fucking broke me?"

"I couldn't." I whimpered as he dragged me across the floor. "I wasn't allowed to."

"What the fuck does that mean?" Reproach flooded his face, and he dropped me like I'd burned him.

"I w-wasn't allowed to contact you." I sobbed, curling into the fetal position at his feet. "We were put into witness protection. My dad tried t-to..." The memories of that night hit, and I couldn't talk. They stole me away from a seething Dillon and pillaged my mind with the darkest moments of my life I'd tried to forget. I was drowning.

"Shit, baby. I'm so sorry. I didn't know." The air moved when he fell to his knees. "Jamie, p-please." I flinched when he touched me, and an agonized sound wrenched from my chest.

"D-Don't... t-touch m-me."

"I'm sorry. Fuck! I'm so—"

"Your words mean nothing to me now," I whispered. "T-tell me what you meant last night by y-you didn't m-mean it to go this far."

Dillon's frozen face contorted in the most gut-wrenching pain, as if what he was about to say would cost him everything. "It was me." He crumbled before my eyes. The mountain fell. "I wanted to make you pay for everything you've done to me. I told them to hurt you. An eye for an eye."

"No." Every word he said landed like a killing blow to my heart. It wasn't meant to be like this. I didn't know if I'd survive this, survive him and the way he broke us. I'd lost so much already, and his betrayal was like the final nail in my coffin.

I didn't know how I did it, but I tied my shattered pieces back together and threw on the first clothes I found discarded on the floor. I was shaking so violently I could barely see and crawled to the door, my heart nothing but scattered ashes on the floor. My hand latched on to the handle, and I hauled myself up. My legs buckled, too weak to hold me up.

"JAMIE!" he roared as I fell through the door and crashed into the one across the hallway. "COME BACK!"

"No," I cried as the maelstrom of my emotions pulled me under and started to run as the world fractured around me. His pounding footfalls followed me, but I refused to look back.

"Jamie, come back..."

I tripped over my bare feet, knees crashing to the ground. Pain lanced through me as I gritted my teeth and pushed myself up. I couldn't breathe, couldn't think. I couldn't be near him. I couldn't look at him anymore. Not when all I saw were broken dreams and bleeding hearts.

"I didn't know—"

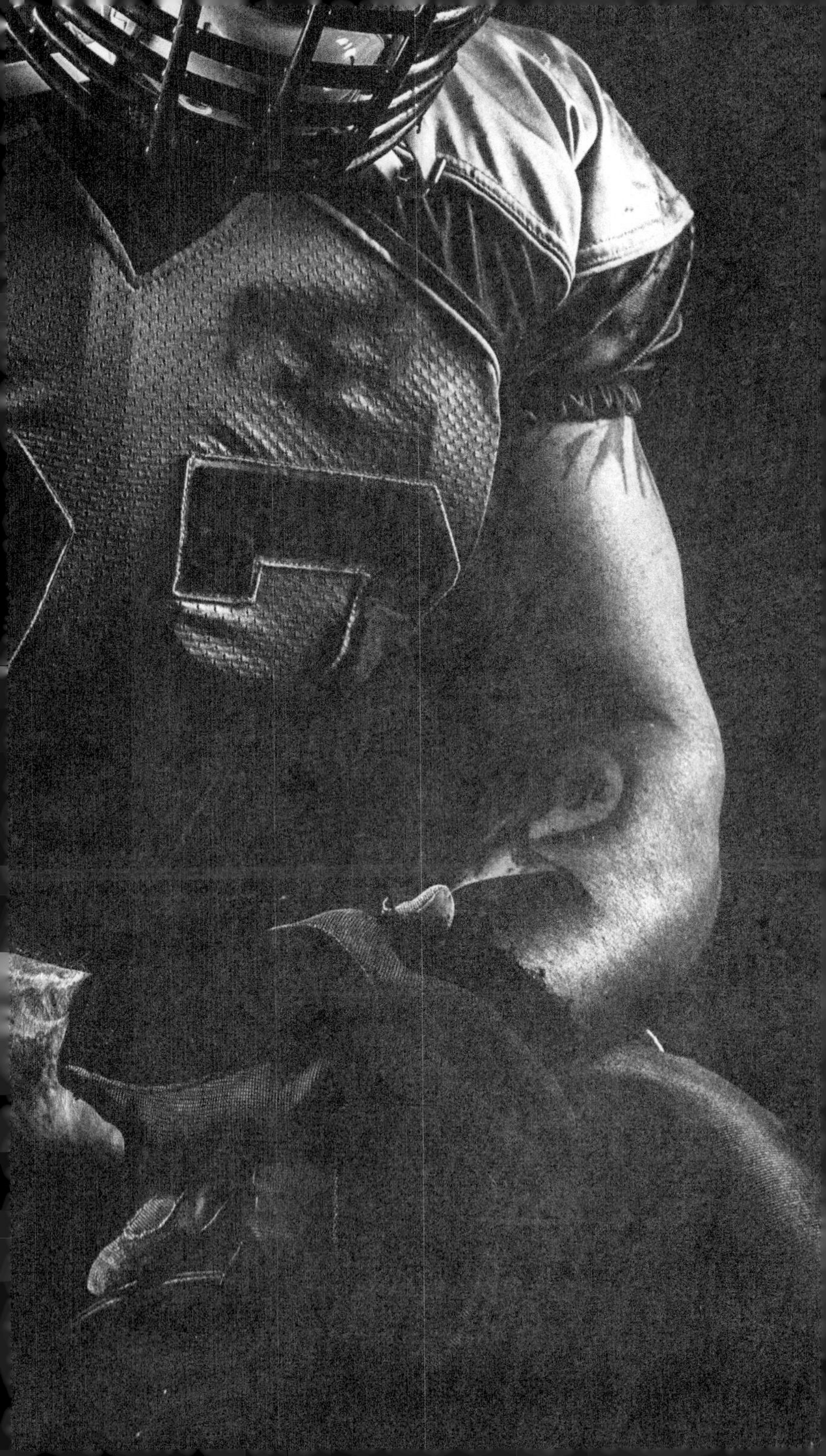

CHAPTER TWENTY-SEVEN

Dillon

"I didn't know..." The finality of the door to the stairwell slamming shut was like a bullet through my heart. I thought I knew what it felt like to have my heart broken five years ago, but that pain was nothing but a dull echo of what consumed me now.

My heart froze in my chest as I fell to my knees, my hands reaching out to him, my fingers clinging on to nothing but air. "What have I done? What have I done?"

"Hey, Dillon. Come on, man, let's get you out of here." I shook my head. I didn't care anymore. I didn't want to exist in a world where he didn't. It was like he'd died and taken a part of me with him when he ran from me. In the silence he left behind, I finally understood how someone could die while still breathing.

I didn't want to breathe anymore.

What was the point?

"Dillon," B growled in my ear as he wrapped his arms around my chest and tried to pull me to my feet. "You weigh a damn ton. Help me get you up. I need to fix your hand again, you idiot."

"What's the point?" I rasped. "He left me..." Shame swallowed me whole, and the last remnants of the adrenaline I'd been running on faded away, leaving me hollow and cold.

"I'm not discussing this with you here."

His words were a harsh slap in the face. "Fuck off, Taylor. Just leave me alone." I was a piece of shit. He didn't deserve my anger, but he was there, and he'd take it like a champ.

"No. You're my friend whether you like it or not, and I'm here for you, no matter how many times you tell me to fuck off. I'm not going anywhere. So shut the fuck up and get your ass on your feet."

"Fine," I gritted out through clenched teeth and let him haul me to my feet. It was one of the hardest things I'd ever done, picking myself off that floor. Letting go of that last lingering connection between us. Every time I closed my eyes, I could see his face, tear-stained and broken.

"Your room or mine?" he asked. His assessing gaze cataloged my face, but I didn't care if he saw my tears or pain.

"Yours. I can't go back to mine yet. It hurts too much." All I wanted to do was go and hunt Jamie down so I could beg him to forgive me for the way I'd treated him. For how I'd lashed out at him. I'd promised never to hurt him. Instead, I ripped his damn heart out and crushed it under my feet. I wanted to smash something to alleviate the rage boiling inside me before it twisted me into something he'd never recognize.

I wanted to do so much but I didn't know how.

"I know, big guy. The ones that hurt the most are usually the ones worth fighting for." I didn't have the capacity to process his philosophical words as he dragged my sorry ass into his room and deposited me on his desk chair. "Sit and stay."

"I'm not a fucking dog," I snapped and carded my hand through my hair.

"Then stop acting like one," he called from the bathroom. The sound of running water and his low hum filled the silence that blanketed the room. Buchanan washed my hand down with a wet cloth, then cleaned the cuts with antiseptic to stop them getting infected, grumbling when he had to pull a few splinters out with a pair of tweezers before wrapping it in a bandage.

"Thanks," I mumbled and stared down at the floor as I toed a loose bit of carpet. My mind churned, and my heart seethed. I couldn't see beyond my own failings.

Buchanan cocked his head to the side and folded his arms over his chest as he leaned against the wall opposite me. "Tell me what you need."

A lobotomy so I could forget him? A time machine so I could go back and undo everything I've ever done wrong to him? "A bullet to the brain?"

"Ha fucking ha, Dillon." He cuffed me around the head and walked over to his closet. "You have two options. Either we talk about whatever the hell just went down, or we drink and then we talk."

I didn't like either, to be honest, because the bottom line was they were the same. I'd just take a different route to get there. B was relentless once he got going. He was like a dog with a bone and would hound me until I gave him exactly what he wanted. I didn't talk about feelings and shit, not really. Not anymore. "*Hargraves don't do therapy.*" My dad's snake-like voice slithered through my mind like the poison it was. I was tired of plugging the gaping holes in the wall that I hid behind and more than anything, I needed to fix things with Jamie. I just didn't know if that was even possible.

"I could drink." B glanced at me over his shoulder, a wicked grin on his face as he pulled out a top shelf bottle of tequila. "Fuck no. That stuff is lethal."

"That's the point, my friend. Loose lips sink ships." He grabbed his laptop and sat on his bed, patting the space next to him. There wasn't much room on the queen-sized bed for the two of us, but this was something we'd done on many occasions over our time here at Briar U.

"You want to get me drunk and snuggle? You can fuck right off," I said as I shuffled over onto the bed next to him. I grabbed the bottle from where he had it propped against his leg, opened it, and swallowed the burning liquid down while he found some inane program to put on.

"Give me that," he griped, ripping the bottle from my hands and swallowing a few gulps, grimacing as it went down. "Ugh. Just because it's expensive, doesn't make it nice, does it?"

A laugh burst out of me, and I sighed before taking another drink. We spent the rest of the day passing the bottle between us and when that one finished, we moved on to another. Mixing drinks probably wasn't the most advisable thing to do in my state, but I didn't give a fuck. Everything that seemed so important at the beginning of the semester now meant nothing.

"I don't know what to do, B," I said, my words starting slurring. The sun had long since set and I'm pretty sure we'd watched every *Friends* episode once already. It all kind of blurred into the background as my mind kept going over everything that had happened this morning. How if I had done things differently, it could have been me and my little crow curled up on my bed watching shit TV programs. I wouldn't have cared, because he'd have been with me, right where he belonged.

"Well." Buchanan hiccuped. "To be able to answer that conundrum, I need to know what happened." He looked at me over his shoulder and sighed. "The truth this time, Dillon. If you even know what that is at this point."

I scoffed and stuck my middle finger up at him before

grabbing a bottle of beer from his mini fridge. "D'you want one?"

"Sure, another can't hurt." He snorted, getting stuck while taking his hoodie off. "Maybe water too."

I rolled my eyes and grabbed two before setting them on the bed next to him. "I can't fucking believe you're making me do this shit," I gritted out between clenched teeth.

"Well, as I see it, Dillon," Buchanan said as he stretched his legs out in front of him. "To be able to fix this, we need to go back to the beginning."

"I don't know what you mean." I focus on peeling the label off my bottle of beer so I don't have to look at him.

"You're not that obtuse, Hargraves. Start at the day you met him and end with today. *Capiche?*"

"I'm not fucking drunk enough for this conversation," I grouched, upending my bottle of beer and draining it in one go. The belch that ripped out of me afterward sent me into a crazed fit of hysterics. Maybe the alcohol is going to my head more than I thought. Still didn't fix a fucking thing though.

"Follow it up with this." He passed me one of those miniature bottles you find in hotel room wet bars. Without giving it too much thought, I drained it and threw it across the room. I was aiming for the trash, but it bounced off the rim instead. "And this one."

I rolled my eyes at him, uncapped it, and drank that too. "Anyone would think you're trying to get me drunk." I leaned into him and tried to cuff his shoulder with my fist, but somehow ended up catching his chin. Buchanan glowered at me before covering his face with his hand and snort laughed until tears streamed down his cheeks.

"Now that we know that you can't hit for shit, talk."

"Do I have to?" I whined and it was my turn to get clipped around the head. "What was that for?"

"Stop fucking bitching and whining and talk. I know you want my help, so spill." Ever the straight talker. Buchanan was right. I wasn't going to be able to sort out my epic fuck up without help, because god knows I was a useless prick who was only good at hurting anyone I gave a shit about. It's not like I cared about anyone but Jamie, and as far as I could tell, we were dead and buried under the Arctic Circle.

Throwing my hands up in the air, I mumbled inaudibly under my breath as I tried to gather my jumbled thoughts. "It all started when..." Other than telling Jamie the truth, this was probably the hardest thing I'd ever had to do. It felt like I was staring down the barrel of a shotgun, waiting for the buckshot to hit me in the face. The more I spoke, the easier the words came, and the deeper I looked into our intertwined history, the more I realized just how deep my feelings ran.

We'd been inseparable as children since I saved him from getting beaten up, but I'd been more than a friend; I was his protector. Eventually, I became his person. I didn't realize it, but every day we spent together, I fell a little more in love with him. Looking back, our love was inevitable, like it was written in the stars we spent long summer nights watching.

Memories, thoughts, and feelings I'd never shared with anyone passed my lips and a slightly hazy B looked at me like he had no idea who I was. As the words flowed, my mind unlocked moments I had shut away and forgotten. As each one pulled forth, it was like a brand on my heart, and another piece of me clicked back into place. I had wiped from my mind how much we used to casually touch each other—holding hands, brushing my thumb over the apple of his cheek, my hand on the back of his neck whenever we watched TV, Jamie wrapped around my back like a fucking koala, his head resting on my shoulder as he whispered in my ear, or how I would stroke my fingers through his hair. I loved how he used to wrap around me at night and rest his head on my chest. The ones that hurt the most and made my eyes burn, were the moments when time suspended as he stared at me with a myriad of emotions playing in his eyes, our bodies close enough to share the same air. It was in those moments he became a part of me, a part that was as vital as my own DNA. That was why it fucked me up so much when he left.

"Then, on his birthday, I told him he could have whatever he wanted." Emotion burned the back of my eyes as I fought to share one of the most perfect memories with a stranger. I touched my tongue to the back of my teeth and took a steadying inhale. "I was late meeting him down at the creek—practice had run late—and he was sitting there reading like he always did, like the world around him didn't exist. His hair looked like it had strands of gold woven through it when the sunlight filtered through the trees. Then he turned to look at me, and his eyes seemed to pulse with an emotion I couldn't name—not then. But now, I realize it was love. He didn't need words as his actions said everything, but I was too fucking stupid to see it—him—for what it was."

"Hey, take this." B handed me a Kleenex, and I looked at him through misty eyes with confusion. "Dude, you're crying," he said softly, a smile wavering on his lips.

"Ugh, thanks." I sniffed and dried my face, but another tear fell as my hands trembled. "He laid himself bare to me that night, and I didn't fucking see it." Self-loathing infected every cell in my body. I hated myself and every wrong thing I'd said and done to my little crow. "I called out to him, and this blinding smile illuminated his face as he set his book down and chastised me for being late. I sat astride the log he was on. He turned to mirror me but shuffled closer and put his legs over my thighs. My hands automatically landed on them and god, his skin was so damn smooth. It felt so good under my rough hands and... and...a...."

"Have a drink, Dillon."

I chewed on my bottom lip, fighting back the urge to cry as I took the proffered bottle of water. It was warm, but it was enough to clear my throat and calm my raging emotions enough for me to breathe.

"What did he ask for?"

"Huh?" My mind was being pulled back to that magical day. The one that started a chain reaction of hurt, anger, and hate. "Oh, umm, he asked for a kiss. It was his first one too—"

"It was yours too, wasn't it?" B interrupted, a knowing look on his face.

I shrugged and rubbed my eyes with the heel of my hand. "Yeah, it was, and it was fucking everything. *He* was everything. I went home that night on a high I'd never experienced before. I couldn't sleep. All I could think about was how soft and warm his lips felt against mine. But then..."

"Then something happened, and it all went to shit?"

I snorted. Yeah, basically. "I went to his house the day after, and he was gone. They all were. The place was fucking trashed, like they'd been robbed. I was so worried, I knocked on all the neighbors' doors, but no one could tell me where they'd gone. Five days later, Mr. Abernathy turned up and beat the shit outta me."

"So that was true, but not the reason why, I'm guessing?"

"Yeah, exactly. He wanted to know where his 'faggot son' was, and was convinced I knew because we were always together. But I was just as much in the dark as he was. I never heard from him again. Days turned into weeks, then months, and then years. Before I knew it, five years had passed and there he was. And he looked..."

"Perfect?" The pained tone in B's voice made me pause. I blinked to clear my vision and saw so much understanding etched into the lines of his face that it stole my breath.

"B?"

"We're talking about you, not me here, Hargraves." He wiped away all traces of emotion off his face, but he couldn't hide what was in his eyes. I didn't push it. "I get why you were hurt, but what made you sic the team and everyone else on him?"

Humiliation seared through my veins, and heat flushed up

my neck. I cleared my throat as it became hard to breathe. "F-fear." Tears poured down my cheeks, and my chin touched my chest as I buried my face in my hands. I was a pathetic scared little boy. Hate. Fear. Jealousy. Anger. Hurt. "I was scared of what my dad would say or do if he knew I was like Jamie. I-I mean, Jamie never said he was into boys, but everyone knew. It was obvious to anyone who knew him. Well, apart from Mr. Abernathy, but he wasn't interested in anything other than himself and his next beer. I knew Jamie better than I knew myself. I'd always known, even if I didn't admit it to myself. I... I should have..." I shook my head. Every word hurt to say, let alone admit. "B-but I thought I-I'd lose my place on the team... a-and I couldn't lose that too! Christ, we both know how homophobic half the team is. Then there's Coach. He'd most likely bench me or kick me off the team. Not surprising really, when we're playing like sad sacks of shit, but—"

"Dillon, you need to breathe. Otherwise, your anxiety is gonna eat away at you, and you'll have a panic attack. Come on, man, just breathe with me." B lifted my hand and placed it on his chest, covering it with his own. "Breathe when you feel me breathe."

I nodded and choked on a sob that felt like it was gutting me. I hated myself. I hated how I'd let fear rule me. How I'd let it turn to hate. It was easier to hate him than face the truth about myself. If I locked it all away in a neat little box and buried it so it wouldn't see the light of day, I wouldn't have to face myself. I let my fucking hate consume me. When I looked in the mirror, I saw someone else. A monster. A petrified child. A fake. A fucking fraud.

I was nothing. I deserved all this and more. I didn't know how to live with myself, let alone face Jamie again. As much as I wanted to fix this, it felt insurmountable. I didn't know if I was strong enough to try.

"That's it Dillon. You're doing great," B said as my breath hitched in my throat. It burned with every breath. Tears and snot poured down my face as I broke. My walls came down, and I was left staring at what I'd become. Putrid. Rotten to the core.

Sometimes, the lies we tell ourselves are the most dangerous of all. They infect your brain and alter reality to fit the narrative your mind created, refusing to see the truth that is right in front of you no matter how much it hurts to keep believing the lie. No matter who is left broken and bleeding along the way. You cling to it—the lie—even as it kills you, because that's better than being wrong. That's the destructive power of a lie.

"Do you know why he left now?" B asked softly, hesitantly.

I nodded and curled my legs up to my chest, hugging them tightly to me. "I do... I fucking do, and t-that's what makes it worse. W-what I did to him, Taylor. I-I fucked up so bad. H-he said that..." My throat closed up the truth, a noose around my neck.

"Shhhh, it's only me, and I'm on your side here, Dillon, no matter what."

""H-he told me... he told..." It was like pulling teeth trying to get my mouth and brain to work together. Every time I tried, my blood grew hotter as my anger rose within me. "He... he told me t-t-that they were... put into... w-witness protection. T-that his dad beat his mum, S-Selene, almost to d-death." I roared as I pushed through the pain of telling him the truth. "I'm a fucking disgusting person. I make myself sick."

I threw my legs over the side of the bed and paced around the room, yanking on my hair as frustration made my skin crawl. My heart shattered, sending shrapnel running through my veins. "He was running for his fucking life and had to leave everything he loved behind. And me?" I bellowed. "I was throwing a fit because he left me and didn't say goodbye. In what fucking world is that a normal reaction? He's suffered and lived in fear for years. And me? I fucked the prom queen to fit in. Then I had you guys… Gah! Everyone targeted him because I hated him. Because I said so." My fist broke through the drywall as my temper got the better of me. Maybe if I got myself locked up, then I wouldn't be able to hurt him again.

"I'm a selfish piece of shit who threw his toys out of his stroller, because I lost my favorite one. I make myself sick." My other fist went through, and plaster dust filled the air. "He hates me, B. He was crying, and I dragged him off my bed and threw him on the floor and yelled at him." My legs gave out underneath me, knees smashing into the unforgiving floorboards. The maelstrom of emotion inside me severed that last thread of sanity, and I screamed at the unjustness of it all. I fucked up. I created a lie I told myself and hurt the only person that has ever mattered to me. My heart thundered against my sternum so hard, I was amazed the bone didn't break. I pounded the floor with my fists until my knuckles were split and bleeding, but it wasn't enough. It would never be enough. I cried because I loved him. I cried because I hated him when he loved me. My body shook as it tore apart, refusing to connect the monster I'd become.

"Hey. Hey, it's okay, Dillon. I've got you." Buchanan wrapped his arms around me and pulled me into his side. The contact grounded me as he soothed his hand up and down my back. He held me until I stopped shaking, until my tears ran dry, and my screams turned to hiccuped sobs. "I'm here, and I'll help you get him back. I know what it's like to love someone who doesn't even notice you exist." I pulled back and looked at him with wide eyes. His sad smile said so much, and his pain echoed mine.

"Tell me who she is," I growled and clenched my bloodied fists.

He cleared his throat and ran a shaky hand through his hair. "He is the most amazing person I've ever met. He doesn't see it, but he really is." He sighed, shoulders slumping. "But he's in love with someone else, and I'll never compete against them."

"Oh, Taylor, I'm so sorry." His face was a complex mixture of emotions I couldn't decipher. "C-can I ask you a question then?"

"You already did!" He grinned, lightening the mood.

"Are you gay?"

Buchanan burst out laughing and wiped a tear from his eye as we laid back on the floor. "You've seen me fuck how many girls?"

"Yeah, that's true. So what are you? I know I'm being blunt—"

"When are you not?" he interrupted with a smirk. "I'm pan. It's all about my connection with the person. Gender doesn't come into it for me."

"Oh."

"You look so shocked!" He laughed, even though his eyes still drowned in pain.

"You kept that from me?" I grumbled, feeling slightly hurt until he pinned me with a look as he turned to face me.

"You're really saying that? After all of this?"

"I guess I did," I croaked. "I told you—I'm a dick. And I guess I feel bad you couldn't tell me."

"It's not like I hide it; I just don't advertise it. It's like when I met Jamie at one of the LGBTQ+ events a while ago. I told him to take a chance on you. Even though..." He rolled his lips to stop himself from talking. "Coach will be fine. He'll support you one hundred percent."

"Really?" Even though I was emotionally drained and physically fucked—I didn't even know if I could pass a ball with my hands in this state. Buchanan's words made me feel lighter. "How? Why?"

"His son, Isaiah, is gay. Coach may have caught us once in a hotel room when we were playing an away game."

"Ah." Buchanan looked at me deadpan before I burst out laughing. "Where were you?"

"Oh god. That memory lives in my read rent free. It was horrifying, but fuck was it funny. He walked into his son's room and found me fucking Isaiah's face." He cracked a smirk. "Coach has never been able to look at me the same again."

"No shit?! That's... you're fucking awesome. But how do I fix this?" I asked, running my tongue over my dry lips.

"That's the hard part. But if you listen, I think we can get him back."

CHAPTER TWENTY-EIGHT

Jamie

November 6th

I didn't walk away to teach him a lesson. I walked away because I'd learned mine. I'd rather have to adjust my life to the absence of him, than adjust my boundaries to accommodate his blatant disrespect.

CHAPTER TWENTY-NINE

Jamie

November 12th

I loved him, and I gave him the power to destroy me. I just didn't expect it to decimate me so completely.

CHAPTER THIRTY

Jamie

November 29th

My thoughts were destroying me one day at a time. I tried not to think. Not to remember. But silence was a killer I'd never expected.

CHAPTER THIRTY-ONE

Jamie

December 12th

"You can't keep going on like this, JJ. You need to talk to us. We want to help you, but we can't if you won't tell us what happened." Mal's pained tone was like sandpaper over my skin. It hurt, but I knew I'd hurt him more. I'd shut down completely after running away from Dillon with my bleeding broken heart dragging behind me. Instead of answering, I grunted, rolled over, and buried myself under my covers.

"Angel, you need to eat," Ava said softly as I curled around myself, hugging the hoodie I'd stolen from Dillon. Food, drink, and life held no meaning anymore. What was the point of living if the one person who you loved—gave your heart, body and soul to—could treat you like that so easily? Like I meant nothing to him after telling me he loved me.

I couldn't breathe anymore, every inhale was more painful than the last. Each beat of my broken heart was too much to bear. I was alone.

I'd been dodging calls from Aunt Clara, Uncle Daire, and even my little sunbeam. I didn't want them to see me like this—my gaunt face deadly pale, dark bruises under my eyes, my hair a limp and matted mess. It took all my energy to go to class and not pass out.

"You're a shell of who you were, sweetie." Ava sighed as she sat on my bed and pulled back the blankets covering my face. "It hurts to see you like this and not be able to help you," she added and wiped away the tears trickling down her face. I'd shut my emotions off the second I'd walked through my door that day, but now they hit me with the force of a Category 5 hurricane.

A whimper ripped its way out of me as tears stung my eyes. I pushed myself up, pulled Dillon's hoodie on, and lifted the hood to cover my face as the tears started to fall. "It was him. Everything...w-was...b-because of him." I pulled my knees up and hugged them to me and tipped my head back against the headboard as I exhaled a pained breath. "I thought...he s-said that... he loved...I loved him."

The bed dipped on both sides of me. My tears turned into a raging torrent as my heart broke all over again. Small arms wrapped around my back, while larger ones—Mal's—wrapped around my shoulders and pulled me into him. My sobs turned to gut-wrenching cries as I let out everything I'd tried to bury that had been eating away at me for the last six weeks. The memories that haunted me when I closed my eyes. I don't know how long they held me in a cocoon of their arms, but I was grateful they did.

After what seemed like hours, my cries abated. My aching eyes pulsed and my throat was sore. Their faces were wet with tears of their own and made me feel like the worst friend in the world. Ava pushed the hood off my head and combed her fingers through the tangled mess. "Will you tell us what happened, Jamie?" I gasped as a fresh wave of pain pummeled me and licked my salty lips.

"Yes," I rasped. "But, can I have a shower first? I'm sure you think I stink."

"There's no think about it, JJ. You reek," Mal said with a chuckle. "Are you hungry? We can order something while you shower and get some clean clothes on."

"And we'll change your bed too," Ava said softly. "Then we will help you anyway we can, okay?"

My gaze ping-ponged between their earnest eyes. I tried my best to smile for them, but it came out more like a grimace. "I don't want to be a burden," I whispered.

"You're not, JJ. We're your friends, and you're hurting."

"And we help pick up our friends when they're down, right Mal?"

He nodded. "Exactly. Now off you go, and we'll get this mess cleaned up and maybe open a window too." He pinched his nose with his fingers, and I stuck my tongue out at him, making him laugh. The first proper one I'd heard in weeks.

"Get moving, stinker!" Ava shooed me from my bed before heading over to my closet to get some sweatpants and a sparkly tee that Mal and I got when we went shopping. God, that seemed like years ago now.

"How does pizza sound?" Mal said, eyes trained on me as I shuffled to the bathroom.

"Sure. Pepperoni supreme and garlic breadsticks with ranch on the side?"

"As if we'd forget your favorite, angel."

"Thanks." My lips curled up as I stepped into the bathroom and locked the door behind me. I already felt drained physically and emotionally. I didn't know how I'd get through explaining to them everything that had happened—there was so much I'd kept from them. What would they think of me? Telling them about my dad and Uncle Daire was one thing; they at least had some distance from that. But they barely knew anything about me and Dillon, except that I had a crush on him and we'd spent the night together on his birthday.

Hot water pummeled my shoulders, working out the knots and washing the stink off my skin. I closed my eyes and braced against the cool tiled wall, letting the steam work its magic and help clear my blocked nose. By the time I'd cleaned up, dried off, and was getting dressed, Ava knocked on the door to tell me our pizza had arrived and to hurry my tushy up before she ate mine. My stomach revolted at the idea of food, but I'd force some down if it made them happy. I'd done enough to hurt them recently.

"Wow! Who do we have here then?" Mal said around the slice in his mouth as I walked out the bathroom in a cloud of steam. "You look like someone we haven't seen in a while."

I stuck my tongue out at him and crawled back onto my bed between them. "Mmm, this smells amazing." And to my surprise, my stomach growled, making Ava snicker and choke on her soda.

"Jesus. Warn a girl before you let that monster out." A beat of silence followed before we all burst out laughing. Pizza and drinks passed in the blink of an eye, and it kinda felt like old times, almost like the last couple of months hadn't happened. But I could feel it blanketing the room, no matter how much my best friends did to lighten the mood. I knew they were concerned about me. It was written all over their faces and in their not-so-subtle side glances. I was waiting for Mal to start pushing seeing a therapist again; it was only a matter of time.

I knew it was because he cared, but it made me feel inadequate, like a burden. Someone who couldn't look after themselves.They once saw me as a ray of sunshine, but now I was hidden behind the storm clouds. I was homesick. Not for a place, but for the person I'm not sure exists anymore.

"Now," Ava said as she dusted her hands off and stacked the empty boxes on the trash can. "We want the truth, angel. What's going on?" Always cutting straight to the root of the problem, she had a knack for getting to the heart of the issue without making you feel like crap.

"I'd really rather not," I muttered, playing with one of my curls and refusing to meet her eyes that I could feel boring in to me.

"Well, tough shit, sweet cheeks. This is a friendervention."

"I think you mean interfriendsion, Ava?" Mal said.

"Nope! No, no, no. It's an intervention." Ava threw her hands up in the air, then snapped her fingers at me. "Whatever! You're talking. Now."

I looked at Mal for support, but he just smiled with resignation, a total contrast to Ava's take no shit attitude. I was really doing this. They left me no other option, and I didn't want to keep hurting them with my silence. They didn't deserve to be treated this way, so I hastily stitched half my broken pieces together and faced it head on.

"It was him." Just saying the words was a blow I didn't know I could survive, but I needed to allow myself to feel it to remind me why I couldn't just ignore what he'd done. "Everything that's been done to me since the opening party, why I've been targeted by students, and... and..."

"I thought things were like, you know, good?" She shrugged.

"Me too, Aves." I yanked on my curls as frustration washed over me. I can't believe I'd been naive enough to think things would pick up between us where they left off five years ago. That we'd still be the same people, and that he'd still be the boy I loved. But time was a cruel mistress. It had morphed him into someone I didn't recognize, yet was callous enough to fill my mind with memories of fleeting glances, lingering touches, and stolen moments.

"So, the blood box?"

"Yup."

"Shit. What else?" She looked between me and Mal. "Judging by the guilty looks on your faces, that's not everything, is it?"

"No." I shook my head, and my shoulders slumped. "The fire alarm in the mathematics building—"

Ava gasped. "Wait, what? What happened then?"

"Well, I was, umm..."

Mal cleared his throat, his Adam's apple bobbing thickly in this throat. "Velecote held him back. When everyone else left, JJ kind of got kidnapped and locked in the janitor's closet with a bag over his head and..." Mal stared at his hands. He'd been furious when I told him what happened. But what didn't make sense was the horrified look on Dillon's face when he rescued me and carried me back here.

"What in the everloving... AHH!" Ava sprung up off the bed and started pacing with her fists clenched. She was practically vibrating with anger. "I'm going to the dean! Fuck this!" She stopped at the end of my bed, tears glistening in her eyes. My heart ached at how angry she was for me. "What else?"

"That's it?" I squeaked. They both pinned me with a glower that had me wanting to crawl back under my covers and hide.

"JJ, we know there's more." The implication of his words wasn't lost on me. They knew me well enough to know when I was being evasive. I was doing it to protect them as much as shield myself.

"Fine, fine." I held up my hands. "There might have been an image of me getting railed by two really hot guys displayed in the middle of a calculus presentation. Then on Halloween, I got chased by guys in glowing masks across campus and hid in the groundskeepers' building until Dil came and rescued me. Then-he-took-my-virginty-and-told-me-he-loved-me," I sucked in a desperate gasp, "and-admitted-he-was-the-one-to-blame-for-it-all."

"Holy shit!"

"Angel, what the hell? Oh my god. That is insane!" Ava threw herself at me, and Mal pulled us both into a massive doggy pile hug.

"Ouch! Aves, get your elbow off my nuts," I said, lost among their limbs, crying and laughing. It was cathartic, like a weight had been lifted off my shoulders. A secret shared was a burden halved, but it still messed with my mind so much.

"Oh, sorry." She snickered, rolled off me, and sat opposite me with her legs crossed.

"I love him and hate him at the same time. It's confusing and draining." I sniffled. "H-he told me he loved me, b-but he was the reason all of that happened. How could he expect me to be okay with it all? It hurt me—*he* hurt me—terrified me. He embarrassed me in front of the whole damn college, and it was like he thought saying 'I love you' would make me forgive and forget. I mean, I do love him, and have done since before I knew what loving someone felt like, but this?" I shook my head. "I don't think I can just put it behind me." I deflated and curled into Mal's side. He pulled me closer and placed a kiss on the top of my wild curls.

"What do you want?" The low tone of Mal's voice sent a shiver through me.

"I don't know." I wanted everything and nothing. To go back five years and never leave. To have never met him. But that thought was like digging my own grave. I didn't want to live in a world where he didn't exist, but I didn't know if I could exist in one with him.

Ava's hand coasted down my arm until she entwined our fingers and gave them a reassuring squeeze. "It's hard when the people we love hurt us." Her voice resonated with pain. "Even if they didn't mean to do it. But you're special, Jamie." She smiled at me in a way that made my heart feel too big to fit inside me. "You're like a wildflower; beautiful and delicate, yet resilient. You flourish no matter what the odds, and nothing can dim your shine. Don't let this beat you. Come back fighting."

I was gobsmacked as I stared at my friend. That was probably one of the deepest things I'd ever heard her say. It was beautiful, heartfelt, and resonated with my soul. I didn't know what to do about Dillon. The wound was deep and bloody, and I'm not sure I had the stomach to look at it yet. Maybe in time I'd be able to, but for now, I'd let myself bleed out. Anything to numb myself.

Love is nothing like I'd expected it to be. It's a constant battle, a war that leaves scars behind, ones that don't always heal. It's a war you choose to fight every day. It's about growing up and admitting when enough is enough. The hardest part about walking away from him was that he didn't follow me. He hasn't fought for me. Not once in six weeks.

We spent the rest of the day curled up under my covers, while Mal selected shitty rom-com movie after shitty rom-com movie for us to watch. It was nice to do nothing but not be alone. I was like an explorer who'd come home after years in the Arctic. I slowly felt like I was coming back to myself. I had the best friends, and with them holding me up, I could get through this. I just had to push the guilt aside that keep chipping away at the happiness I clung to by my fingertips. Those photos and that damn USB stick whispered my name every time I closed my eyes, but I shoved in my ear plugs and ignored them.

"Oh, oh, oh, I have a great idea." Ava bounced across the room to her bag. Mal and I looked at each other with mirroring expressions of confusion. She heaved a dramatic sigh and placed her hand on her hip. "You've heard of the revenge body, right?"

"Yup."

“Yes,” Mal and I said at the same time.

“Well, we’re going to do a revenge makeover, and then we’re going to make you a star, Jamie.” She squealed and started talking to someone on her phone at a million miles an hour.

“Not sure I like this, Mal,” I whispered.

He chuckled, and his face lit up. “You’re aboard the Ava express now, JJ, with no stops until the end of the line. So you better buckle up and enjoy the ride.”

“Well, shit.”

“Oh, Ava, I’m so glad you called. This is just perfect. I was actually looking...” Levi’s voice died as he turned into our room and saw me and Mal curled up on my bed. He came rushing over, his hands frantically waving in the air. “Oh, babe. What’s happened?” He sat on the bed by my feet, pulled my hand into his, and started petting me.

“Levi,” Ava snapped. “He’s not a dog. Stop petting him.” He grinned like a deranged pixie before turning to blow her a kiss but didn’t stop.

“Boy trouble,” Mal said, giving me a tight squeeze before releasing me so I could sit up properly.

“Ah, they’re all assholes. Don’t worry, babe, Ava and I have a plan.” Levi smirked. “He’ll be down on his knees begging for forgiveness when I’m done with you.”

“Oh god.” I hid my face in my hands. “Do I even want to know?”

“Babe, we are going to revenge make-you-over. I’m going to help you become your most fabulous self. I have an idea of what you like from when you were at my house, and with a body and bone structure like yours.” Levi made a chef’s kiss motion and started talking at a million miles an hour. I couldn't do anything but smile. He was like a spark of infectious energy.

"Thank you," I murmured, my cheeks blooming under his undivided attention. It was like he was inspecting me under a microscope. It was a little unnerving, but he was kind, so I let myself get swept away in his whirlwind.

"Oh. Oh, babe." He squealed. "Please, please, please, say you'll do this for me." He steepled his hands under his chin. "Please walk in my show?! I want you to be my Christmas star."

His pleading eyes seemed to grow bigger the longer I stared at him and considered his offer. "What would I have to do?" I asked tentatively.

"Oh babe, it's so simple. I promise, you were born for this. There might even be some scouts coming to my show too. I'm hoping to get an internship at Matthieu Montoya. It's kind of a done deal, but they want to see my final collection."

"Sounds great, right?" Ava beamed as she sat next to me. "You'll have the world at your feet, and he who shall not be named will be beside himself." I sighed and gave her an exasperated look. "I know you, angel. You love him but need time to work through everything that's happened."

"If it helps at all," Mal added. "I don't think he was implicit in anything that happened. I saw his face with the blood bomb and that didn't look like someone who knew what was going to happen. Plus, he was the one who saved you every time."

Mal's words took root in my mind and hope flickered in my heart. "But what if that was all part of his plan? What if he's just that manipulative?" I tipped my head back and closed my eyes as my mind whirled.

"Hey, butt out, Mally chops. This is the Levi show." Warm fingers grabbed my jaw and gently shook my head until my eyes opened. "Jamie, sweetie, I'm gonna pop downstairs with Aves and grab the outfits I've brought for you to wear.

These are just a few everyday things that you can interchange with each other for different looks. Then I'll go through your closet and put some pieces together for the next couple of weeks, okay?"

"Sure. Okay. And yes, I'll walk in your show if you tell me what I have to do."

"Oh my days! I adore you, my little honey bear." He lurched forward and wrapped his arms around me, the smell of cotton candy smothering me. "This is going to be amazing. Trust me."

With those parting words, Levi and Ava left, leaving the room looking like some kind of natural disaster had struck. I couldn't decide if I'd made the right choice or not. I guess only time would tell, and it sounded like I had an evening of fun with a now orange fluorescent-haired pixie to look forward to. At least for a few hours I could be a normal guy, enjoying his college experience with his friends. But Mal's words clung to me, and I couldn't let them go.

"Were you serious about what you said?"

"Huh?" Mal's brow furrowed before the confusion cleared. "Oh! Yeah, I overheard one of the footballers saying that Olli Stevens and Chad Prescott had it out for your guy, and they were taking shit too far. It didn't mean anything to me at the time, so I brushed it off. But now..."

"You're wondering what they actually meant?"

"Kinda, yeah."

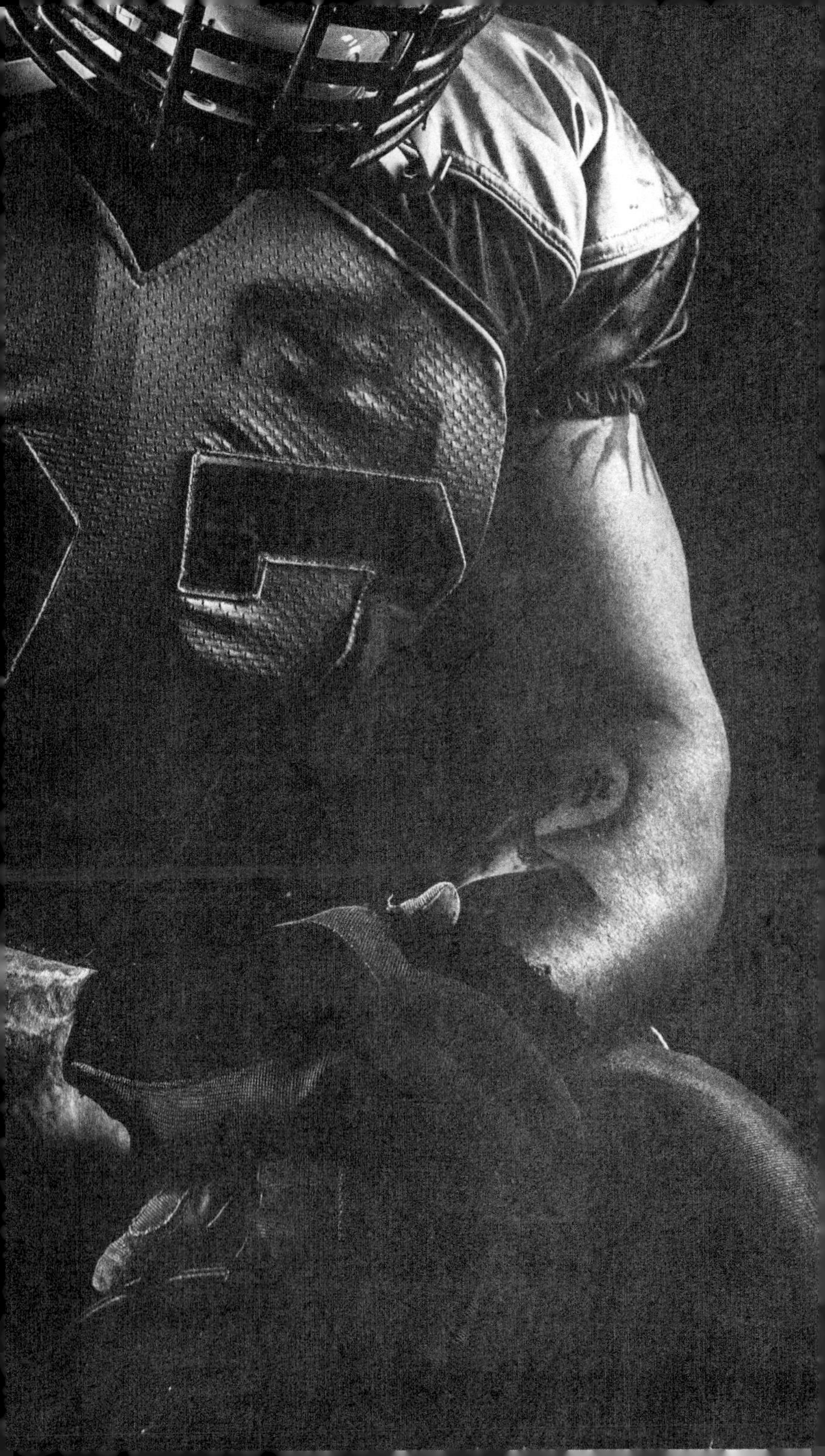

CHAPTER THIRTY-TWO

Dillon

Winter had finally set in and temperatures had plummeted, my glass heart along with it. I knew I deserved what I had gotten—karma fucked me in the ass and made me its bitch. It hurt to keep my distance, but Buchanan said I needed to give my little crow time to find his wings again. As much as I hated him for saying it, I knew in my heart he was right. I would have been at Jamie's dorm that same day, banging his door down if I'd had my way, but B convinced me it would do more harm than good. Hurting Jamie more than I already had would have pushed me over the edge.

Watching him suffer and become a shell of who he was though—fuck! It was nearly killing me along with the unrelenting guilt eating away at me inside. I didn't think I would ever be able to bleach my mind enough to remove those memories. It was like watching someone slowly die and not being able to save them. Day by day, little bits of what made him who he was faded away until there was nothing left. First, it was the glowing aura that made you feel like he'd encapsulated you in sunlight. Then, the life drained out of his face, and his skin turned ashen and dull. His one vibrant ice-blue eyes were consumed by shadows, just like my soul. Every change irreparably broke a piece of me that I didn't want to fix if I couldn't have him. Hold him. Love him.

If I thought I'd stalked him across campus before, it had nothing on what I did now. I didn't just wait outside his classes, I became his shadow. Wherever he was, even in his dorm, I was there watching. My grades nosedived, and I was on the verge of being benched, but I didn't give a fuck. Coach understood—to a certain degree—but told me my puppy love infatuation had to stop, and if I didn't pull myself together after Christmas break, then I'd lose my captaincy.

Chad, the fucking waste of space, started parading around campus like a prized peacock, telling everyone he was going to be captain next year. Thankfully, no one took him at his word. Revenge was a dish best served cold, and it was epic to watch him blow up when people scoffed or laughed in his face. The one thing I couldn't wrap my head around was how Elise was suddenly glued to his side with hearts in her eyes. Not that I minded. Anything to keep that psycho bitch away from me was a win.

Cold wind stung my cheeks as it carved a path through the trees while I waited for my little crow to leave the dorms and head to Bean There to meet Ava like he did most mornings. The overcast sky was thick with churning shades of gray that threatened snow but so far had held off. Jamie had always been obsessed with the white shit when we were younger, and a crazed grin cut across my face as memories of past winters with him floated through my mind.

My breath caught in my throat as he slipped through the open door and buttoned up a thick dark gray peacoat. My heart beat its way out of my chest as my eyes roved over him from head to toe and back again, taking in every detail of his appearance. "Fuck." I scrubbed my hand through my stubble as I tried to reconcile the Jamie before me with the one I'd seen close up on Friday.

He looked fucking edible, and my mouth watered. He was glowing, more radiant than he had been in months. His hair looked like spun gold, his face flawless, but it was his eyes that drew me in. Even from my vantage point, they smoldered, and it made my dick twitch in my pants. "Shit," I ground out as I pushed the heel of my hand against my growing bulge. I needed to kiss him, claim him, and stop anyone else from thinking they had a chance.

He was fucking *mine*.

Since I'd called off my idiotic idea of scaring the shit out of him to get him to leave, I'd noticed just how much attention my little crow garnered. I mean, I'd picked up on it before, but it had grown exponentially. And because I'd broken his heart, I was terrified he'd choose someone else, and I'd never be able to convince him to give me a second chance.

"Fuck that," I muttered as I slinked through the trees on the far side of the lot, following him to meet Ava. I didn't think she'd noticed me yet, but she was hyper aware of what was going on around them if they were out in the open too long. I didn't know why, but both her and Mal had closed ranks around Jamie recently.

I could only assume it was because of what happened on Halloween. I'd beat the shit out of Chad for that epic fuck up when I found out it was his idea. I was livid that the bruises and swelling had all but faded, but it was winter and accidents happen all the time. He could fall down the stairs and break his nose. That dick deserved more than what I gave him, but luckily, the dean had received an anonymous email with attached video footage. Cory had turned out to be very useful, and now Chad was on probation.

A growl rumbled in my chest as Ava wrapped her arms around Jamie and pulled him in for a hug. My reaction might be irrational, but I couldn't deny my need for him. After six weeks, I was like a thirsty man in the desert. The only sustenance I needed was him, and I was going to do whatever it took to get him back. Jamie pulled his phone out of his pocket, swiped across the screen, and slipped it back in. I knew it was his ten minute alarm, and when he got up and blew Ava an air kiss, my skin started to tingle. This was my chance, and I was going to grab it with both fucking hands.

On silent feet, I followed him into the building. There were only three rooms that had classes at eight in the morning, and I knew which rooms would be free. I slipped through the open door before it shut on his heels. "Jamie?" I called out. His shoulders hunched, and he ignored me. Oh, that would not do. My little crow didn't get to walk away from me again. "Jamie, please." My heart hammered against my ribs. "Please."

He froze as if he was about to spin around but was struck by indecision with one arm slightly outstretched. I took my chance, my hand ghosting down his arm and latching onto his wrist. His breath hitched in his throat, loud enough to resonate through the empty corridor.

"I really need to talk to you." I laced my fingers with his, and my body sung at the contact as electricity danced over my skin. "Fuck," I breathed out at my body's potent reaction to him. His sweet caramel scent grew stronger, and I took a deep inhale before dragging him into an empty room.

"Jesus, Dillon," he grumbled as I pushed him up against the door. He looked like he wanted to fight me, but his body was pliable in my hands.

"I missed you." My voice was pained as I saw nothing but devastation in his shadowed eyes. "I'm so sorry, baby. But I can't stay away from you any longer. I can't b-breath without you, little crow," I murmured as I closed the space between our bodies until my hips pinned him to the door, and my arms bracketed his head.

"D-Dil," he groaned, and his length thickened against me. His breaths hit the side of my neck in short sharp pants as the temperature in the room rose.

I rolled my hips against him, desperately seeking friction for my pulsing cock without realizing Jamie moved with me. It was euphoric after not touching him for over six weeks. I unwound the scarf around his neck when he tipped his head back and groaned. The sound reverberated straight through me, like a bolt of lust to my balls. "Fuck, you smell so good, baby." I moaned as I ran my nose along his arched neck, deeply inhaling his scent.

"D-Dillon." His hands rested on my shoulders, tension radiating off him like he was going to push me away. I would have stopped if he had, but instead, he laced his fingers in my hair and pulled my head closer. "Fuck. We s-shouldn't be doing this." He gasped as I sucked biting kisses across his jaw to his ear. I teased the shell with the tip of my tongue, making him shudder before sinking my teeth into the lobe until he groaned long and low.

When I went to pull away, he held me in place, tightening his hold in my hair and guiding me back to his neck. I licked from the base of his neck to his fluttering pulse and smiled against his skin as goosebumps bloomed across it.

"Oh, baby, I've missed you," I said between drugging kisses on his slick skin as I worked on unbuttoning his coat and slipped it off his shoulders. It fell to the floor with a finality that gave me the confidence to continue to take from him. To give to him. To mark his perfect skin with my bruises, so everyone would know he was mine.

"Oh god. Oh god." He pulled my head back and fused his mouth to mine, and a jolt of lust-filled adrenaline surged through me, because he wanted me as much as I wanted him. His tongue teased across the seam of my lips, begging for entry. The frenetic need pouring off him only served to fuel the burning need flowing through my veins. Jamie had me so wound up, I couldn't breathe as he owned my body. I didn't care that my lungs were screaming at me. Who needed oxygen anyway?

I groaned as Jamie speared his tongue through my lips. He tasted and teased me to within an inch of my life, and we devoured each other with an unmatched hunger as our teeth clashed with desperation. Our tongues wrapped around each other in a sensual dance as I coasted my hands down his sides. The feel of silk beneath my fingertips was as delicate as his skin.

He pulled my bottom lip between his teeth and bit down hard enough for me to taste copper.

"I need to taste you, little crow," I murmured, my lips brushing his with each syllable. Pulses of electricity skittered across my skin. My fingers hooked into the waistband of his pants and trailed around his sides before I pushed down inside and felt the smooth heat of the perfect globes of his ass. I sank my fingers into them as I dropped to my knees and pulled his clothed groin into my face. I rested my forehead against his hard erection, loving the heat radiating off him and looked up at him through my lashes. "Please." One powerful word, both a plea and a promise.

"Yes, Dillon." Jamie bit down on his lip, lust blazing in his eyes as he watched me flick open the button and slowly pull the zipper down. I knew Jamie had a thing for lace, and I couldn't wait to see what surprise he was wearing for me today.

"Oh fuck, baby. You're perfect. Just fucking perfect for me." I buried my face into the delicate white lace snowflakes and licked along his shaft from root to tip, savoring his musky taste before sucking his leaking tip through the barely there material of his thong.

Jamie's hands carded through my hair, and his blunt nails

scraping over my scalp made me shiver. I nipped the top of his thong with my teeth and pulled it down his cock. "Oh god, that's hot. Why is that so damn hot?" He groaned as his length broke free and slapped against his abdomen. His cock glistened in the soft light from the partly shaded windows, and I could just make out a string of precum hanging between his glans and stomach.

I licked my lips, and saliva pooled in my mouth as I ached to swallow him down. "Fuck, little crow. You have no idea how much I need you in my mouth. I want to feel you fuck the back of my throat." I grasped his base and lapped at the wetness dripping down his shaft. Holding him still, I circled his glans with my tongue before dipping it into his weeping slit. "Fuck, baby, you're so wet for me." Jamie's head hit the door as he groaned, his abs tightening under my hand as I slid it across his soft skin. "Is your greedy little hole begging for me? Is it clenching around thin air?"

"Stop talking, and suck my dick," he bit out. Fuck, he looked like the best wet dream, with his cheeks flushed, skin covered in a sheen of sweat, and wild eyes pinned on me. *Fuck, yeah.*

I chuckled and pulled him closer. "Don't be grumpy, baby. I'm gonna make you feel so good." I flattened my tongue, pulled his flushed head down so it was facing me, and licked at him like he was my favorite flavor of ice cream.

"Dillon, I swear to god, I'm gonna leave if you don't—" I wrapped my lips around him and sucked him all the way to the back of my throat in one go, moaning as his velvety length slid along my tongue. "Oh god. Yes, more. More."

Your wish is my command. I smiled around his length and hummed my approval as he pulsed in my mouth. I licked my way up his shaft until just the tip rested on my lips and flicked my tongue over his slit, making him shudder. I hollowed my cheeks, increasing the pressure around him as I sucked him back down my throat. "That's it Dill. So good. So, so, good."

My hands slid up his thighs as I continued to lick and suck him like my life depended on it and reveled in the feel of his straining muscles. As my hands cupped his ass, he trembled beneath me. I dug my fingers into the supple flesh before tracing them along his crease. Jamie's hold on my hair tightened to the point of pain. His hips rolled, chasing my mouth, forcing his length farther down my throat. His cock grew thicker in my mouth as a whimpering moan worked its way past his parted lips.

I watched his fluttering lashes closely as I pulled his cheeks apart. He gasped as cool air hit his perfect hole, and his length jerked in my throat, making me gag. "Damn, that's hot. You gonna cry for me, babe?"

Fuck. I loved it when he let go, and his baser instincts ruled him. My little crow was a filthy fucker underneath all that perfect beauty. I wanted him to fuck my throat so hard I couldn't talk. I wanted to feel him all day. If this was all he'd give me, I would hold on to the memory of him for as long as I could.

"I-I'm close." His length thickened even more, stretching my lips to the point of pain as he pulled my head down so my nose was nestled against his silky flesh. I pulled back enough to suck in a gasping breath before doubling down and swirled my finger around his pucker, making him whine.

"Oh god. Oh, shit. More...more..." His whimpers set my skin alight as they turned to stuttering inhales and exhales, his words becoming nothing more than a garbled mess. I pushed my finger against his tight entrance, forcing myself inside him.

Jamie let out a scream and clamped down on my finger. *Fuck.* I moaned around him as his muscles spasmed around my finger. I pulled off his length and begged, "Come on my face, little crow. Come on me and show everyone who I belong to."

He stroked his cock, and I tipped my head back, opening my mouth just as the first thick rope of cum lashed across my face. "Oh, fuck. Dillon! Yes. Yes. Yes," Jamie bellowed as he covered my face in his cum. It dripped into my mouth, and I groaned as his taste filled my mouth.

"More. Give me all of it. I want you inside me. Fuck, your ass is crushing my finger." Another spurt landed on my extended tongue, and Jamie collapsed against the door. Utter bliss resonated through me as I drank him down and licked what I could off my face.

He was the picture of ecstasy as he leaned against the door, his chest heaving with labored breaths, legs shaking, and his hand still holding his softening dick as one last pearl of cum leaked from his slit. I leaned forward and licked him clean, pulled up this thong, and did up his jeans.

When Jamie opened his eyes, the blue depths were blotted out by pools of black, but as soon as we made eye contact, he shrunk back into himself. Guilt and shame washed over his features before they settled into neutrality. "This shouldn't have happened. It was a mistake," he said, brushing his curls off his face and picking his jacket up off the floor.

"Jamie," I rasped, my throat raw and aching. "It wasn't me. I didn't do those things. I didn't know—"

His glare had me eating my words; it was like I was strung up by a noose. "No." He shook his head and slipped his arms into his peacoat before tying his scarf. "You might not have planned what they did, but you gave the order and set the precedent. So don't tell me it wasn't you. Guilt by association is still guilty, Dillon."

His words landed blow after blow, perfectly timed for maximum impact.

"Fuck, Jamie I'm sorry. I was—"

"Hurt? Two wrongs don't make a right, Dil." He turned on his heel and disappeared through the door. It clicked shut with a resounding thud. My heart stopped beating as I knelt there, covered cum and with tears streaming down my face.

"I never meant to hurt you, little crow. I'm so sorry," I whispered into the silent room.

CHAPTER THIRTY-THREE

Jamie

"Do you know where you're going, JJ?" Mal peered over at me from his desk as I pulled on my coat, a black envelope burning a hole in the pocket.

"I, umm? The exhibition center is on the other side of the sports area, right?"

Mal chuckled and pushed back from his desk. "Here, take this. It might help." He winked.

"What is it?" I asked, taking the open booklet from him.

Mal rolled his eyes at me. "It's a campus map. Didn't you even look at the package they sent you when you got accepted?"

I shook my head. I hadn't had time due to getting a last minute acceptance here. Uncle Daire had tried two colleges out of state first, but they refused to take someone under my circumstances at such late notice.

"Uh, I must have missed it, or Aunt Clara kept it as a memento."

"That explains so much." Mal grabbed my beanie off my bed and placed it on me before arranging some of my curls around my face. His eyes snagged on something that made him gasp.

"Jamie, what the fuck are those?" He pulled the collar of my coat down. "Hickies? You have fucking hickies on your neck!" Stepping back so he could look me in the eye, Mal glowered as he waited for my response.

I rolled my lips between my teeth while I tried to come up with an explanation. "Well, you get hickies when someone sucks on you skin hard enough to break the blood vessels, and that creates a bruise—"

Mal held his hand up, looking at me agape. "Christ, Jamie." He scrubbed a hand down his face. "I know how you get a hickey, but how do *you* have one?" He eyed me suspiciously and leaned back against his desk with his feet crossed at the ankles and arms folded over his chest. I could feel his impatience growing with every second that passed.

"Oh, um, you know, just some guy," I said flippantly and shouldered my bag. "Thanks for the map. I, erm better be going. Don't wanna be late, do I?"

My hand was on the handle before Mal spoke. "JJ, please wait." I stepped out into the corridor and spun around. "Look, I'm sorry. That was out of line. I-I'm just worried about you. You've got so much going on at the moment."

I sighed and itched my head under the beanie as perspiration formed underneath it. "I know Mal, but I'm a big boy, okay?" I looked in his sea-glass green eyes, begging him to understand.

Huffing out a breath, he wrapped his arms around me. "I do, JJ. I just worry about you when Ava or I aren't with you, so I got you this. Please take it."

I snorted. "I'm walking across the playing fields in broad

daylight. I think I'll be fine." I released him and squeezed his shoulders. "Thanks for caring, Mal." I planted a chaste kiss on his cheek, took the pepper spray from his proffered hand, and walked away, waving over my shoulder.

The frigid air slapped me in the face when I stepped out of our building. It felt like I got ice burns on my cheeks. "Shit!" I muttered, pulling my beanie down and my scarf up to cover my nose. It looked like I was wearing a multi-colored ski mask. I cast my eyes over the parking lot and down the sidewalks out of habit at this point. I'd felt eyes on me a lot over the last two months, and while it didn't feel sinister—like they were gonna jump out and stab me in the back—it made me uncomfortable and jumpy all the same. I had my suspicion that it was Dillon stalking me from the shadows, but as I hadn't spoken to him since I came all over his face at the beginning of the week, I wouldn't know for sure unless I caught him. And one thing Dillon was good at was lurking in the shadows.

I could still picture his flushed face covered in my cum, cracked and shattered before me when I left him in that room. I couldn't forget the way he slammed me up against the door, or the way I lost myself in the electric feel of his hands on me. The way our bodies gravitated to each other was otherworldly and so addictive. I craved him more than my next breath. But every time I think I've gotten past our issues, something happens to send me spiraling down that black hole again, and I end up spending the next few days trying to pull myself out of it. Every time leaves more cuts and scars on my heart, and I don't think I can take it anymore.

As I walked, I noticed posters for the Winter Gala stapled on every available surface. The buzz about it was palpable, but it had nothing on the fashion department's annual showcase. Levi said the theme for the year was Winter Wonderland and would contain formal and casual outfits. I still couldn't believe I was doing this, especially since I didn't know what it entailed. Ava said all I had to do was look pretty and smile, but

Levi quickly shut her down. He reminded her that it was far more complicated than that, and that I should ask her about the time she tried to walk freshman year. Safe to say, that conversion ended abruptly.

The wind whipped through the deserted quad as I crossed it, and I debated whether I had time to stop at Bean There, but the reminder of the envelope in my pocket made my mind up for me. I checked my watch and glanced around to make sure no one was looking too closely at me. Feeling confident I wasn't being followed, I stepped up under the overhang of the library and pulled out the offending item.

My heart pounded in my chest as the cold air burned my lungs, tremors racking down my arms.I know I should have just put it in the box in my closet and ignored it, but it felt thicker than the others I'd received, making alarm bells ring in my head. With one final look around, I slipped my finger under the lip and upended the contents into the palm of my hand. I stared at it, the images not registering in my head.

"Oh holy shit." I gasped. My free hand covered my mouth as bile scorched the back of my throat. "What the..." I shook my head and flipped through the images, each one worse than the one before. If Dillon saw these, he'd lose his shit. He's not out—in any capacity I know of—and this could ruin him. My heart turned to lead and plummeted through my gut, and the backs of my eyes burned with such intensity that the world around me blurred and darkened. I sucked in a sharp breath, wincing at the pain as my legs gave out and I crashed onto the ice-cold cement.

"Who would do this? Why? Why?" A whimper worked its way up my throat as I looked at the photos again. They were taken from different places and nausea rolled through me at the thought of multiple people stalking me around campus. The hair on my neck stood on end, and blood filled my mouth as I chewed the inside of my cheek.

Fifteen photos of me and Dillon. Him chasing me into the

building, arm outstretched. Him pinning me against the door in the empty classroom. Him on his knees, staring up at me. Me fucking his face with my head thrown back, mouth parted as I yelled. "Shit. Shit. Shit." My bottom lip trembled as I shoved them all back in my bag and hauled myself up.

Another wave of nausea hit me, and I retched over the stair rail into the evergreen bushes. "F-f-uck." I flushed hot and cold as my breaths stuttered in and out of my dry throat. I focused on my breathing, trying to slow my inhalation rate enough so I could actually get some oxygen into my lungs before I passed out.

My phone vibrated in my pocket, letting me know I only had ten minutes till I had to meet Levi at the exhibition center. How long had I been lost in a dazed heap on the ground? Too long, obviously. Today was meant to be a good day, one filled with positivity and fun—not a goddamn pile of shit. The skies seemed to have darkened along with my mood, and the cold feral wind whipped around me. I stuck my hand in my bag, grabbed a bottle of Mountain Dew, and downed a few mouthfuls, hoping the sugar would help calm me.

I closed my eyes and counted to twenty as the sugary goodness worked its way around me, then counted back down to zero and focused on locking the memory away. I put each photo into a black lace box, placed the lid on top, tied it with a silver lace bow, and dropped it in the black cave in my mind. Locking it away from my conscious thoughts helped lift the weight from my shoulders. Compartmentalizing my memories and body's responses to certain stimuli was the only way I'd managed to survive. Was it healthy? Definitely not. But I couldn't afford therapy, and I didn't want one of Uncle Daire's recommended colleagues doing it for fear of them reporting back to him. It was the best I could do.

The sports fields were frozen under foot, and the crisp crunch of the grass brought a smile to my face. It took me a moment to hear a second set of footsteps behind me. I screamed and reached into the front pocket of my bag, grabbing the pepper spray Mal gave me. I spun on my heel, held the bottle out in front of me, and said, "Don't touch me, or I'll spray."

"Shit, Jamie. I come in peace." I cracked my eyes open, not realizing I'd closed them, and took in the guy smiling back at me with his hands raised in the air. His dark blond hair was styled in the effortlessly messy just-got-out-of-bed look I could never achieve with my wild curls, and his bright blue eyes sparkled with mirth. But it was his disarming smile that got me to lower the pepper spray and sparked my recognition.

"Oh my god." I scratched my itchy head as a bout of nervous energy hit. "I'm so, so sorry. I'm just a bit..."

"Jumpy?" he added.

"Yup." I nodded and put the bottle back in my bag. "I don't mean to be rude, but I can't remember your name. I know we've met but, yeah. My mind's blank."

He snorted. "It's alright. I'm kinda forgettable."

"Shut up. You're not, and you know it." He smirked back at me and winked. *Jesus.*

"The name's Taylor. Taylor Buchanan." I cocked my head and waited for the words I could almost see on his lips. "I'm on the football team."

Bingo. "Hell no." I turned away from him and walked away. I didn't want to deal with any of those assholes. *Really? None?*

"Jamie, please wait. Dillon doesn't even know I'm here," he huffed and jogged to catch up with me, which took all of zero seconds. "Please?" He reached for me, and I flinched.

I stopped so abruptly he almost crashed into me, making a chuckle slip through my lips. "Fine."

"Really?"

"Sure, why not? It's not like I've got anywhere important to be." My words had far more bite than I intended. Taylor looked me up and down with confusion on his face.

"But you don't play sports, so why would you be here?"

I rolled my eyes. "I'm walking in the Winter Wonderland fashion show." I shrugged. "I'm meant to be there for fittings and shown how to walk, because apparently, it's not like normal walking... who knew?"

"Ha! Rather you than me." Taylor licked his lips as a crease formed between his brows. "How about I walk you to the exhibition center and make sure you get there in one piece?"

"Uh, fine. Might as well." I buried my hands in my pockets as it felt like my fingers might freeze off. I could feel Taylor's gaze on me as I waited for him to say whatever he came here to tell me.

His breath fogged the air with his weary exhale before he cleared his throat. "I'd like you to just listen to me, Jamie, without interrupting me. Do you think you can do that?"

I shot him an incredulous look. "Don't see why not," I grumbled and pulled my shoulders up to my ears as the wind picked up.

"I've known Dillon since we met on the first day of freshman year. He's always been singularly focused on his studies and football. It was like nothing in the world existed to him." The whimsical note to his voice pulled at something inside me I didn't quite understand. "He was strong and brave but closed off and hostile to everyone. On the field, he was a power house. But off it, he grunted rather than talked to people, you know? Until I got sacked really badly one game and got knocked out. He helped me, kept me talking so I'd stay conscious. Apparently, I kept blacking out."

"I get it, alright? He's wonderful and the sun shines out of his ass."

Taylor snorted. "You said you'd listen."

"I did. Sorry," I said, suitably chastised.

"Anyway, he didn't make friends. I think he tolerated most of us. I know his dad constantly gives him shit. He speaks to Coach, and then tears Dillon a new one. But I'd never seen him act like he had no feelings until the night you popped up. He looked like he'd seen a ghost and was terrified. I now understand why, and that's what I really wanted to tell you. When you left, it fucked him up—"

"That wasn't my fault," I growled.

"Hey, I know, okay? And so does he now. But the point is, what he shared with you—he's never had with anyone. He might have been with girls, but that was because he was terrified that if people found out he was into you, that his dad would fuck him up worse than yours did."

"Excuse me? What did you just say? What the hell did my dad do?"

"He didn't tell you?" I shook my head, furrowing my brows as trepidation crawled over my skin. "Just...you didn't hear this from me, k? A few days after you left, your dad showed up at Dillon's house, demanding to know where you were. Since Dillon couldn't tell him, your dad beat the shit out of him, breaking his arm and putting him in the hospital."

The world spun around me, and I swayed on my feet. "No."

"That's what he told me."

"Fuck!" Tears fell from my eyes unbidden as the image of a beaten fifteen-year-old Dillon filtered through my mind.

"And when you turned up, the hurt and devastation he felt toward you morphed into anger. Plus, he was terrified about losing his spot on the team. He thought—stupidly, I might add—that the best way to solve his problem was to scare you into leaving."

"It's not that simple," I whispered as the wind basted us with ice cold air.

Taylor glanced at me with sadness swimming in his eyes. "But it is, Jamie. Dillon told the team he'd been bullying you, so you sicced your dad on him. The lie he told blew out of proportion. He only suggested knocking into you, trashing your books, or sending you to the wrong building so you'd be late for class."

Tears streamed down my cheeks as guilt threatened to devastate me. "But—"

"All the nasty shit that's happened was orchestrated by Stevens and fucking Chad. They hate Dillon, because he has what they want. They might be assholes, but Stevens isn't stupid—despite how he pretends to be—and he figured out Dillon's secret. He thought targeting you would break Dillon and get him to fuck up, thus getting him off the team."

"But thats... thats..." I couldn't find words for what I was hearing. "Barbaric."

"It is. Dillon beat the shit out of Chad for what happened on Halloween and sent incriminating evidence to the dean. One more fuck up, and Chad will get kicked out."

I stopped and looked Taylor right in the eyes. I needed to see if he lied. "Have you been part of any of the fucked up things they've done?"

He shook his head but kept his eyes trained on me. "No. The things they've done made me sick. Plus, Dillon..."

I rocked back on my feet as the realization hit me. Stabbing pains pierced my chest, and I swallowed down the lump forming in my throat. "Oh my god! Does he know you're in love with him?"

Taylors eyes glistened as tears filled them. "No, and he never will. You're here, and he loves *you*, Jamie. These last six weeks have just about killed him. I've never seen him suffer like this before." He placed his hand on my lower arm. "Just give him another chance. He's willing to do anything to win you back. Anything, Jamie. You ask, and he'll do it."

My heart squeezed in my chest, stealing the breath from my lungs as tears pricked my eyes. "I just need time. I lost my mom two years ago. When Dillon said he was the reason for all this madness, it was as much of a gut wrench as my mom's death. It's all too raw, y'know? So yeah. I need time."

"I do. I got you, okay? I'll talk to Dillon."

"No, I've got it." I licked my lips. "I will." Taylor nodded, gave me a small smile, then walked away, leaving me standing outside the exhibition center.

I couldn't work out what part of that little talk broke my brain more—that Dillon wasn't, in fact, the manipulative unfeeling monster I'd made him out to be, or that his best friend was in love with him and Dillon had no idea. The truth was, Dillon was just a terrified broken boy who came from a cold loveless home, and had a dad who forced him to suppress all his emotions. That Dillon didn't have any social skills or the ability to read people's intentions made sense. My heart broke in a whole new way for him. For the experiences he'd denied himself out of fear and how he forced himself to conform.

Mal thought I might be demi, but I knew I wasn't. It was just my heart belonged to one person; always had, always would. We were as inevitable as the sunrise and as sure as the changing tides. But the way Dil explained his prom night makes me think he might actually be demi but not know it. Our friendship grew over five years before we kissed, and he was only then starting to acknowledge there was something more than friendship between us.

I cast a final look at Taylor's back vanishing across the field and sighed. One more thing to tuck away and think about later. I had a meeting with a frenzied pixie I couldn't be late for.

CHAPTER THIRTY-FOUR

Jamie

"Oh, there you are, babe." Levi's voice was barely audible over the screeching of rusted door hinges.

I turned to see him leaning out of it and burst out laughing. "Oh my god, Levi! You do realize it is freezing out here, right?!"

"Yup." He shivered and rolled his eyes at me before motioning me to come inside. "That's why I'm inside and not out there."

"But this is just, there's like nothing there." My eyes bugged out of my head at the black lace hot pants and chucks he wore. "Do you need to put a shirt on?"

"Jamie, I'm in a harness. One doesn't wear a harness under a shirt."

I chuckled and followed him into the glass building, my nerves swarming in my gut like angry wasps.

"Baby cakes!" Ava squealed as we stepped into the biggest room I'd ever seen, with a huge runway in the center. I was immobile as I stared at the thing, feet welded to the floor and absolutely terrified. I was so focused on the glowing white plank, I didn't see Ava coming. So when she crashed into me, we both went down with a bang on the marble floor.

"Oh shit!" I laughed and collapsed backward as she scrambled to haul herself off me. "What are you doing here?"

Ava dusted herself off. "My dance group are doing the opening number before you strut your little tushie." She cackled and bounded over to a group dressed in black leotards and rainbow leg warmers while I was still trying to get up off the floor.

Clearing his throat, Levi appeared next to me and held out his hand. "If you think she's nuts now, just wait until performance time. She'll blow your mind."

I smiled as he led me behind the glittering white curtain to what I could only assume was the backstage area. "No matter what, I love her."

Levi gave me an indulgent smile before launching into the plan for the day. The number of costume changes I'd have, what they were, and how to wear them. Looking at some of them on the hangers, I thought I'd look naked under the lights they had rigged up, but who was I to argue with greatness? So I just nodded and agreed to everything he said. The day faded away under Levi's tutelage, and I actually felt excited for the show the following weekend.

My eyes burned and my legs ached. Who knew walking up and down the runway so many times would cause this much pain? The blisters on my feet had blisters because none of their shoes fit my small feet, so instead, they packed the shoes with god-knows-what to make them fit better.

The bitter cold cut through my clothing like it was butter the second I limped out of the center, despite how wrapped up I was. My teeth chattered, and I was sure I'd be every shade of blue by the time I got to the dorms.

"Thank you so much, babe." Levi grinned as he hugged me. "I knew you'd be perfect. See you Friday." He blew me an air kiss before sauntering off to his car, likely as desperate as I was to get out of the cold.

A small smile played on my lips. Despite the aches and pains I had, I'd had a great day. It was an amazing insight into what Levi and the other guys did. The passion they had for their work was inspiring and had me thinking about what I really wanted to do in life. I still wasn't sure, but maybe one day I would be. I needed to live before I could find my true calling.

I popped the collar up on my peacoat to block the icy wind, regretting once again my lack of gloves. I fished my beanie out of my pocket and pulled it on before brushing my curls out of my face and sighed thinking about the long walk home.

The air changed, growing thicker around me, and the hairs on my arms and the back of my neck stood on end. I glanced around but couldn't see anyone. The pools of light from the street lights weren't large enough to illuminate much of the parking lot or surrounding space. I shivered as the slamming of a car door rang out in the otherwise quiet night.

"Little crow?" I whipped around. Dillon strode toward me, wearing a puffer coat, and that faded rainbow beanie. The sight of that beanie brought forth a thousand memories of our childhood. I gave it to him for his tenth birthday, and my heart squeezed knowing he'd kept it all these years. "Can I take you for a drive?"

"I'm only heading back to the dorms. It's fine," I said, brushing him off.

His shoulders slumped, his whole body seeming to sag as he peered at me with wide pleading eyes. "Please, Jamie. Let me take care of you."

Talk about being stuck in a catch twenty-two; I wanted to go with him. I wanted to drown in him until he saturated every atom in my body, but I also needed time and distance to process everything that had happened. I hadn't had a chance to really think about what Taylor told me. I only knew my head was a mess, while my heart begged to be closer to its counterpart.

A cool finger lifted my head until I found myself drowning in the swirling darkness of his eyes. "Please, baby," he whispered, his lips brushing mine. I shivered at the contact and the intensity in his eyes. He was bewitching. "Let me. Please, Jamie."

His soft husky voice broke through my hastily built defenses, and I nodded before I realized what I was doing. Dillon laced our fingers together and pulled me along with him, his heat radiating into mine. "Straight to the dorms?"

A wicked grin curled his lips. "I want to show you something first. Then yes, I'll take you to the dorms."

"You're not gonna kill me, are you?"

Dillon stopped abruptly and yanked me into his body so my arms landed on his chest. I felt his thundering heart through his layers as if my hand was on his bare skin, touching the gorgeous crow tattoo on his chest.

"What kind of a question is that?" he demanded and wrapped a hand around my throat, giving it a gentle squeeze. Electricity covered my skin and lightning pulsed through my veins as he pulled us until our bodies were pushing into each other. "I love you, Jamie. I'd never do anything to intentionally hurt you. You're too precious for that."

A groan built in my chest, and I pushed up onto my

tiptoes, closing the distance between us and melding my mouth to his. His firm lips yielded to me as I pushed my way into his mouth and wrapped my tongue around his. That first touch ripped through me like an earthquake. All reason melted away as I was consumed by lust. My skin felt white hot, and his hold on my throat tightened as he took control of the kiss. He owned my mind and body. I craved him with an intensity that short-wired my brain.

My hands glided up his chest and looped around his neck as I hooked my leg around his hips and pulled him in closer. It wasn't enough. I whimpered, and it was like Dillon could read my mind as his hands landed on my ass and lifted me so I could wrap my legs around his waist.

"More Dillon, I need more." I moaned as I plundered his mouth, tasting every inch of him, trying to fuse us together and failing. My body ached for him, and my hole clenched as lust ran through me like liquid fire.

"I've got you, baby," Dillon whispered reverently against my lips and kissed a path down my jaw. His hot panted breaths teased against my ears, making me shudder. The rocking motion of his steps ratcheted up the burning desire that consumed me, providing a teasingly light friction against my erection. I lost myself in his kiss, in the feel of him against me, surrounding me. I felt safe and wanted, owned and craved as he kissed me with the same frenzied fever.

My back crashed into a solid surface, pulling an abrupt grunt from me. I broke the kiss, gasping for air, and sucked greedy lungfuls down. "What the fuck?"

Dillon grinned, his lips puffy and spit-slick from where I'd been devouring him. The click of a lock and the orange flash of lights allowed my brain to fill in the missing pieces as Dillon opened his truck door and pushed the passenger seat back as far as it would go.

We were lost to our carnal desire—nothing existed beyond us. Our hands scrambled to rip our clothes off, consumed by the need to get closer. Buttons flew off my coat, while Dillon's landed on the blacktop. "I need you, Dillon. I need you inside me. Want it. Want you." Incoherent words babbled from me as I drowned in him, his mouth refusing to be parted from me longer than it took to remove a layer of clothing.

"Fuck, little crow." He groaned as he pulled my pants down and teased a finger along my black fishnet thong, my dick twitching and leaking, begging for him as much as I was with my hands and mouth. "Fuck, need to be inside you. Now. Fuck!"

One minute I was kissing him, the next I was face down on the passenger seat with my ass up in the air. My legs were held together by my jeans around my thighs, pinning me in place. His hot breath ghosted over my ass as his finger pulled the thin strip of my thong away from my puckered hole. "So fucking gorgeous," he murmured before licking across my entrance.

"Oh, god." I moaned as he licked and flicked around my rim while his fingertip pushed against the tight ring of muscle. Waves of electricity pulsed through my channel as he sucked on my hole like he was making love to it with his mouth. My hips rocked against him, chasing the feeling of euphoria I would get when he sunk into me.

"Dillon. Now. I need you now." His finger breached me, and I screamed at the intrusion. He hadn't softened me enough for it not to hurt, but the burn was exquisite. "More... yes..." I rode his finger as he slowly pulled it out and pushed it back in with force. My back bowed with the onslaught of sensations. My hands grappled to find something to hold on to for when his thick cock finally sunk into me.

"Such a needy little hole." His gravelly tone felt like a physical caress on my slick skin. His spit landed on my hole, the hot liquid squelching as he pushed it in. My walls clamped down on his finger, refusing to let him go.

"More. I need, I need..." My breaths tore from my lips in harsh pants as my hard cock leaked all over his seat. I didn't care. I was singularly focused on Dillon and what his fingers were doing to my insides. I needed his cum. I wanted him to fill me up so I could keep a part of him with me at all times.

The sound of his zipper being undone was loud above our labored breathing. “Look at your greedy hole gaping open for me, little crow.” Dillon moaned as the blunt head of his cock notched against my entrance.

“Now. Now,” I demanded, wiggling to get him to slip inside me, but he smacked my ass as his other hand pressed down on my lower back to keep me still. The stinging heat only intensified my arousal and made my balls draw up so they hugged the base of my cock.

“Fuck!”

“What?” Desperation made it impossible to think. My body pulsed with need, and my empty hole clenched around nothing.

“I don’t have any lube. I won’t—”

“I don’t care,” I gritted out between panted breaths. “If you want to fuck me, Dillon, fuck me now! I want you inside me. I want it to hurt, so when I wake up alone in my bed tomorrow, I’ll ache and still feel you there.”

Spit trickled down my crease, catching on my rim and making me moan at the sensation. “You asked for this, little crow. I won’t be gentle—it’s been too long since I’ve been inside you.” The slick head of his dick notched against my rim, pulsing a teasing pressure that was just enough to stoke the fire inside me. Another drop of spit hit my entrance, and a low guttural groan rumbled through Dillon as he punched his hips forward.

“Ahhh!” I startled as he forced his way through the tight ring of muscle. The pain was instant, but as he rocked his hips back and forth with shallow thrusts, it dissolved into drugging pleasure as he worked his way in.

“Jesus, baby. You feel... sooo...damn...good.” His words were low and filled with sinful desire as he bottomed out inside me. I felt so full, fuller than before. This was raw, dirty, and animalistic, and it was more than my brain could process. My body was in heaven.

I licked my lips as perspiration dripped off my nose. "Dil? Fuck me." I circled my hips in a figure eight motion and reached through my legs, tugging on his balls. Dillon snarled. With one touch, I'd frayed the last thread of control he had over himself, and he devolved into an animal.

The slap of Dillon's hips against mine was a symphony to my ears as he pistoned in and out of me. The truck rocked from the force of his thrusts. My man was lust personified as he fucked me like he hated me. He pounded my ass within an inch of its life as he took out his emotions on me, and I couldn't get enough.

"Jamie, your ass is heaven, but I'm going to take you to hell and punish you for how you've treated me." His fingers sunk into my hair, and he wrenched me back until my head rested on his shoulder. My arched back changed the angle, making him hit my prostate with every thrust. Teeth skimmed along the column of my bare neck, and I shuddered when his tongue lapped at my salty skin.

"D-Dil... please," I begged, and my eyes fell closed as I was lost to the feel of his thick shaft. "Oh, god... oh...god...yes!"

"You want to come for me, my little crow?" he murmured, his tone was taunting and cruel. "You don't get to come until I've filled you with my load and it's dripping down my cock."

"Oh, shit." His filthy words turned my insides to liquid fire, and lightning raced down my spine as my orgasm came careening forward. My body shook, my ass flaming every time his hips snapped against my skin. "I-I c-can't..."

It felt like he was going to split me in half as he punched into me like a man possessed. "I'm so close, little crow," he whispered, eliciting a shudder from me as his lips brushed the shell of my ear. "I'm going to fill you with my cum. Eat it out of your wrecked hole and feed it to you when I fuck your mouth with my tongue."

I was a rag doll in his arms, my body only moving thanks to his powerful body. I felt owned. Consumed. Adored. Dillon's hips stuttered, and he sunk his teeth into my shoulder to quieten the shout he set loose. Warm cum filled my ass as he came, and I pinched my tip to hold my orgasm back. It was harder than I'd ever imagined as his slick heat filled my ass, my walls clenching around him.

"Down," Dillon ground out and pushed me back onto the seat. My head spun. My body was alive, my aching cock pulsing. I was in a lust-filled haze, right on the edge of orgasm.

"Ah!" I jumped as the flat of Dillon's tongue laved over my wet hole.

"Feed me my cum, little crow." He growled at me and the sound rippled over my sensitive skin. I clenched my walls, then bore down to force his cum out of my hole. "That's it. Good boy." His chest rumbled against my thighs as his release trickled out of me and into his waiting mouth as he slurped it up.

In the blink of an eye, he spun me around and fused his mouth to mine as he fucked his cum into me with his tongue. I moaned against his lips as spit and cum flooded into my mouth. Sucking in a harsh breath, I sunk my hands into his hair, holding on to him as if he would slip through my fingers like a filthy dream.

"You taste so good, Dil. I love your cum in my mouth, down my throat, and in my stomach." He pushed me back, and I fell against the cold seat. He kissed his way down my body before looking up at me through his thick lashes with a devilish smirk on his face. "What are..."

He stole my words, my breath, and my dreams as he sucked my sensitive length all the way to the back of his throat. The tight wet heat of his mouth and a single roll of my balls was all it took for my orgasm to make me splinter to pieces and black out.

"Fuck." I gasped as I swam back to the surface, my whole body quaking with aftershocks from the most mind-blowing orgasm I've ever had. Dillon rumbled before his lips sealed wth mine, and we tongue fucked my cum between our mouths until the taste of both of our essences lingered on our tongues. "I think you broke me, babe," I whispered as my eyes fluttered closed.

Dillons rasping chuckle settled into my bones like a weighted blanket as I started to drift off, my body boneless and sated in a whole new way. A rough palm cupped my cheek and stroked my skin reverently, like I was precious.

"I love you, Jamie." Dillon's lips brushed mine. "I would never do anything to hurt the love of my life. Will you be mine?"

His words were like something out of a fairy tale, and my heart backflipped as my insides lit up like the Fourth of July. "As your boyfriend?" I breathed, so happy, I felt high.

"Boyfriend, partner, whatever you want to call it. But I hope, one day, it might be my fiancé..." Sleep pulled me under before Dil could finish, but those words wrapped around my heart and that final missing piece clicked into place.

CHAPTER THIRTY-FIVE

Dillon

"Seriously?" I muttered under my breath. I stared at myself in the bathroom mirror, trying to tie my damn bowtie, but I just kept fucking it up. Why we had to dress up as confused ass penguins for this thing was beyond me. All I wanted to do was watch Jamie look like a fucking god on that runway, but I'd gouge anyone's eyes out who looked too long. That boy was mine.

My phone pinged, and I swiped it off the counter, my mouth twisting into a grin when I saw it was Jamie.

JAMIE

Can I have a sneak peek of you in your suit?

What do I get?

JAMIE

....

JAMIE

....

Fine

photo

JAMIE

My man is hot!!!!! GTG see you later xoxoxo

See you at 7!

"Yo, Cap, open up!" Vieck bellowed as he hammered on my door. I rolled my eyes and stormed through my room, wrenching open the door my teammates were crowded around.

"Dillon, you can't tie it, can you?" Buchanan said with a laugh.

B snorted and gestured to his perfectly tied bow tie and then at Vieck and McCormack who all wore manic grins. The smarmy fucktards. "What do you think, Cap?" They fist bumped and laughed at my expense as I ran a shaky hand through my hair.

"Fuck!" I had to walk away from the idiots, or I'd end up putting my fist in their faces as they filed into my room. Tonight wasn't just a big night for my little crow, who was the star of Levi's collection, but it was our first official night out as boyfriends. I didn't want to keep him hidden in the shadows like some dirty little secret, but some fears were so deeply ingrained in you, that they were almost impossible to push past. I just hoped that in time, I could walk up to him without an ounce of fear in my blood and kiss him in public. But for now, I'd be tentatively hopeful.

"Hey, hey, come on, Cap. It's all going to be fine," Vieck said, leaning against the door jamb scrolling through his phone. "Buchanan will sort it for ya. He did ours, and we look shit hot!"

I rolled my eyes and clenched my jaw as my hands shook. "Dillon, it's going to be fine." B put his hands on my shoulders and squeezed. "We've got you, man. The three of us have your back no matter what." I pulled a smile on my face and let out a relieved breath. It was scary to put my trust in other people. It was no problem on the field, but in real life, I'd been burned so many times I found it almost impossible.

"Thanks, guys. That means a lot." I looked at each of them in turn. My throat felt tight, and my eyes stung as I came to realize I actually had some really good friends around me. I felt like shit for being such a cold bastard to them most of the time.

"That hurt to say, didn't it, Cap." McCormack snickered into a bottle of beer he pulled out of nowhere.

"Uh, yeah." I closed my eyes as B ordered me to lift my head so he could finish fixing my bowtie.

"You know, it all makes sense now," he added.

"What does?"

"Why you had it out for Goldilocks." McCormack wiggled his eyebrows, and I glowered at him. "They do say love and hate are two sides of the same coin, after all."

I sighed, my shoulders sagging. "I was an asshole."

"You can say that again," Vieck added, not looking up from his phone while B snorted in my face. *Jerk.* "So, you gonna tell us about your boy toy?"

"He's not a fucking toy," I growled. "Jamie's it for me. Always has been, but I was just..."

"Terrified of the ramifications? Worried about how people would react? What might happen to you and the team?" Three pairs of eyes turned to Vieck who finally glanced up from his phone. "What?"

"Dude, that was deep." McCormack looked at our friend like he'd never seen him before. I felt the same, but I guess everyone had layers—you just didn't get to see under them most of the time.

With a deep sigh, Vieck pocketed his phone and crossed his arms over his chest. "Look, I know we all get sucked into upholding the heteronormative culture that gets pushed down our throats, but not all of us fit in it."

"What are you saying, Jordan?" B asked softly.

"I'm bi, okay? I might tip more towards boobs, but I love a bit of dick too." Vieck smirked, and the ambiguous tension that had been building in the room dissipated.

I couldn't help but laugh, and the guys wore matching smirks. "Guess I got myself into a shit situation when I didn't need to. If I'd known..."

"You'd have had to talk to us then, Cap," Vieck added as he snatched and drained McCormack's beer before asking if he had another. McCormack wiggled his eyebrows and held a fresh bottle over his head, taunting Vieck, and the two started bickering.

"Done," B said and smoothed down the shoulders of my jacket and gave me a small smile. "Tonight is gonna be fine. Trust in us and your boy. He's going to look amazing. Levi is incredible at what he does. The real question is—can you keep it in your pants?"

"Fuck you," I muttered, but it held no heat because he wasn't wrong in the slightest. Jamie had described some of the outfits he would be walking in, and fuck me.

"It's alright, I've got Kleenex," McCormack joked, and Vieck slapped him over the head.

"Don't be a dick. There's some fine ass going to be up there tonight, trust me." Vieck winked.

"Jesus. I'm surrounded by horny fuckers." McCormack groaned and checked his watch. "We need to get going if we're going to make the pre-show drinks." He rubbed his hands together. "I've never been to a pre anything before. This is going to be so cool."

"Child. You're a damn man-child." Buchanan laughed and motioned for us to get out of my room. "Let's go. We're taking my car, because I am not getting this suit wet for no one."

We filed out of the building and jumped into B's car. The wind and rain were picking up, and what should have been a quick drive took us nearly fifteen minutes. My nerves were eating away at me, and no amount of deep breathing was helping. My knee bounced erratically, my heart hammered a chaotic staccato rhythm against my ribs, and I had to keep rubbing my sweaty palms on my trousers. By the time we stepped onto the blacktop by the exhibition center, I was ready to puke.

A line had already formed on the white carpet they'd rolled out, and the windows looked like snowflakes were falling down them. The excitement level was palpable as we straightened our suits and headed in, flashing our passes to the guys on door. The outside display had nothing on the transformation that had taken place on the inside of the hall. The glass walls were draped with swathes of white fabric with twinkling lights behind them, giving off a muted glow. Small tables were littered around the edges of the space. People I didn't recognize stood around them, having quiet conversations with drinks in their hands. But it was the ceiling that captivated my attention; it resembled a cloudy night sky with falling snowflakes. It looked so real you just wanted to touch it and capture one of the snowflakes in the palm of your hand.

"This is good shit," McCormack said as we took in the freshly decorated space with awe. "I'm going to get some drinks."

"See you when the show starts," I said, but he was striding away, heading toward one of the waiters with a tray full of drinks like a man on a mission.

"Have you seen him yet?" Buchanan asked as he grabbed a drink for both of us from a passing waiter.

"No." But as soon as the words left my mouth, the twinkling lights caught on golden curls, and my heart stopped.

Jamie looked amazing in a simple white suit that hugged his body to perfection. As if he felt me looking at him, he stopped talking to whoever he was with and our eyes locked. Even from this distance, I could feel the appreciative heat in his gaze. A smile lifted the corners of my lips, and some of my nervous energy abated just from knowing where he was. Jesus, I was whipped. But he was so fucking worth it.

"Dillon? Dillon?" A hand waved in front of my face, breaking our connection. "Ah, I see you've found him. Shall we go see the star? Or should I say, snowflake." My gaze snapped to B, my smile morphing into a sneer.

"Snowflake?"

B choked, spitting his drink all over the place before he covered his mouth. "Man, your face. It's a winter wonderland. I thought snowflake was all kinds of fitting."

I grunted in response, ignoring his laugh and somehow dodging his elbow too. "Who's that prick who thinks he can touch what's mine?" I said between clenched teeth. I fisted my hands to hide the violent fury pulsing down my arms.

The guy in question had Jamie backed against a wall in a semi-dark corner. His arm was braced next to Jamie's head, like he was caging him in. Jamie's eyes darted back and forth with increasing frequency as we weaved our way through the growing number of people gathering for the show. "Fuck this."

"Dillon, calm down. I'm sure it's nothing," B whispered in my ear. "Don't go making a scene and fucking this up for him." I glared at him, and he held his hands up in surrender. "What? You're a possessive son of a bitch, aren't you?" Unable to answer, I nodded as we finally broke through the crowd, only a few feet separating me and Jamie.

His wide eyes flicked up to mine just as the jackass trailed a finger down his cheek, making him freeze as the color drained from his face. The pained look in his features and the twitch at the corner of his left eye had me ready to smash the douchebag's head in with my foot.

"Oh fuck, this isn't good." Buchanan's voice sounded faint as the world around me faded away and narrowed down to the two figures in front of me. Blood whooshed in my ears, and my knuckles cracked.

"What's going on here?" I growled and slipped my arm round Jamie's waist, pulling him into me, and effectively moving him out of the douchebag's reach. Bloodlust took over when my little crow looked up at me with tear-filled eyes, genuine fear swimming in their blue depths.

"D-Dillon...t-this is—" I silenced him with a kiss. My chest heaved as I tried to wrangle my emotions under control so I didn't scare him, but as our lips touched, the frantic energy bleeding from him subsided as he melted into me. My tongue dipped into his mouth, and he moaned as it wrapped around his. The rage inside me quietened until the rude fucker cleared his throat. My eyes snapped open to see him glaring at me with his lip curled back in a sneer.

"I've got you, baby." I placed a chaste kiss on his lips once, and then once more. "Let Taylor take you backstage, okay? I'll be there in a minute. I just need to take out the trash."

Wide glistening eyes stared into my soul. Fuck, I loved him. Jamie licked his lips, and a slight touch of color bloomed on his too pale cheeks. "Okay." He placed a hand over my thundering heart. "Just be safe."

The twat next to us scoffed, and I turned my ire on him. "Got it, baby." I forced a congenial smile on my face, and Jamie rolled his eyes at me. "Go get ready. I can't wait to see you in action."

"Thanks!" He kissed my cheek and let Buchanan lead him through the crowd and away from this sad sack of shit.

"You!" My hand shot out and wrapped around his throat, pinning him to the wall. His fingers scraped against mine, trying to gain purchase. A malicious smile cut across my face as I allowed my jealousy and anger to consume me.

"Do you know who I am?" He whimpered like the pathetic limp dick he was.

"You could be Jesus for all I care. No one, and I mean fucking no one, lays a hand on my boyfriend without his permission."

"He was begging for it, willing to do anything to get a contract with me. Levi invited me here tonight to check out the models. If you hurt me, he'll know."

I stepped into the jackass and pinned him against the wall, my nose brushing his. "Levi won't give a fuck what I do to you when I tell him what you were doing to that sweet boy. Fuckers like you make me sick."

"It's the industry. Stuff like this happens all the time, and no one will care what you say."

I snorted at his arrogance. "You think I care? We're going to go have a chat somewhere a little more private. That's what you like, isn't it? Private places with little boys?" He made me sick. The dick must have been in his late forties, with his thinning hair and terrible teeth.

"You're not really my type." He squeaked as I yanked him off the wall and dragged him through the fire exit.

"Well, you're not mine either, but tonight I'll make an exception." I spat at him as the door crashed open. The cold wet air hit me like a wall of ice, and the idiot fell over his feet and face-planted on the ground. I wrapped my hand in his hair and yanked his head back. "You touch him again, and this will look a lot like love," I said and punched him hard enough to hear a crack. Warmth flowed over my hand, and I smirked.

"AHH," he cried, scrambling to cup his hand over his face. But because of how he'd fallen, all he could do was whimper.

"Pathetic." I dragged him by his hair and threw him against the solid brick wall. "When you wake up, you're going to leave and never come back."

"W-w-what?" He looked at me with dark bloodshot eyes that swirled with fear. Blood poured over his lips too fast to lick away. He shook in my hold and groaned as the scent of urine filled the air.

"What the fuck?" I looked down in horror at his pants. "You sick fuck! Remember what I said?" He nodded. "Goodnight." I punched him in the temple so hard he blacked out instantly and fell to the ground in a heap. He wouldn't be getting up and time soon.

"Shit." I was a mess. My knuckles were split and covered in blood. The door slammed into the wall as someone stepped out. "Fuck." I clenched my fists, feeling the burn of the split skin and whirled on whoever was coming for me with a snarl on my face.

"Chill, Cap," Vieck said as McCormack stepped up beside him. "We thought you might need some help cleaning up and taking the trash out."

Vieck smiled and passed me a wet cloth to wipe myself down with. The cool water stung my knuckles but was definitely welcome as I cleared that fucker's blood off me.

"What d'you want us to do with him?" McCormack asked as he kicked the lump of man flesh to see if it would move.

"Don't care. Just get rid of it and this." I handed him the cloth which he stuck in a bag.

"We got you, Cap," Veck said, pulling keys from his pocket. "We'll get rid of him. Enjoy the show. I'm sorry we'll miss it though."

"You should stay," I muttered halfheartedly, desperate to get back in there and check on Jamie.

"Don't." Vieck held up his hand. "This is far more important."

"Exactly. We've got him. Go support your boy." McCormack grunted as he lifted the sack of shit off the ground. "Vieck, bring the car around, and Cap, fuck off!" He smiled as he moved into the shadows away from any prying eyes that might come our way.

I hurried back inside and slipped into my seat next to Buchanan just in time to see the dancers and Ava, one of Jamie's best friends, disappear behind the curtain looking like winter fairies. The lighting dropped to a muted glow as the runaway cleared. I sighed as the tension in my muscles ebbed away, and I flexed and my aching fingers. I couldn't wait to see my man up there. I loved him so much. Now I've finally gotten him, I'll never, ever let him go.

"All sorted?"

"Yup. Was he okay?"

Buchanan sighed and ran his hand through his hair. "I think so? He seemed shaken, but Levi nabbed him as soon as we got through the curtain and pulled him into makeup. So hopefully, he'll be too distracted to think about it at all until after the show, and then you'll be there."

"Okay, that's good. I hope. I'm glad I haven't missed anything." I gave B a tentative smile, even though I couldn't shake the feeling that tonight wasn't done with throwing us into the line of fire.

"Nah, the good stuff is about to start."

A voice boomed through the room as they announced the winter wonderland showcase and the order of the designers that would be presenting their lines. The lights lifted and a dry icy smog floated over the base of the runway, setting the scene. According to Jamie, we had some of the best seats in the house, right at the end of the runway. Music started to play as a silhouetted figure broke through the curtains and took to the stage. Applause rang out as Jamie's figure cut through the smog, and my world narrowed down to him. Always. Only. Him.

"Fuck," I groaned and scrubbed my hand down my face as my eyes roved all over Jamie's body.

"He looks good."

I narrowed my eyes at B, and he smiled right back. "Fucking dick," I muttered, but my attention was captivated by Jamie as he walked down the runway like he owned the place. His golden curls took on an icy edge to fit the theme, and his face glittered like it was covered in a million crystals. His pale-blue eyes looked luminous under the lights, but it was the fact that they were locked on me that heated the blood in my veins and had me adjusting my hard dick before he'd made it halfway. My eyes dragged down his body to the sheer net shirt draped over his torso. Long sleeves encased his arms right down to his fingertips and draped around his neck. The small pearl and crystal detail that covered it reminded me of freshly fallen snow glittering in the sun.

"Wow," Buchanan said as Jamie stopped in front of us and winked. When a whoop rang out behind us, a fucking epic blush stained his cheeks.

"Mine!" I ignored B as I watched my little crow's ass sway in his fitted white pants as he sashayed back up the runway.

CHAPTER THIRTY-SIX

Jamie

"Holy shit! Holy shit," I chanted as adrenaline coursed through my body, making me vibrate with the overabundance of energy. I felt like I was soaring and falling simultaneously.

"JJ, babe. You're magic! Just magic out there. I'm so proud of you." Levi squealed as he wrapped me up in his arms. "Did you have a chance to chat to Derek before the show? He was eager to meet you after I sent him some of the pictures of our dress rehearsal."

I gulped as my stomach fell through the floor. "Uh, ah, y-yeah." I started to shake, and the world swirled around me. I flushed hot and cold, and my throat tightened.

"Shit! JJ? What's wrong? Can someone get me some water?"

"L-Levi...h-he... tried..." I heaved in a gulp of air.

"Here." A cold metal straw pressed up against my lips.

"Drink this, Jamie, it'll help. Just focus on taking little sips, okay?"

I gulped down a few mouthfuls of cool water and it eased the tension that had suddenly ripped through me. With each swallow, I came back to myself and was able to order my thoughts properly. "H-he propositioned me and h-he touched—"

"He did what?!" Levi cried in outrage and started pacing in front of me, waving his hands around frantically. "I mean, I've heard rumors, but I've never known... I've never..." He shook his head and knelt at my feet, taking my hand in his.

"I-it's okay, he didn't tou... Dillon was there, he..." I bit my lip and silenced my words. I didn't know what he did after I left, but he took care of me, and that was all that mattered. He was my very own hero. No, that wasn't right. I knew he'd burn the world down to save me. That made Dillon my villain, and I loved him for it. Every possessive touch and word just did it for me, in a way nothing else ever has. It was him. It was always him and always would be.

"Good. I can't believe I'm saying this, but I'm glad that oaf was there."

I barked a laugh and slapped his shoulder. "Dillon is anything but." I sighed, probably with hearts in my eyes even though they stung with tears I refused to let fall. I was stronger than that; nothing happened. It just shook me that Derek was so brazen. The full room didn't deter him in the slightest. I shuddered at the thought.

"He's a beast on the field, and I bet he is in the bedroom too!" I gasped as Levi wiggled his eyebrows. "Some of those players are amazing, especially when they're throwing you around the room." He sighed, fanning himself.

I cocked my head to the side, eyeing him with suspicion. "And who on the team have you 'exercised' with?" I used my fingers to make air quotes as a teasing grin lifted my lips. Levi bent over double, clutching an arm over his stomach as he laughed at me. With me? Who knows.

"Jesus, Jamie, you're too much," he wheezed. "Anyway, I'm a good boy—I don't kiss and tell. Most of them are so far in the closet, they're not ready to be discussed like this."

My shoulders slumped, and I nodded, because I got it more than he knew. "Yeah. I totally get that. I think that was a massive part of the issues Dil and I had." I rolled my bottom lip between my teeth. "But now, I think we've come through that. I've seen all his ugly parts, and I know all his mistakes. I know he's sorry for what happened."

"You mean siccing his friends and everyone else on you?" The serious look on his face told me he didn't approve one bit.

"Yeah. That. But," I held up my finger as he sucked in a sharp inhale like he was about to speak. "It came from a place of fear—I'm sure you can understand?" Levi's eyes dropped to the floor, and he scuffed his boot against my chair. When he looked back up at me, his eyes swam with painful memories.

"I totally do. Growing up, I always knew I was different. I always liked boys. Girls were pretty to look at and all, and I love them, but boys...ugh, their muscled arms. Forearm porn is a thing, and if anyone tells you differently, they're lying." He snorted and smirked as I rolled my eyes. "And dick. You can't beat dick."

"I guess not. Dil's is—"

Levi slapped his hand over my mouth, so I licked it. "You can not tell me about your man's dick!" The outrage in his voice buoyed my spirits even more. "That man is a beast. His arms. *Oh my god!* His ass, damn...that thing looks like it's carved from marble." I snickered and finished my drink as Levi drooled over Dillon. I was surprised I didn't feel a hint of jealousy, because I did daily when people looked at him. But with Levi? Nothing.

"Oh it is, and his dic—"

"Shut up! I can't take this," Levi whined and placed his

hand on his forehead like a dramatic fainting maiden. "I bet it's goddamn perfect, isn't it? Thick and long, hits all the right places when he's pounding—"

"Now it's your turn to shut up." Heat flushed from my chest to the tips of my ears. I blew out a heavy breath and smiled. "Thank you, Levi."

He wrapped his arms around me, giving me a tight squeeze. "I've got you. Doesn't mean I'm not insanely jealous you bagged the second hottest guy in school."

"Only second?"

"Yeah, in my eyes anyway. You two make the hottest couple though. Chad and Elise have nothing on you." He cupped his hand over my ear and whispered, "Just don't tell her that. I can't lose my runner for the night."

I blinked up at him in confusion. That bitch was here? Thank every star in the sky I hadn't seen her. She made my skin crawl. It made me so damn angry the way she'd acted all proprietarily over Dillon, the way she clung to him and touched him all the time, even though a blind person could have seen he wasn't into her.

"Ten minutes, you two," Kaileigh said as she scampered past, wheeling a loaded clothes rail. "Justin is waiting in makeup for the final look. I suggest getting it on before you see him."

I looked over at Levi's large grin and narrowed my eyes. "This is the only outfit you haven't shown me. Why is that?"

Levi blushed—something I didn't even think was possible for him—and sighed, plopping down in the vacant seat next to mine. "One, because I only finished it this morning, and two, because it is the most sensual thing I've ever created, and I designed it with you in mind."

"It's in the changing area." Kaileigh scurried past with a beaming smile on her face before I could question him further about it.

"I really want to know, but I also like that it's a surprise." I chuckled half-heartedly as my heart rate picked up and sweat slicked my palms. This was what excitement felt like; a drop of anticipation and a dash of trepidation. I'd never thought I would walk in a fashion show, let alone wear the design his collection centered around. But to find out he'd designed it with me in mind, before he'd even asked me to model, felt like an honor I couldn't refuse.

"Everyone will want you after this, and I don't doubt there are a few straight men questioning themselves after seeing you out there tonight." I hummed in agreement, but I didn't care —I only had eyes for one man. As long as he liked what he saw, it didn't matter what anyone else thought. This was just some fun for me, but for Levi, it counted toward his final grade, and I would never let him down.

"It's an honor to be the last to walk, to close the show, Jamie. And considering this was your first time?" He shook his head. "You've shone like the brightest star in the sky. I hope you've enjoyed it."

"Oh my god, don't." I fanned my hand in front of my face as tears pricked my eyes. "You're getting me all emotional. How dare you!" Levi smiled and held out a hand for me. Thank god he did, because my legs felt like Jell-O under the weight of expectation. What if this outfit looked dreadful on me? What if I fell on my face and made an ass out of myself?

He held back the curtain and ushered me into the small changing area. There was a silver garment bag hung on the rail and a mirror propped against the only solid wall. "Stop stressing. You'll be fine. Just look at your man and focus on him. Trust me when I say you need to look at him, because he won't be able to take his eyes off you."

My eyes fluttered closed as I inhaled deeply and counted to ten and then back down again. When I peeled them open, I felt nothing but excitement zinging through me. "Alright. I'm ready."

Levi clapped his hands together in excitement, unzipped

the bag, and slowly peeled out my next outfit. My heart was in my throat when I saw nothing but the finest net glittering in the lights. It took a while for my eyes to adjust to the minute intricate details that made up the garment. It was exquisite. Tiny snowflakes glimmered next to diamantés and a smattering of pearls. But one thing didn't escape my notice. "Ah, Levi?"

"Yeah, babe?" The devilish look in his eyes said everything.

"I-it's see through."

He threw his head back and belly laughed. "It's not entirely, babe."

"Everyone will see my dick!" I pointed out, and the little shit snickered again.

"I've got something for you that will cover it." He dived back into the bag and pulled out a micro G-string that only had enough holographic material to cover my dick; everything else looked like floss.

"I'll break that putting it on!"

"You won't, I promise." His eyes glinted with mischief. "I can always help you put it on."

A giggle slipped past my lips. "Yeah, thanks, but no. Dillon would have something to say about that."

He laughed and nodded. "But I will help you with the main piece. You'll never be able to button it up on your own." He rolled on the balls of his feet. "You good?"

"Yeah," I squeaked and swallowed as a lump caught in my throat. "I've got it. Now get out and let me get in this teeny-weeny thing. I'll shout when I'm done."

Beads of perspiration dotted my brow and trickled down my spine as I stripped and folded my clothes into a neat pile, setting them on the back of the chair. I took a few calming breaths as adrenaline spiked through me, making my hands tremble. I shook my head at the tiny piece of material posing as underwear. *I'm going to hell for this.* I stepped into it and pulled it up, terrified the strings on the side would snap and I'd end up flashing myself to the audience. Once it was in place, I looked at myself in the mirror and grinned. Maybe I could keep this for Dillon.

"I'm ready. I think?" I called out and Levi chuckled while talking to Kaileigh about where my boots were. I'd never worn heels before the dress rehearsal. I'd ended up with bruises in places I didn't think possible from wearing shoes, but he promised they'd make the outfit along with the wings.

Excitement eddied through me as Levi appeared with boots in hand. They'd been upgraded since I last wore them. They were now a shimmering silver with the same beadwork as the outfit I was going to be wearing. He looked up at me with eyes so bright they glowed. "They look incredible, if I do say so myself."

"Did you make them?"

"No." He shook his head and dragged a small stool over, sitting down. "I gave the design to Kaileigh, and she did the beadwork while I finished this showstopper and the wings."

"I can't wait to see it all finished," I said as I stepped into the outfit Levi held out for me. I dared not breathe for fear of the fine lace splitting. "Did you manage to get the lighting working?"

"I did, and they look..." He brought his fingers to his lips and gave a chef's kiss. "Now, step back slowly and hold your arms out while I slip this on for you."

The piece Levi designed fit like a second skin, and the soft lace felt like silk flowing over my skin. The material was loose enough to move freely, which prevented the many embellishments from chafing. Levi positively radiated excitement, and I could hardly stand still while Justin applied my makeup. He used cool blue, silver, and gray tones to accentuate my eyes and swiped a shimmering sheen across my cheekbones.

I picked up a host of tips from him, and couldn't wait to put them into practice and bring Dillon to his knees.

By the time we worked the delicate gladiator-style knee-high boots up my legs, I was bouncing on my toes, ready to go. All the trepidation and fear bubbling under my skin melted away, and I felt like I was flying.

"Two minutes," Kaileigh called from the curtain. "Fog's up and lights are lowering runway side." She turned to look at me, and her mouth fell open on a gasp.

"Does it look okay?" Insecurity bled through me as I chewed on my lip, earning a slap from Justin who had to touch up my lip gloss.

"Behave, Jamie," he muttered as he covered my face with his hand and sprayed my hair with glitter spray. I felt like every femboy's dream, and I loved it.

"Jamie, you look...you... wow! The design was good to begin with—"

"Thanks, babe," Levi interjected, strolling past her with my wings.

"But honestly, you complete it. You look like a fairy. No. A snow angel."

Levi snickered as he guided the straps over my arms and clipped the harness over my chest. Thank god for the addition of padding, because these things weighed a ton. They stood two feet above my head and trailed on the ground, even with my four inch heels on. They were the most elegant piece of construction I'd ever seen, with layer upon layer of sparkling white feathers covered them. They really did look like angel wings. I turned in a slow circle when Levi made a circular motion with his finger and made his final checks.

"Comfortable? Does the weight feel evenly distributed?"

I nodded, unable to speak as nerves shot through me. It didn't matter I'd done this four times already tonight; this was the show stopping showcase design, and I dreaded messing it up for him.

His hands landed on my shoulders, and I looked down at him. "Just remember how we practiced. The room is dark right now, so they will see you silhouetted once you're behind the curtain. Kaileigh will pull them back, and the runway will be illuminated under the smog. Focus on your man and walk straight down the middle. Take it slow, because these babies are heavy. Most of all, remember to breathe and enjoy it. Okay?"

"Fun, right." The air whooshed out of my lungs as I stepped up behind the curtain and a hush fell beyond it. I sucked in a deep breath and closed my eyes to center myself before nodding at Kaileigh. Levi gave me a thumbs up, and I cracked a smile. My heart thundered behind my ribs, and exhilaration uncoiled inside me. My arms braced against my wings, and I focused on Kaileigh counting down with her fingers before the curtain pulled back. I could see before me was the glowing smog of the walkway. I lifted my eyes and searched for Dillon. Even though I knew where he was, I still searched until that instinctual pull between us locked on to him.

My first step was tentative, and I feared the floor beneath my feet was an illusion. But once I knew the ground was solid, my nerves bled away. After my second step, the wings on my back glowed, and the audience gasped. Dillon was out of his seat, halfway to the stage, his dark eyes burning with lust. He looked like he wanted to devour me. A smirk lifted the corner of my lips as I drew closer to him. Catcalls sounded around me as I stopped at the end. I bit down on my lip when Taylor and Mal had to hold Dillon down in his seat as I peered down at him.

I winked at him before turning and walking back up the runway, his deep groan ringing in my ears. The rest of my walk faded away, like I was lost in a dream. Nothing seemed real—not getting hugged by Levi and Kaileigh, not doing a final walk with Levi, not receiving rapturous applause, or doing too many interviews to remember. I vaguely recalled a guy named Matthieu Montoya who raved at Levi and begged me to work with him, but it all flowed around me like an ocean current.

By the time I wobbled back through the curtain with aching feet, I was exhausted. All I wanted to do was fall into a chair, drink a million bottles of water, and have Dillon carry me away. I couldn't walk another step. "Wait up, Jamie." Kaileigh ran after me with a broad brown-haired guy. "We need to get your wings off before you collapse and break them and end up hurting yourself."

I waved her off, staggering a bit as my burning feet turned numb. "I'm good," I lied, my eyes heavy as the adrenaline crash hit like a Mack truck.

"No you're not. Prescott, grab him for me before he collapses," Kaileigh said, frantically undoing the harness before slipping it from my shoulders.

"Ahh," I groaned as the weight dragging me down was gone, and I was suddenly floating.

"Let's switch," she said to Prescott, handing him the wings for him to put away before leading me to a chair."Just a couple of minutes, and I'll get your boots off, Jamie. I promise. I've got some water for you to soak your feet in too. I bet they hurt like a bitch."

"You can say that again." I huffed a laugh and grabbed the bottle of water that was on the stand beside me and downed it. Kaileigh snorted and set a bowl of warm water at my feet and fuck, did it feel amazing. She studied me for a second and glanced around the backstage area before turning to me with a bright smile.

"You did so well out there, Jamie. Levi is over the moon." She looked over her shoulder again and sighed. "He said he was gonna come back and talk to you, but he must have gotten held up. You can catch up with him during the gala. I'm sure he'll fill you in on all his news there."

I flexed my toes in the water as the feeling slowly came back to them, but my legs still felt like rubber, and the idea of standing around drinking was growing less and less appealing by the second. I rolled my head, the muscles in my back aching. A wave of exhaustion washed over me, and my eyelids felt heavy. "We'll see, but to be honest, I'm beat and just want to Netflix and chill." She snorted and guided me forward so she could unbutton the back of my outfit. "Could you get Dillon for me? I don't think I can walk."

She pressed a kiss to my cheek when she was done and smiled at me. "You got it, hun. Oh, before I forget, this was left for you. I'll leave it here with a fresh bottle of water and go and get your man."

I focused on stripping out of my outfit and managed to get it off without damaging it or dropping it in the bowl of water. I pushed it away with my foot, because knowing my luck, I'd trip over it and end up face first in the damn thing. I snorted at the image of Dillon's horrified face when he found me floundering in three inches of water.

Once dressed, I put the garment back in its bag—sans cute teeny-weeny G-string—and pulled on a pair of Dillon's sweats and his hoodie. The soft material felt like butter on my skin as I slipped my shoes back on. I stumbled over to my chair and snagged the bottle of water Kaileigh left me and downed that too. Exhaustion ate away at me, piece by piece. My eyes shuttered as I sighed. Why was Dillon taking so long? As I began to drift, Kaileigh's words ran through my mind, and my eyes popped open.

The black envelope on the table in front me wavered before my eyes. It couldn't be. I snatched it up with trembling hands, nearly dropping it as I tried to open it. Bile stuck in my throat, the taste getting stronger with every breath I took and it made my eyes water. I upended the envelope, and four Polaroids and a card fell out.

"Oh, fuck no!" The first tear fell as my mind recognized the image. Someone in the audience took a picture of me with glowing wings and a beaming smile on my face. My heart fought its way up my throat. The next was of me standing in front of Dillon with his face scored out and the word *slut* written across the bottom. The last two were of me before the show, getting ready backstage. Ice sheeted my skin as a violent shudder rocked through me.

"This can't b-be happening." My voice was hoarse as it pushed past my lips, and I tasted my tears on my tongue. I released a tremulous breath and turned over the black piece of card, as I read the words.

I'VE FOUND YOU!

It slipped from my fingers as I frantically scrambled off my seat. My feet slipped out from underneath me as I tried to run to the backstage door, my heart and head pounding a staccato rhythm. The walls wavered around me. My slick palms slid off the handle, unable to open the door. Darkness crawled across my vision.

"Not like this. Not like this. Please...not like this," I muttered and tried to yank open my bag and get my phone to call Uncle Daire.

Tears burned down my cheeks. Sobs ripped my throat raw as unintelligible sounds passed my lips. I swiped my hand across my eyes, trying to clear the darkness. My fingers latched around the burner at the bottom of my bag just as the door opened. "T-thank g-god, Dil..."

"There's no god here," a shrill voice cackled. "It's time to meet your maker." My heart froze. *No. No. No.* "Pick him up. Chad. I want my money. and that sick fuck's not going to pay until we hand him over."

"Ugh. I hope I don't end up covered in fucking glitter." The world around me blurred. I felt like I was at sea, the rough water rocking side to side as lights flashed around me. *Dillon...*

The loud bang of a door jolted me awake. The faint thudding of music reached my ears, but everything was black. "About fucking time, young lady," a dark voice growled. "Take it and fuck off."

“I’d say it’s been a pleas...” The voice trailed off as two loud shots rang out. I was floating. Falling. Cold hard ground hit my face.

My head was wrenched backward, and my eyes flung open. “Hello, son.” Pain exploded in my head. My dad’s vile sneer was the last thing I saw before it all went black.

CHAPTER THIRTY-SEVEN

Dillon

"Dillon? Hey, excuse me?"

I turned around and glowered at the redhead tapping my shoulder. "What?" She retreated a couple of steps back and wrung her hands. "What did you want?"

"Dillon, be nice," Buchanan scolded me, handing me another beer. Jamie was taking forever to get changed, but whatever. I could be patient. I did have my limits though, and if another five minutes went by, I'd storm backstage to find him.

"Oh, umm. Jamie asked if you could go backstage and help him? His feet are kill—"

"When did he tell you to ask me?" I bit out. Was she for real? The show finished almost forty minutes ago.

"Errm." She glanced at her watch and winced. "Like forty minutes ago?

"Fuck!"

"S-sorry, I got distracted." I stepped right up in her personal space and bent down so we were eye level. "If he's upset, or worse, hurt…" I poked her in the chest. "I'm holding you personally responsible."

"He'll be fine, he was soaking his feet when I left him." I ignored her fumbled words, tapped B on the shoulder for him to follow me, and cut through the crowd toward the side entrance for the backstage area.

"Why are *we* doing this, Dillon? He wanted *you*."

I glanced at him over my shoulder. "Call it trusting my gut. Something isn't right." I didn't know how to explain it, but as the minutes ticked by, the tension in my body coiled tighter and tighter. After that slimy twerp earlier and now this… it felt like things were working against me and my little crow. Nothing on this goddamn green earth was going to keep him from me.

Jamie liked to think of me as a good guy. And to him—minus my fuck-ups the last few months—I was. But to everyone else, I was a deranged man child with a hair-trigger temper. The only people to ever cross me were Stevens and fucking Chad, and they were about to realize revenge was a dish best served cold. When I was through with them, they would no longer be on the team and most likely kicked out of Briar U altogether.

Cory was worth his weight in fucking gold. He found out about their sex game and how Stevens got so many conquests. The guy had been drugging girls left and right to get the highest points in a night. Fucking savages! Disgusting. I couldn't believe I once thought Stevens was a decent guy. It turned out I was a shit judge of character, unlike my little crow. He surrounded himself with people who would go to war for him. They were drawn to him like moths to a flame.

The door looming in front of me snapped me out of my thoughts, and I pulled down the handle. It didn't open. What the fuck? Irritation and a flash of fear coursed through me. "Fuck this door," I ground out and slammed my shoulder into it. Buchanan laughed behind me, muttering "Fuck that bush. Fuck that bush." Fucking child. It took our combined forces to open the door, and once we got through, it all made sense. Someone had barricaded it with storage shelves and prop shit.

"This ain't good."

"You can say that again, B." I grunted as I kicked a pile of boxes out of the way.It was like a fucking rabbit warren around here, and was dark as night. "Fuck!" I yanked my hair as the door slammed shut behind us, and my skin crawled with frustration.

"I'll get the... shit."

"What?"

"The lights don't work." He pulled out his phone and switched on the flashlight. Thank fuck one of us was thinking straight. I pulled mine out and did the same.

"Which way?"

"Call him. If he's here, you can follow his ringtone." He paused. "Assuming you know it, that is."

I punched him in the shoulder. "Of course, I fucking know it. It's some Falling In Reverse song he's obsessed with." I tapped the speed dial, and his phone rang in my ear, but I couldn't hear anything in the space around us. Buchanan muttered something, but I didn't catch it as I was too focused on the fact my call went to voicemail.

"Levi said to go straight ahead. It's the last door on the right."

Levi? He must have texted him. I shook my head at myself. I needed to stop letting my emotions get in the way of rational thought.

"Come on," I replied, picking up my pace. Buchanan followed, hot on my heels. My heart was hammering against my ribs, but I ignored it, trying to keep my mind clear and focused as I tried Jamie's phone again.

"He also said there was no issue with the lights."

Well, that was just fucking great. I knew something was off. "Fuck me! This damn door is locked too. Step back!" I braced against the wall opposite the door before charging it and kicking it in. It crashed into the drywall, the sound reverberating through the large room.

B flicked the light switch. "Still no lights."

Jamie's phone went to voicemail for the fourth time, and I still couldn't hear his ringtone. I wanted to punch the damn wall as frustration ate away at me, but I couldn't. I refused to let him down again, like when I almost hurt him in my room. Fuck, that killed me to think about, and it probably always would. It was my cross to bear; my penance for being a broken piece of shit too scared to embrace what was right in front of me. I would spend the rest of my life begging for his forgiveness.

"Voicemail again. I say we start by the runway entrance and work back. There must be another exit somewhere in here, right?" I turned to look at B and nearly blinded him with my flashlight. "Right?" He shrugged and followed behind me as we swept our phones in an arc, looking for any sign of him, but there was nothing. What the hell? He wouldn't have left without me. He'd have called or texted me to let me know if he was going to leave, that much I was sure of. The space was empty apart from a few chairs in front of dressing tables and the odd empty box. I glanced at them before moving on, not seeing anything.

"Uh, Dillon? Come 'ere."

"What is it?"

"Just fucking get over here. Now." Buchanan stood by one of the chairs, the hysterical edge to his voice making me rush over. "Here. Look at these." His voice wavered as he passed me four Polaroids.

"What the fuck?! What the hell is this?" I looked at him wide eyed.

My chest felt so tight, it was like my heart was on the verge exploding as I flicked through them. A photo of Jamie on the runway, one of him with me, and two of him backstage.

My hand covered my mouth as bile seared a path up the back of my throat and coated my tongue. I scrunched the photos in my fist as anger and fear pulsed through me. This was a fucking pile of shit. I tucked them in my pocket in case we had to call the police if we couldn't find him. I refused to accept that outcome.

Jamie was fucking *mine!* No one took what belonged to me and got away with it. Fuck that shit. I'd burn the world to the ground before I lost him again. Five years without him was like being stuck on death row. I refused to contemplate another stay in that hellhole.

"Where did you find them?"

"Here on the chair and on the floor. Uh, hang on." He dropped to his knees and pulled something out from under the bowl of water. "Got it." Buchanan handed me a card.

I'VE FOUND YOU!

"Fuck. What does this mean?" My knees buckled and collapsed underneath me. I braced my hands on the floor and dry heaved with each gasping breath, but couldn't stop rereading the damn message as it stared up at me. A hand landed on my shoulder, and I flinched as my mind spiraled.

"Pull yourself together, Dillon. You're not going to be any help to him like this." B sighed as he straightened, pulling me up by the collar of my shirt. He grabbed my jaw and forced me to look at him, his face swathed in shadows. "Look, we don't know what's going on, but we will find him. Focus on that and get your head in the game." He pushed his forehead into mine. "Focus, Hargraves."

Focus? I wanted to kick the shit out of something and make some fucker bleed. Instead, I grunted and pulled away, stalking to the corner we hadn't searched yet and using my phone to search the area."Oh shit." My heart froze mid-beat, and every muscle in my body locked up as tight as my eyes snagged on Jamie's bag. My feet moved of their own volition, and I tore through his bag before realizing what I was doing. I yanked out his phone, tapped the screen, and saw seven missed calls. Four from me and three unknowns.

"Can you hear that? That buzzing?"

I couldn't hear much above the ringing in my ears. B dropped down next to me and emptied the contents of Jamie's bag on the floor while I shined the light from my phone on it. Papers, books, makeup, and an old-style phone skittered across the floor.

"I've got it." The illuminated screen went dark just as I grabbed it, but it started to ring again immediately. I glanced at the screen to see who it was, but it was a withheld number. Thankfully, there was no password or face recognition; all I had to do was press the green phone button.

I pushed it and held it to my ear. My heart throbbed behind my ribs and blood pounded in my ears. "Thank fuck, Jamie! Where the hell are you? I need to get to you right now! He's there. Jamie—"

"Who the fuck is this?" I growled as my stomach lurched. Why was another man calling Jamie? He sounded older, powerful. Was my little crow…? Tears stung my eyes. No. He wouldn't cheat on me. He wouldn't! I sunk my teeth into the bottom of my lip as I tried to make sense of what the hell was going on.

"Where the hell is Jamie?"

"Shut up, asshole. I asked first! Who are you, and how do you know Jamie?" The phone slipped from my sweat-slicked hand, but I caught it before it hit the floor. "Fuck."

"…again. I'm FBI agent Daire Whitlock, Jamie's uncle."

"Jamie doesn't have an uncle!"

"There's a lot you don't know, punk. He has a whole

damn family. Now tell me where he is, or I'll arrest you for wasting police time." Uncle, family? Jamie had all these people in his life and didn't tell me? How could he keep this from me after everything? I thought things were good between us, but it seemed my little crow still had skeletons in his closet I didn't know about.

I licked my dry lips. I didn't trust this guy as far as I could throw him. I wasn't going to give him anything easily. "W-who's he?" I knew what he was going to say before he took a breath. But fuck me, I wanted to believe a beautiful lie right now, because the truth was going to be a damn hard pill to swallow. And I didn't want to, because that would make everything real and meant my little crow was in serious danger.

"That's between me and him." Agent Whitlock said with no room for argument. "I don't know who you are. You could be a stranger on the street or working for..."

"For fuck's sake, I'm Dillon. I've been his best friend since he was eight."

"Until he left and stopped all contact with you."

"Yes, but—"

"No buts, kid. I don't know you from Adam, so no dice. Pass me to Jamie."

"Fucking listen." My voice shook with the force of his fear. "Did you know Mr. Abernathy beat me up after they left? Put me in the hospital with a broken arm and concussion? Because I couldn't tell him where Jamie and Selene had gone?"

"I did." His voice was softer, filled with regret. "I'm sorry, kid but I need—"

"Don't you think I'd have given Jamie the damn phone if he was here?" I bellowed and broke. Tears flowed from my eyes in torrents. "I-I don't k-know where he i-is..." My breath hitched, stealing my words as my world shattered around me. Memories of Jamie telling me what his dad had done to Selene flashed through my mind, along with all the times Jamie had unexplained bruises and split lips. I screamed because he wasn't here to hold. If he wasn't in my arms, he wasn't safe. I didn't know where he was. My heart splintered all over again, and all I had to cling to was thin air. I pounded my fist on the floor as if it would give me the answers I needed, only to be met with silence and my labored breaths.

"Dillon, we need to go." My gaze zeroed in on B's face. "We need to go. Now! I've messaged Mal and Ava to meet us at Jamie's dorm." I stared at him as his words flowed in and out of my ears. He could have been speaking another language as nothing made sense. I was numb.

I licked my lips, catching my tears on my tongue and blinked as if it had the power to clear the storm in my mind. Vivid image after vivid image bombarded me. Some were memories I could place, others were possibilities I didn't want to think about. My whole body shook from the force of them, like I was being shot by a firing squad.

Buchanan's eyes bored into me, trying to give me the strength of conviction I needed to keep going. He was trying to patch me up with Band-Aids, but I was bleeding out faster than he could plug me. He fisted the front of my suit jacket and shook me. "Get. The. Fuck. Up! You want to save him?" I nodded. "Then get up. The others are meeting us there."

"How do you...?" I pushed up onto unstable feet and let him drag me through the door next to Jamie's bag—the only one that wasn't locked.

"I took the phone off you when you had your little meltdown and spoke to Agent Whitlock. He's meeting us and already has men on campus searching for your boy." I looked at him, my vision hazy from the water filling my eyes. "You good?" I gritted my teeth and nodded. I had to be. I would be for him.

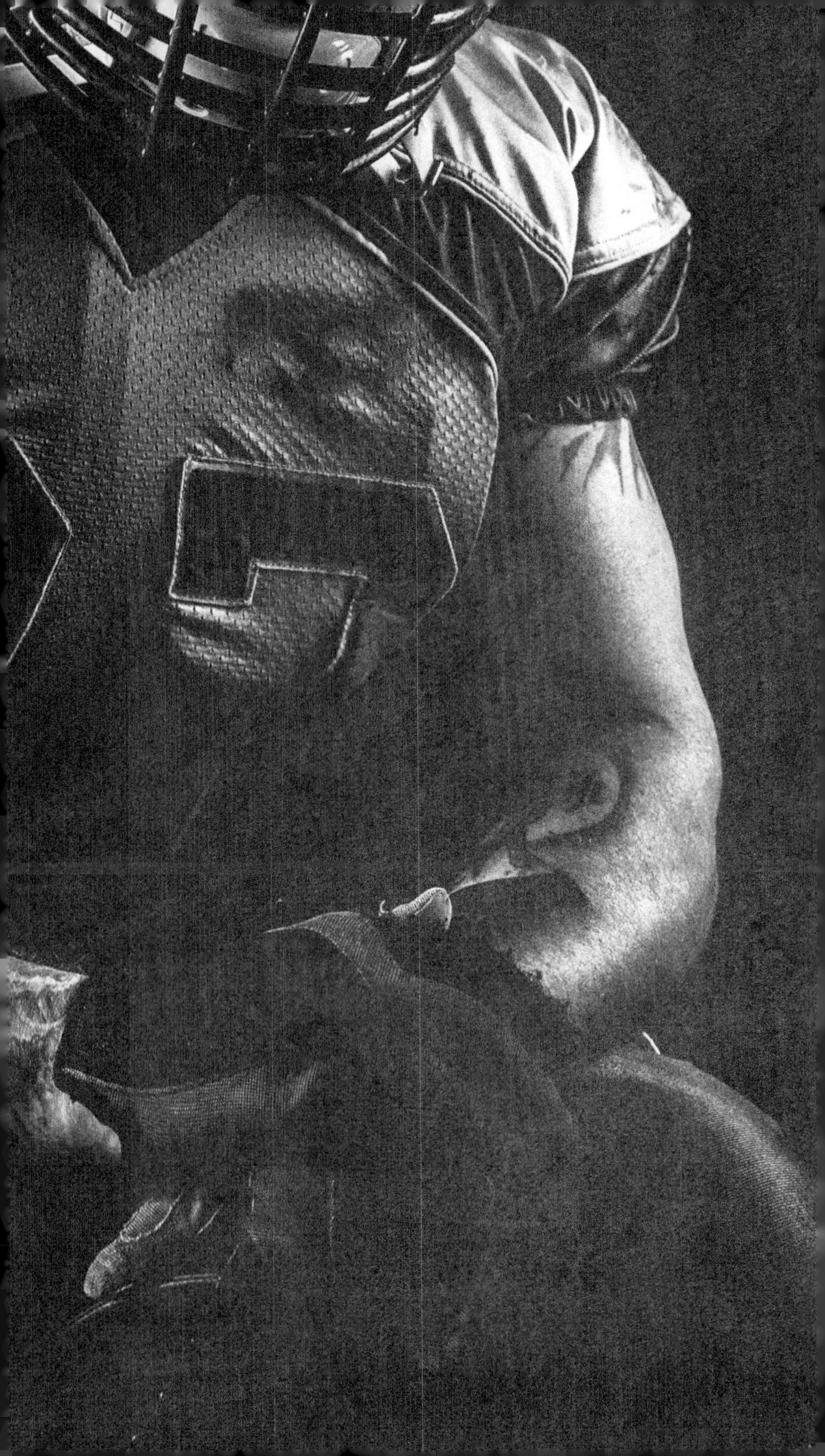

CHAPTER THIRTY-EIGHT

Dillon

I was out of the car before the wheels stopped and left the door open as I charged across the lot to the front of Jamie's dorm building. I barged through people and ran for the elevator, but the doors shut just as I reached it. I punched the buttons, but none were coming down. "Fuck!" I shouted in frustration, pulling on my hair. I ripped off my stupid bow tie and threw it on the floor, crushing it under my foot.

"Stairs!" B yelled from behind me. I turned and sprinted to them, my heartbeat thundering in my ears as the steps blurred beneath my feet. I was singularly focused on my destination and my need to get him back before his piece of shit dad did something incomprehensible that Jamie couldn't come back from. I needed my little crow to live. He was my air, my reason for living. I'd be an empty husk without him. There was no life without Jamie in it. I'd chain him to me if that's what it took to keep him safe.

Adrenaline surged through my veins, and I vibrated with the overload to my system as I swung around another landing and pushed up the next flight of stairs. My legs burned, the muscles straining under the pressure. A stitch pierced my side, the stabbing pain increasing as I gasped for air, but I didn't slow down. I couldn't. Even if my body failed me, I'd drag myself up on my hands and knees. I'd keep going until my fingers were bloody stumps, worn down to the bone.

The door at the top of the stairwell flew open as I barged through it, making the crowd of people behind it jump. I stood frozen for a split second as I took in the sheer volume of bodies wedged into the tight corridor. I shoved men and women out of the way, ignoring their shouts of protest. I didn't give a shit; they were in my way and they needed to get the fuck out of it.

A fat balding dude stood in front of Jamie's door with legs spread and arms crossed over his chest. He shoved me as I tried to get past. "Can't go in there, kid."

A guttural growl tore free from me, and I spat in his face. "That's my fucking boyfriend they're discussing. Either you let me pass, old man, or you'll end up on the floor." I stepped into his personal space, backed him up until he hit the door, and gripped the front of his jacket, pulling his face to mine so our noses were almost touching.

"I wouldn't do that, kid. I'm—"

"I don't give a fuck if you're the next fucking messiah. You're. In. My. Fucking. Way." I punctuated each word with a sharp yank, making his head wobble like a rag doll. "Move, or I'll make you." I released him with a shove, and his head smacked into the door with a thud. A low groan slipped past his lips as he rubbed the back of his head.

"You little punk—"

I snorted. "Fucking try me." I raised my fists, adjusted my

stance so my weight was on my back foot, and turned my hips so I could put my whole body into my punch.

In the next breath, the door opened and porky fell backward, landing on his ass with a shout. "What the hell is going on here?" A well-built older guy wearing a navy-blue jacket with wavy salt and pepper hair and a trimmed beard eyed me. His gaze roamed over me and ping-ponged between my raised fists. "Not the most intelligent person, Dillon." His condescending tone made my skin itch, and my lips pulled back in a sneer.

"Fuck you! Daire, I assume?" The pompous dickwad grinned at me, and it drove me insane. My boy was missing, and this tool was impersonating the Joker.

"Maybe not as stupid as I thought. Get in here and talk me through what you know."

"Hang on, I'm coming. Get out of the damn way, ma'am. I'm with..." Buchanan's voice faded away as I cocked my head and looked more closely at Daire. His amber eyes swirled with anger and frustration. The tight set of his lips and the deepening crow's feet at the corners of his eyes were the only indications that this situation was affecting him.

"Not without him." I chucked my thumb over my shoulder to where B was fighting to get past a female officer without shoving her into the wall.

"Constantine, let him through. He's one of the friends." The grimace on his face made it look like the words had cost him, but if he had any brain cells in his head, he'd know we were some of his strongest leads.

"Well," I pointed to the doorway he was blocking. "What are you waiting for?" He muttered under his breath and moved out of the way so we could enter.

"Thanks," B said as we stepped into the room. He walked straight over to where Mal and Ava were curled up on Jamie's bed and wrapped his arms around them. Their crying faces buried into his neck as he offered them a comfort I wasn't capable of giving. I was filled with rage, everything tinged red.

I turned my gaze onto Daire. "What do you know? Have you found him?"

"Not yet, but we found two people with gunshot wounds." He tapped on his phone before flashing it in front of my eyes. "Can you identify them?"

"Where were they found?"

"Outside the back of the exhibition center. The female had a GSW to her stomach, and the male had one to the shoulder. They're being transported to the hospital with a police escort. We can't interview them until they're out of surgery, so we won't know if they were involved until then."

I held out my hand for Daire's phone. If I could identify them, maybe I would be able to offer something useful. "Oh you stupid little bitch." I pointed to the screen. "This is Elise Estrada. Her father is a senator." I flicked to the next person. "This fucker is Chad Prescott."

"Thank you. Do they have anything against Jamie or anyone he might know?"

Buchanan's snort cut though the shitty small talk. "Elise is obsessed with Dillon and is pissed that he turned her down. Chad is a spoiled little shit. He'll do anything for cash, and he hates Dillon."

"Why does he hate you?"

I slipped my hands into my pockets to hide how badly they were shaking and rocked on the balls of my feet. "Jealousy. He wanted to be varsity captain, and I got it. Not much more to the prick, honestly."

"Okay, thanks." He stepped away and made a quick phone call, speaking too low for me to make out what he was saying. With him distracted, I made my way over to Jamie's bed and collapsed on it. I pulled his pillow to my face and inhaled deeply. I missed him so fucking much. My raw eyes burned, but it didn't stop a fresh wave of tears from spilling down my cheeks. I felt weak and useless, and I hated it. I was supposed to protect him.

My phone vibrated in my pocket, and I yanked it out, pulling out the photos and note along with it.

"Daire!" I barked. His head shot up, his sharp eyes pinned on me as I waved them at him.

"What are they?" he inquired as he covered the mic on his phone and strode toward me. "Shit! Chief, I've gotta go. I'll update you in an hour."

"We found these backstage after a redheaded woman told me Jamie wanted me." Acid filled my mouth as I looked at the images again. I felt violated. They were only grainy photos taken from a distance, but they made what had been an amazing night feel dirty.

Daire sat next to me on the bed and expelled a breath. He pulled out a notepad and pen. I tried to smother my snort but failed, and he smirked right back at me as he clicked his pen. "I need all the details as concisely as you can. Alright?" I nodded and recounted everything I could remember, even the description of the girl.

"Oh, that's Kaileigh Waters. She's in my dance class." Ava sobbed. "I think I have her phone number, and I can tell you where her off campus apartment is."

"Excellent...?"

"Oh, uh, Ava, sir." Her red-rimmed eyes looked like fresh blood. She licked her lips and nodded as Constantine walked over and crouched down in front of her. They talked in hushed tones while Daire went over the photos and the note.

Daire sighed. With his elbows braced on his knees his head hung low between his shoulders, defeat radiated off him. "These don't make sense," he said as he spread the Polaroids out on the floor by his feet.

"What do you mean?"

"These don't feel like the first ones. They're too violent and threatening."

A memory surged forward in my mind, propelling me onto my feet and into Jamie's closet. I searched around, moving clothes, boots, and boxes. "I know it's in here somewhere. Come on, Jamie. Come on." I kicked a large cardboard box and the side split, revealing another box inside. "Fuck! Yes!" I crawled on my hands and knees and ripped the bigger box open and pulled out a wooden box with a mother-of-pearl inlay. It was one Selene had given him years ago.

"What have you got there, kid?" Daire sounded worn down, like hope was slipping away from him.

"Um, when Jamie and I were younger, we'd write each other little notes. He always kept his, said he was like a dragon and they were his treasure. So I thought maybe... if he's had other photos like you've hinted at, they might be in here."

"That's great kid, thanks." The shrill ring of his phone needled, making it feel like my eardrums were bleeding. I scrubbed my damp hands on my pants, my eyes tracking Daire as his body tensed. I slipped off the bed as shadowed his footsteps so I was close enough to hear what he was saying. "Left... Bean There? I want two teams combing that whole..."

"Buchanan!" I grabbed his shoulder and shook him. "Let's go. I think I know where he is." A wicked grin carved across his face.

"Let's go." He extracted himself from Mal and Ava and trailed behind me as we slipped from the room without anyone noticing us. We turned in the opposite direction of the crowd and headed to the fire escape. "Are you going to tell me where we're going?"

"I'm sure you can work it out," I said as we raced down the stairs, glancing up periodically to make sure no one was following us. "If the car's been abandoned by Bean There, where would he go that's far enough removed from everything?"

"Shit. Jerry's storage shed?" I snapped my fingers, just catching B's grin as we stepped out into the dark night. Silence enveloped us, broken only by our labored breaths and the calming pitter-patter of raindrops splattering on the ground around us.

We broke into a run, weaving through the trees, using them for cover in case any of Daire's men spotted us. We made it to the sports fields without encountering anyone. It seemed way too easy, but I wasn't going to look a gift horse in the mouth. Sweat poured down my face, intermingling with the rain drops. I'd lost my jacket at some point, but I didn't care as I unbuttoned and rolled up my sleeves. I cracked my neck, rolled my shoulders, and flexed my fingers.

"What's the plan, Dillon?"

I looked at B and realized I couldn't put him in the position of getting injured. I didn't care about myself. If I went down trying to save Jamie, it was well worth it. But I wouldn't risk anyone else.

"When we know for certain that he's there, I want you to run to Bean There and tell them where we are. Don't let them shoot me." I swallowed down the thought that I might already be a dead man walking. My last few breaths tasted like ash in my mouth. Mr. Abernathy hated me on principle, and nothing and no one could dissuade him from something once he'd made his mind up. But I knew I could use his rage against him, force him to make mistakes as I backed him into a corner he couldn't get out of.

"Dillon..."

"No, Taylor. I need you to do this for me, okay?" I wrapped my arms around the guy I'd come to realize was my best friend and bit back a fresh wave of tears. I blinked them away before looking into his watery eyes, the muted light from the parking lot glittering in them. "Please?"

"You got it, Cap."

We crouched down low as we ran behind the tennis courts and across the field to where Jerry's shed stood at the edge of the woods. A rasping guttural cry filtered through the cracked open window. I spun on my feet and grabbed his arm. "Be safe. Look over your shoulder until you hear from me again. We dont know if this fucker is on his own or not." B nodded and squeezed my shoulder before helping me through the rotting window frame. "Good. Now go!"

Jamie's muted cries grew louder the farther into the space I went. My breath caught when I saw him. I had to blink to make sure it was real. Jamie's wrists were bound with thick rope that was suspended across the wooden beam pulling them up. The strained tension in his arms was apparent. His toes skimmed the cement floor, swinging in a pool of dark liquid. His torn shirt lay in tattered pieces on the couch behind him, and cuts and bruises bloomed across his skin. But it was the blood trickling down his sliced torso that locked my feet in place. The metallic scent of copper, sweat, and urine permeated the air.

Please be okay. Look at me, little crow. I'll spend every second of every day worshiping you, if you just lift your head and look at me. Please, Jamie. Breathe. Our story doesn't end here.

"Jamie, please." I crouched down behind a shelf filled with old paint cans, moving them a little so I could see. Jamie froze, his muscles clenched in fear, his mouth twisted in a grimace. Out of nowhere, something lanced across his skin. The sound of it slicing through his flesh was now etched into my memories. Jamie's cries were the worst thing I'd ever heard.

"You fucking little faggot. Just as bad as your whore mother." Mr. Abernathy stepped out of the shadows. "Disgusting," he spat and raised his arm for another strike. I retched silently, bile pouring from between my lips. I spat it out and wiped the back of my hand across my face.

I glanced around, looking for something I could use as a weapon. If I could get close enough to that vile excuse for a human, I'd use every ounce of my rage to take him out. Something metallic crashed on the floor, the sound shattering the silence. I crawled toward a tool box and pulled out a hammer and a couple of wrenches. These would have to do.

Jamie screamed as a low thud echoed in the enclosed space. I swear I heard something crack. My heart was beating its way out of my chest, my breathing nothing but shallow pants. But I felt a wave of calmness wash over me as I prepared to strike.

Metal dragged across the cement floor like an old horror film. The hair on the back of my neck stood on end as a metal baseball bat glinted in the moonlight coming through the far window. Mr. Abernathy looked like a bloated pile of shit. He was drenched in sweat, and the scent of his body odor grew stronger by the second.

"I don't know how you two managed to evade me for so long." His guttural laugh was unnatural. "But now your time is up. Any last words?" He lifted Jamie's head with the tip of the bat.

"Fuck you, old man. I love him. I fucking love him, and even if you kill me now, I'll love him until I'm nothing but a memory."

"You make me sick. You piece of filth. You dirty little faggot." He raised the bat above his head as I charged at him with a roar. The sound of metal hitting bone rang out just as I let the hammer fly into the back of his skull. The sickening crunch made my stomach churn, but it was the splatter of blood over my face that made me jump back and expel the contents of my stomach.

"Shit. Jamie? Little crow?" I clambered over the lump of lard at my feet and cupped Jamie's face, brushing my thumbs over his cheeks. Tears streamed down my cheeks, and I whimpered. "Jamie? Baby? Please look at me."

Nothing. He was stone cold and immobile. My hands flittered over his body, down his sides, over his chest. Trembling fingers searched for a pulse, but I couldn't find one as he hung limply by his arms.

"Jamie?" I cried and wrapped my hands around his hips,

lifting him to remove the pressure on his arms. The scent of urine grew stronger, but I didn't care. I just needed him back. "Jamie?!" Hot wetness engulfed my fingers. "Oh fuck. Oh fuck."

I clung to him and cried from all the time we'd lost over the last five years. For all the time I took from us over the last few months, and all the time the grunting sack of shit has taken from our future.

"I'll fucking kill you if you've taken him from me," I roared until my voice was nothing but a rasp. "I'll fucking kill you!"

CHAPTER THIRTY-NINE

Jamie

"Come back to me, little crow. You can't leave me."

The drugging darkness had sunk its claws into me, and no matter how much I fought its hold, it didn't want to let me go. It was like I was fighting against a riptide, expending all my energy to get away, but it just dragged me back into the depths. Indistinct images and memories flickered through the darkness, but I couldn't discern if they were real or part of a fractured illusion.

Snippets of conversations and phantom touches had me clinging to the hope that I would find my way out of this rabbit hole and back to myself. I didn't want to give in to it, even though it felt like the easiest thing to do. My heart burned to be reunited with its other half, and as trapped as I was, I didn't forget him. He was the anchor I was searching for, and the one thing that could tether me and bring me back.

"Can anyone hear me?" I screamed into the dark void, but

there was only silence. Always present and unending. It was suffocating, and I… I…

"How much longer is he going to be like this?" Agony stained every word.

"It's hard to tell. It's up to him now. The swelling has gone down, and his vitals are stable. Hang in there. He's young and strong. He'll fight for you."

Warm wet drops splashed on my forehead. I wanted to wipe them away, but I couldn't move. "Please. Please come back to me Jamie. I… I don't know how much more I can take, baby…" It was fading. He was fading. Even with my arm outstretched, reaching for him, my fingers were swallowed by the darkness as it pulled me back under. *No! No. No. Let me go…*

I felt lighter, like the crushing weight holding me down had dissipated. I sucked air into my lungs and it burned. White-hot pain engulfed me like a tsunami, flooding my limbs. Any little movement intensified the pain. I tried to pry my eyes open, but they were welded shut.

"W-what's happening?"

The steady beeping increased its tempo, getting more frantic as I tried to pry my eyes open.I needed to be free. I shook the bars of the cage holding me prisoner. I wanted to be free. To be back with them.

"Doctor? What's going on?"

Footsteps echoed and the ground shook beneath me. Coldness swept through me, chilling me to the bone.

"What did you do?" His rage was palpable, even as I started to drift.

"He was fighting too hard. We've sedated him so he can't cause himself any more damage. The swelling might have receded, but he's still in a very delicate state. You should try and get some rest."

"I'll rest when he's back."

THE CLOYING SCENT of bleach and disinfectant seared my nostrils and coated my lungs with every inhale. The rhythmic *beep beep beep* grated against my nerves like sandpaper. I managed to open my eyes a crack, but it was nothing but a grainy haze. The bright lights made my brain ache and pulse in time with the beeping. Tears pooled in my slitted eyes and flowed down my face. I still felt numb, or maybe disassociated was the right word? But I was grateful, because it held back the avalanche of pain I knew was waiting on the other side.

The air moved and pressure increased somewhere on me. It was like feeling heat on the other side of a barrier that tempered it. I couldn't move my head or anything else, and it was quickly becoming too hard to keep my eyes open. I sighed when the blackness blanketed me.

A DOOR CLICKED SHUT and soft footfalls moved around me. The rich aroma of coffee overpowered the bleach and it made breathing easier. The scraping sound of a chair being moved pierced through me, and I tensed.

"Dillon, darling. You really should go and get some rest.

You need to eat and sleep. He'll still be here when you get back. You haven't left his side."

"And I won't fucking leave him, not until he tells me to go. I-I promised I'd protect him… t-that I'd keep him safe, and I f-failed him, Clara. I can't leave him. I'll grab a shower and a change of clothes, but I'll be back. Thanks for the coffee." Heavy footsteps faded away, and my heart dropped as his presence dissipated.

"Oh, Jamie." She sighed. "Your man is one of the most amazing young men I've met. He's told me everything that happened between you. I'm so proud of you for taking the leap and giving him another chance." Her breathing stuttered. "You didn't deserve what he did, but fear is a powerful thing."

I wanted to answer her, but I didn't have the strength to fight against my body. Her soft voice accompanied me as I drifted in and out of consciousness. Other people came and went, talking in hushed tones like they were afraid I could hear them. I'd always laughed at the idea of talking to coma patients, but now I understood. It was like listening to a CB radio—sometimes clear, sometimes garbled, and there was no real frame of reference besides the images your imagination conjured.

SLOWLY, I became aware of every ache and pain that flashed and rolled through me, and the enormity hit me all at once. Everything I'd felt up until this point had been nothing but a faint echo. Now, the pain burned with an intensity that consumed me like a wildfire, and I longed for the cool dark abyss of my previous semi-conscious state.

A heavy weight was draped over my right arm. The heat radiating from it permeated my cool skin, making me shiver. I tried to flex my fingers, but something tightened around them with the slight movement. I was too scared to open my eyes, because what if I was wrong? What if I wasn't awake, but in heaven? My heart stuttered and my body jolted at the realization that I could be dead. I didn't want to have had my chance at a life with Dillon ripped away from me by my vile dad. I wanted years of waking up next to him and watching him sleep. I wanted many more stolen moments between us as our lives sped on around us. I wanted and I wanted. I wanted my dreams to come true. I wanted a house. A husband. Memories of our lives and children growing up. I wanted to sit on the porch swing when we were old and gray and watch our family around us.

I wanted it all. And if that bastard has taken my chance of happiness away from me, I'd go down to hell and kill his ass myself.

Tears welled behind my closed eyes, making the pressure unbearable. I had to either feel them trickle down my face, or be brave enough to face whatever reality confronted me. I could do this. I knew I could. Trepidation rolled through me. I sucked in a stuttering breath and slowly opened my eyes. Anticipating the bright lights I'd seen before, I squinted as my vision slowly cleared and breathed a sigh of relief when a darkened room came into focus.

My eyes darted over the small space. Dull off-white walls, a muted TV hanging opposite me, and a small table at the end of my bed with empty snack wrappers. A white closed door with a small window in the middle showed a dark corridor beyond, and if I strained hard enough, I could hear the nurses chattering. The window on the opposite side of the room had a slatted blind, but it was open enough for me to see the parking lot beyond it. Orange street lights illuminated the cars, and odd shadowed blobs moved around.

My tears fell when I managed to turn my gaze on the weight I'd felt on my arm. I hiccuped a breath as my heart grew a millions times too big for my body. Every one of Dillon's words and protests echoed in my mind. He refused to leave. He stayed and guarded me when I wasn't there to do it for myself. *My heart, my soul, my body is yours, baby. Always and forever. I'm yours.*

I'd follow him to the ends of the earth and beyond like he had so willingly done for me. A smile flickered at the corners of my lips as I traced the rose on the back of his hand that was wrapped around mine. His skin felt rough under mine, the hairs course, but it didn't do anything to dampen the electricity that ignited from such an innocent touch. "I love you, always," I breathed, my throat aching and raw.

"I love you too, little crow," he muttered, his voice thick with sleep. I couldn't see his face, but I mapped its sleeping form in my mind. How I'd trace my fingers across his brows, down his nose, and along the bow of his full lips. Every part of his body was imprinted on my memory, but I hungered to taste him again, to feel his solid muscles under my fingertips.

"I'll be here when you wake up, Dil." Time moved slowly as I slipped in and out of a sleepy doze, but Dillon's hold on me never wavered. It filled my heart to bursting. The sky beyond the window went from an inky black, to indigo, to the pale blue of a new dawn. When oranges and reds chased the darker shades of night away, Dillon started to stir. He moved his head onto my lap and wrapped his arm around my legs. He couldn't have been comfortable. His unrelinquishing hold kept my overwhelming emotions at bay. I carded my hand through his hair, trailed my fingers around the shell of his ear, and down to the roman numerals on his neck. It was the date we first met; when I was eight and he saved me from an ass whooping.

"How's he doing?" Aunt Clara's voice was soft, but the tiredness that laced her tone hurt. My eyes slowly fluttered open. Bright sunlight shone through the slatted blind and made my head pulse, so I closed them and stayed still so I could listen to them talk. Partly because I wanted to know what was going on, and partly because I'd alway been nosey.

Dillon sighed and stretched, rubbing his neck. "You know I dreamed he spoke to me last night?"

"Oh?"

"Mmm. He told me he loved me, and he'd be here when I woke up. It was so real. I could almost believe he traced the rose on my hand." His voice grew thick, and his breathing stuttered.

"Oh, baby. You know I felt like I knew you that night when we all ended up here. Selene spoke about you so much, and you're exactly as she described you. Strong, loyal, and totally devoted to him."

"I let him down, Clara. I hurt him, and it's inexcusable."

"We all make mistakes, kid. Even Jamie isn't perfect. He kept the stuff about his dad from you because he thought he was protecting you, but all he did was make both of you vulnerable."

"No. His heart was in the right place. He always put others before himself. Even if that means he has to suffer."

"I know. He's so like his mom in that way. She hid her pain at the end."

"He never told me what happened to her. That's why I..." He huffed out an exasperated breath. "I'm sorry I yelled at you, demanding she be here."

"Water under the bridge. Anyway, I need to dash back for Zack and Jessie. I thought I'd bring them by after dinner to see him. He's always loved his little sunbeam."

"Sounds good. I can't wait for my hugs."

Aunt Clara chuckled. "They adore you just like they do Jamie." She kissed my cheek and ran her fingers through my hair. It took everything in me not to react. Selfishly, I wanted Dillon and I to have some time alone before the rest of the world barged in and burst our bubble.

The door clicked shut, and I opened my eyes. They were

drawn to Dillon's face like they instinctively knew where he was. His profile was as stunning as the rest of him. His strong jaw was hidden under a dark beard that hid its sculpted lines, but he was no less impressive. I breathed him in for a minute and felt the melancholy coming off him in waves. He was staring blankly at the door and hadn't noticed me move. "Dil?" I rasped.

His chair flew out from under him and went skidding across the room as he jumped to his feet and faced me. Disbelief flickered across his face seconds before his eyes started leaking.

"Are you crying?"

"Nah, it's just allergies."

I snorted and winced. "Y-you don't have them." My voice wavered as mine started to water too. The air thickened, and the next thing I knew, he was blanketing my chest, and I was in his embrace. I inhaled his musky sea salt scent and finally felt like I could breathe through the unending pain.

He gave me a watery smile and cupped my face, thumbs stroking over my cheeks. "Is this real, or am I dreaming?" He inched closer until his lips brushed mine.

"If it's a dream, it's just about the most perfect one I've ever had." I chuckled and felt his wicked grin against my lips, but I couldn't pull my eyes away from his. My tongue ran across my bottom lip, teasing him with the barest touch and making him groan.

"Oh, baby, I want to kiss you so badly, but I don't want to hurt you." Instead of answering, I closed the distance between us and melded my lips with his. As his lips brushed mine, I felt whole. Dillon completed me on a molecular level; his atoms merged with mine, fusing us together in a way not even death could take from us.

I lifted my hand and stroked my fingers along his nape as he sunk into the kiss. It was chaste, with only our lips teasing against each other, but I could feel the ramifications in my soul. Nothing had ever felt so perfect. I pulled back when my neck started to ache, and my lungs screamed for air. "I need to brush my teeth," I whimpered as I choked on emotion. "My throat hurts. Do you think I can have a drink?"

Dillon looked at me like I had two heads, and that cute little furrow formed between his brows. "I have no idea, little crow. Let me get the doctor. She'll want to know you're awake, and then I can let—"

I held up my hand to stop him. "Can't it just be us for a little while?" And oh, how he melted into a puddle of goo before me and turned into a blundering fool unable to get his words out. When I laughed and wheezed, he gave up, nodded, and went to get the doctor, promising to return with a drink.

The day passed in a blur of doctors, tests, and random people stopping by to see me. I didn't recognize them, but I felt deeply indebted to each and every one of them. Without them and their help, I might not be here, so I could suck it up and be polite. I plastered a smile on my face until I was losing the battle against my heavy eyes, and Dillon growled at the last nurse that came in to remove my drips and catheter. Ugh. That is a process I don't ever want to repeat. I'd made Dillon leave the room and get me a latte so I wouldn't have to live with the embarrassment of him watching. After that ordeal, she gave some of the good stuff, and I faded away into a blissful painless sleep for a few hours.

When I finally woke, my eyes immediately darted to the window. The sky was an array of pastel shades; the yellows, reds, and oranges merged into deeper blues that announced the onset of night. A yawn split my face, and I heard a loud squeak that had me wincing as my heart took flight.

I blinked a couple of times to clear the last remnants of sleep that clung to me and focused on the little princess bouncing like the Energizer Bunny at the bottom of my bed. Her curls danced across her shoulders, but it was her shimmering amber eyes that had me fighting the damn waterworks again.

"Hello, my little sunbeam."

"JJ!" she cried and jumped up onto the bed, which shook with the force of her exuberance. Luckily, Dillon caught her before she landed on me and sat her on his hip to keep her weight off of me.

"Hey, beautiful." I held my arms out and wrapped them around her. Her body shook with the force of her emotions, and her tears soaked my chest. I held on to her until her cries turned to whimpers. She looked at me through glassy eyes. "I was so scared, JJ. I didn't want to lose you like Auntie Selene." Her words landed like a punch to the solar plexus and stole the air from my lungs.

"Me either, sunbeam." I cupped her face and smiled. "I just need a little rest, and then I'll be home so we can celebrate Christmas." The silence in the room was a dead weight. I looked at everyone gathered in my room and saw them visibly wince. "What?"

"Christmas has been and gone, Jamie," Zack said as he sat down on my other side and gave me a gentle hug.

"Oh." I chewed the inside of my cheek. "H-how long?"

"That's probably best for the doctor to talk to you about, Jamie," Uncle Daire said, guilt shining in his eyes. "Having us all here is a lot for you to cope with, considering you only woke up a few hours ago."

"But he's been napping all day!" Jessie grumbled as Dil set her on the ground. Aunt Clara pulled my little sunbeam into her side. "He's fine, right?"

"He will be, little lady, but Jamie still needs lots of rest and time to heal. So how about we head home and get the house ready for when he can leave?"

"Yay!" She squealed and clapped her hands. "Can we decorate his room too?" Aunt Clara cast me a worried glance, and her lips thinned.

"Of course, you can. Just don't make it too bright because I don't have any shades." Jessie chuckled and dragged Zack and Aunt Clara to the door, telling them what they needed to buy.

"She doesn't have an off switch, does she?" Uncle Daire said, smirking. "Glad you're out of the woods, Jamie. I was really worried I wouldn't get there in time."

"But you did, right? Or I wouldn't—"

"Don't!" Dillon barked. I opened my mouth, but he covered it and shot me a warning glare. "I said don't, little crow." Effectively silenced, I nodded.

Uncle Daire slapped Dil on the shoulder. "You've got a good one here, Jamie. Let him tell you what happened. Just know it's not me you need to be thanking, he's the real hero."

Nerves swarmed inside me like locusts. "Will h-he ever..." I couldn't force the words out, even if it was imperative that I knew if I would be spending the rest of my life looking over my shoulder.

Understanding dawned on Uncle Daire's face. "No one leaves hell once they enter, Jamie. He's never coming back, and he will never hurt anyone you love again. He's gone."

I grabbed his hand and pulled him in for a hug—our first one ever—and held him tightly. I'd resented him, hated him, and feared him, but he'd done everything he could to keep me and my mom safe. "Thank you. I-I don't know..."

"You don't have to say anything, Jamie." His large hand cupped my face in a tender gesture that made my throat feel thick. "You're family, and I'll do anything to protect mine. Let me know when you're home, and when Jessie decides our Christmas will be, and I'll see you then. But if you need me, my number is now in your proper phone."

"Thanks, Uncle Daire." He waved goodbye, and it was just Dillon and I left, holding hands in the silence that remained.

"When I get home..." I licked my lips as my eyes roved over

the tight Henley hugging his chest. I could see the visceral reaction his body had to mine.

"Nope. Don't you dare!" He slapped his hand over my mouth to silence me. "When we're home, we'll talk about things like that. Until then, any S. E. X. talk is banned, so we don't face a nuclear meltdown. Understand?"

"Yes, sir."

Dil threw his head back and groaned as his pants tightened, making me snicker. "I need to take a long walk, you little shit. Doctor Aimes will be here in a second to talk you through everything."

"But..."

"I'll bring you back another latte." He kissed my lips and slipped out the door just as a short raven-haired lady came in with a gentle smile on her face.

I WAS UP EARLY and dressed before breakfast was served. After nearly four weeks in the hospital, I was ready to get out of here. I was both excited and terrified about going home. Well, back to Aunt Clara's. I was looking forward to not spending another night on the itchy hospital bed but feared not being able to cope with the pain, brain fog, and bouts of patchy memory I still suffered with. Doctor Aimes said it was still early days, and with time, I should regain my full memory. Although after Dillon explained what happened the night he rescued me, the state I was in, and what he did for me, I'm not sure I want to remember.

Sheila chuckled as she walked in with my oatmeal and fruit. "Release day, is it?"

"It sure is, and it can't come soon enough." I beamed as she set it down on the table and wheeled it over the bed for me.

"How's the pain, Jamie?"

"It's alright," I said, opening the pot and pouring the small sachet of honey on top of the oatmeal, making sure to keep my eyes trained on my hands.

"Sure it is, young man." My shoulders slumped and she laughed again. "Broken ribs and a serious concussion are no joke, especially when you had to be placed in a medically-induced coma."

"I know, I know. I just hate the way they make me all sleepy, y'know?"

"I do, Jamie, but that man of yours sure loves you all sleepy and snuggly."

The door opened at that exact moment, and Dillon snickered. "I sure do." He walked around Sheila and took the seat next to the bed while I shoveled food in my mouth and prayed they weren't going to pick on me anymore.

"I'll leave these here for you, Jamie." I rolled my eyes and smiled at Sheila as she waved goodbye and left me to Dillon's scrutinizing attention. I glared at him and continued to eat until he turned away and started flicking through the channels on the TV. Elise and Chad's photo flashed across the screen, and Dillon's shoulders stiffened before he changed the channel. They both made it through surgery and were promptly arrested for kidnapping and assault once they were in recovery. At least I wouldn't have to see them when I returned to Briar U. Stevens was also expelled due to the part he played in my bullying and the sexgate scandal with Chad. We could thank Taylor for that development.

"It's going to be okay, little crow. I promise."

Tears stung my eyes and my bottom lip wobbled as I nodded. "I know, it's just..."

Dillon pushed the table away and sat next to me. I collapsed into his arms, seeking the comfort only he could offer. He was my home. It wasn't a place or a memory anymore. It was a person. My person. Dillon.

“I know, baby.” He cupped my nape and pressed my head against his formidable chest, his steady heartbeat soothing me. “I do have some good, albeit morbid, news to share.”

I sat back and blinked away my tears. “Do tell.” I laced his fingers with mine as he got this faraway look in his eyes, and his grip on my hand tightened. I stroked my thumb over his knuckle and traced the patterns in the rose with the other.

“I got a call from the sheriff back home. He told me d-dad was involved in a drunk driving accident. He was the only casualty, thankfully. He drove into a tree and died instantly. They think the high blood alcohol level coupled with the icy road conditions and lack of skid marks, that he didn’t have a chance to react,” he said clinically. “Just drove eighty miles per hour straight into a tree.”

“Are you okay?”

Dillon’s face was a war of conflicting emotions. “I… I don’t know, to be honest. Am I sad he’s dead? Not really. The guy was a controlling asshole, but he was my dad.”

“And you miss who he should have been?”

His sigh broke the shackles holding his emotions back. It was a palpable thing, like a current moving through him. Dillon buried his head in the crook of my neck and wrapped his arms around me, holding on like I was a fragile thing that was going to be ripped away from him. *Oh, my sweet baby.* “Something like that.” His gravelly voice cracked as he choked on a sob.

“Let it all out, babe. You’re entitled to feel your feelings without having to explain or justify them to anyone.” I ran my fingers through his hair as he shuddered in my embrace. His tears slid down my neck, and I clutched him closer to me. *I’ll never let you go.*

“I-I’m so glad you gave me another chance, Jamie.” Dillon looked at me through wet lashes, and it was like seeing through a window into his soul. He wasn’t perfect—he’d made mistakes, but I loved every part, even the ones he hated.

"I love you so much, Dil. Broken pieces, mistakes, shitty dads, and all. I don't want to live another day without you by my side. You complete me in every way. You're my home."

He sealed his lips against mine, and I lost myself to the drugging sensation of his tongue wrapping around mine. I drowned in the depths of the feelings his possessive touch invoked. He was the air in my lungs, the blood in my veins, and the marrow in my bones. We had been to hell and back together since we'd met as kids and again as adults. We'd faced more challenges than most couples did in a lifetime, and it only served to make us stronger as individuals and as a couple. Even death had knocked at our door, and we'd sent him packing.

We had a lifetime of memories to capture, and we would —one day at a time. This was our new beginning, and I couldn't wait to see what our futures held.

EPILOGUE

Dillon

Five Years Later

"Tell me something," Jamie said, his fingers teasing down my chest, making my heated skin prickle with goosebumps.

"Anything." I looked at him with wonder, the same way I'd done since the day I met him, and the way I planned to for the rest of our lives together. The scent of sex and cum filled the air as Jamie ground against me. He still had the face of an angel, but no one but me knew the nympho living beneath the surface.

"I've always wondered this." He bit his slick bottom lip. I pulled it out with my thumb and kissed him, because I could never get enough of his lips. "Why *little crow*?"

I gave him an indulgent smile. "Because a murder of crows is a dangerous thing."

Jamie rolled his eyes at me, crossed his arms over my chest, and peered up at me with those beguiling blue eyes. "Why? And I want the truth this time."

I sighed and ran my hands through his wild curls. Even all these years later, they were still a force of nature. "Because... because crows are seen as a symbol of transformation, positive change, and intuition. And I knew in my heart that you changed me the day I met you. Even if it took me years to truly understand what it meant."

"I have no idea what to say to that. I never...I never knew it meant that much to you. I just thought you had a thing for birds."

I gasped in mock outrage. "A thing for birds? You little shit. I'm going to get you for that." Jamie burst out laughing and jumped off the bed, running toward the bathroom with me hot on his heels. "Don't think the shower will save you..."

I stepped into the bathroom and froze. My little crow was on his knees in the shower, water droplets kissing his golden skin as they slid down his chest and clung to the hard nubs of his nipples. His eyes glowed with a heat of their own. "Unless?"

"Unless you're on your knees, willing and waiting for me." I stepped into the shower cubicle that was big enough to hold at least six men, and tapped my straining erection against his lips, teasing a bead of precum across them. Jamie's tongue lapped it up before dipping into my slit.

"I want you on the field today knowing I can still taste your cum when you make your first pass. I want you hot, sweaty, and hard for me when you meet me afterwards. And I want you to fucking ruin me when we get home."

I wrapped his wet hair around my wrist and thrust into the tight wet heat of his mouth. A guttural groan rumbled in my chest as his tongue teased the vein on the underside of my shaft, the crown nudging the back of his throat. I was already a throbbing mess, thanks to his filthy words. I wouldn't last long. This needed to be hard and fast as I had to get to the stadium for today's game.

"I'm going to fuck your face, baby, and fill you with my cum because I need to go." Jamie moaned as I set a punishing rhythm, pulling out until the tip rested on his lips before snapping my hips and bottoming out. Nothing beat the feeling of his throat constricting around me. His slick fingers teased along my taint, rolled my balls, and gave them a tug.

Lightning flowed through my veins, my orgasm barreling closer with every slurping suck as he made love to my cock with his talented mouth. "Oh shit. That's it, baby." Jamie smiled around my dick as tears fell down his flushed cheeks. He flicked his tongue over my slit, and my balls pulled up tight.

"Oh fuck, oh fuck. Swallow me down, baby." I grunted as I thickened his mouth, his lips stretched impossibly wide. It was the undiluted hunger in his eyes that pushed me over the edge as thick ropes of cum poured down his throat.

Jamie cleaned me off before catching the drops that had dribbled down his cheeks. He stuck his tongue out to show me the thick white liquid and crooked a finger, demanding a kiss from me. He moaned as I slammed my lips down on his, and he fucked my cum into my mouth with his tongue until it was all gone. "Such a filthy boy."

"Only for you." Jamie groaned as he washed himself off under the shower, while I dried off and brushed my teeth, unable to take my eyes off him. "Go, or you'll be late. I want you to win your second Super Bowl for me."

"I'll do anything for you, little crow." I blew him a kiss and darted to our room, pulling out the little black box that had been taunting me from my sock drawer for weeks. I shoved on my clothes and made it to my car with fifteen minutes to spare.

"Wow, Bill, today's Super Bowl was an absolute blow out. The New York Kings slaughtered the Milwaukee Mutants 73 – 0. Why do you think that was?"

"There is only one reason here, Larry, and that's the King's star quarterback, Dillon Hargraves. He is on target to crush the legendary Tom Brady's all-time record by next year if he continues to throw like he is. That man is a machine. And as one of the most high profile out players, he's a beacon of hope for everyone that you can achieve your dreams if you keep focused and push yourself."

"He is going to be one of the greats, Bill! But today, we have been asked to make a special announcement at the end of the game. We'd like everyone to stay in their seats for a once-in-a-lifetime show."

"Are we ready?"

Fuck, I had never been so nervous in all my life. My heart was on the line, and if it all went wrong...

"Don't look so worried, Dillon. You know he worships the ground you walk on."

"Yeah, Cap, you've got this." The guys in the huddle slapped my back and gave me more words of encouragement as the brass band started playing "A Thousand Years" by Christina Perri. I swallowed down my nerves as the group broke away from me. As one, we pulled out our microphones, and I started to sing in front of a full Super Bowl crowd.

The stadium fell silent, and all you could hear was my voice and the rest of the team harmonizing along with me. Sweat poured down my back as I belted out line after line. The confusion in the crowd died away as I spotted Jamie on the large screen. Tears glistened on his flushed cheeks, and his hand covered his mouth as he made his way out onto the field.

A deafening roar from the supporters, staff, commentators, and fans threatened to make my ears bleed, but I focused on the words and breathing techniques the vocal coach gave me and kept going.

Jamie owned the field as he sauntered toward me with his model swagger. He might be one of the most famous faces in the world these days, but he will alway be my little crow, and I'll always be the only man he's ever loved. He's mine. Just fucking *mine.*

Tears pricked my eyes as he stood ten feet in front of me, Coach guiding him to the exact spot. Every set of eyes and every camera in the stadium were trained on us. My heart was on my sleeve as I lay myself bare for him, all that I am, I gave to him. Now and always. As the song drew to a close, I dropped to one knee. A collective gasp rang out before the stadium fell silent.

My heart skipped a beat as the man who owned my heart walked slowly towards me. His brilliant smile and radiant glow stole my breath, and I almost forgot my words. I held out my hand to him, and he slid his hand in mine.

"Jamie Bowen, you are unequivocally the most amazing person I have ever met. You changed my life the day I met you, and it has never been the same since. You are my north star. My guiding light. My heart beats only for you." I wiped the tears from my face and sucked in a sharp breath.

"You are my home. The one who guards my heart. I know I'm not an easy man to love, but you make loving you a gift. I want to spend the rest of my days waking up to see your smile and falling asleep in your arms."

Jamie chuckled and fanned his face, but I could see the way his body trembled. I squeezed his hand and mouthed, *"Look at me, little crow."*

"Jamie, you are all of my yesterdays and all of my tomorrows. I'll give you my heart forever if you'll grant me the honor of being your husband."

I held my breath, waiting for his response, but he seemed incapable of speaking. "Oh shit. Sorry, kids, cover your ears. I forgot the ring." Jamie burst out laughing and fell to his knees in front of me, golden hair glowing like a halo. I pulled the box out of my sock and held it up to him. He launched himself at me and nearly knocked me off my feet, kissing the breath from my lips.

Laughing, I pulled him up, slipped the ring on his finger, and held his hand up to the crowd. If I thought I'd been deafened before, it had nothing on the thunderous applause that made the ground shake beneath our feet.

"I love you, little crow." I hugged him and felt the shudders that racked his body. I held his face between my hands and stared into his beautiful eyes. "I love you."

"I love you too, babe. Can't wait to be your husband."

YOU ARE FORMALLY INVITED
TO THE WEDDING OF
DILLON HARGRAVES
& JAMIE BOWEN.

PLEASE KEEP AN EYE ON MY
SOCIAL MEDIA FOR A
NOVELLA OF THEIR
WEDDING DAY AND FIRST
NIGHT AS MR. & MR.

The honour of
your presence is requested
at the wedding of

DILLON HARGRAVES

and

JAMIE BOWEN

22 JUNE

Saturday, at 4 o'clock in the afternoon
Lake Tahoe, California

RSVP: Ava Mitchell
rainbowfairy@net.com

AFTERWORD

Thank you for reading Jamie & Dillon's story. These two grabbed hold of my brain and demanded their story be told their way.

What I had intended to be a light bully with angst novel, grew into something so much more, and I couldn't help but love them more with every word I wrote.

I went through every emotion writing this book, but I wouldn't change a thing. No one ever tells you how isolating it can be sitting and writing for hours on end, but luckily for me, these boys were loud and kept me company. They will always hold a special place in my heart.

ACKNOWLEDGMENTS

Thank you to my amazingly supportive alpha team: Jenna, Kait, Michelle, and Louise. Your comments and feedback were invaluable.

Amy V, you are the most wonderful beta. Your comments are life!

Michaella, thank you for holding my hand when I wobbled and reminding me that commas are a real thing!

ABOUT THE AUTHOR

Skyla Raines is obsessed with romance and broken boys. She's an avid reader and a sucker for hard-fought happily ever afters.

When she's not bringing to life the characters in her head, she's watching her family grow and cherishes every moment with them.

ALSO BY SKYLA RAINES

Without Limits Series

The Lies We Tell Ourselves

The Lies We Believe

(Coming December 2024)

CONTENT NOTE

Please note this book has dark elements and contains themes which some may find difficult to read. Triggers are personal to each individual, but I have listed the main ones below. I have tried to handle these topics with care.

Mental health rep
Bullying
Homophobia
Domestic violence (off page/memories)
Physical childhood abuse (memories)
Graphic sex
Dub con
Drugging
Kidnap
Attempted Murder
Beating

Printed in Great Britain
by Amazon

52235562R00255